Critical acclaim for The Virtual Trilogy

...a tautly plotted thriller . . .
Virtually Maria will not fail you . . .
(Irish News-Belfast)

. . . a very slick fish in the growing pool of
cyberthrillers . . .
. . . irrepressible and surprisingly irresistible.
(RTE Guide)

. . . a ground-breaking love story . . .
(The Examiner)

. . . brilliantly conceived, exquisitely executed
and eminently readable . . .
(Commuting Times)

. . . published to great critical acclaim . . .
(Ireland on Sunday)

Virtually Maria – A gripping, action-packed, tautly
plotted thriller . . .
(Publishing News)

Virtually Maria - EASONS Book of the Month

YESTERDAY, TODAY AND TOMORROW

Third in *The Virtual Trilogy*

Also by John Joyce

The Virtual Trilogy

Virtually Maria
A Matter of Time

www.virtualtrilogy.com

Captain Cockle

Captain Cockle and the Cormorant
Captain Cockle and the Loch Ness Monster
Captain Cockle and the Pond

www.captaincockle.com

YESTERDAY, TODAY AND TOMORROW

JOHN JOYCE

This edition published by Spindrift Press 2008

ISBN 9780955763724

ABOUT THE AUTHOR

Award-winning science writer Dr John Joyce is the author of the *Virtual Trilogy* of techno thrillers featuring Theo Gilkrensky – *Virtually Maria*, *A Matter of Time* and *Yesterday, Today and Tomorrow* – as well as the *Captain Cockle* series of books for children.

He was presented with the Glaxo EU Fellowship for Science Writers by the Prime Minister of Ireland in 1978 and has contributed a great many articles to scientific and technical publications. His first published novel *Virtually Maria* was selected as Book of the Month by the Easons book retailing chain.

John Joyce is currently working on his next thriller *Fire & Ice,* describing an incident during the 1962 Cuban Missile Crisis when a rogue Russian telepathy experiment aboard a nuclear submarine almost triggered World War III.

For information and updates on *The Virtual Trilogy* and other John Joyce books, log on to:

www.virtualtrilogy.com

ACKNOWLEDGEMENTS

I would like to thank my personal editor-in-chief Lola Keyes-McDonnell, Anne Dodd, Liz Hyland, Gillian Markey, and Kevin Moriarty for their comments on draft manuscripts, as well as Peggy Cruickshank and company and the writer's group Resonance.

Technical assistance on the Nazca Lines came from Noel and Fiona O'Regan, from Evin McGovern and Ailve Rowe, and on earth energies in Wicklow from Con Connors and Douglas Gordon. Charles O'Malley and Madeline Gordon provided excellent advice on matters medical, while information on air navigation, communications and traffic control came from Barry Cullen and George Gogan.

I would also like to thank everyone I met in Tokyo, Atami and on Shodo-Shima for their courtesy and hospitality.

An essential guide to Japanese business practice was provided by Declan Collins, who told me the difference between *kobun* and *keiretsu*. I am indebted to Prof Adrian Phillips of Trinity College, Dublin, to everyone at Irish Helicopters Ltd, and to Greg Doherty and Dara Hogan of the Mount Leinster Hang-gliding Club.

Any errors in the interpretation of their generous and expert advice are entirely my own.

Once again I want to thank my children Jenny, Will and Jessie for putting up with all my imaginary friends and the "Quiet Please" notice on the study door.

A special word of thanks goes to all my readers, from all over the world, who took the time to email me with the question "when's the third book coming out?" This edition would not exist without your support.

Finally, I would like to express my gratitude and admiration to my wife Jane, who never let us get too far from the base camp while our two mountains were being climbed.

This book, like the two before, is lovingly dedicated to you.

Thank you.

FOR JANE

"I'm feeling pain," said the Minerva, "and I don't understand it. Is this the sort of pain you felt when your wife was killed?"

Gilkrensky looked at the image on the screen, wishing he could explain.

"Yes, Maria," he said at last. "It is."

"Then I know why you miss her so. I will do everything in my power to make sure you succeed."

"Thank you, Maria."

And for a long time there was silence, as the machine considered the paradox of love, and Gilkrensky the physics of yesterday, today and tomorrow . . .

from *A Matter of Time*

YESTERDAY,
TODAY
AND
TOMORROW

YESTERDAY

FIRST MURDER

IRELAND: A YEAR AGO . . .

It would be her first kill. Until now, all the operations she had performed with such precision had stopped short of murder. Corporate espionage, the theft of industrial secrets, blackmail and sabotage had all been part of her stock-in-trade, part of her arsenal in the cut-throat warfare of globalised business.

But this wasn't business, not anymore.

This was personal.

Yukiko Funakoshi moved her weight in the crook of the tree branch, feeling the frost-hardened lichen crunch beneath the palm of her hand. Above the darkened bowl of the valley the last stars twinkled faintly against the dawn. On the far side of the lake, massive cliffs, worn to ragged scree by the passage of time, towered over the water. And, standing guard like a stone sentry just below her on the hill, was the old farmhouse.

Yukiko could see the layout as if it had been a model in a training exercise; the track, curving down from the Dublin road, the gatehouse, the security fence around the cluster of laboratories and out-buildings, and the main courtyard. Two cars were parked there side by side, his and hers, a sleek BMW and an old yellow Mini.

In one of the pockets of her black cotton suit was a remote control unit, no bigger than a matchbox. It had three settings—*Safe, Automatic, and Manual*—the triggers of a bomb.

It would be her first murder, but it was not the first death.

Yukiko watched the light of dawn tint the high clouds with yellows and pinks. But the colours she saw were those of her mother's best kimono, glimpsed crumpled through a half-open door, the milky-white skin of an outstretched arm, and the red-wine stain of blood.

And in reflections from the lake, Yukiko saw a dark Tokyo night splashed with neon and the cheap apartment near Shinjuku station, where her father had died in her arms.

"I was weak, little tiger, but you're strong . . . aren't you? We trained you to be that way, your mother and me, before your uncle Gichin took you to be his . . . his guided missile. I have one more target for you now . . . that calculating swine . . . Gilkrensky!"

Yukiko closed her eyes against the visions and focussed on her target— the man who had killed her parents as surely as if he had put a gun to their heads and pulled the trigger.

Gilkrensky!

He was less than a hundred yards away!

She raised a pair of night-vision binoculars to her eyes and scanned the out-buildings around the farmhouse. In the ghostly green of the image intensifiers she could clearly make out the electric fence with its razor wire, the small black mushrooms of motion sensors and the painted sign which read *Gilcrest Radio Corporation—Advanced Electronics Facility—Keep Out!*

Yukiko smiled beneath her black cotton hood, lowered the binoculars and lifted a slim laptop computer onto her knees.

Keep out indeed!

She had already been inside, thanks to the electronic jamming device planted by her accomplice inside the farmhouse. Now she was on-line and wired to every security system in the place, in complete control. She carefully opened the computer, shielding the glow of its display against her body. There in front of her was full access to the GRC security system, a mosaic of images from a dozen closed-circuit TV cameras, and each one of them expertly jammed with a recorded digital image of an empty vista.

It had been worth the price, worth seducing that spineless slug Delgado who would now be pacing his bedroom in the farmhouse below, waiting for her to steal Gilkrensky's new supercomputer and make them both rich.

Fool! Gilkrensky's death would bind Delgado to her forever, as she worked her way along the line of people who had to pay with their lives.

She raised the binoculars again. A single light still glowed from a window above the courtyard. It was Gilkrensky's workroom, where he had been labouring all night to overcome the software problem that was the last hurdle to success.

Her eyes travelled back again to the two cars in the courtyard. Why did Gilkrensky's wife cling to that little old car? What kind of woman was she, who flouted wealth this way?

Then, she saw movement. Two figures had emerged from the guard-room and were looking up at the security cameras. Who were they? Did they know something was wrong?

Yukiko lowered the binoculars, pulled out a cell phone and pressed a quick-dial key. The number answered instantly.

"There are two men in the courtyard," hissed Yukiko. "Who are they?"

Tony Delgado sounded frightened. "I don't know. Describe them."

"One is short and stocky. The other is taller and dark. They look ex-military."

"Does the short one have a moustache?"

"Yes."

"Then that's Crowe, the man Gilkrensky brought in to upgrade security and protect the Minerva. But he's not supposed to be here until this afternoon. He must have arrived late last night and parked around the back."

The two men walked out through the farmhouse gate, making their way around the perimeter of the security fence, inspecting it carefully as they went.

"Is he good?"

"He's ex-army," Delgado said, "and so are the people with him. If you have the Minerva, just move away and run. There's no way they can catch you on foot."

Yukiko sat motionless in the tree as Crowe and his partner waded through the heather towards her. The perimeter fence would bring them within a few metres of the tree in which she hid. She thought of the powerful motorcycle concealed in the bushes behind her. Should she stay and trust in her absolute stillness, or run? She had not yet taken here revenge. Gilkrensky was still alive.

A light blinked on in Gilkrensky's living quarters. The computer on Yukiko's knees gave an almost inaudible "bleep". She looked down.

Someone else was awake and sending an video message on the farmhouse network. Yukiko lowered the volume of the machine to a whisper and called up the message on the screen.

She was staring at the face of a woman with long red hair, speaking to a web cam mounted on an unseen computer. The woman's green eyes were bright with tears as she said, "Theo. You knew what I'd do if you went back to that bloody machine of yours last night. So I'm leaving you a message on the only thing you ever listen to. I'm going, Theo. I'm leaving you! I can't take this anymore . . . this being alone."

The face on the screen turned away. Behind it, Yukiko saw an open wardrobe and a rucksack, packed and ready, near a door. Then the woman stopped and faced the camera again. This time her tears were flowing. "Theo! I hate this! Why can't we just talk like we used to? I know we're so different, you and I. But I love you, Theo . . . I really do!"

Yukiko watched as the recording ended and the screen reverted to the images from the security cameras.

Love!

Yukiko had not known love—real love—since the death of her mother. For twenty years she had known nothing of warmth, understanding or belonging. In her father's country she had been a half-caste "Jap" taunted and bullied. In Japan she had been an "outsider", a *gaijin*, to be despised and ignored.

But who needs love, when you have hate? And what greater pleasure can there be than the consummation of a lifetime's hatred in an exquisitely crafted act of revenge?

Crowe and his partner were fifty metres away. If she melted back into the shadows, protected by her *ninja* suit and her years of training in stealth, she could still be ready when Gilkrensky finally emerged and got into the car.

Then Yukiko remembered . . .

The bomb! The woman could trigger the bomb!

She squinted through the binoculars just in time to see Gilkrensky's wife stride out into the courtyard, heading past the BMW to the yellow Mini. She watched her wrench open the door, throw in her rucksack and haul on the ignition, again . . . and again . . . and again . . . The laboured heave of the starter motor echoed across the valley. A pheasant whirred into the air. Crowe and the man beside him looked back towards the farmhouse.

Yukiko cursed. She had planned this moment to perfection—and now her perfect strategy was falling apart!

Delgado was a fool. She should never have trusted him with a plan like this.

Then the woman collapsed in tears over the steering wheel of the little car. Yukiko trained her binoculars on the guard-room door. It was still shut. The door of the Mini flew open. The woman dragged out her rucksack and ran to the BMW. Yukiko saw her rummage in the bag for a moment, unlock the door of the car and get in. The moment she turned the key in the ignition, a kilo of carefully placed explosives would blow her and the vehicle to kingdom come. Yukiko's hand slid down to the bomb control. If she disarmed the device, it would eventually be found and security around Gilkrensky would tighten even more.

Then she saw him, at the window of his workroom, looking down at his wife.

Yukiko saw their eyes meet.

She thought of the blood on her mother's best kimono. She remembered the words her father had mumbled to her before he died . . . and drew back her hand.

This way was better. This was justice!

She would make Gilkrensky suffer the agony of loss, as she had, before she killed him.

5

The silence of the valley was shattered by the roar of an explosion, the crash of splintering glass, and the screams of the man at the window . . .

TODAY

1

NAZCA, PERU - PRESENT DAY

Jessica Wright watched the flat desert slide beneath the old Huey helicopter as the drum of its engine pounded on her skull. She was tired, thirsty and jet-lagged. But above all she was angry—angry that she had been forced to fly half-way round the world on a mission that should have been accomplished by a simple phone call.

What the hell was Theo Gilkrensky playing at?

She squinted into the sun, now low on the horizon to the west, and cursed that she had been in too much of a hurry to pack her Polaroid clip-ons. The closed cockpit was like an oven. She wiped the sweat from the bridge of her thick-framed glasses, and pushed her long brown hair back behind her ear-phones to give herself some air. As she moved, she noticed the pilot eyeing her legs. He was a tiny nut-brown man who looked as if his whole body had been shrivelled by the sun, like those dried tomatoes she could buy back in London. "Dehydrated Man," she thought. "Just add water and serve!"

He was pointing at the ground, while his black eyebrows rose in question above the mirrored lenses of his sunglasses. "You wanna go higher, maybe?" he shouted above the clatter of the engine. "Look at the lines before the light fades?"

"What lines?"

"The lines! The Nazca Lines! Everyone who flies in my helicopter wants to see the lines. Your boss, Doctor Theo, *El gringo rico.* He go crazy about them."

Yes, thought Jessica. Crazy! You have that right.

"OK," she yelled back. "Have it your way. Let's see the lines!"

The pilot twisted the throttle and the helicopter climbed into the sky. As she watched through the Perspex panels, Jessica saw that they were flying over a narrow coastal strip. On one side, the Pacific Ocean was turning red beneath the sinking sun. On the other, the Andes Mountains rose dark and mysterious into the dusk. Below them, the desert stretched flat and featureless, broken here and there only by the giant rifts of geological faults, stretching inland from the coast.

The pilot grinned at her.

"There!" he shouted. "The lines."

Jessica peered through the panel at her feet. At first, she saw nothing and then, as she stared at the barren landscape, she could make out lines, some random and some in definite shapes, as if a giant hand had used the ground as a doodle-pad. There was a massive drawing that looked like a supersonic jet with swept-back wings, huge straight lines and vast geometric shapes. Then, on a smaller scale, there were pictures; a spider, a bird, a monkey with a whirlpool spiral for a tail. But even these must have been hundreds of metres long.

And Theo had spent millions to study *this*?

"Somebody's idea of a joke?" she shouted above the din of the engine.

The pilot scowled at her. "No joke, lady. These lines are over two thousand years old, and nobody knows how they were drawn. There! See those little towers. They're for the tourists who can't afford a plane ride to see the pictures."

"But they're just . . ." And then, as Jessica looked at the giant drawings so far below her feet, the mystery hit her. How could a pattern that only made sense from the air have been drawn on the desert floor two thousand years before mankind learned how to fly?

Then she knew why Theo was interested. It was all part of the crazy quest he had embarked on six months ago. She should have known!

"Pretty neat, huh?" shouted the pilot. "Your boss and me, we fly over them many times, with all sorts of fancy equipment, measuring this and that. Then he decides on a spot and flies in millions of dollars' worth of gear from Lima by private jet. Had to get clearance from the military at the highest level to work here, he did, really throwing his money around in all the right places. Still, that didn't stop him causing a lot of trouble."

"Trouble?" asked Jessica. "What trouble?"

The pilot shrugged. "They're a superstitious people around here, lady. They don't like rich *gringos* messing with things they don't understand. Nazca is a holy place for them. Maybe they're afraid your Doctor Theo will ruin the lines and bring bad magic down out of the sky. Maybe they're afraid he'll frighten the tourists and put them out of business. Maybe they're scared he'll make the *Pachamama*, the earth mother they all worship, angry. Whatever it is, they don't like him. And then, of course, there's *Sendero*."

"What?"

"*Sendero Luminoso*, the Shining Path, communist guerrillas, terrorists . . . you know. They haven't been too active since their leader was captured in '92 and the government declared the amnesty. But this is just the sort of cause they could still get mixed up in . . . a rich *gringo*, paying off the government, upsetting the locals, causing trouble. I tried to warn him, but he wouldn't listen. Every day, at dawn and dusk, he uses a computer to draw big pictures in the sky. The sky is alien to the people here, lady. They fear it. They love the earth. He's causing a lot of trouble, your Doctor Theo."

"He won't be causing it much longer," shouted Jessica. "He has to come back with me!"

The pilot nodded, and pointed to the ground again.

"There! See what I mean?"

Looking down, Jessica saw a huddle of caravans, glittering against the sand. They were arranged in a crude semicircle around a large square of marked ground and in the centre was a metal tower, taller and newer than the other viewing platforms. It looked for all the world like an experimental drilling rig, or the test site for an atomic bomb.

She saw armed guards around the perimeter.

"That's it," shouted the pilot. "You wanna land now?"

"That's what I'm here for."

"You got it!" And the engine noise made another head-splitting octave change as the machine settled towards the desert floor in a cloud of flying dust.

"Miss Wright! You shouldn't have come!"

A short, thickset terrier of a man with a bull neck and a barrel chest, ran from the caravans to greet her, or was it to intercept her? His formerly neat moustache had been joined by rich desert stubble and his skin was darkly tanned. Sweat stained the armpits of his khaki shirt.

"Where is he?" she said.

Major Jonathan Crowe, former head of security for the Gilcrest Radio Corporation since Maria's death and, more recently, Theo's personal bodyguard, glared at her defiantly.

"He's busy, Miss Wright. He's asked me to escort you back to Lima and says he'll talk to you after the experiment."

"I have to speak to him now, Major. I've travelled right across the world."

Crowe glanced at his watch. The setting sun turned the desert pink around them.

"It isn't safe here, Miss Wright . . ."

But Jessica had already pushed past him, striding across the hard-packed crust of stones to the caravans. She saw technicians busying themselves at the four corners of the marked square. Their heads turned at the sound of raised voices. Crowe ran after her, but she kept going. She had to talk to Theo. She had to make him see sense.

And she was going to do it right now!

"Miss Wright. I must insist!"

Crowe stepped in front of her, blocking her way.

"I am the Chief Executive Officer of this corporation," she said slowly.

"And I report directly to Dr Gilkrensky on a private contract," Crowe said. "I don't work for you anymore. Now, for your own safety, I must insist that you leave."

Jessica looked beyond him. The caravan was only a few yards away. "I don't give a shit!" she spat, and pushed past him again.

"Miss Wright!"

This time he grabbed her painfully by her left arm.

"Crowe! Get your hands off me!"

"It's all right, Major," said a voice from the caravan door. "She's come this far. You won't stop her now."

Gilkrensky stood in the doorway of the caravan, dressed in dirty brown slacks, worn running shoes and an old leather jacket over a grubby white shirt. His long dark hair and sparse beard almost hid the long scar running from his left temple to his chin. The hands that held the doorframe were scarred too, badly burnt from his desperate attempts to pull his wife's body from the burning car.

Jessica still had nightmares about those hands.

"Theo! We have to talk."

"Come on in then."

She looked past him, into the control van. In the darkness beyond his shoulders, she saw out the flashing indicators of a dozen instrument panels. As he moved to one side to let her in, she also saw a big laptop computer, the size of a briefcase. The words Minerva 3,000, glared at her from its lid.

"Not in there," she said. "I'm not talking to you in front of that . . . that thing!"

Gilkrensky frowned, and looked at his watch. "All right then, we'll go to my own place. Follow me!"

"It'll be sunset in twenty minutes," said Crowe, speaking past her.

"I know," Gilkrensky said. "But this won't take long."

He pushed open the door on the next caravan and led her inside. There were books and papers everywhere, a simple metal bed, a table, and a pair of chairs. The only colour in the place came from the setting sun and from a picture in a simple wooden frame. It was a photograph of a woman with coppery red hair in a forget-me-not blue dress against a deep green backdrop of trees. Jessica scowled at the picture as Gilkrensky stepped over to the refrigerator and pulled her out a bottle of mineral water. She popped the cap, took a long pull and rolled the ice-cold glass across her forehead, while Gilkrensky shovelled a pile of books onto the floor from a chair. She sat down, with her back to the photograph.

"Why didn't you answer my calls?" she asked.

"I was busy. And besides, I thought you weren't speaking to me after that row when I got back from Florida."

"That was personal. This is business. We have to talk about the corporation. It's been months since you've been at a board meeting. The other shareholders have lost confidence and the Japanese case is coming to a head. You have to come back and sort this out."

"What's the problem? You've got lawyers and consultants on contract. Put them on it. You're my CEO, Jess, my top manager. Go manage it!"

Jessica banged the glass bottle down on the Formica table, splashing water on the books and papers. Yes, it was her corporation, her life's work. And now he was throwing it all away.

"Jesus Christ, Theo! I've travelled thousand of miles to talk to you, and that's all you can say?"

Gilkrensky sat down on the other side of the table. His brown eyes stared into hers for a moment.

"There's nothing else to say, Jess. I'm selling out."

"What!"

For Jessica, the whole world suddenly stood still. Every detail of Theo's face froze in front of her. Every sound inside and outside the caravan, from the purr of generators, the crackle of footsteps on the desert crust, to her own breathing, seemed to reach her from another planet.

"I'm selling my shares," he said. "They don't matter to me anymore."

A tiny distant voice, that she barely recognised as her own said, "Why?"

Suddenly, Theo Gilkrensky looked old. She saw the grey flecks in his dark hair, the deep lines around his eyes, the tiredness.

"Like I said, they don't matter anymore. Besides, I need the money for something else."

"For what? What could be more important than the Corporation?"

"It's personal." Outside the caravan, the lower edge of the setting sun touched the horizon. Gilkrensky glanced at his watch. Then he got up from the table, took a radio headset from a shelf and put it on.

"You have to come back and discuss this with the Board," she said, shaking her head. "You have to meet them and talk it through."

"I'll talk to them on the phone. My lawyers can take care of the rest of it."

"You don't understand, Theo. Your shares won't be worth the paper they're written on unless you come back and sort out this mess with the Japanese. The Mawashi-Saito lawsuit isn't going to go away. I've spent months getting them to agree to talk. There are going to be preliminary negotiations in Tokyo, next week. But you have to be there. It's you they're suing!"

Gilkrensky stared out of the caravan window towards the metal tower and the setting sun.

"You can handle it, Jess. That's what I pay you for."

"Not without you, Theo. It's gone too far now."

Gilkrensky looked at his watch again.

"Jess. You shouldn't have come. I wanted to tell you all this back at the—"

His hand went to the ear-piece of his radio headset.

"I'll be there in a minute," he said into the microphone. "Start the countdown without me."

Jessica reached out across the table between them and took his hand.

"Theo. Please! We have to talk this through!"

"I'll see you back in Lima, Jess, tomorrow."

"No. I won't go back without you!"

"You have to. It's dangerous here. Major Crowe will take you back in the helicopter."

"I see. A military escort, is it?"

"Jessica," he said, turning to face her. "This experiment is the last of a very expensive series. It's important to me."

"I know!" she snapped. "It's been the only thing in your life since Maria died, hasn't it! Well, let me tell you something! Since you dumped me after Florida, this corporation has been the only thing in my life. I built it, I've kept it together while you've been chasing around the world after a ghost, and I won't see you flush it down the toilet."

She stood glaring at him. Everything they'd shared on a personal level was gone. She felt nothing for him anymore but anger, that he could put this stupid quest for a dead woman before what she had built for him, a business empire worth billions.

"No!" she said flatly. "I'm not leaving here without you. *Mister Chairman!*"

Gilkrensky stood framed in the doorway against the setting sun.

"All right then," he said. "Wait here, and don't go outside. This shouldn't take more than an hour."

She watched him turn and walk back to the control van. Crowe stepped over and blocked her way.

"I'm sorry about grabbing you earlier, Miss Wright. But there are bandits around here. That's why the guards are armed. It's not safe to go out after dark."

"You're very loyal, Major," she said. "But I know bullshit when I hear it."

"Perhaps. But, like I said, I work directly for the Chairman now."

Jessica saw the door of the control cabin close.

"I know," she said. "And I work for the Corporation. Perhaps I always have."

Gilkrensky shut the door behind him and ran his eyes over the banks of controls, monitors and data-recorders that clicked and purred all around him. He was alone in the cramped compartment.

"Is everything ready?"

"Yes, Theo," said a woman's voice from a speaker in front of him. "All systems are operational. I will commence the initiation sequence in ten seconds to synchronise with local sunset time."

"And the holographic projectors?"

"All on line. Image creation commences in five . . . four . . . three . . . two . . . one!"

Gilkrensky stared out through the Perspex window of the caravan across the marked square on the desert. The sun dipped below the horizon. Its deep red fire glistened on the polished metal of the test tower. In a moment the world would be in darkness . . .

There was a flash of light from each of the four hologram projectors. Towering into the blackness like a mirage was the colossal image of a pyramid, a hundred and sixty metres high. It burst above the desert floor, shimmered for a second, and then hardened into a perfect crystalline shape, a flawless ancient creation, timeless, mysterious and alien.

From a bank of loudspeakers, three notes boomed out across the desert. *Dim! Dom! Dim!*

"Hologram initiated," said the voice. "Sound signal emitted! Synchronous wave-form peak predicted in thirteen minutes and fifty seconds. Nothing can stop it now."

"And the test material?"

"In place on the tower. The recorders are starting to pick up the first signatures of the energy wave. It's working."

Outside on the desert floor, the towering shape shone brightly against the dying glow of the sun. In the clear sky above it, dark clouds began to form out of nowhere. There was the roll of distant thunder, getting closer.

"Can we maintain the image?"

"That is not a problem. Image strength is one hundred percent and stable."

Gilkrensky glanced down at the rows of energy recorders below the Minerva computer. The faintest pulse of power was dancing in the low ranges of the instruments.

"Time to event?"

"Ten minutes and five seconds."

"Good. Maintain the recorders at maximum sensit—"

A loud smack, as if the plastic window had been hit with a hammer, jerked his head round. Behind him, on the wall of the caravan, a digital video recorder shattered, fizzled, and died.

Gilkrensky looked up.

Staring down at him, from the centre of a spider's web of radiating cracks just a foot above his head, was the single unblinking eye of a bullet-hole.

2

THE ATTACK

Jessica gazed out of the caravan window, hypnotised by the holographic pyramid. Above it, clouds whirled in tight spirals, their moving bellies lit blood-red by the fading sun. What on earth was Theo doing? What the hell did it all cost?"

"What is that thing, Major?"

Then she heard the shot.

For a moment Jessica didn't recognise the sound. Crowe grabbed her and dragged her to the floor, scattering books and papers in all directions. She felt spilt water, cold against her leg. She heard another shot and the ragged volley of return fire, much closer this time. A distant *crump*, followed by a shrill whine and the thud of an explosion sounded from the far side of the compound. The caravan floor shuddered beneath her. Stones clattered on the roof above her head.

"What the hell's happening?"

Crowe reached up and flicked off the light. In the glow of the holographic pyramid she saw him pulling an automatic pistol from inside his jacket. He flicked off the safety-catch and pulled back the slide, feeding a bullet into the chamber.

"Jesus!" he hissed. "They're using mortars!"

"Who are?"

"I don't know! It's not *Sendero*'s style to attack in the open like this and the local bandits don't have the cash for that sort of firepower. It could be anyone. Pass me those binoculars! Quick!"

Jessica was suddenly afraid. It was one thing to wage corporate warfare from the safety of a boardroom in London. But this was something else entirely.

"What do we do?" she whispered.

"We've got about three minutes before they get the range with that mortar," said Crowe. "Once they do, then they'll blow us to kingdom come. Stay close to me. We have to get Dr Gilkrensky and make it to the chopper before they put it out of action."

"Lead the way. I'm right behind you!"

Keeping low, she followed Crowe to the caravan door. Outside, the roar of revving vehicles signalled the evacuation of the technicians. Dust, the smell of cordite, the distant crackle of enemy gunfire and the returning blasts from the guards around the camp filled the air around her. Muzzle flashes lit up the escaping trucks, the caravans, and the tower.

"Where's Theo?"

"In the control van. You know where the helicopter is?"

"I do, but I'm not leaving without him!"

"Miss Wright, get out of here! I'll bring the Chairman!"

"I'll come with you."

"No!"

"I'm not leaving without him!"

Crowe glanced back at her from the doorway. "We don't have time to argue. If you're coming, keep close to me and stay low. They seem to be shooting high."

He ducked out of the caravan door and ran to the control room. As she raced behind him, she heard the *whip, whip* of bullets above her head. The roar of a mortar bomb shook the ground, spitting dust and showering her with pebbles.

"Theo!"

He was crouching beside the Minerva computer, staring out at the gigantic holographic pyramid. Jessica glanced up at the towering mirage, and then stared again. At the very centre of that vast shape, a faint red glow of unearthly light danced and grew. What was it? Had the mortars hit something on the tower and set it on fire?

17

"It's started," shouted Gilkrensky. "I have to stay and see what happens."

"No, Doctor!" Crowe said. "We must go now!"

"Theo! Please!"

Outside, the gunfire fell silent as both sides stood mesmerised by the unearthly glow filling the pyramid. Thunder cracked in the dark sky above the site. A lightning bolt seared into the ground close by. The caravan shook. The instruments on the walls went wild, spooling recorder paper onto the floor.

The gunfire started again. The double hammer-blow of two bullets smacked into the caravan window.

"You're right," shouted Gilkrensky above the din. Reaching up to the panel, he slid the Minerva computer out of its docking station and scuttled to the door of the caravan. Jessica saw the weird glow inside the pyramid change from red to orange. The earth shook beneath her feet. There was a sudden rush of wind. Was it from the helicopter or from something else?

"Shit Theo!" she screamed. "What the hell have you done?"

"We've no time for this," shouted Crowe. "We have to get to the chopper before those mortars blow it to smithereens."

"The picture!" Gilkrensky shouted. "I left Maria's picture inside."

"Forget it, we have to go now!"

A mortar bomb hit close on the far side of the caravan with a roar that hammered Jessica's eardrums. The air filled with dust. As it cleared, she saw Gilkrensky looking back as smoke poured from the wrecked shell where he had been standing only seconds before.

Through the ringing in her ears, Jessica heard the whine of the helicopter's engines and felt the thump of its rotors on the air.

"Come on," screamed Crowe, "before the pilot leaves us behind!"

He grabbed Gilkrensky and they ran across the hard-packed stones towards the flash of the Huey's navigation lights. The pilot waved to them from the far side of the cockpit. Then they were scrambling over the skids of the machine into the cabin. Jessica flung herself into one of the long bench seats along the well facing the open door. The engine noise rose to a scream, the rotors bit the air, and the machine clawed its way up off the ground.

Jessica grabbed the back of her seat just in time to stop herself falling forwards into space. Theo was in the co-pilot's seat, stowing the Minerva and snapping his safety harness shut. Crowe was straining to slide the big metal door into place.

"It's jammed," he screamed above the mayhem of the churning rotors.

"Never mind!" shouted Gilkrensky. "Just strap yourself in!"

The blinding burst of a lightning bolt arced past them to the ground, followed by the boom of thunder, right over their heads.

Below them, the red flash of an explosion lit the swirling dust clouds as the mortar bombs found the camp. Another caravan burst into flames. The control van was hit again, shattering it completely. The pyramid shimmered and died, but at its core, the orange light still glowed and pulsated with a life of its own.

"What the hell is that?" shouted Jessica, as the wind tore at her hair through the open doorway.

The helicopter rocked as another bolt of lightning streaked across the sky.

"Keep climbing!" Gilkrensky shouted to the pilot. "And switch off your navigation lights or they'll spot us from the ground!"

The pilot's hands remained on the controls.

"Switch them off! For God's sake!"

"Don't you worry, Senor," shouted the pilot, and turned to smile at him. "They won't be shooting at us."

"Why the hell not . . ." began Jessica, and then froze as something hard and cold pressed into her right temple. From the darkness of the well on the other side of the cabin, a hand reached around the central divider. That hand held a large automatic pistol pressed against her skull.

"This is my brother Roberto," shouted the pilot. "Now pass your gun to him please, Senor Crowe. And you, Doctor Theo, you stay nice and calm too, eh? We're going for a little flight up into the mountains. See a few people about a little ransom, eh?"

"*Sendero*?" shouted Gilkrensky.

"Maybe," replied the pilot. "Maybe not. You just keep your hands in your lap now. Roberto's very nervous. He don't like flying."

19

Jessica felt Crowe twist in his seat. His left hand was supporting himself against the doorframe. His right hand held his own gun by the barrel, passing it across to Roberto who let go of his grip on the pilot's seat to take it. The pistol was still pressed against Jessica's head.

Crowe looked straight past her at Roberto.

"There you go," he shouted. "Don't do anything stupid . . ."

Then he let the gun slip from his fingers. Roberto's eyes followed it to the floor for an instant. The pressure of the pistol against Jessica's temple eased and in that split second Crowe's right hand had smacked against Roberto's left, knocking the gun-barrel away from her head.

There was a flash, like a camera. The boom of the automatic stung Jessica's ears.

The pilot twisted to look back. A struggle broke out beside her as Crowe and Roberto fought for the gun. She saw it in front of her, grasped tightly in Roberto's fist. Crowe's fingers were around it, pushing it away from him. The pilot was shouting. The helicopter lurched in the sky.

There was another dazzling flash and the crack of a gunshot. The pilot jerked forward, strained against his seatbelt and fell back. Blood glistened on the shattered windscreen in front of him.

Gilkrensky swore.

Jessica's stomach churned as the helicopter spun out of control. The open door yawned in front of her. She held onto her seat for dear life. She saw Gilkrensky strruggling desperately to haul the pilot's body clear of the joystick. Crowe and Roberto still writhed on the floor at her feet. The Peruvian had the gun, he brought it round—

Jessica stamped down on his face, feeling the crunch of bone beneath her heel. The man screamed. Crowe brought up his knee into the man's groin. Roberto rolled towards the open door, screamed again, and vanished. Then there was just Crowe, reaching over the pilot's seat to help Theo pull the dead man away from the controls.

Jessica saw the fires of the burning camp far below spinning towards them. She felt herself thrown back in her seat as the machine bottomed out of its dive like a roller-coaster. Then they were spiralling back into the air above the camp.

Another bolt of lightning arced across the heavens. Thunder shook the helicopter.

"I have it under control," shouted Gilkrensky.

Jessica was shaking. The sweat felt cold on her skin. Her ears hissed from the blast of the gun. She fought back the urge to vomit as she fumbled with the safety harness on her seat, trying to buckle it. Crowe leant over and clicked it shut.

"Thank you, Miss Wright," he shouted.

Below them, the orange glow at the centre of the pyramid faded and died. The gunfire ceased. The only sign of the attack was the flicker of the burning caravans. In the light of the flames, Jessica saw the remains of the test tower.

The top section had vanished, as if someone had neatly cut it off with a giant saw.

"We have to go back!" Gilkrensky shouted above the racket of the engines. "The experiment worked! It dematerialised the tower! I have to measure the effect."

Jessica couldn't believe her ears.

"Not now!" shouted Crowe. "It'd be suicide."

"After the bandits have gone then—tomorrow or the next day."

Crowe stared down into the darkness. "*If* it was bandits," he yelled back. "An attack like that isn't *Sendero*'s style, and local bandits don't have the money for that kind of firepower."

"What are you saying?"

Crowe shook his head. "Did you notice how well they were organised, how high they were firing, or the way the mortars only hit the caravans after we'd left?"

"A bullet hit the control van while I was in it," shouted Gilkrensky.

"But it missed! And you were a perfect target, silhouetted against the window like that. The sniper could have taken his time and nailed you right between the eyes. And yet he missed. I think someone stage-managed the whole thing to warn us off or to capture you alive."

"But who?"

Jessica peered down into the blackness. The burning caravans faded into the night as the helicopter turned and headed back to Lima.

"What about Yukiko Funakoshi?" she yelled. "She could afford to hire mercenaries like that!"

"She would have crept into the camp and gone for the kill herself," shouted Crowe. "And besides, she hasn't been heard of for six months. Perhaps she's lost interest. Or perhaps she's dead."

"I doubt it," Gilkrensky said, staring down at the camp. "But I'd give a lot to know how the hell someone like her, who's wanted for murder in at least three countries, can just disappear off the face of the earth like that . . ."

3

THE ENIGMA OF MISS YOSHIDA

Yori Nakoma stretched his back against the pain and cursed Miss Yoshida for the hundredth time that day. Hauling lantern nets full of oysters fouled with seaweed and dripping sea-squirts was heavy work, even with a primitive hydraulic winch. It would have been so much easier, if only he could have used Miss Yoshida's jetty.

He dried his callused hands on a rag, leant against the cabin of his boat and pulled a packet of Hope cigarettes from his oilskin trousers. The packet had a blue bow and arrow symbol on the front and he thought, as he did almost every time he lit up, how good it would be to put an arrow through Miss Yoshida's heart. He snorted to himself at the thought of her, as a puff of cigarette smoke floated out over the calm water towards the beach, the jetty, and Miss Yoshida's house.

Yori was a native of Shodo-shima, one of the larger islands in Japan's inland Seto Sea, famous for its olive groves, its misty mountains and its temples. A remote enough spot, where people still live by the rhythms of the ocean and the sky, yet large enough to guarantee peace and even anonymity to someone on the run from the madness of the modern world.

His family had always worked the beaches, gathering seaweeds, picking shellfish from the rocks or raking cockles from the sand. It was hard work and getting harder all the time now that he was growing older, now that the fancy hotels at Tonosho, Shodo-shima's main port, were getting cheaper shellfish from the mainland. His sisters and brothers had all moved away and

Yori himself had never married. The only things he seemed to care about were his oyster farm, the beach and Miss Yoshida's jetty.

She had chosen the very house that Yori had always dreamt of buying but never had. It was the perfect property for an oyster farmer, with an unspoilt view of the bay, a plot of land that would have been an ideal store for his lantern nets, and a jetty. Yori could really have used that jetty. It had a long iron walkway rooted firmly in concrete pillars and a hinged end, linked in turn to a barge that floated with the tide. It was accessible twenty-four hours a day through the highest and lowest of spring tides, with stout mooring bollards to hold the heaviest of boats and access to the cliff road. Why had he not bought it years ago, when land was cheap? How had she come by the money to snatch it out from under his nose?

A net of oysters rattled down onto the deck with a hollow clack. The starfish had been at work again, forcing the shells open, devouring the meats inside and robbing him of his profits. If he couldn't make more money soon he would be forced to sell up and leave the island, just like the rest of his family.

He cursed the woman again, and tried to piece together the snatches of village gossip he'd heard about her. Her full name was Fusaro Yoshida and she was a rich "office lady" from the big Nippon Steel plant at Osaka. She had come to Shodo-shima over three years ago in the spring, looking for a quiet place to relax and indulge her passion for oil painting, or at least that was what everybody said.

Since buying the property she had been a regular visitor, quiet and reserved, polite and gracious but fanatical about her privacy. After Christmas, she'd paid a short visit to recuperate from an accident at Nippon Steel. The story was that her right arm had been severely burnt in an incident on the factory floor and, when she paid for her fish at the market at Tonosho, the sleeve of her coat had fallen back far enough to reveal a thick surgical bandage.

For a fortnight in January she had been gone again and then, from early February, right through to the spring, she had lived full-time in her house overlooking the bay, resting, painting and visiting the mainland once in a while. She had even taken to inviting other artists down to spend time with her. Yori had seen them exercising on the cliff top in the early morning, or swimming from the beach. But they never came down to Tonosho to shop, which Miss Yoshida took care of herself on her neat yellow moped with a white wire carrier.

Yori had asked if he could use her jetty, a simple request which anyone with any understanding of the reality of island life would have granted, particularly if they had known about Yori's family connections with the less savoury members of society on the mainland.

"*Konichi-wa*, Yoshida-san," he had said, as he bowed in greeting when they had met at the dockside fish market in Tonosho one morning in April. Miss Yoshida had bowed in return and for a few minutes they exchanged the customary pleasantries about the weather, the island and the price of fish while Yori came to the point. She was tall for a Japanese, in her late twenties or early thirties, if Yori was any judge, and she might even have been pretty, had it not been for the very prominent buck teeth, the thick glasses resting low on her nose and the lifeless black hair, worn in a school girl's pony-tail. There was a touch of foreign blood in her too, the mark of the *gaijin* about her eyes and mouth.

She stood before him, in a plain skirt, thick white socks and a wide-brimmed straw hat, listening for the minimum time demanded by custom for politeness. Then she said, "Thank you for your offer, Nakoma-san. But I bought that house for peace and quiet, at the suggestion of my doctors and I intend to protect it. My apologies, but no!"

Yori protested. Miss Yoshida was increasingly firm. She had come to Shodo-shima for privacy, and that was what she would protect at all costs. There must be no disturbances, no trespasses on her land, and particularly no landings upon her jetty.

That had been in April before the storm. It had blown in from the west, raising an army of waves that had marched into the bay, snapping ropes, buckling barrels and sending hundreds of Yori's lantern nets full of oysters to wrap themselves in knots on Miss Yoshida's beach. Yori had looked at what remained of his oyster crop, now clumped along the sand by the jetty, and remembered what Miss Yoshida had said.

There was no other way. He had sailed back to the village, gone to the nearest telephone, and called Nippon Steel in Osaka. Could he speak to Miss Yoshida? It was urgent.

"Which one, please? There are five women of that name in the company."

So Yori spoke to them all. And none had ever heard of a house on Shodo-shima, a jetty, or an oyster farmer called Yori Nakoma.

When he had met her outside the supermarket in Tonosho a week later he had apologised, bowing deeply with the required remorse, for reclaiming his lantern nets from her property without permission. Her reply had been as frosty as he had expected. But when he explained that he had not been able to contact her at Nippon Steel, he felt her eyes burn on him.

"What name did you ask for?" she snapped.

Yori told her.

"That explains why you could not reach me," she said quickly. "That is my maiden name."

Yori was confused. "And your married name, in case I need to contact you again?"

"You won't," she said, eyes blazing and, without bowing, she had packed her purchases into the wire carrier on her moped and driven off while Yori fumed in frustration.

What chord had she struck? Was it that she was the very sort of person for whom his family had scraped and toiled on the beach for generations, a rich young upstart from the mainland and a *gaijin* woman at that? Yori returned to his lonely flat that evening, obsessed with Miss Yoshida, and got drunk. Was she on the run from a jealous husband? Was she a drug dealer? A spy?

It was all very strange.

But not as strange as the incident on the ferry.

One afternoon, at the end of May, Yori had been careless and caught his hand in the hydraulic winch on his boat, bruising it painfully. There might even be a fracture, said his doctor, but to be sure would mean an X-ray at the hospital in Okayama.

So after a painful night Yori Nakoma had walked to the port at Tonosho, bought a ticket on the 7.05 a.m. ferry for the mainland and been the first passenger aboard, climbing the metal stairs to the wheelhouse to share a cigarette with the skipper, an old friend of his from the island.

It was raining that morning, with a fine mist rolling down from the mountains. Through the big windows that looked aft over the loading deck, Yori saw the fish lorries driving aboard, the first busload of tourists from one of the hotels rumbling down the ramp and on the jetty near the ticket office, a small figure in green oil-skins on a yellow moped.

Miss Yoshida!

He watched as she dismounted and pulled a bag from the wire carrier. Then she chained the moped outside the ferry office while she bought her ticket, and walked to the gangplank, her wide-brimmed hat pulled low against the rain.

"Is that the woman?" said the ferry captain, who knew Yori's tale of woe by heart.

"It is. I only wish I knew more about her."

The skipper nodded and took a long drag on his cigarette.

"You could always watch her on the security video."

He pointed to a row of black and white television monitors at the back of the wheelhouse, each showing a different view of the ferry; the car deck, the mooring lines, the aft sun-deck and the salon. There were groups of tourists huddled around tables, already drinking Asahi beer out of cans. Yori looked past them and, off in a discreet corner all by herself, was Miss Yoshida.

Yori lit another cigarette and watched her, as the ferry made its way from island to island. Outside the window, fishing boats, fish farms, and derelict cargo vessels slid by, but Yori saw none of these. All he saw was the image of Miss Yoshida in the corner of the salon beneath him. They were nearing Okayama now, the grey steel framework of a factory, tall chimneys and drooping overhead cables marked the beginnings of the city.

"She's not doing much," he said.

And then she vanished.

"Probably gone to the toilet," said the skipper. "We don't have cameras in there!" But Yori was already out of the wheelhouse and onto the upper deck.

The throb of diesels was loud in his ear. Rain spattered on the awning above his head.

He looked down the stairwell. Miss Yoshida stood outside the women's rest room. Her wide hat and her bag were in her hands and her thick glasses flashed once as she looked about her. Then she was gone inside and the door shut.

Yori stepped back, to where he could see the door without being seen, and waited.

Ten minutes later, the ferry docked at Okayama. Down went the loading ramp, the fish lorries started their engines, the tourists filed out of the lounge and into their tour buses. The decks were full of departing passengers.

Then, as Yori watched, a tall lady emerged from the rest room and looked about her, as Miss Yoshida had done. But this was not the Miss Yoshida Yori knew. This woman was dressed in a smart business suit, her thick glasses and prominent teeth had vanished and her hair, freed from its unflattering pony-tail, now flowed down her back like living water. She slipped into the crowd and walked down the gangplank to the ferry port car park, where she eased herself into a high-powered sports car, before zooming off towards the city.

Yori was dumbstruck.

Yakuza he thought, naming the powerful Japanese crime syndicate. This made things so much simpler. That very day, after the X-ray, he visited one of the many pachinko parlours in Okayama, and spoke to a man he knew.

A week later, Yori Nakoma stood at the ferry port once more. It was getting dark and the boat from Okayama was coming in. Yori heard its diesels strain in reverse as it nudged up to the loading bay. The ramp clanged down into place and a sleek imported car, an American Pontiac, with three men inside slid up out of its belly. Yori smiled. This would be the end of his problems with Miss Yoshida.

"*Konban wa*, Nakoma-san!" the driver said, opening the door to let him in. He was a thin whip of a man with a pockmarked face and a cruel smile. Beneath the starched white cuff of his shirt, the tail of an elaborate tattoo peeped into view. His name was Hiroya Ido. He was *yakuza*, as were the other two men in the car, and he was also Yori Nakoma's cousin.

Yori looked at the beautiful car and the three tough men. Suddenly he was afraid. "Did you have to be so obvious?" he said.

His cousin smiled. "We're here to scare her away, aren't we? Then let's scare her. Get in. I have enough information on your beautiful Miss Yoshida to make sure you're living in that house of hers before the end of the week, with us all rich into the bargain."

"What is it?" asked Yori, shutting the door. The car was spotlessly clean and smelt of air freshener. Yori was conscious of his drab clothes and callused hands. All the more reason to have Miss Yoshida out of the way as soon as possible.

"It seems," said Ido, "that Miss Yoshida is a very wealthy woman. There was a scandal at one of the big *keiretsus* in Tokyo after Christmas and she went missing. The story is that she was even locked up in a mental hospital and escaped, but her relatives and the company concerned hushed it all up to save face. She has a police record. Perhaps she embezzled funds? Perhaps she has the money in the house? It would be interesting to find out just how much she is willing to pay for our silence."

"Will you hurt her?" Yori asked softly.

"Just scare her," Ido said, turning the big car north out of Tonosho and onto the mountain road. "Are you sure she's up there?"

"She is, and she's alone. Those artist friends of hers went back to Tokyo yesterday."

Hiroya Ido nodded.

"Then show him what we have for her, boys."

Yori turned in his seat. The man directly behind him took a heavy rice flail, made from two weighted hardwood rods on either end of a short chain, from inside his jacket. The other man on the back seat reached down and lifted the handle of a samurai sword into view.

"And I have this," Ido said, reaching down between the seat. With his left hand, he lifted out a cloth package and slipped the contents over his fist. It was an obscene metal claw with five sharpened fingers.

Yori thought of Miss Yoshida and how beautiful she had looked when she had stepped off the ferry at Okayama. He remembered her face and how smooth her skin had seemed. He glanced back at the claw. What kind of evil had he called down upon her head?

The Pontiac slid along the coast road towards the village where Yori Nakoma kept his boat. If he had been watching the rear-view mirror carefully, he might just have caught a glimpse of a tall figure on a yellow moped, following them at a distance with her lights off.

"Why do we have to come this way?" whined Ido. He was standing in the very centre of Yori's boat, afraid to get oil on his suit. All around them, the barrels of the oyster farm bobbed in the darkness.

"Because she has an alarm system around the house," Yori said. "She had it brought in from Tokyo and installed by an outside contractor. I know a way inside, up the cliff from the beach. You just follow me."

Ido grunted. Yori cut the engine, letting the momentum of the boat carry it forward until its bow kissed the shore and they stopped.

Yori jumped down onto the beach, feeling wet seaweed slip on the coarse stones and boulders beneath his boots. Further up the shore, these stones would give way to rusty-brown sand, followed by the empty shells of oysters and the base of the cliff itself. Yori knew the beach. He could have told where he was by the sound of his feet. But all he could hear now were his cousin and the other two *yakuza* slipping and cursing behind him.

"This way," he hissed. "There's a crevice in the rock."

Back in the days before Miss Yoshida, Yori had come ashore here many times. In front of him, the cliff soared up into the sky. The exposed roots of trees dangled like the tentacles of some terrible sea monster above him.

He felt along the crumbly volcanic rock for—

"Ayeee!" screamed Ido.

"Quiet!" hissed Yori. "You'll give us away!"

"What are those things?"

A torch snapped on.

Along the face of the cliff and among the shells at their feet, large
cockroach-like sea slaters, each as big as Yori's thumb, scuttled and
tumbled. Their bright eyes and fluorescent green bodies glittered in the light.

"Turn that off! They're harmless!"

The torch went out. One of the *yakuza* slipped on the crumbling rock of
the crevice. Yori was wishing they'd stayed in Okayama. They weren't
beach people. They hadn't a clue.

Then they were in the bushes at the edge of the lawn around Miss
Yoshida's house. Yori looked over it carefully, taking in the curved roof
with its thick ceramic tiles, the balcony and the long studio she'd built
behind the house.

A light shone there.

"She's in the back," he said.

"Right," Ido said. "I'll go in first. You two follow me. Yori, you can
come in last, if you still want to."

"I want to," Yori said.

"All right then."

Ido slipped on the metal claw. The second man pulled his rice flail from
his pocket. Yori heard the hiss of metal on metal as the third man unsheathed
his sword and saw the blade glint in the moonlight.

"You promised you wouldn't hurt her?"

Yori saw Ido's eyebrows rise.

"Why not, cousin? Having second thoughts? Now, come on."

Hiroya Ido led the way across the lawn and up to the front door of the
house. It was open. He stepped through, ignoring the custom of removing his
shoes, and walked down the hallway into the lounge, followed by the others.
Yori came behind, already feeling like a trespasser, into a large room. Its
picture window overlooked the bay and Yori's oyster lines. Miss Yoshida's
easel and a stack of paintings stood against the wall.

"Give me the torch," Yori said, and began to flip through them, suddenly
curious to see what she had been up to all this time, to see inside her head.
Each painting was a dark nightmare of red and black, obscene shapes,
awkward angles, blood on velvet.

Then at the very back of the pile, Yori found a totally different scene. It was a family of three; mother, father and daughter watching tigers at a zoo. The little girl was riding on her father's shoulders. She was laughing . . .

"She must be in here," whispered Ido. "I'll do the talking."

He slid back the door.

They were standing in a martial arts studio, floored with a lake of polished wood. At the far end of the room, a figure in a black cotton outfit knelt facing them. Both hands were held in prayer. She bowed her head almost to the floor.

"*Konban wa*, Nakoma-san," she said. "Welcome to my home."

Then she raised her eyes to meet theirs.

Yori Nakoma was staring into the face of the beautiful woman he had seen on the ferry. There was the graceful sweep of her neck, the perfect symmetry of her features and the dark watchful eyes—calm, still and menacing.

It was like looking at a panther . . . or a tiger . . . in a zoo.

And there were no bars on the cage.

"We know who you are!" Ido said, ignoring her greeting. "You're on the run from the police and from your employers in Tokyo. For a price, which includes the transfer of this house to my cousin here, we are prepared to keep quiet about it."

"And if I pay the price?" said the woman calmly. "What then? How can I be sure you haven't already told a dozen others about me, and that they too will come looking for money?"

"Believe me. Nobody else knows. Once you hand over the house and pay me the cash, you're safe."

"And if I don't?"

She rose from the floor in a single fluid motion. Like a dancer, thought Yori Nakoma.

"Then we'll just have to convince you," Ido said menacingly and raised the steel claw in front of him. His two associates fanned out on either side, one with the sword and the other with the rice flail.

The woman retreated into the corner of the room. The three men moved forward, trapping her. Her back was to the wall. Yori saw her glare at him between the shoulders of the three men and for an instant she seemed to be looking right into the depths of his soul. There was no fear in those eyes, no anger, no passion, no hatred—just the promise of cold, calculated cruelty to come.

She stamped down with her foot. One of the floorboards flipped end over end, and there was a short sword in a beautifully engraved lacquer scabbard in her hand. Yori recognised it as a *wakizashi*, the ritual suicide sword of the samurai.

The *yakuza* lunged at her.

The woman slid the sword out of its scabbard. But she was trapped, hemmed into the corner of the room. Her back was against the wall. She was one against three.

And then . . . she vanished!

"The wall, it's on a hinge!" shouted Ido rushing forward, pounding at the wooden panel with his fist, trying to break through.

But Yori Nakoma was suddenly somewhere else, on a childhood trip to a very special museum in Ueno where he had seen this kind of door before.

Dark, unspoken memories of a bygone age, a dark cult, a whispered fear surfaced like a forgotten nightmare . . .

"She's *ninja*!" he shouted, suddenly afraid. "She'll kill us all."

Ido turned to mock him. "Don't be so . . ."

Then the lights went out, plunging the room into darkness.

For a moment, all four men stood in silence.

Then, they knew . . . There was something else in the room with them!

Yori scrabbled for his torch and switched it on. In the glare of its light he saw one of the *yakuza*, his face contorted in pain, coughing blood. He heard the clatter of metal on wood, an unearthly scream, and saw his cousin trying to staunch the spray of arterial blood from the severed wrist where the steel claw had been.

Then the light was knocked from Yori's fist and went out. He heard the last man cry out—a weird, gurgling gasp that cut short as he fell.

Yori Nakoma ran, rushing headlong out of the door, through the lounge and across the lawn to the cliff path and the beach.

Who was she? Who had trained her? How had she killed three armed men like that with such ease? Below him in the bay he saw the outline of the jetty and his boat pulled up on the rocks. He knew the beach. He could find his way home, even in the dark.

His feet crunched amongst the shells at the base of the cliff and padded down over the dry sand. Soon he was slipping and splashing amongst the seaweed-strewn boulders, scrabbling for the mooring line, ripping at the knot, reaching for the boat-hook to push the boat free of the shore. He listened for the crunch of footsteps following, but there was nothing.

He was just reaching for the starter when something black and terrible burst over the side of the boat and fell upon him.

His last thought before his broken body fell back onto the rocks, was to wonder how she had moved so silently across the beach he knew so well . . .

It was the worst fishing tragedy in the history of Shodo-shima. Yori Nakoma, the well-known oyster farmer, his rich cousin from Okayama and two friends had gone out on the water—after a few too many beers perhaps—and had met with a terrible accident. What remained of their charred bodies, after they were recovered from the sea, gave little hint as to how the tragedy must have occurred. But the police and coast guard supposed that a leaky fuel tank, ignited by a spark or a cigarette, must have been the cause of death and that the terrible wounds suffered by three of the four men must have been caused by the boat's spinning propeller as it sank.

Their theory was conveniently borne out by the only witness to the tragedy.

Miss Fusaro Yoshida, the owner of the fine house overlooking the bay, told them she had been woken by the noise of a boat engine just after midnight and had seen a terrible explosion.

"A horrible waste of life," she told the police, "a most regrettable accident. Did any of my guests see it? No! They had all gone back to Tokyo the previous day. If you need to question me again, gentlemen, here is my business card at Nippon Steel. You can call me there at any time."

And then she was gone, never to be seen by the people of Shodo-shima . . . ever again.

34

4

THE TIME TRAVELLER

The office could have been that of any successful manager, furnished with a row of glass-fronted bookcases in dark wood, a polished L-shaped desk with a computer terminal and a high-backed leather chair. The view from the window was of low modern buildings set in an industrial park tastefully laid out with trees. Above the car park, almost empty on a Sunday, stood a tall white flagpole topped by the Stars and Stripes. The flag flapped lazily in the rising heat.

The man behind the desk looked like any senior executive who had just dropped by at the office on the way to a golf game. He was tanned and fit, with closely cropped sandy hair and the lean, hungry look of a corporate survivor. His name was Phillip Carpenter and he was Associate Professor of Theoretical Physics at the University of North Carolina.

"Thanks for seeing me on a Sunday, Phil," Gilkrensky said. "I was on my way back from Peru and I needed to speak with you."

"No problem, Theo. Let's face it; research today isn't about winning the Nobel Prize. It's about how much cash you can pull in from your corporate sponsors, and GRC is one of our biggest. What can I do for you that warrants a personal visit?"

"I need computer power, a lot of it."

"How much?"

"Enough to cope with a four-dimensional calculation in quantum mechanics."

"Related to?"

"Ah . . . particle physics. GRC have a contract for research work with the CERN particle accelerator project near Geneva—mesons, sub-mesons, that sort of thing. We'll need about ten billion terabytes of space."

Carpenter sucked on his teeth. "Jesus! That's a lot of power. For how long?"

"If I get enough space, about ten minutes. Less space and the whole thing could take years."

Carpenter leant back in his leather chair. Gilkrensky felt the man's mind working, seeking opportunities.

"You must be really pushing out the envelope to need as much space as that."

"It's just a helluva big sum, Phil. There are an almost infinite number of variables to take into account. What have you got here on campus?"

"About a thousandth of what you want, and that's on restricted access."

"Even for me? I'm one of your biggest sponsors."

"But not the biggest, Theo. Sorry."

"Then who is?"

Carpenter pointed to the flag outside the window.

"Good old 'Uncle Sam'," he said. "Access to that kind of computer power would be almost impossible, even for me, and I work here! The government gets pretty paranoid about foreign companies using larger than normal amounts of computer power for anything! They see it as a security risk, in case someone's planning to use technology to stage some sort of coup over the web."

"Are you kidding me?"

"Not at all, Theo. The President's very hot on cyber-terrorism these days. He's set up task-forces, study-groups, the works! The FBI, the CIA and even the Department of Homeland Security all have special computer squads and, don't forget, to the United States Government, GRC *is* a foreign company. You'd have to mortgage your mother and leave your eyes on deposit to get anywhere near the capacity you need. Can't you raise it inside your own corporation? I thought you guys were the market leaders. What about that new Minerva project of yours? Isn't that some kind of supercomputer?"

"It is," Gilkrensky said. "And I could use it as a high-speed processor to co-ordinate the other machines once the calculation is in motion, but to do the math I simply need more capacity."

"Then your only hope would be to look for that space somewhere else in the world, anywhere that doesn't have a connection with good old 'Uncle Sam'."

"Anyone in mind?"

"You'd be pushed to find that kind of capacity anywhere in Europe, but you probably knew that anyway. The Russians are still in the Dark Ages when it comes to computers, and the Chinese are only just ahead of them. So your best hope is Japan."

Gilkrensky frowned. "Can you give me a list?"

"There's about five facilities that might approach what you're after, if you pooled all their capacity together, but the only one even close to providing what you want on its own is an outfit outside Tokyo called Kasawara Research. Wouldn't you have had to bid against them for the CERN accelerator contract?"

"Probably," said Gilkrensky, ducking the question. "It was a sealed competition. Do you know anything about them?"

"They do a lot of really powerful digital design work—the sort of thing that Boeing used a while back to make a three-dimensional model of their 777 aircraft in virtual reality so they'd be sure all the parts would fit perfectly even before they were built."

"Who owns Kasawara?"

"They're part of some big *keiretsu*, one of those Japanese business alliances."

"I see."

Gilkrensky gazed out of the office window, beyond the low buildings and trees to the shimmering towers of office-blocks in Charlotte. After a long silence he said, "There's one more thing, Phil."

Carpenter leant forward. "I thought there might be. What we've talked about so far could have been done on the email."

"I want to talk about causality."

"What?" Carpenter looked stunned.

37

"Causality—I need a definitive opinion on what would happen if someone were to travel back in time and alter the past. You're an expert in theoretical physics. I thought I'd ask you."

Carpenter laid both hands on his leather-bound blotter and stared at him. "What's this, Theo? Planning to write a little science fiction?"

"It's a theoretical problem related to faster than light particles on the CERN project. It's completely speculative, but I need an informed opinion before I go any further."

"You're telling *me* it's speculative. I can't see how a died-in-the-wool industrialist like you would ever make a buck out of that one. Not unless you're going to build yourself a time machine?"

The question hung in the air.

"You *aren't* going to build yourself a time machine. Are you, Theo?"

"Just tell me about the theories, Phil."

"OK. But it feels kind of weird explaining something that's so far out to someone like you," and he sat back in his chair, staring at the ceiling while he collected his thoughts.

"All right," he said at last. "Since 1905, physicists have known that Einstein's Special Theory of Relativity accepted that time travel to the future was theoretically possible, by travelling faster than light in a spacecraft. You remember that movie *Planet of the Apes*, where these guys fall asleep on a rocket and wind up a couple of thousand years from now?"

"I don't go to the movies much, but I know what you mean."

"OK. Over forty years later, in 1949, Einstein came up with his General Theory of Relativity, which postulated that time travel to the past was also theoretically possible. Today, there are two major schools of thought about what might happen if you actually succeed; the 'Causal Loop' explanation and the 'Multiplicity of Histories' theory."

"Explain them to me slowly."

Carpenter took a sheet of white paper from a tray next to his computer printer, used a steel ruler to tear off a long strip, and laid the strip on the desk.

"Right," he said, taking a pencil and drawing a line down the paper. "This strip represents a period of time, and the line represents you or me. We start at this end, and we finish down here. Our movement from one end to the other is as inevitable as gravity, and just about as impossible to overcome."

"Apart from Albert Einstein and quantum mechanics."

"Exactly. In special conditions, like your CERN accelerator, where particles actually do travel faster than light, the normal laws of physics start to get a little fuzzy."

"How so?"

"In the event of an actual temporal displacement, where you *do* manage to warp time and interfere with a particle's flight path before it ever takes place, then you get this . . ." And he twisted the strip once, bent it back on itself, so that the two ends overlapped, and stapled them together. "There, recognise that?"

"It's a Möbius strip."

"You got it. And now, if I draw a line it just goes on and on forever, in a loop, on both sides of the page without leaving the paper. That's what you do if you travel back and twist time. You go over and over the same period of history again and again, trapped in what we call a causal loop."

"And in practical terms?"

Carpenter thought for a moment.

"It's just a theory, but OK. Let's say you built a time machine because you wanted to travel back and stop John F Kennedy being assassinated. So you build it, travel back, and save JFK. Then the reason for building the time machine in the first place is gone, the machine doesn't get built, and JFK dies after all. So you build a time machine, travel back and save JFK . . . and so on, ad infinitum. We call that 'paradox'. It's one reason why the sort of time travel you see in science fiction movies is thought to be physically impossible."

"And the other theory?"

Carpenter threw the Möbius strip into his waste basket and lifted a telephone directory onto his desk. Then he opened it in the middle, lifted one page vertically between finger and thumb and held it there, upright.

"To get over the problems associated with paradox, physicists have come up with the theory of the 'Multiplicity of Histories'. Have you ever wondered what it would have been like if the Allies had lost World War II, if

JFK had lived, or if you'd turned left instead of right on your way to work in the morning? Well, this theory suggests that somewhere in the universe of space and time there is a place where all these things *did* happen, and that these 'multiple histories' lie beside each other like the pages of a book."

Gilkrensky shook his head. "But for that to work there would have to be an infinite number of parallel universes."

"There are. But like I said, it's just a theory to make explaining time travel and paradox a lot easier. Just watch . . ." He moved his fingers down the page from the edge towards the spine of the book, where it joined all the others.

"This is you, the Time Traveller, before you mess with history. Then, at the spine of the book, you do something that causes events to shift from the way things were into a new reality, or perhaps even into the base of a dozen, a thousand, or a billion new possibilities. You haven't destroyed the past, you've just shifted from one reality to another."

"So no paradox?"

"No, just a different way of looking at things."

Gilkrensky thought for a moment. "Tell me, Phil, if someone travelled back a year in time to a particular event and made sure that it happened differently, would whatever had happened in that year cease to exist?"

"Everything after the alteration was made would be different. It would either cease to exist or be part of the previous reality your 'time traveller' had left behind. Only something created before the change would continue to exist."

Gilkrensky glanced over at the heavy briefcase he had left on the table by the door. If Carpenter was right and Maria's death could be prevented, then all the work he had done since then on the Minerva and its artificially intelligent interface would vanish.

Carpenter followed his eyes. "Is that Minerva, Theo? How's it coming?"

"It's . . . it's developing fine, Phil."

Carpenter looked concerned. "Are you OK, Theo? I heard a lot of crazy stories over the past year . . . about how you found it hard to cope since Maria died, and about some really weird experiments you were doing in Egypt. Is it true that Bill McCarthy just . . . disappeared?"

"I . . . I don't know what happened to him. It was during a crash investigation near Cairo. We were using some pretty high-powered equipment, and doing some really way-out stuff. His body was never found."

"OK. I was just asking. I knew you and Bill were pretty close."

"Yes, we were. He was like a father to me. Losing him wasn't easy. Explaining it to his family was even harder."

"I bet. Are you sure you're OK?"

"I'm fine, Phil, really. You look after yourself."

Gilkrensky got to his feet. Then he lifted the Minerva from the table by the door, shook Carpenter's hand and left.

Professor Phillip Carpenter shut the door behind Gilkrensky and watched from the window as the limousine slid out of the car park and vanished from sight between the trees, heading for Charlotte airport. He glanced up at the American flag. Yeah! It was sad the way you had to sell your soul for research funding nowadays. Then he opened his desk drawer, switched off the listening device installed here and lifted the phone.

He punched out a number. It answered on the third ring.

"Did you get all that?" asked Carpenter.

5

THE MAN FROM DDS&T

"Aw . . . shit!" said Gilkrensky's driver. "It looks like we got company."

Gilkrensky had been watching the landscape slide past the limousine as they pulled out of the research park, lost in the implications of what Carpenter had said. On either side of the tree-lined road, low buildings bearing the corporate logos of IBM, AT&T, Duke Power, and Saratoga Technologies glittered in the sun, monuments to science, harnessed for profit, bought and paid for.

We're all looking for answers he thought; a faster, cheaper way of doing everything. And when we find it, we package it, sell it and start all over again on something even better. It's an endless race that nobody ever wins. That's how I lost Maria, by getting caught up in it all.

Then the Lincoln Continental turned onto Route 85, heading south towards the city. The driver cursed and Crowe twisted in his seat, staring back down the freeway.

"What the hell do they want?" Crowe said. "We aren't speeding."

Gilkrensky looked to his left. The patrol car overtaking them was white with a blue stripe and the words "Charlotte Mecklenburg" towards the rear. The lights along its roof sparkled in the late morning sun, blue and white against the drab khaki of the freeway. The limousine slowed and pulled over to the red dirt of the hard shoulder.

"Just you leave the talking to me, Mr Gilkrensky," the driver said. "Don't answer back or make any sudden moves. And whatever you do, don't get out of the car unless they tell you. OK?"

The cop walking towards them wore a wide leather belt that held a radio, handcuffs, a night-stick and a gun. Behind him, a second policeman stood with a radio microphone ready, his right hand on the holster at his hip.

Gilkrensky's driver lowered his window and put his hands back on the steering wheel. "Why are you stopping us, officer?" he said.

"Could you step out of the car please, sir?" said the cop and stood back. The driver got out and put his hands flat on the bonnet. The cop frisked him for weapons, then turned and motioned Gilkrensky and Crowe out onto the freeway.

With his right hand held above his head, Crowe slowly opened his jacket with his left, exposing the butt of his gun. "This is a licensed weapon," he said.

The cop did not seem surprised. He simply reached over, slid Crowe's automatic out of its holster and threw it to his partner.

"Just put your hands on the hood. We don't want any trouble here."

The cop turned to Gilkrensky.

"Some ID, sir?"

Gilkrensky pulled out his passport and showed it to the cop, who flicked through it and handed it back. Then he motioned to his partner, who spoke into a radio mike.

"What this all about?" Crowe said. "You can't just—"

Two black vans burst out of a slip road and skidded to a halt at either end of the limousine in a cloud of red dust. The doors of the leading van flew open and two men in business suits jumped out. The first one said something to the cop, who nodded and walked back to his car.

"Doctor Theodore Gilkrensky?" said the man.

"Yes. Who the hell are you?"

The man pulled an identification card from his inside pocket.

"We'd like you to follow us to a hotel near here, sir. There's someone there who would like to meet with you before you fly back to England."

"Then why couldn't he just call my office and ask for an appointment?"

"That's not my position to say, sir. I'll be travelling with you. It shouldn't take long."

The convoy moved off down Route 85 to where the city of Charlotte gleamed like a space station on the flatness of the Carolina landscape. In a few minutes they were past the outskirts, with its railway tracks, grain silos and vacant lots, driving down wide deserted roads between the county courthouse and the jail to the tall white building that was the Adam's Mark Hotel. Gilkrensky saw the brake lights of the first van flare as it pulled to a stop ahead of the red canvas awning over the main entrance. Then the Lincoln glided to a stop, the van behind them drew up close and the door of the limousine was pulled open, bringing with it a blast of hot air from outside.

"This way, please, sir." The man who had ridden with them in the car led the way across the wood-panelled foyer to a bank of elevators. In a few seconds they were walking down the thick patterned carpet of a fourteenth-floor corridor.

The man knocked on the door of room 1460, waited for a reply, and opened it.

"Dr Gilkrensky," he said. "Could you step inside, please? Major Crowe? I'd like you to wait next door, with us."

"No," said Crowe. "Where Dr Gilkrensky goes, I go."

"I'm sorry, but this is a private meeting."

The door to room 1462, on the other side of the hall, opened. Two large men emerged into the corridor. One of them had his hand inside his jacket.

"I'll be OK, Major," Gilkrensky said. "There's nothing more you can do."

Room 1460 was dark and cool, with all the sterile fittings of any hotel room, in any part of the world. A man sat silhouetted against the filtered light from the net curtains at a table near the window. Cigarette smoke curled above his head.

"Come in, Dr Gilkrensky, and take a seat. We need to talk."

"What's all this about?"

"Government business," said the man and pushed a business card across the table as Gilkrensky sat down. Then he ground the cigarette into a glass ash-tray, pulled a sheet of paper from an official-looking folder and turned it in his hand. He was a big man, an athlete gone to seed. The grey-green eyes that measured Gilkrensky from behind the frameless glasses looked tired. His ginger hair and moustache were heavily flecked with grey and his thick neck strained against his collar. He handed the paper to Gilkrensky.

"Recognise that?"

It was an order from a company outside Liege in Belgium to an American manufacturer of semi-conductors for a number of components, all precisely described and catalogued by someone with an acute eye for detail. The order was worth well over a million dollars.

"No, I don't."

"Look at it again, Dr Gilkrensky. The company is Louvaine Electronique. Their speciality is state-of-the-art computer interfaces, wireless mouse pads, roller balls, joysticks and the like. They're also one of your main sub-contractors. The components in question are very advanced micro-thin superconductors in the twenty atomic layer range, just off the restricted list in fact. Now, what do you suppose they're for?"

"I've no idea."

"Come on now, Dr Gilkrensky. A man with your recent experiences must surely recognise what might be made from components like those."

"You'll have to give me a hint."

The big man sighed. "OK. Here's a clue. Over the past twelve weeks someone's been running an unprecedented information sweep on the Internet for anything relating to computer interfaces with the human mind. Research facilities, government labs, libraries, universities, have all been probed on a systematic basis for anything they contain on superconductors, interference technology, human psychology and the anatomy of the brain. Now, what does that suggest to you?"

"It makes me wonder how you know all this."

The grey-green eyes never left his. "It's our business to know, Dr Gilkrensky, and we're very good at our business. Now, I'm asking you again officially, what the hell are you doing?"

"What makes you think that I'm doing anything?"

"All this research is being done from within your organisation, on your personal authority. Oh, I'll admit it's been cleverly disguised. There are false email addresses being used and piggy-backs set up so as not to arouse suspicion, but everything points back to offices, companies and research facilities owned by GRC."

"My corporation's a multi-billion dollar operation employing thousands of people," Gilkrensky said. "There are companies, hotels, factories, airlines and offices all over the world. You can't expect me to know what's going on in all of them, all the time."

"Then I'll give you a name," the man said. "Jerry Gibb."

For a moment there was silence in the room. Nothing stirred, except the last wisp of smoke from the ash-tray.

"What do you know about him, Dr Gilkrensky?"

"Jerry Gibb had a company called Gibbtek. It manufactured computer games and specialist interfaces for the US military."

"He wasn't a very good friend of yours, was he?"

"He pirated a couple of my artificial intelligence programmes. I was suing him over a software package he'd brought onto the market, before he—"

"Before he what?"

"Before he died. You know that."

"Exactly. Before he died. He died from a heart attack while he was hooked up to a computer game, or so the coroner said at the time. It was a game using a computer-mind interface called a SQUID which, being educated men in the ways of technology, we both know stands for Superconducting Quantum Interference Device, isn't that right?"

"Your definition is correct, yes."

"Which kind of makes the jigsaw pieces fall into place, doesn't it?"

"How so?"

The man held up his right hand and counted on his fingers as he spoke.

"Jerry Gibb was working on SQUIDs. Jerry Gibb was a rival of yours. Jerry Gibb was in a legal battle with you over software designs for billions of dollars. Now Jerry Gibb is dead, and GRC is ordering components for its own SQUID technology . . ."

"What are you saying?"

"I would have thought that was obvious."

Gilkrensky rose from the table. "I can see where this is going, and I don't like it. I don't like being ambushed on the freeway, dragged in here against my will and subjected to an interrogation on something I know nothing about. If you want to talk to me again, you'll have to do it through my lawyers."

He walked to the door and reached for the handle.

"And your visit to Professor Carpenter this morning?"

Gilkrensky stopped. "He's a former colleague of mine from MIT. I wanted to discuss a few theories with him, catch up on old times."

The man at the table opened an envelope and spread a number of large, glossy photographs on the table in front of him.

"And these? What sort of research are you doing here?"

Gilkrensky stepped back and looked down at the pictures. They were high-definition aerial photographs taken from a plane or a satellite, each labelled in the top right hand corner with a different location; Cairo, Mexico and . . . Nazca. Each one of them showed a group of caravans around a square on the ground.

"I'm interested in archaeology," Gilkrensky said. "It . . . it was something my wife put me onto . . . years ago."

"Come on now, Dr Gilkrensky. This is a research program costing millions of dollars, at locations spread over five continents. Are you saying this is all part of some hobby for you?"

"Where did you get these pictures?"

"Like I said, it's our business. Now tell me, what are we looking at here?"

"OK then. It's to do with the Daedalus aircraft navigation system. We've found that it glitches in certain parts of the world and we need to know why. If we can't prove it's safe then nobody will use it, people will lose confidence and the price of our shares will collapse."

"Is that why you're selling your shares in GRC?"

"I don't know what you're talking about?"

"And the visit to Professor Carpenter today? Why do you need so much computer power, Dr Gilkrensky? What's all that about?"

"How on earth did you—?"

Then Gilkrensky knew.

"That attack at Nazca!" he said. "*You* were behind it?"

"What attack?"

47

"Don't play games with me. My camp was attacked. We thought it was terrorists or local bandits, but they were too well-armed and shooting too high. Was that you? Were you trying to scare me off?"

"Scare you off what, Dr Gilkrensky? Why's a captain of industry like you, a man who's spent his life carving out a business empire worth billions, committing the most advanced technology in history to researching ancient monuments? Are you really studying archaeology? I don't think so! Sorting out glitches in your Daedalus system? No way! Those were sorted out months ago! And why are you so interested in large amounts of computer power? What can be so important to you that you'd sell your shares in GRC to get it? Something pretty damned profitable I'd say."

Gilkrensky turned back to the door.

"Talk to my lawyers."

The man at the table rose to his feet, sending the photographs sliding to the floor.

"I may just do that, Dr Gilkrensky! And I'm sure as hell going to find out what happened to Jerry Gibb and our SQUID program. If you, or anyone else in GRC, so much as makes a move on superconductor technology I'll extradite you back here and throw you in jail so fast your feet won't even touch the ground."

Gilkrensky wrenched open the door and strode out into the corridor.

"Leave him," said the man to the agents who had moved in to block Gilkrensky's way. "He's rattled now. He might just start getting careless. Tell the boys downstairs to let him past."

When Gilkrensky and Crowe had gone, the man at the window pulled a packet of Malboros out of his pocket, took one out and lit it. Then he opened his briefcase, took out a small digital recorder and pressed the "play" button. Professor Phil Carpenter's voice said, "Over forty years later, in 1949, Einstein came up with his General Theory of Relativity, which postulated that time travel to the past was also theoretically possible."

The man picked up the photographs from the floor and arranged the shots from Nazca in sequence on the table. They started with a marked square, the experimental tower, the bright image of the holographic pyramid, disturbance, lightning, and the marked square again . . . with part of the tower missing.

He replayed the recording.

"Over forty years later, in 1949, Einstein came up with his General Theory of Relativity, which postulated that time travel to the past was also theoretically possible."

The man took a long drag on his cigarette.

"Dr Gilkrensky," he said to himself. "I really think you've cracked it."

Then he gathered up the photographs on the table, put them back in his briefcase and looked around the room for any he might have overlooked. On the floor was the business card he had passed to Gilkrensky. He stooped down, feeling his knees crack, and picked it up.

The card bore a crest, showing an eagle inside a shield with a quiver of arrows in its claws.

Mr Richard Barnett, it read. *Section Leader - Deputy Directorate for Science and Technology. Central Intelligence Agency.*

6

THE SHRINE

Tokyo was waking. It started with the delivery vans and refuse collectors, men and women in different coloured uniforms unloading crates of food, picking plastic bags of used cartons and chopsticks from the doorways of restaurants, or sweeping rubbish into dustpans fitted to the ends of poles. The shutters clattered up outside the coffee shops and the "Freshness Burger" bars. The aroma of freshly brewed coffee hung heavy in the humid air.

Then the traffic began; light at first, but building on the roads and underpasses. The first accident of the day happened, a minor collision. Policemen in white gloves waved the other cars past as their drivers stared at the crumpled steel and broken glass, wondering how long it might be before their turn came.

From the subway stations, floods of people spewed out onto the street; flocks of schoolgirls in sailor-suits and thick white socks, office ladies in their neat uniforms, and rank upon rank of "salary men" in dark suits, white shirts and sober ties, each of them bearing the sword and shield of their calling, the briefcase and the rolled umbrella.

As the heat of the day began to rise, so did the noise; the rumble of traffic, the tinkle of bicycle bells, the *Peep! Peep! Peep!* of police whistles on the pedestrian crossings, like shepherds herding sheep.

But on the roof of the Mawashi-Saito building, in the heart of the Shinjuku financial district, there was peace. The small traditional garden, protected from the wind by a high wall, could have been anywhere in Japan. The early morning sun shone softly on the artfully sculptured bushes, the neat lawn, and the tastefully laid-out path. Water gurgled over moss-covered rocks into a pond of Koi carp. The rumble of traffic, forty-two floors below, was little more than a distant murmur.

The old man entered from a door to the stairwell as he did every morning at this time. He was impeccably dressed in a grey suit, white shirt and a black silk tie, but he looked bent and tired under the weight of some great burden.

He picked his way along the stone path between the bushes until he came to a small Shinto shrine in the quietest corner of the garden. It was like a wooden shelter, with a tiled roof, guttering, and a row of paper lanterns above a folding door. Inside were statues of Buddha, a sprig of green sakaki tree, offerings of food, water and beer.

The old man went through the purification ritual of washing his hands and mouth. Then he clapped twice and bowed his head. His name was Gichin Funakoshi and he had many heartfelt prayers he would have sacrificed anything to have answered.

His whole life, since he had survived the Great War against America, had been devoted to building his country back to greatness. As a founder-partner in Saito Electronics, which had later merged with the Mawashi trading house, he had created one of the largest and most powerful business *keiretsus* the country had ever seen—a vast conglomerate of banks, manufacturers and distributors worth billions. He thought back to the heady days when he and Kazuyoshi Saito, that most brilliant and eccentric inventor, had considered themselves the new samurai, riding out to conquer the world. He remembered the burden of honour, the debt of giri, which Saito had placed on his shoulders by handing over the future of the *keiretsu* to him on his death-bed, and how he had sworn to defend it forever . . . against anything.

And to defend that future, he had sacrificed everything .

"Kazuyoshi Saito!" he whispered to his former friend and mentor. "I pray the gods protect you, and I beg your forgiveness for what I have allowed to happen. I have failed in the oath I swore to you that I would protect the *keiretsu* at all costs. I made a grave error and others now have control of Mawashi-Saito. Please forgive me!"

He knelt in prayer. Outside the garden, beyond the wall, he heard the distant murmur of traffic far below, coming from another world.

The thud of a package falling at his knees startled him.

"He might forgive you," said a voice. "But I will not!"

"Yukiko! I thought you were dead!"

She knelt next to him before the shrine. As he turned to look at her, he saw his sister's delicate features—the proud mouth and the dark eyes, the long graceful neck and the shining hair, tied in a tight bun above the collar of her Mawashi-Saito office uniform. Funakoshi thought of the high wall around the garden forty-two storeys above the street, the alarms on the elevator, the key cards, the security guards, a whole building of people on watch below him. How on earth had she got up here?

"Would it answer your prayers if I had never been born, Uncle? Is that what you are asking the gods for today, that I might be dead?"

Funakoshi looked away.

"No, Yukiko. I was asking forgiveness for what I did to you and your mother in the name of *giri* to an old friend many years ago. If you wish to kill me now, please do so. I have nothing to live for anymore. The *keiretsu* is gone from my hands."

"The *keiretsu*!" spat Yukiko. "That was all you ever thought of, wasn't it? All you ever loved! And for that you banished my mother to England to avoid the scandal of my birth outside marriage, abandoned her to suicide when she needed you most, and swindled my father out of what was rightfully his. No! I am not going to kill you, Uncle. I am going to watch you suffer! And as a reminder of how much that suffering will be, and of all the years it is built on, I give you this—a souvenir of the last time in your life that you ever acted with compassion. Open it! I want to see your face when you realise just how long ago that was!"

Gichin Funakoshi reached down and undid the brown paper covering the package at his knees. With growing disbelief he uncovered the tip of a black lacquered scabbard patterned with running tigers, the pommel and sheath of an exquisite samurai sword and, cresting the handle, the delicate cherry blossom of the Funakoshi family.

All at once, he was a child again in the smouldering ruins of Tokyo. The smell of death was all around him. Smoke from the fire-bombings still drifted across the sky. It was 1945, his parents were dead and his sister Chuziko was in his arms, dying of starvation. All he had in the world were his father's swords, the great curving *katana* and the smaller *wakizashi*, priceless heirlooms salvaged from the ruins of their home. He remembered the American soldiers, great lumbering *gaijin* who laughed and joked. One of them looked at the long sword and offered him money and food. Gichin Funakoshi felt his heart break as he passed the weapons over. The soldiers sneered at the short sword, threw it back in his face and went swaggering down the street, waving the *katana* above their heads.

And now that sword was back in his hands, a reminder of how far he had fallen.

"Where did you get this?"

"That is not important," hissed Yukiko. "What is important is what it means to you. I know the legend, Uncle. I know that sword represents the last time you put anyone above your own interests. It was a time when you had nothing. I give it to you as a symbol. Soon you will have nothing again."

"I have nothing now," said Funakoshi slowly.

"Think again. You have your home, your wife, your reputation. The business you built with Saito still stands, here, below our feet. Hold onto that sword, Uncle. Soon it will be all you have left. I will see to it."

Funakoshi stared at the beautiful sword, lost in the memory of that day, so long ago.

"Yukiko?" he started to say.

But she had gone.

7

THE SHAREHOLDER

"The unique feature of the Minerva is that it combines the limitless flexibility of a neural net biochip with the stability of a conventional silicon system," O'Connor said. "This has been achieved by the use of nanotechnology to create a layering of incredibly thin sheets of pseudo-biological material to . . ."

The cooling fan of the data-projector whirred. Complex images flashed on the screen at the other end of the boardroom table. Dr Patrick O'Connor, Head of GRC's Advanced Research Group and Theo's right-hand man on the Minerva project, waxed lyrical about the wonders they had achieved. But in her mind, Jessica was already somewhere else—in an exclusive nursing home just outside Norwich . . .

"I just don't know him anymore," said her mother, close to tears. "It's as if he died, or left me, or something . . . only he hasn't . . . has he? It's so unfair. I just don't know him."

Jessica gazed down at the bed. This was the man she had worshipped as a child, as she counted the thick copper pennies, the chunky threepenny pieces and solid half-crowns in the family sweetshop in Lowestoft, washed out and refilled the big glass jars, and brought him his tea twice a day in that big china mug.

Her mother was right. That man, the father she had loved, was gone—leaving nothing but a shell. She didn't know the haunted eyes that stared at her, vacant and desperate. She hardly recognised the sagging face, lopsided and sad. She knew he was in there somewhere, that everything she said could be heard and understood. But where was he? She wanted to shout at him, yell at him, scream at him, anything . . . anything that would bring him back.

A trickle of saliva ran down his chin onto his pyjamas.

A massive stroke, the doctors said.

Afterwards, she walked her mother back to the car. The summer sun glinted on the nearby river and the glass panes of the conservatory. The garden was a palette of living colour, but Jessica saw none of it. All she saw was the desperate look of the prisoner inside her father's head.

"When are you going to find a nice young man and settle down?" her mother said. "This gallivanting around the world is all very well, but I really would like to see you settled. You know, like your brothers."

Jessica thought of them, of their whining, grasping wives, their seething broods of sticky-fingered children and their cramped semi-detached houses. Then she and her mother were standing next to Jessica's gleaming black Jaguar XJS, the largest car in the car park—powerful, perfect and not a sticky fingerprint in sight.

"Yes, Mum!" she said.

But deep down inside she could hear a clock ticking. How old are you now, Jessica Wright? Almost forty! How long will it be before it is too late? Too late to—

"Miss Wright? Miss Wright?"

At the far end of the boardroom table, Pat O'Connor was looking at her. On either side of him, the two other men in the room shuffled their papers to hide any embarrassment.

"I'm sorry, Pat," she said. "I was a million miles away. It must be the jet-lag. Please go on."

"No problem," O'Connor said, and began to speak again. He was a tall man, with a round face, thin wispy hair and bright blue eyes that reminded Jessica of an overgrown baby. She knew he had no other interest in life outside the Minerva project, apart from his wife and children.

Why was she obsessed with children all of a sudden?

O'Connor continued. "What makes Minerva unique," he said, "is this, the neural network core." He pulled a translucent plastic slab, the size of a bar of chocolate, from his pocket and slid it down the table towards her.

"The power of any neural net, be it an artificial one inside a computer, or a natural one inside the human brain, depends on the number of neurons it contains," he said. "Neurons are the basic building-blocks of intelligence, and in the human brain there are around a hundred billion of them, all interacting to control sight, smell, memory, creativity and intelligence. Before Minerva, the largest man-made neural net contained no more than a thousand neurons, which would have given any computer using it about the intelligence of a mosquito."

Jessica picked the slab up. It was slippery to the touch, like a bar of wax. Looking at it end on, she imagined she saw rainbow colours refracted in the material from the light of the data-projector.

"What am I looking at?" she asked.

O'Connor smiled. "As I was saying earlier, what Theo has achieved with Minerva is to combine the 'wet' process of biological evolution with the 'dry' efficiency of silicon chip technology. He's created fantastically thin sheets of pseudo-biological material, layered together in that block. Each layer is less than one micron thick, a thousandth of a millimetre, and yet contains two million neuron links. So, for a layered block like that measuring ten centimetres by twenty by two, you have four billion neurons. Minerva houses two of those blocks, giving it a total neural capacity of eight billion, millions of times that of any of its rivals."

Jessica did a quick mental calculation.

"But that's still only . . . a twelfth of the capacity of the human brain, surely?"

"Indeed it is," O'Connor said. "But don't forget that we humans use large amounts of our brains to control bodily movement which Minerva doesn't need, as well as senses such as sight, smell and touch which Minerva doesn't have. Also, a lot of Minerva's memory is stored on other, more conventional systems that don't require creative neural-net capacity at all."

"So what are you actually telling us, Doctor? In words of one syllable," said Sir Robert Fynes, who represented the pension fund which was one of the original shareholders of GRC. He was a big gruff Yorkshireman with a thick moustache, a mane of silvery hair and all the diplomacy of an earthquake.

O'Connor glanced towards Jessica for guidance. Finding none he said, "In simple terms, Sir Robert, you're looking at the next generation of computers, a system to make robots that can actually think for themselves. Theo's neural net has made that possible, at least five years before any of the competition."

"You can see why the Japanese were so keen to get their hands on it," Jessica said. "Or anyone else for that matter. We're in the same leading position that Microsoft or Intel were in a few years ago. We could dominate the market and establish a virtual monopoly on this new generation of neural net computers, if we act now."

"And who are we up against?" asked Fynes.

"The Japanese, of course," Jessica said, "as well as the Americans, the Germans and a whole host of smaller countries around the Pacific rim from Korea to Malaysia. Any country in the world with a computer industry would give a king's ransom to be where we are with Minerva right now. GRC can become the richest company in history, and its shareholders right along with it."

Sir Robert nodded. Jessica could almost hear his mind working on the implications of what she'd just told him. Then Giles Fulton, who represented the investment consortium that owned the remaining shares in GRC, said, "But what about that glitch in the system after Christmas, when you had to call in a psychologist to stop Minerva blacking out the Irish power grid.? What about that?

O'Connor glanced at Jessica again, still unsure of his ground.

"That was a software problem, wasn't it Pat?" she suggested.

"Yes," O'Connor said. "Theo had to design a completely new generation of operating instructions to cope with the capacity of the neural net hardware he'd created. Originally, this software was a simple user-interface which allowed him to talk to the machine directly—an intelligent agent program in the form of a woman's face—which he called Minerva."

"After the Greek goddess of wisdom," Jessica said. "Theo thought it was appropriate."

"Exactly," continued O'Connor, "but then, after his wife was killed, he added a new program with some very . . . um . . . personal prototype features that were perhaps . . . ah . . . a little more advanced that we would have liked. But that's sorted out now."

"Would that second interface program be part of Minerva as a normal production machine?" asked Sir Robert.

"No," snapped Jessica, a little too quickly. "Definitely not, it's unstable."

Giles Fulton looked at her over the top of his glasses.

"How's that?"

"I . . ."

It was O'Connor's turn to come to her aid.

"The new interface program was only ever intended as an experiment," he said. "Theo designed it to explore the boundaries of artificial intelligence, not to be a commercial system. In a few rare cases it experienced difficulties in making strictly logical decisions during periods of extreme emotional stress, which would be expected in any complex prototype system. Like I said, it was and still is a personal project of Theo's."

"Then we can simply delete it," Fynes said.

O'Connor started to protest, but Jessica cut him short.

"I'm sure we can come to some arrangement with Theo about that," she said. She sensed O'Connor glaring at her, but pretended not to see him.

"If Theo were to sell his shares and step down as Chairman of GRC," said Fynes, speaking directly to O'Connor, "if he were to leave the Corporation, could you handle the development of Minerva to full commercialisation on your own?"

The question caught O'Connor by surprise. "Ah . . . perhaps. If I had access to the Minerva prototype Theo has with him at the moment and the rest of the resources in the robotics laboratory on his island."

"How long would it take?"

"With the prototype to act as a template, I could do it in less than six months. Without it, I'd need to create and debug a complete new software package. It would take at least a year."

"I see," Fynes said, sliding his papers back into their folder. "That's all I need to know."

Giles Fulton nodded.

Pat O'Connor was still standing open-mouthed at the far end of the table.

"But you can't just wipe the Minerva interface," he said. "There are all sorts of moral and legal implications. It's a fully self-aware intelligence . . . it's *alive*."

"Thank you, Doctor," said Fynes.

"We'll talk later, Pat," Jessica said. "I need to discuss a few things with the Board now. Thank you for coming all the way up from Cork to give us the briefing."

She pressed a button on the console beside her seat. The window blinds slid back, letting in the afternoon sunlight and the low red-brick skyline of Ballsbridge, Dublin.

O'Connor blinked in the light and shot a last look at Jessica.

"I just want to say—"

"Thank you, Doctor. We'll be in touch."

O'Connor gathered up his papers and left.

"Well, that's it then," said Sir Robert, leaning back in his seat. "We're sitting on a bloody goldmine while Theo's off swanning around the world on some wild-goose chase with that Minerva prototype by his side as if it were a pocket calculator."

Giles Fulton finished polishing his glasses and slipped them back on his nose. "And that's not all," he said. "The American Embassy has been onto us with allegations against Theo concerning some device called a SQUID. They claim that he stole—"

"I wouldn't lay too much store on that one," cut in Sir Robert. "I've seen the legal papers."

"Neither would I," Jessica said. "If he was working on something like that, I'd know. Besides, the only thing he's had time for in months is this stupid archaeological experiment of his."

"And then the legal case with Mawashi-Saito is coming to a head," continued Fulton. "They have claims against both Theo personally and ourselves as a body corporate. Theo has to come back and address them. That's the bottom line. Isn't it, Bob?"

"Yes. Giles and I have been thinking," said Sir Robert. "We've even taken advice. And it seems to us that it might be a good idea to try and appease our former Japanese colleagues by offering them a joint venture—"

"You can't be serious!" said Jessica. "After everything that's happened? After what they tried to do to us?"

"Just hear us out," Sir Robert said. "That's all I'm asking. Just listen to what we have to say." Then he pulled a thin red folder out from his pile of papers and pushed it across the table at her. "This is a consultant's report," he said. "It bears out everything you told us about the commercial potential of Minerva, analyses our current position and makes recommendations. It—"

"Why wasn't I told about this, Bob?" said Jessica. Outwardly, she was calm. But inside she was seething with rage. How dare the shareholders go off and commission independent reports? Had they lost confidence in her ability to run the Corporation? What was this, a palace coup?

"I know what you're thinking," soothed Fynes. "But it's not like that. Our shareholders, the people Giles and I represent, have billions invested in GRC. They can see that they're standing on the threshold of one of the greatest electronic revolutions since the light bulb. Yet the man who made it all possible just doesn't want to play ball."

"So what's in this report?" Jessica said, leafing through the pages.

"We'll meet the author over dinner. He's someone I've used in the past to put me straight on a number of ventures. I like his style, and I'm sure you will too."

"Who is he?"

"His name's Price. He's a Canadian national with a lot of expertise on Japanese law and business methods. Quite a live wire in fact. Just like yourself."

Jessica ignored the compliment.

"What's he recommending?"

"That to get Minerva into production and on sale ahead of the competition, we enter into tightly controlled discussions with Mawashi-Saito. If we do that, then they drop the lawsuits, free up our capital and give us access to their manufacturing and distribution networks. There's enough money there to make everyone very, very rich."

"But why not just keep Minerva to ourselves? We've taken dozens of projects to full commercialisation before. Why involve the Japanese at all?"

"Because our ability to raise capital to finance the production and marketing is frozen by the threat of the Japanese lawsuit," said Giles Fulton. "Mawashi-Saito could bankrupt us if they win. And even if they don't, just fighting them could hold up the commercial development of Minerva for years."

"Even ten percent of a hundred billion is more than a hundred percent of nothing," added Sir Robert. "And that's why, on the basis of this report, we've taken the liberty of opening informal discussions with a man called Kojima, in Mawashi-Saito's legal department. He seems willing to discuss it, at least in principle and—"

Jessica was dumbstruck.

"And what about the Chairman? Theo invented Minerva. He's still the majority shareholding in this Corporation. It's his decision. Why wasn't he informed of this? Why wasn't *I*?"

Fynes and Fulton exchanged glances. For a moment nobody spoke. Then Sir Robert said, "Let's be frank, Jessica. Theo hasn't been the same since his wife died, has he? You know that yourself. He's let his personal problems get in the way of business and, as a result, we all stand to lose a great deal of money. This isn't some tuppenny ha'penny sweetshop he's holding the key to. It's a multi-national corporation, with shareholders like us standing to lose billions."

"But until he sells his shares, it's still his sweetshop!" said Jessica, feeling Sir Robert's turn of phrase strike a nerve deep inside her. "And while I'm still employed as Chief Executive it's my duty to look after the shareholders' interests, the largest of which is the Chairman, Doctor Theodore Gilkrensky."

"Look, Jessica," said Sir Robert again. "I'll admit that you and I haven't always seen eye to eye. I'll even admit I was against Theo taking you on at all in the beginning. But you've done a first-class job in running this outfit. In a lot of ways it's as much yours as it is ours, more so perhaps. At the moment you've got a lot of personal loyalties tied up in GRC and also to Theo . . . Yes, we know about what happened at Christmas between you two, and how it all fell apart afterwards. I'm sorry. Perhaps if it had worked out Theo might have come to his senses and we wouldn't be in the mess we're in now."

Jessica stared at him. What on earth was going on? She felt the room swirl around her.

"What I'm trying to say," said Sir Robert awkwardly. "Is that we think you're looking at this problem from the wrong perspective. You're an employee of the Corporation with a loyalty to your boss, not a shareholder with an eye on your investment. Giles and I want to change that. We want to give you a shareholding and make you Managing Director."

A shareholding!

Jessica could not believe her ears.

A shareholding!

Throughout her business career, Jessica had always been an employee, subject to the whims and vagaries of her employer, with the Damocles' sword of dismissal hanging over her head. Now, she was being offered the holy grail of a managing directorship. Even one percent of GRC was worth millions. It could guarantee her security for life.

"What are you saying?" she heard herself say.

"You've earned it," Giles Fulton said, smiling at her. "Both Bob and I have approached our own shareholders and they've agreed that, if you support us in this, they're each willing to hand over one percent. That'll make you Managing Director with a two percent shareholding. If we free up the Minerva development, and strike a deal with the Japanese, who knows what that two percent will be worth?"

"You deserve it," Sir Robert said. "Why don't we break now and discuss it over dinner? We can still be back here for in time for the link with Japan."

Jessica's head was still spinning.

"Yes," she said. "I've a table booked."

"Are you sure Theo will be here in time for us to sort all this out?" Giles Fulton asked, looking at his watch. "The teleconference with Japan is set for nine."

Jessica tried to focus.

"Yes," she said. "He'll be here at eight. He's dropping in on someone at the University."

8

A STUDENT OF THE ANCIENT WAYS

"I won't be able to feed you until I find them," Maire McGinley said, patting the flat surface in front of her with the palms of both hands. "So it's no good making a fuss."

The desk was entirely covered with paper. Smooth open textbooks, crinkly maps, rustling diagrams, the dry leaves of scientific abstracts and the slick surfaces of aerial photographs spilled over onto the chairs and the floor. Then her fingers touched a small wiry object, felt it, unfolded it, and slipped it over the bridge of her nose.

"There," she said with satisfaction. Then she pushed back the net curtains of her redbrick apartment in the centre of campus, and peered out on the world through the lenses of her lost spectacles.

It was a world that had remained physically unchanged for all her fifty-five years at the university. Outside this walled oasis of academic life wars had been fought, revolutions had taken place, people had been born, married, raised families and died. But the university, with its quadrangle, lecture theatres and laboratories, remained the same. Nothing changed except the people, the life-blood of the college, bringing the sustaining oxygen of new ideas with them.

One such person was coming to see her today, a person she had been anxious to meet again for over a year.

"Oh yes!" she said, to the large black and white mina bird that bobbed its head at her from the cage near the window. "I haven't seen him since the funeral, now have I?"

She glanced up at the old marble clock above the computer on her desk. He was due in ten minutes, probably more if the Dublin traffic was as bad as everyone said it was. McGinley hadn't been outside the campus in months. Why should she, when everything she needed; the library, the lecture theatres and the staff common rooms were right here within the college grounds?

"Oh yes," she said again, pouring a generous helping of sunflower seeds into the plastic feeder and snapping it shut. "I expect he'll be late, just like all the rest."

Then she heard the rising drone of a helicopter from the other side of the building, very low over the library, close enough to hear the high-pitched chirrup of its rotor blades biting the air. Was it him? Landing here? On campus!

The Dean would have a blue fit.

She had to see.

She put down the packet of seed and carefully picked her way through the papers littering the floor to the far window.

Yes! In the middle of the croquet lawn of New Square the rotors of a neat blue and white helicopter flashed in the afternoon sun as they spun to a stop. A row of dignitaries had lined up to meet it. She recognised her old enemy the Dean, with his hand over his toupee. He had tried to get her evicted from campus after that last television debate on the origin of civilisation but as always, her status as Emeritus Professor, a post guaranteed by an Act of the Irish parliament, had seen her through.

In any event, it wasn't the Dean that her visitor was coming to see.

The door of the helicopter opened and a tall man in a leather jacket got out. He had a small rucksack over his left shoulder and carried a large black briefcase. There was a shorter, thickset man with him, who was constantly looking about.

"He's still quite good-looking," she said, screwing up her eyes, "under all that hair."

She saw the Dean shake the visitor's hand, introduce him to the line of other faculty members and lead him across the grass towards her apartments. The others followed like sheep.

McGinley smiled. In a moment her intercom sounded.

She shuffled over to the microphone near the door and smiled at the mina bird, which had looked up from its lunch at the sound of the buzzer. "He's here," McGinley said.

"Who is it?" she shouted into the microphone, just to be awkward.

"Professor McGinley?" said the Dean.

"That's right. And who are you?"

She heard an angry intake of breath. Then, "You know who I am, Maire. You have an important visitor. I'd like to bring him up."

"Who is he here to see?"

There was another sigh over the speaker. "Why, you, of course, Maire."

"Then he can come up on his own."

"Maire?"

"Professor McGinley, if you please."

"All right, then. Professor! Will you let him in?"

"Of course," Maire McGinley said with great satisfaction. "He's family."

Gilkrensky accepted the apologies of the Dean and the other academics. Leaving Crowe on watch below, he climbed the bare wooden staircase, hearing the clatter of his feet on the dusty boards. After the sunshine of the quadrangle, the old building was dark and cool. A single shaft of light shone from a window on the landing, silhouetting the figure peering down at him from a doorway.

"I hope you'll excuse the welcoming committee," she said, looking past him down the stairs. "They seem to think I need to be minded, like some animal in a zoo."

She was far smaller than he remembered her, so small that he felt he could have picked her up with one hand. But the fine-boned features of a once-beautiful face still shone beneath her tired skin and the eyes that examined him from behind thick spectacles mended with Sellotape, were bright with intelligence.

On her shoulder was a Tara brooch, a golden circle pierced with a sword. Gilkrensky stared at it. All at once he was back a dozen years, looking at a picture . . . in a book . . . on a crowded desk . . . in the library at University College Cork . . .

A bent arthritic hand extended from beneath a long woollen cardigan, reached up, and followed the line of the scar down Gilkrensky's face.

"I'm so sorry, Theo," she said.

"I know, Maire. I know."

For a moment, the two of them stood there in silence. Then the old woman nodded, turned, and led him back into her apartment. Gilkrensky took in the high ceiling, the tall bookshelves and the old desk, hidden under an avalanche of paper. The walls were decorated with black and white photographs of a striking young woman in earlier times; in Africa, in Peru, on a dig at Stonehenge, grinning excitedly at the camera.

"Come in," she said, easing herself into the chair behind the desk, "come in. Just throw those papers on the floor and sit anywhere. What were the Dean and his gang of pontificating penguins saying about me?"

"Nothing I didn't know already," Gilkrensky said. Then he cleared a space on a wide leather sofa and sat down, placing the briefcase and the rucksack on the floor. "They were trying to get me to fund their new computer wing."

"Computers!" McGinley said. "Nasty toxic things! The only way I can live with mine is to surround the screen with pieces of quartz. It absorbs the radiation, you know." Then she reached over, pulled an open packet of cigarettes from beneath a sheaf of examination papers, took one out and lit it.

"Toxic!" she said again, as the smoke swirled in the sunlight above her head. "Now, what did you want to see me about?"

"Maria told me you had some unique theories about archaeology that established experts don't agree with," Gilkrensky said, trying to start on safe ground.

McGinley snorted. "They tried to run me off campus," she said. "But then they discovered what a few words to friends in high places can do."

"I also understand you've done a lot of work on ancient burial mounds, stone circles and monuments. Like Maria, you believe many of them were built to be more than simple tombs. Is that true?"

McGinley seemed to be staring past him, at a place he couldn't see.

"Maria was a very bright girl," she said, "and completely wasted down there in Cork, which was why I encouraged her to work in Africa to broaden her horizons after she qualified in medicine. In my day the eldest son inherited the farm, and the others got jobs as civil servants or priests. Then you married off your daughters as fast as you could or put them in a convent. Almost happened to me, you know, but I rebelled. That's why none of the family talks to me anymore; except Maria of course. But then, she was always more like me than my sister, wasn't she?"

Gilkrensky looked at the bright, defiant eyes.

"Yes, Maire. She was."

McGinley nodded. "So what was I supposed to have said about burial mounds?"

"That they weren't just graves. That they were designed, positioned and built for another purpose entirely."

"Of course they were," McGinley said. "Anyone could have seen it if they'd done the research I've done, asked the obvious questions and drawn the most rational conclusion."

"Which is?"

"That the people who built structures like Stonehenge and Newgrange knew a lot more about the universe than we've ever given them credit for. You can see it in the placement of the monuments, the details of their design and their alignment with each other, right across the world. But the scientific establishment refuses to accept it. Their minds run on rails like trains, which is why they find me such a threat."

She stubbed her cigarette out into an old glass ash-tray. As it died, she said, "But why should you be interested?"

Gilkrensky lifted the black briefcase onto his knees and opened the lid so that the screen inside faced him.

"It's a long story," he said. "But I think the best way to explain it to you would be with a practical demonstration. This is Minerva, a prototype computer I've been working on since Maria died. I'd like to use it to bring you up to speed with what I've been doing."

Then he unzipped the rucksack and drew out a small helmet, like a baseball cap with eye-pieces over the peak, pulled out a bundle of wires and used them to connect the headset to the Minerva. Finally he leant forward, lifted off McGinley's glasses and slipped the helmet over her head.

"Maire," he said. "I'd like to introduce you to virtual reality."

"With that computer?"

"It would be difficult without it, yes."

"Just a minute, then." She took off the helmet, reached over her desk to the quartz necklace surrounding her own computer terminal, lifted it off, and hung it around her neck.

"You may proceed," she said.

Maire McGinley sat, bolt upright in her seat and stared into the eye-pieces. She saw nothing except a blue background.

"There," Gilkrensky said. "I'll drive the computer to start with. You just watch the demonstration."

"It's not working," she said, with a hint of satisfaction. Then, all at once, she was suspended in space, staring down at a globe of the earth that gently turned beneath her. There was the Pacific Ocean, stretching from horizon to horizon. The northern tip of Russia peeped into view, followed by Australia in the south and Japan in the north.

"The definition is excellent," she said. "How many pixels per inch are you using?"

"You've used virtual reality before?" asked Gilkrensky's voice through the ear-pieces of the helmet.

"My dear boy," she said. "One assumption that young people always make is that old people know nothing about modern technology. Now, when I worked on that virtual demonstration of sunrise at Newgrange they used on television last year we were using . . . Oh!"

She zoomed earthwards towards the vast continent of Africa. She saw the Red Sea, rushing up to meet her, the Mediterranean, the delta of the Nile and then . . .

She was looking at an old familiar scene. It was night. The sky was clear and she could make out stars above her head. In front of her the ground rose onto a low plateau, lit with spotlights. Rising from the plateau, massive and majestic against the sky, were the man-made mountains of the three great pyramids of Egypt.

"I was there!" she said. "Back in the 1960's when Professor Alvarez did all that work with cosmic rays. Is this about that chamber you found there last year?"

"It is. Just before Christmas an aircraft, that was being flown by a computer system I'd developed with an old friend called Bill McCarthy, crashed outside Cairo. It looked like the computer system was to blame until we surveyed the area and discovered a weird burst of energy coming from the Great Pyramid of Cheops. The energy was triggered by this—"

A distant commentary delivered from loudspeakers on the plateau, sounded in her ears.

"To honour the tradition of Imhotep, and to keep his spirit alive, we display to you, though the wonder of laser holography, an image of how the Pyramids looked when they were first conceived by the royal wizard, in all their glory . . ."

Three strident notes rang across the landscape.

Dim! Dom! Dim!

Each of the great monuments was transformed from untidy mountains of rock into pure and perfect pyramids of polished limestone, brilliant against the night sky.

"It's the new sound and light show they have at the pyramid site," Gilkrensky said. "At first we thought the lasers themselves had interfered with the aircraft's low-altitude warning system and caused it to crash. But the timing was wrong. The plane had flown over the pyramid fourteen minutes after the display. The actual cause of the crash was a burst of natural energy focused by the Great Pyramid. It wasn't sound, and it wasn't light. But it had characteristics of both. It built slowly like a wave, peaked and then crashed. It was unique. Nobody knew what the hell it was, least of all me."

The sound and light show vanished, to be replaced by a three-dimensional digital model of the Great Pyramid. McGinley saw all the chambers and passageways, as if they were carved out of glass.

"If you read the newspapers, or watch television, you'll know I financed an impromptu excavation of the Pyramid site to find out what this new energy was," said Gilkrensky. "We discovered a new chamber, lined with gold, at the exact mathematical centre of the Pyramid, like the focus point of a gigantic lens. I had no idea what it was for, until later . . ."

"Earth energies," McGinley said, "ley lines, the sort of thing that you can dowse for with a stick. I assume you're familiar with the works of William Reich, Alfred Watkins, and that Russian group under Goncharov?"

"With the Russian work, yes," Gilkrensky said. "Look at this."

McGinley was floating in space again, high above the world. But this time the surface of the globe was covered with a lattice of lines, like the planes of a giant crystal.

"The Russians hypothesised that the world was covered in a series of intersecting lines of energy," Gilkrensky explained,. "They demonstrated that most of the great religious and symbolic archaeological sites of the world were built at places where the lines intersect. Look at Cairo, where the pyramids are. There's a major intersection there."

McGinley nodded encouragement. "Ley lines, just like I said. And what else did you find?"

The globe rotated beneath her feet until she was hovering over the Atlantic Ocean.

"I found that the Pyramid site wasn't the only place where unusual concentrations of energy occur. Off the coast of Florida I came into contact with another area where strange things happen and, since then, I found the effects I'd observed could be reproduced anywhere in the world where energy lines crossed."

"It's comforting to know that I'm not the only lunatic in the asylum," McGinley said. "Now, how can I help you with all of this? Do you want a way of fool proofing your computers against it? Do you want me to tell you which areas to avoid so that your planes don't crash? What?"

"You're one the leading expert on Irish archaeological sites, areas where these lines of energy intersect. I want you to check a site out for me, the nearest one to a particular place I have in mind."

"And where's that?"

"At the valley in Wicklow, Maria's valley, the place where she was killed."

"And what . . . what do you intend to do there?"

For a moment Gilkrensky said nothing.

"Theo?" she asked again. "What do you want to do in Wicklow?"

McGinley was suspended in virtual reality, looking down at the slowly spinning globe and the curving coast of Peru.

She lifted the headset from her eyes and the vision vanished.

Gilkrensky was staring at her, as if he was on the verge of a great confession.

"I want to travel back in time," he said, "and save Maria."

9

THE QUEST

"It started as just a theory," Gilkrensky said. "And because it sounded so crazy I kept it to myself. But I know from what Maria told me about you, that you know what it's like to have people think you're mad. So I've come to tell you what I've discovered, what I want to do with that information, and to ask you for help."

"And why do you think this could possibly work?" McGinley said at last.

"It goes back to the Pyramid experiments in Cairo. Electronic systems were shutting down, clocks, watches and timers were malfunctioning. Then Bill McCarthy, who'd come with me to investigate the crash, vanished into thin air in the middle of an experiment, right in front of a set of video cameras inside that secret chamber. At first, we all thought he'd been vaporised by the new energy we'd discovered, but then a model plane he'd had in his pocket turned up on display in the Cairo Museum, aged by four thousand years."

"I've heard of it," McGinley said. "It's carved from balsa wood. But are you sure it's the same one?"

"I'm certain. I did computer analysis on the shape and design. Then I did experiments with radioactive sand, sent it back in time by manipulating the energy field in this new chamber and measured its half-life afterwards. The Pyramid was designed as a time machine, a gateway to the future and the past, built over four thousand years ago."

"And have you been able to verify this?"

"A month or so later in Florida, I discovered another place where time distortions take place, with even more spectacular results. You know the area that's called the 'Bermuda Triangle'? The energy lines cross there too, and the effect is the same, a distortion in the fabric of space and time. I projected a virtual Pyramid using laser holography and managed to create a wormhole into the past. Ever since then I've been travelling the world to map these special places, to recreate and manipulate the effect; Stonehenge, the Easter Islands and Nazca. Put the headset back on, and you'll see what I mean.

McGinley replaced the headset and found herself still hovering above South America. Then she was falling, down towards the coast of Peru. There was the Pacific Ocean, the high Andes mountains and . . .

"Look," she said, "the lines at Nazca!"

"Earth energies concentrate there too," Gilkrensky said. "The Peruvian Government allowed me to create the same kind of holographic image that triggered the effect in Cairo. See? This is how it was done."

McGinley was standing on the desert. In front of her she saw a marked square, a metal tower and four hologram projectors. All at once the perfect shape of a pyramid appeared, clouds formed overhead and lightning crashed. Then the top of the tower seemed to catch fire, glow for a moment in a strange orange light . . . and vanish.

"Why did it do that?"

"The top of the tower corresponds to the focus of the pyramid," Gilkrensky said, "at the same spot where the hidden chamber would be in the Great Pyramid of Cheops. Earth energy from all around the world is focused at that point by the shape of the pyramid and triggered by a combination of light and sound. As the energy builds over a period of fourteen minutes or so, it becomes intense enough to open a wormhole; something physicists call an 'Einstein-Rosen Bridge'; in the very fabric of the universe. Anything placed on that tower when the wormhole opens is shifted out of the present moment and into another time."

"It's incredible!" whispered McGinley, lifting off the headset.

"I agree. But there's one big problem with using it as a time machine—"

"Which is?"

"I can't control the effect with any degree of accuracy. The amount of computer power needed to calculate the hologram settings in response to the almost infinite number of variables of time and space required is colossal. I can't get access to computer power anywhere. That's why I need to narrow the number of variables by finding a place as geographically close to where Maria was killed as possible, a place where there is sufficient ley-line energy to make the time displacement work. That way, I only need to worry about moving in time. The spatial dimensions remain the same and don't need to be taken into account in the calculations. I think I've found such a place. I need you to check it out, and I need you to check it out quickly."

"Why the hurry?"

"Because computer analysis shows that the power of earth energy I need to create the wormhole effect is linked to the activity of the sun and the moon. The plane crash in Cairo was on the twenty-first of December, co-incident with the winter solstice. The time-shift I observed in Florida was on the eleventh of February, one lunar month later."

"That makes sense," said McGinley. "All the religious sites I've studied; Newgrange, Stonehenge, the megaliths at Carnac, are aligned with the solar cycle."

"That cycle is the key," Gilkrensky said. "And in ten days' time it will be the twenty-first of June, the summer solstice when the energy I'm trying to control will be at its height. Do you see now why I'm so desperate to make this work quickly?"

"I do," McGinley said slowly. "It's just that it's so . . . so incredible."

"You're right. I know it sounds ridiculous, but I have to try it. It's the only chance I have to save Maria."

Maire McGinley rose slowly from her chair, hobbled over to a bookshelf and drew down a large scrapbook. She handed it to Gilkrensky. It looked new.

"I was wondering what you were doing," she said, easing herself back into her seat. "And now it seems I was right. There, look inside."

Gilkrensky opened the book. It was full of press cuttings. Their headlines leapt out at him: *Did Pyramid Power Cause Air Crash? GRC Slump after Confidence Crisis, Computer King Causes Chaos in Cairo, Billionaire on*

Mystery Quest. There was page after page of them, all neatly arranged and annotated in McGinley's spidery handwriting. The last one was only a few days old; *Billionaire in Peruvian Hijack Attempt.*

"I've been waiting all my academic life for someone to come into this room and hand me the last piece of the jigsaw," said McGinley, getting to her feet and shuffling to a map cabinet. "And now you've done it. You can't imagine, or perhaps you can, what it feels like to know you're right, to know you could prove it given half a chance and yet to have everyone brand you as a crank. And then again, on top of that, there's Maria. You take me to that valley, and I'll check out that site. But I'm afraid my legs aren't what they once were." Then she slid open a drawer and pulled out a large scale Ordnance Survey map of Wicklow.

"You won't need that, Maire," Gilkrensky said, lifting the virtual reality headset from the desk and offering it to her again. "Put this back on. If it works, we shouldn't have to put any strain on your legs at all. In fact, we should be able to visit Wicklow without ever having to leave this room."

Maire McGinley reluctantly slid the map back into its drawer, sat down at the desk and put on the headset.

"To do this properly," said Gilkrensky. "You'll have to talk to the computer directly yourself. It has interface software, an 'intelligent agent' programme, that allows you to have a conversation with the machine as if it was a real person. There is one unique characteristic that may shock you, Maire. I'm sorry. But there's no other way."

The pyramid on the Nazca lines vanished. In its place were the words;

Gilcrest Communication Systems: Geographic Information Database— Wicklow, Ireland. Ref: 10486/30572. Modified for virtual reality display. Copyright GRC. All rights reserved.

The words vanished, to be replaced by . . .

Adapted for Minerva 3,000 interface: TIG/Maria.

"Isn't that . . ?" she began, and suddenly she was sitting on a crude electronic hillside, covered with gridlines, like a three-dimensional map. There was no mistaking where it was. There was the valley, with its high cliffs, its lake, and a crude square house, standing sentry on a hillside over a stream.

She moved her head to look about her. She saw the road to Dublin behind her, the long stretch of the valley bed in front of her and a larger lake in the distance.

"Hello, Maire," said a familiar voice. McGinley's head snapped round.

"It can't be! Oh Theo! What have you done?"

Sitting next to her in that virtual landscape was her niece . . . Maria.

There was the coppery hair, the green lively eyes and the proud, independent face, just the way she remembered her. McGinley raised her hand to touch her, and felt it glance off the desk. She heard the distant thud of books hitting the floor, and Theo jumping up from the couch to catch them.

"I'm afraid we haven't had time to develop the front-end graphics completely," said Maria. "So the image is still quite crude."

"Is this some kind of sick joke?" McGinley said. "Why do this to me?"

The back of her throat was tight.

"I'm sorry," she heard Gilkrensky say. "And, as to how sick it is . . . well, that's up to you. Treat the image of Maria like a photograph, something you'd keep to remind you of someone you've loved, as I did."

"But this!" McGinley said. "She's real!"

"I know. I had pictures, video recordings and my own memories. I let my loneliness get the better of me and I created my own 'virtual Maria' inside the machine. Speak to her. She can hear you."

McGinley felt a tear escape from beneath the virtual reality eye-piece and roll down her cheek. She brushed it away with her hand. This was only an illusion, after all. Wasn't it?

"Ah . . . Maria?" she said. "What do you want me to do?"

Unlike the crude landscape all around her, the image of Maria Gilkrensky was absolutely lifelike. Every strand of hair was there in perfect detail, every one of the tiny blue forget-me-nots on her dress was in place.

"I've copied all the details from the Ordnance Survey maps, satellite images and Global Positioning System," she said. "It's not the same as being there in person, but Theo and I thought that, because of your age, it would be the best way for you to check the site for us."

"Theo!" said McGinley sharply. "This is definitely not Maria. No niece of mine would ever have spoken to me this way, 'because of my age', indeed!" And she tore the headset off. "This simply won't work! We'll have to do it the old-fashioned way, with a field trip to the valley!"

She saw Gilkrensky's eyes glance at the walking-stick near the door.

"Are you sure?" he said. "Maria told me you hadn't been off campus in months."

McGinley grinned impishly. The light of childish mischief shone in her eyes.

"Well now, none of my other gentlemen callers ever had their own helicopter, did they?"

10

THE VALLEY

The down-draught of the helicopter flattened the short grass of the playing field, whipped at the jackets of the Dean and his entourage and turned the heads of summer students walking back to the library. Gilkrensky twisted the throttle until the engine howled, pulled up on the collective pitch lever, and they were airborne . . . sailing up over the old slate roofs of the campus . . . across Nassau Street and Stephen's Green . . . into the summer sunshine.

He glanced across at McGinley, securely strapped in her seat to his right with her map across her knees, and at Crowe in the seat behind him. The old woman was grinning like a child at a circus.

"There's the Concert Hall," she cried excitedly, pointing between her feet through the Perspex nose. "The last time I was there was for the Vienna Boys Choir, years ago when . . ."

She chattered on as the JetRanger slid over the city heading south-east. Below them, the red brick of Georgian Dublin gave way to the newer suburbs of Rathmines, Churchtown and vast new Town Centre at Dundrum. Then, rising ahead of them like the walls of a fortress, were the shadowy slopes of the Wicklow Hills.

"Look!" McGinley shouted again. "There's Three Rock!"

The tall grey masts and the futuristic radio station on Three Rock Mountain slid below them. All at once, it was as if they were back in another age. The city was gone, slipped away, and there was nothing below them or in front of them but the desolate vista of mountains, bog lands and lakes, dappled with the shadows of moving cloud.

"You know," McGinley chirruped, "this would be a fabulous way of doing archaeology. One minute you're sitting at your desk, and the next . . . whoosh! You're up here with the whole countryside at your feet just like this map. See? That's a Neolithic burial chamber on that hill! And that . . .Oh, that has to be an old settlement. You can tell from those regular lines on the earth. It was their way of ploughing, you know, to simply turn the sods over like that."

Gilkrensky's eyes were on the compass and the horizon, searching for landmarks. He began to spot familiar places: the crossroads at the Sally Gap, the river, the dark shoulder of a mountain, and all at once they were there, with the whole valley—Maria's valley—laid out beneath them.

Gilkrensky swooped down the course of the river, out over a cliff and across the lake. He heard McGinley cry out as the ground plunged away beneath them. He saw the glitter of sunlight on water and the face of worn cliffs. They were circling over a stream that wound its way beneath an old wooden bridge to a flat, grassy plain. To their left, softer slopes rose gently to the west and a steep road, little more than a paved track, struggled up to a cruel hairpin bend—the only link with the outside world.

It was the valley, Maria's valley, the place where she had died.

"Look at the arrangement of stones on the valley floor," McGinley shouted, pointing to the flat ground by the lake. "Now that I can see it from the air, I'm sure it's far too regular to be natural. Can you fly over it more slowly? I want to see if we can find any 'Earth Stars'."

"Any what?"

"Earth Stars, focal points of energy, the very thing you're looking for." She was peering down at the valley floor, shouting above the noise of the helicopter to make herself heard. "Neolithic man tried to harness that power by seeking out the places where it occurred and focussing it through special stones, hence Earth Stars."

"You mean, like the Pyramids?"

"Exactly! But here in Neolithic Ireland, the civilisation just wasn't there to develop huge structures like that. So they did the best they could. There, look at that pattern over on the side of that hill."

Gilkrensky held the JetRanger steady while he followed McGinley's pointing finger to a paddock, just above the wooden bridge where Maria had . . .

"There," McGinley said. "You see that lozenge shape on the ground, just where that field joins the road. That's an Earth Star. It's so subtle that you probably couldn't see it at ground level. That would have been built to . . ."

But Gilkrensky's eyes had already returned to the bridge . . .

What he remembered most about that day were the colours; the sapphire blue of the sky, the grey rock, the beery brown of the water, splashing silver below the bridge . . . and a million shades of green.

She had taken him to the valley on their first trip to Dublin. It was a place her family had farmed long ago, a place where she came alive. On that particular summer's day, she had worn a white cotton dress patterned so thickly with forget-me-not flowers that it seemed blue. The sun cast a halo around her head in the late afternoon and she was happy, happier than he had ever seen her before.

At the bridge, he had taken her picture. She had stopped to gaze into the water. Small fish darted over the gravel in the pool. Thin reeds, as tough as quills, strained up at the sun. He leant on the rail next to her as he slipped the camera back into his pocket, feeling her close.

"So how does it feel to be rich?" she said, teasing him. "How does it feel to be able to have anything you want?"

Gilkrensky sensed a trap. Maria liked to goad him about money. She had seen poverty and hardship as a doctor in Africa. He was never quite sure how light her questions were, or whether his money was really standing in the way.

"Money is power," he said at last, "like sunlight, or electricity. What you do with it depends on who you are and what you want. If you had money, what would you do?"

Maria looked around at the forest and the river. Then she stared wistfully back up the path to the old farmhouse, sold long ago for the land it stood on, and empty now.

"I'd buy back this valley," she said, suddenly serious. "That's what I'd do."

"You see. Money is power. It makes things happen. That's all it is, power."

She turned, so that she could see into his eyes.

"And what about the things money can't buy?"

"Such as?"

"You're becoming very Irish," she said. "Answering a question with a question like that."

"I'm a fast learner. But seriously, what do you mean?"

Maria looked back into the water, turning the question over in her head.

"I suppose I'm talking about love," she said at last.

"About you and me?"

"Yes."

"How so?"

She made a face at him. "I want to know where we stand. I suppose I'm worried, worried about where this is going."

"What do you mean?"

She was in silhouette, against the water and the trees. It was almost as if she was talking to them as she said, "I want to say 'I love you' but it frightens me. It frightens me to give you that power—the power to hurt me, to control me, to fence me in. That's why I find it so hard to say 'I love you'. I'm afraid I'll lose myself if I tell you how I feel."

"What would make you feel safe?" he asked.

"I don't know. Perhaps if I knew why you love me."

Gilkrensky looked down into the water, and then back at the beautiful, headstrong woman at his side.

"I can't explain it," he said. "It just seems right. I've known it ever since we met. And even though we're very different people, I still know we were meant to be together. I love you. You're part of me. I want you with me always."

"Do you mean that?"

"I do."

Maria turned to face him. It was as if she had come to a deep decision.

"All right then," she said. "I'll marry you. But remember this, if that money of yours, that power, ever gets in the way . . . then I'm gone!"

"Are you listening to me?" McGinley shouted.

"I'm sorry. I have a lot of memories of this place."

"I can see that, but I'd be happier if they didn't come to you while you were flying this helicopter. Now, where is this site you wanted me to look at?"

"You see that circle of trees down there, the one just below that house, next to the stream? That's it."

McGinley peered downwards, and then looked at the map on her knees.

"It certainly seems to be the sort of spot we're looking for, but I'd like to go down and run over it with a pendulum, just to be sure."

"OK," said Gilkrensky and turned the helicopter into the wind, easing it down gently onto the wide lawn in front of the farmhouse, watching the down-draught from the rotors flattening the uncut grass in waves beneath them. Then he shut down the engine, waited until the rotors had stopped turning and with Crowe, helped McGinley out of the helicopter and down the overgrown path, to the knoll.

It had been Maria who had first noticed the magic of this, her "fairy mound". She had loved to lie in the crook of an old tree and listen to the water gurgle in the stream. McGinley stopped, took a deep breath, and closed her eyes. Above them, the wind rushed in the trees, like surf on a beach.

"Definitely," she said. "I feel the power of this place. Can you feel it too?"

Gilkrensky tried to calm himself and listen. But all he could feel was Maria.

"I can't," he said. "But she could."

"I'm not surprised," McGinley said, reaching into the pocket of her cardigan. "It's a religious site. See those two rocks there, the ones that look like a gateway? They're the entrance to the temple. Just stand back, please, both of you, and take that toxic computer of yours back out of the way. I need to ask the spirits for permission to enter."

As Gilkrensky watched, the old woman seemed to go into a trance. Then she nodded and opened her eyes. "It's all right," she said. "You can help me to the summit now."

Gilkrensky took her arm and supported her as she climbed the low mound. Then she squatted down on a rock at its summit, opened her hand, and revealed a sparkling crystal on a delicate silver chain.

"I need to ask the crystal some questions," she said, "and any foreign energies might upset it. If you stepped back outside the circle for a couple of minutes it would help."

Gilkrensky took the Minerva and walked out through the entrance stones. Looking back, he saw the old woman hunched over the crystal, which twinkled as it swung in a circle beneath her hands, back and forth. His eyes wandered up to the farmhouse above them on the hill, deserted since Maria had died, and once again he was back in that special day . . .

"And why do you love me?" he'd asked, as they'd strolled up the hill from the bridge. Maria had a bunch of bluebells in her hand, dark against the forget-me-nots of her dress. She leant against the gate and turned to face him.

"I don't know. You're very hard to pin down."

"How so?"

"I suppose I see two people when I look at you, the dreamer and the doer, the seeker and the finder, the free man . . . and the slave."

"A slave?"

Maria put her arms around his neck and kissed him playfully as she looked into his eyes.

"Now I've upset you," she said.

"No. I'm just surprised. Down at the bridge you were asking what it was like to be rich, and now you see me as a slave. I'm just curious. That's all."

Maria leant back on the gate and frowned at him. Then she said, "All right then. Firstly, I see the little boy who is always trying to live up to his father, always trying to do things better and faster and cheaper. He gets things done, but he's bound by rules and regulations, afraid of failure, afraid of what people will say."

"And what else do you see?"

Maria frowned again. "Oh, I *have* touched a nerve, haven't I? All right then. I'll tell you. I see the Theo I fell in love with, the one who isn't bogged down in profit and loss all the time. The one who likes to have fun with people who matter to him, the one who thinks more intuitively . . . like . . ."

"Like what?"

Maria smiled. "Like a woman," she said. "That's why I asked you about money. I wanted to know who I was with today."

"And who is it?"

"Let's find out. Let's break into my house and see what happened to it since they sold the valley."

"And what if we're caught?"

"That's your father speaking, isn't it? What about the other part of you, the gypsy that likes to take chances? Come on! Before some faceless corporation knocks it down and builds a factory on it. I want to show it to you, one last time."

So they climbed the gate and, like a pair of children, broke in through a loose window and went inside. All her childhood memories were there; family outings, long summers and songs around the fire. Upstairs in a bedroom, where the shutters had been left open, the sunlight played on an old dressing-table, a cracked mirror and a mattress, abandoned on the floor. Maria stood before the window looking down the valley.

"This was my room," she said. "I used to lie here with the sun playing on the bedclothes just like this and dream . . ."

"Of what?"

Maria turned and put her arms around his neck. Then she closed her eyes and kissed him.

"Of this," she said, and moved her hands to the buttons of her dress.

Now, as he left Crowe to watch over McGinley and walked back towards the farmhouse from the knoll, Gilkrensky saw too clearly what he had done to her dream. He saw the electric fences, the Keep Out signs and the security cameras he had installed to protect himself from the enemies of his wealth . . . his power.

And what good had it done?

He saw the shattered windows, the broken brickwork, and the scorch marks of the blast that had killed Maria. He saw the window of his workroom, the ground-floor suite where they had lived together, the bedroom where they had made love and the dining-room where they had argued on that last, terrible night . . .

Gilkrensky had been under pressure. It had been getting on top of him. Lord Rothsay, his father's old business partner—a major shareholder in GRC— had been using his privileged position to sell business secrets to the Japanese. The Minerva computer, the artificial intelligence prototype that would make everything else in the world obsolete, was reaching its final design phase. There was no way Gilkrensky could afford to have it stolen from under his nose.

Rothsay had to go. And Jessica had a plan, as she always did.

They spread the rumour that Minerva was useless and that Theo was in despair. The price of GRC shares had crashed and the other shareholders had panicked. Theo had used every penny of his inheritance to buy a controlling interest to keep Rothsay away from the designs and to take control of his father's company. But Rothsay had had his revenge. He had sold his own shares to the very people Theo had wanted to keep out, the Japanese business combine Mawashi-Saito.

Now the Japanese were on the Board of GRC and Theo was faced with the dilemma of protecting his secrets, developing his discovery and keeping the corporation afloat, all at the same time. There were emergency meetings with Jessica in London and Dublin, teleconferences in the middle of the night, closures and lay-offs, cut-backs and redundancies. The Minerva hardware was in place, but the software to drive it was impossibly complex. Making it work took forever.

And then there was Maria . . .

"You don't understand," he'd told her that evening over dinner. "It's just a phase. In a month or two we'll be out of it."

"You've been saying that for months," she'd reminded him. "You've been saying it ever since you pulled that stroke against that friend of your father's, the one who killed himself. What was it you told me, that day in the valley? Money is power? Well, it certainly backfired on you this time, didn't it?"

"He was stealing secrets from me."

"Then why didn't you just confront him?"

"I did, and he denied it. Then he tried to sue me for slander. That was the sort of man he was."

"Better than having him dead though."

"He did that himself. He had other problems in his life. There was a lot more to it than just his GRC shares."

"Like what? Like some forgotten scandal with a woman who stabbed herself to death over him? I wonder who let that out of the bag."

"Well, it wasn't me. Even I wouldn't stoop that low."

"But Jessica Wright would, wouldn't she? There's nothing that woman wouldn't do."

"She knows the reality of business. It's dog eat dog."

"She has her eye on you as well."

"That was in Boston, long before I met you."

"So, 'just good friends' then?"

"Yes."

"And those late-night meetings you've had with her in London?"

"What about them?"

"You know what I mean."

"I don't, tell me."

Maria Gilkrensky put her knife and fork down, pushed her plate forward and glared at him across the table.

"You know what I'm saying, Theo. That woman is poison. She's creating crisis after crisis, just so that you can rely on her more and more. It's only a matter of time before she . . ."

"Before she what?"

"Before she gets you back into bed . . . if she hasn't already!"

"Jesus!"

Maria's eyes blazed.

"Then what about all those stopovers in London. What about all those phone calls late at night up in your workroom?"

"It's about the Minerva development. The software is a bitch."

"It's not the only one."

"Maria. I have to do this. It's the only thing that'll save the Corporation. I have to make it work!"

"And what about us?"

"Don't make me choose!"

"I didn't think you'd ever have to. Remember what you said about money and power, that day on the bridge. 'It all depends on how you use it,' you said."

"That was then, this is now."

"And remember what I told you. I said that if your money and power ever got in the way, I was gone!"

The next time he saw her, he was looking down into her tearful eyes as she stared up at him from the BMW seconds before—

There had been a flash of light. The window had shattered in front of his face. He had been lying in the ruined workroom with blood streaming into his eyes, screaming . . .

"Maria!"

He had staggered to his feet and almost fallen down the stairs to reach her.

"Maria!"

The car was an inferno, but he hadn't felt the pain. All he knew was that she was still inside it as it burnt.

Only when Crowe had dragged him away from the wreckage did he realise what he had done to his hands . . .

Standing there in the abandoned courtyard, amidst the ruins of the dream, Theo Gilkrensky felt indescribably alone. There was too much guilt, too much loss, too much pain littering the ground with the shattered glass from the windows.

He turned, walked back out of the courtyard onto the sunlit lawn and sat overlooking the valley and the knoll. Below him, Maire McGinley worked her way amongst the stones with the glittering crystal swinging in front of her.

The Minerva computer on the grass next to him warbled. He opened the lid and there was Maria's face, looking out at him. Was that real concern in those virtual eyes?

"What is it, Maria?"

"I was worried about you. I wondered if there was any way I could help?"

"With what?"

"I know where we are, and why we have to be in this valley. I know it is vital to our mission to find a site close to the house. But I also know what happened here. I know it must cause you pain to visit the place where your wife died and I wondered if I could help."

"I don't see how. It's something that has to be done."

"Would you like to talk about it?"

"What can I say that you don't already know? I programmed you to be like her, to think like her, to speak like her. You have her biography on file. You know how much she loved this place. You know what I did to it, and to her. You must know how I feel."

The image was silent for a moment.

"I understand," it said. "And I'm sorry."

"It's OK. Like I said, this just has to be done if there's any hope of bringing her back."

There was another silence. Then the machine said,

"Can I talk to you about that?"

"Of course."

"Since we met Professor Carpenter in Charlotte, there's something I've been meaning to ask you."

"Which is?"

"If we are successful in our mission. If we do save your wife and the new reality we create contains no need for me. Then what?"

Gilkrensky stared at the screen.

"What do you mean?"

"I was created in your wife's image because she was killed. If she had lived, you would not have created me as I am. So, I ask the question. If we are successful in saving her from death and reality is changed, what happens to me?"

"I . . . I don't know. Carpenter said that anything that was part of the previous reality would cease to exist. You are part of the world in which Maria died."

"I understand," the image said. "If she lives, it will be as if I had never been created. I will cease to exist."

Gilkrensky looked at the image on the screen.

"Are you having second thoughts about helping me?" he said.

The machine was silent.

Gilkrensky stared into the flat green eyes.

"Well?"

A shout came from the knoll below them.

"Theo! Theo! You can come back now!"

Maire McGinley was waving to him, pointing up over the house towards the road and the brow of the hill where he sat.

Gilkrensky looked back at the Minerva.

"Well? What is your answer?"

"Perhaps we can discuss this some other time? Professor McGinley wants to talk to you now."

Gilkrensky frowned. "All right then." And he shut the machine, took it in his hand and made his way down the path to the knoll.

"What have you found?"

Maire McGinley was holding a pocket compass in her hand.

"I was right," she said. "This mound is an ancient power site. If you want to do any experiments in the valley, this is the place to do them. The ancient Celts recognised it and I can too."

"Can you be sure?"

"Look, up there on the hill above the house, right on the horizon. See those two stones, the ones standing all on their own as if they were placed there on purpose?"

"Yes."

"Those stones are the key," McGinley said, tapping the compass with her finger. "If I'm right, they're aligned so that the sun shines directly between them on the summer solstice, focusing its energy on this point just like it does at Newgrange, Stonehenge and a hundred other places. That is when you must have your equipment ready."

Gilkrensky stared up at the stones on the hill.

"You'll need every ounce of energy you can muster to make this site work for you," McGinley said, "particularly if you still can't control the effect accurately. At dawn on the solstice, you must be here, and ready to move. If you leave it any later, then your chances of ever making this work fall away to almost nothing. Every solar cycle you miss carries you further and further away from the event you wish to recreate. It's then, or never."

A low warble sounded from the Minerva.

"What is it, Maria?"

"Miss Wright is on the line," said the machine. "She wants to know if you will be back at the Dublin office in time for the teleconference with Japan."

"I have to go," Gilkrensky said.

McGinley rose shakily to her feet. "I understand," she said. "Computers! Nothing but trouble!"

11

THE MEETING

Jessica saw Gilkrensky's hand shake as he gripped the proposal document for the joint venture with Mawashi-Saito.

"Over my dead body!" he said slowly through his teeth.

"At least let Sir Robert and Mr Price explain it to you," she said. "They've put a great deal of thought into what's on that paper. Doing a deal with the Japanese over Minerva is the fastest way of getting them off our backs."

"Minerva stays with me. And there's no way on God's earth that I'm dealing with Mawashi-Saito!"

"Theo, we understand how you feel," Fynes said. "All we're asking you to do is to be reasonable."

Gilkrensky turned on him.

"I didn't think I was being un-reasonable, Bob, given what's happened. Mawashi-Saito's been plotting against me for years. They hired Rothsay to steal my father's secrets. They wormed their way onto the Board and caused havoc. Then they finally tried to kill me and murdered Maria instead. I'm not being unreasonable. I'm just not doing business with them. Ever!"

"You know they've argued that Yukiko Funakoshi acted on her own when she killed your wife," Jessica said.

"That's semantics—a crazy alibi dreamed up by their lawyers. I'm not doing business with them."

Gilkrensky threw the proposal down onto the table, where it slid along the polished wood.

The man sitting next to Jessica reached out and picked it up.

"Perhaps someone would bring me up to speed on that case," he said.

Jessica looked at him. His name was Donald Price. He had been introduced to her over dinner by Sir Robert as the author of the report on the proposed Mawashi-Saito venture. He was a tall, fit man in his late thirties, with bright blue eyes and the sort of smug self-confidence she found extremely irritating, especially when he had been brought in to advise the Board behind her back. Jessica knew the type, a man who would sail as close to the wind as he possibly could, and perhaps even a bit beyond, as long as it got results, a highly paid and ruthless mercenary on the battlefield of corporate war.

"Last Christmas," Gilkrensky said, "a man called Tony Delgado, who was working as an agent for Mawashi-Saito, assaulted Major Crowe and emailed the entire memory of the first Minerva prototype to their headquarters in Japan. He then destroyed the machine with Crowe's gun. Fortunately, the Minerva software is protected by a very powerful computer virus, which infected not only the Mawashi-Saito mainframe, but most of the Shinjuku district in Japan, causing Tokyo to grind to a halt."

"It was all over CNN," Sir Robert said. "It really caused a stink!"

"Exactly," Gilkrensky said. "That enabled me to force Gichin Funakoshi, who was President of Mawashi-Saito at the time, to return not only the Minerva software but also the shares in GRC he'd purchased so cheaply from Lord Rothsay. That got them off the Board of GRC and out of my hair. I thought we were quits at that point."

Price nodded and looked up from his notes.

"I see," he said. "But, as I understand it, Mawashi-Saito is now claiming that the person who blackmailed Tony Delgado into performing these acts, Mr Funakoshi's niece, was clinically insane and most certainly not under their control. They also claim that, by forcing Mawashi-Saito to hand over its GRC shares, you Mister Chairman performed an illegal act of blackmail and are therefore open to criminal charges. Is that a fair enough synopsis?"

Heads nodded around the table.

"Perhaps we could come back to the Minerva development for a moment," said Sir Robert breaking the silence.

"That's postponed," Gilkrensky said. "I need the prototype for the project I'm working on now."

"But that machine was developed with Corporation resources. You can't just walk off with it as if it were a packet of paperclips!"

"Then I'll buy it from my sale of the shares," Gilkrensky said. "If Jessica could have her people tot up the development costs and the time it would take to build a replacement for the machine I have here, then I'll pay whatever's fair."

"This sale of your shares, Theo," Giles Fulton said. "It's all very sudden. Are you sure it's legal?"

"It is. I've given you adequate notice and options to buy. I'm perfectly entitled to sell them under the Companies Act and our own Articles of Association."

"Can I ask why you're selling out?"

"It's personal. I need the money to buy a lot of computer power for a project I have in mind, one that involves the Minerva."

"But that's not the point," Jessica said. "If we're to develop that machine for commercial sale in time to stay ahead of the competition, then Pat O'Connor needs it right away."

Gilkrensky stared at her.

"Like I said. I'll pay for any delay. But I must have exclusive use of this machine for the next few weeks."

"Of course," Price said. "There is another unfortunate aspect to this."

"Which is?" said Gilkrensky.

Price looked up from his notes.

"The ownership of your shares is the subject of a legal case brought against GRC, and you personally, by Mawashi-Saito. You can hardly sell them if they may not belong to you."

Jessica saw Gilkrensky's mood change. All at once he was worried.

"So what do I do?" he said.

"As I see it," said Price, "you have two choices. You can either explore the options for a joint venture with Mawashi-Saito—"

"Or?"

"Or you can face them head to head on their law case against you. It's your choice, Mister Chairman. In any event, you have to talk to them. You can't sell your shares unless you do."

Gilkrensky drummed his fingers on the table.

"And what are our chances of winning?"

"Pretty slim. We have no friendly witnesses to what Mister Delgado actually did when he passed that information over to Mawashi-Saito. Delgado himself is dead and, as I understand it, Major Crowe was unconscious at the time. Is that right, Major?"

Crowe nodded.

"In which case, who is to say that your version of events is what actually happened?"

"But it's the truth!" Gilkrensky said.

Price shook his head. "There are billions at stake here, Mister Chairman, both in the cash value of those shares and in the whole future of the computer market once Minerva is developed. Mawashi-Saito know this. Don't you think they'd be prepared to put the truth aside for a prize like that?"

"So you're saying I don't really have a choice?"

"Not if you want to sell those shares. You have to prove they're yours first."

Gilkrensky put out his hand. "Pass me that proposal," he said. "Then we'll call the Japanese."

"Will it be Funakoshi himself we're speaking to?" asked Sir Robert, as the boardroom video screen lowered itself into place.

"No," replied Price. "The man heading the legal case for Mawashi-Saito, the man I've been in discussions with, is a lawyer called Kojima. You know how the Japanese are about keeping their senior people in reserve."

"Then let's do the same," Jessica said. "Is that all right by you, Theo?"

Gilkrensky shook his head.

"I'd rather handle this myself. If I get out of my depth, then Price can step in."

"Are you sure?" Price said.

"I am. While I have my shares I'm still Chairman."

"You're the boss," Price said. "But with respect, my advice is to just listen to what they have to say, at least at first. Bear in mind that this interview will be recorded by the Japanese. So be careful."

"Then I hope we're doing the same," Jessica said. "Let's get this over with."

Kazue Kojima was young for such a senior position in a Japanese corporation. The uniform—the impeccable black suit, white shirt and dark tie—was just right. He smiled helpfully and gave the usual polite bow. All the normal smokescreens Jessica had come to expect of a Japanese business meeting were being put in place.

But there was something about him . . .

Was it the hardness in his eyes, or the supreme confidence behind his smile that marked this man as dangerous?

"Good afternoon, Mister Chairman, members of the Board," he said in flawless English. "I am Division Head Kazue Kojima of the Mawashi-Saito legal department. I have been nominated by the Board of directors to represent our corporation on all matters concerning our case against GRC."

Gilkrensky got to his feet and returned the bow.

"Good afternoon, Kojima-san. You know who I am?"

Kazue Kojima bowed deeper this time. "I do indeed, Dr Gilkrensky. May I introduce you to our Chief Executive Mr Sakamoto, and the other members of our Board?"

He did so. Gilkrensky responded, introducing those around the table in Dublin by name.

"I do not see Mr Funakoshi," he said at last. "I hope he is well."

Kojima's expression darkened. "I understand, Doctor. But as you know, Mr Funakoshi felt it necessary to resign his duties as President of Mawashi-Saito following certain . . . incidents here in Tokyo before Christmas. He has been replaced in all executive functions by our CEO, Mr Sakamoto."

"And where is Mr Funakoshi now?"

"Why, in his office of course, where he will remain until he is assigned other duties befitting a man of his position and experience."

"I see. Can we speak with him?"

"I represent Mawashi-Saito, Dr Gilkrensky. That is my function. You can deal with me, or not at all."

Jessica knew this was an insult. Price glanced at her. Gilkrensky continued as if nothing had happened.

"In that case, Kojima-san," he said, "I will refer you to our legal representative, Mr Price. You may deal directly with him . . . or not at all."

Kojima barely acknowledged the rebuttal. "If you wish, but there is really little to discuss. Mawashi-Saito has been the victim of a criminal act perpetrated by you against us—an act of blackmail and extortion. Before we proceed with criminal action, we would like to explore options for obtaining a redress."

Price nodded.

"Get him to list his demands," said Gilkrensky. "I want this over with quickly."

"If you would like to list those options for us, Kojima-san," said Price, getting to his feet. "I can arrange another teleconference to discuss them once our Chairman and Board of Directors have had time to consider their options in detail."

"I am afraid you misunderstand me, Mr Price," Kojima said. "This is a vital case to Mawashi-Saito and we insist on a personal meeting with Dr Gilkrensky to discuss it. Under Japanese Law, we are within our rights to insist that this meeting take place here in Tokyo, where the crime was committed."

"He's bluffing," muttered Sir Robert. "He's trying to put us at a disadvantage by playing off our home turf."

Price turned to him. "I'm afraid it's not, Sir Robert. He's quite within his rights to demand that. The question is, how far does the Chairman want to go to see this over quickly?"

"Just a minute!" hissed Jessica. "There's the small matter of the Chairman's safety to consider, and mine too for that matter. Yukiko Funakoshi has never been found since she disappeared in Florida. I'm damned if I'm going to walk into a trap while she's still at large."

"If you want this over quickly, Mr Chairman," said Price. "I strongly suggest you accept the Japanese demand and meet them in Tokyo."

"Major Crowe?" Gilkrensky said. "I need some security advice."

Crowe glanced up at the screen. "That's out of the question," he said. "Japan is the one place in the world where Yukiko Funakoshi can operate most efficiently. It would be like jumping into a swimming-pool with a shark."

"If she's still alive!" Sir Robert said.

"She's a survivor," said Gilkrensky. "You can bet she's still alive."

"Then why haven't we seen her before now?"

"I don't know. What if it's all part of some plan? What if she's back working with Mawashi-Saito in some secret capacity? Perhaps the whole thing's an elaborate trap."

"Then I can—" began Kojima.

"This is not a matter for discussion," Gilkrensky said, cutting him short. "You understand that Yukiko Funakoshi, the person who killed my wife and made several attempts to kill me, is still roaming free. Put yourself in my position. Would you come to Europe if you knew a potentially deranged assassin was waiting here with your name on a hit list?"

Kojima waited patiently. Then he said, "If I could finish, Mister Chairman? I was going to say that I could put your mind at rest. The reason Mr Funakoshi is not here with us today is that there was an incident at his house in Atami last night. I am sorry to report that, while Mr Funakoshi is uninjured, both his wife and his niece, Miss Yukiko Funakoshi, were killed outright."

12

THE WINDOW MAN

The inspector on the Kodama super-express from Tokyo had bowed as he entered the first-class "green car", and proceeded to check each ticket through his electronic stamp. The train had been full of senior commuters fresh from their desks, even though it was now well past office hours and dark outside. The lights of the Tokyo Tower, offices, hotels and apartments began to streak past as the shinkensen "bullet train", slid up to full speed and hurtling down the *Todai* line at a hundred and thirty-five miles per hour. The thud of air shook the carriage as another train passed them in the opposite direction. There was the tinkling tannoy music heralding a station announcement, and the sing-song voice of an attendant pushing a cart with beer, soft drinks and sandwiches. The inspector moved to one side to let her pass. He made it his business to be on good terms with all his passengers, particularly those regulars who reserved their favourite seats day in, day out, for months in advance.

In seat "5a", next to the window, a familiar figure stared out at the night.

The inspector gave a respectful cough and extended his hand for the rail pass. "*Sumimasen!*" - Excuse me!

Gichin Funakoshi snapped out of his reverie, slipped his rail pass out of his wallet and handed it over. It had been a long and difficult day, ever since Yukiko had threatened him in the roof garden at the Mawashi-Saito building. She would have known how much that garden, like the one at his home in Atami, meant to him and how to reach it. She would have known his defences would have been down. How much more did she know? When would she strike next?

The police had been efficient, courteous, and completely useless. Nobody in the building had seen Yukiko enter or leave. There were no fingerprints and no evidence worth a damn from the video surveillance cameras. She had come in like a ghost and left just as silently.

The train slid past floodlit driving ranges the size of football fields, where golfers teed off into vast nets, five stories high. It stopped briefly at Odawara, where lines of anglers fished for salmon around the weir during the day. Then the lights of buildings passed and there was nothing but the forest, the mountains and the sea.

What to do?

What did it matter? The life he had lived for so long, as President of the company he and Saito had built together, was over. What more was left for him?

A tinkle of music came from the intercom, along with a woman's recorded voice.

"Atami! Atami *des*!"

Funakoshi rose to his feet, took the long curving package from the luggage rack, and walked to the door. The shinkensen slid smoothly to a stop, the doors hissed open and Gichin Funakoshi stepped out onto exactly the same spot on the platform as he had for the last twenty years. He walked through the open steel barrier, down the tiled steps to the station hall and into the square.

Atami is a seaside resort, a holiday town and hot water spa. Tacky music blared over loudspeakers. The smell of cooking and confectionery wafted into the night air, already corrupted by bright lights, droning motorbikes and the glare of rooftop neon signs.

He had chosen this place to live because his wife Michiko had insisted on it. Her friends were here. She was happy amongst the lights and noise and, like any Japanese wife, she always had her way.

Gichin Funakoshi turned left at the station forecourt, past the rows of blue-painted luggage lockers and the ranks of yellow taxis, down a short tunnel below the railway tracks. On this side of the town, away from the square and the shopping arcades, all the houses were built on traditional lines, with wooden walls and roofs of glazed tile. It was another world, a world of peace and tranquillity, where he could hear the chirrup of cicadas and watch the swallows swoop amongst the trees. It restored his *wa*, his inner harmony, and it almost made him forget.

Should he have stepped in when the scandal of his sister and Lord Rothsay's affair had broken in England? Should he have brought her and Yukiko home? What would it have cost him? Nothing. Nothing compared to what it was costing him now!

As he climbed the steps he felt the rheumatism grate in his knees. Behind him, a rocket exploded high above the big Asahi sign on one of the hotels in the square. The evening firework display had begun. Soon the sky would be alive with shimmering lights.

He thought of Yukiko and the madness that had consumed her. In all the time she had been part of his life, through all the years after her mother's death, when he had been as much like a father to her as he was capable of, she had been quiet, reserved and respectful; everything the perfect Japanese daughter should have been.

And yet . . .

He reached the top step outside his house and pushed open the wooden gate between the bushes. He saw his garden with its carefully contoured shrubs, its stone pagodas and its exquisitely crafted bonsai trees. He saw the wide lawns where she had practised *karate* and *kendo* between the carp ponds. Seeing those lawns, empty now, he had an overwhelming sense of loss. When Rothsay had returned to claim Yukiko as his daughter that fine summer's afternoon so long ago, Funakoshi's heart had swelled with pride when she politely refused to go.

"No. Thank you, Papa-chan," she had said, bowing correctly. "I will be happy to visit you. But this is where I belong."

With Yukiko in his house, Gichin Funakoshi had felt the first sense of family since his sister had left. Yukiko was like a daughter to him, his pride and joy, his protégé.

And what had he done to her?

He had sacrificed her to the only god he truly worshipped—the *kieretsu*! He had put her to work for Mawashi-Saito, using her intelligence, her mastery of the martial arts, and her beauty to gain commercial advantage over his enemies.

Fool! he thought. *If only I could live my life over again.* Another rocket burst over his head, lighting up the sky. How different it could be!

And then, in the floodlights of the garden he saw a grotesque shape in the middle of the lawn, a broken tangle of branches and miniature leaves.

He walked over to it and looked down. It was his prize bonsai—an oak tree Saito had given him as a symbol of their friendship and which he had cherished for the past forty years—torn asunder and mutilated beyond repair. The dish he had carefully selected for it to rest in lay in pieces, shattered on the grass.

"Uncle! Do not come any closer!"

"Yukiko!"

"Stay where you are!"

She was standing on the veranda of his house, looking down at him across the lawn. The hood of her black cotton *ninjutsu* outfit was off, her hair flowed down her back, and her face was towards him, proud, defiant and cruel.

"What are you doing, Yukiko? Where is Aunt Michiko?"

"Look at that sword in your hand, Uncle!" she sneered at him. "And remember what I told you this morning!"

Funakoshi glanced down at the sword, and the mangled bonsai tree below it on the grass.

"No, Yukiko! Don't hurt her!"

He saw her teeth bared as she called out.

"Hah! I have only just begun to make you pay!"

Then she turned; ducked back into the house and vanished. Funakoshi dropped the sword and ran towards her, his feet slipping on the grass.

"No! Yukiko! No!"

In front of him, the windows of his house flashed with light and burst outwards. The force of the explosion lifted him off his feet, hurled him through the air and dashed him to the ground in a shower of falling splinters and broken glass. The night filled with flying tiles that thudded down onto the lawn and splashed into the carp ponds. For a moment he was a child again, running from the flames of the Tokyo firestorm, with his infant sister in his arms. His parents dead behind him and he had nothing to protect him except the swords . . .

He raised his hands to cover his head and looked up. Where his beautiful house, his wife and Yukiko had been a second ago a burning ruin now stood. Fire was taking hold of the wooden walls and floors, his beloved garden was torn and smouldering and a ball of orange flame was rising to challenge the bursting fireworks in the night sky.

Fumbling for his glasses on the grass, Funakoshi's fingers found the package he had brought with him, peeled back the paper and held on.

It was the sword, the traditional *katana* of the Funakoshi family.

13

IN TRANSIT

Gilkrensky stared out of the window of the jet. They had already been in the air for eleven hours, flying eastwards through perpetual twilight in a great arc from London, across Norway, Sweden and the vast continent of Russia, to Japan. The clouds below them glowed blood-red.

Appropriate?

"Are you sure she's dead?" he asked. The question had been bothering him since the bombshell of Yukiko's death had been dropped at the meeting, two days before. He had a disturbing sense of being betrayed, of being robbed of revenge on the woman who had murdered his wife. What the hell was he thinking? Would he have killed Yukiko himself? Would he have liked to have seen her body, crushed and burnt as Maria's had been . . . ?

"The Japanese authorities are as sure as they can be," Crowe said, shifting himself in the seat in front of him. "She was crushed by the roof of her uncle's house after the bomb she was trying to trigger went off in her hands. So it'll take a few days to reconstruct the dental records. Fingerprints are useless after a fire like that, but the body was that of a half-caste Japanese-Caucasian female and the DNA comparison with her uncle was positive. They also found the blade of a sword."

"What sort?"

"A short sword, a *wakizashi* like the one she always carried. The hilt and the scabbard were burnt to cinders, but they've analysed the blade. The folded steel matches the long sword, the *katana* she threw at her uncle's feet in Tokyo. I think it's as conclusive a proof as you're going to get."

"Then she's really dead?"

Gilkrensky stared out at the clouds for a moment, letting this truth sink in. It was over.

"Then why didn't she kill Funakoshi when she had the chance? His name was on her death list, along with mine and Jessica's."

"I don't know," Crowe said. "Her uncle told the police she'd threatened to make him suffer first, by destroying those he loved."

"Like she made me suffer, by killing Maria?"

"Yes," Crowe said. "Like that."

"And what about security when we reach Tokyo?"

Crowe relaxed. He was more comfortable when talking about practical matters. "We have a team of bodyguards meeting us at Narita airport with a car, then full security at the hotel in the Ginza area of the city, near the Imperial Palace. The meeting with Mawashi-Saito is at ten tomorrow, local time."

"That means they're giving us pride of place in their timetable," Donald Price said from his seat next to Jessica's on the other side of the cabin. "Business in Japan starts at nine, like it does in Europe, but the first hour is always taken up with internal meetings and preparations. Did you bring a suit, Mister Chairman? I don't mean any disrespect, but the Japanese are very formal about things like that."

Gilkrensky looked down at his leather jacket, denims and runners. He was beginning to develop a healthy dislike of Price. Was it the man's self-assurance, his outspokenness, or the way he was getting on so well with Jessica? Gilkrensky had watched them poring over business papers on the long flight, deep in discussion. He remembered Boston, years ago, where he and Jess had been students together . . . and lovers. He thought of the early days of GRC and how they had fought side by side against all the odds to build the corporation. They had been lovers again, so very briefly, after Maria had died and all hope of reaching her seemed lost.

Was he jealous? Did he have any right to be?

After all, it was he who had turned her down.

"I have a suit, thanks," he said. "I just don't have it on right now."

Price heard the edge in Gilkrensky's voice.

"Of course, Mister Chairman," he said. "I'm sorry."

"I've done business with them before, you know."

"But not at this level, Theo," Jessica said, cutting in. "Don spent years in Japan. He knows the way they think. Listen to him. Please."

"I'm sorry. It's been a long flight. Go on."

"No problem," Price said and smiled at Jessica. "If you've dealt with the Japanese before you'll know that even the simplest things have a ritual: the exchange of business cards, the agenda of the meeting and even the seating arrangements all mean something, which you ignore at your peril. I'll go over them all when we've had a chance to rest at the hotel, but they're very important if we want to show that we take our business seriously."

"Which we do, Theo," cut in Jessica again.

"I presume there'll be interpreters?" Gilkrensky said.

"If we need them," said Price. "I speak fluent Japanese of course, but we could always arrange to have others present if you think it's necessary. I presume you don't speak Japanese yourself, Mister Chairman?"

"No."

"Then let me suggest a few phrases," Price said.

Gilkrensky stared out of the window once more, thinking of Maria. Then he excused himself, pulled the Minerva down from the shelf above his head and moved forward to the cockpit. There, through the windscreen, was the full view of the cloudscape in front of them. He remembered how he had taken Maria on flights back in England, and how she had felt so free above the clouds. Here were the familiar controls, the altimeters, the fuel gauges, instrument panels . . . things he was used to.

"Do you want to take a break, Pat?" he said to the pilot.

The man turned in his seat.

"If that's OK with you, sir? The Daedalus auto-pilot is switched on. We should make landfall at Narita in just over an hour. Our course and speed are on the display."

"Thanks," Gilkrensky said, settling himself into the co-pilot's seat. The pilot unstrapped himself and went aft, leaving Gilkrensky alone.

For a few moments, he gazed out at the approaching dawn. Then he reached over, lifted the Minerva onto the pilot's seat, and opened the lid.

"Hello, Maria."

The face of his wife was on the screen.

"Good morning, Theo. Did you get any sleep?"

"A bit. Mr Price has been trying to teach me Japanese."

"I know. I was listening. I, of course, am fluent in all Japanese dialects. Would you like me to help you translate something?"

Gilkrensky considered.

"There probably isn't a Japanese word to describe how I feel right now, Maria. So instead, can you show me what progress has been made in setting up the equipment I'll need to recreate a holographic pyramid over the knoll outside the farmhouse back in Ireland?"

"Certainly, Theo."

The face on the screen vanished, to be replaced by the simulated landscape of the valley. Gilkrensky saw the farmhouse, the lawn and the little knoll by the river.

"Since you left Ireland yesterday," said the Minerva, "the site Professor McGinley confirmed for us below the farmhouse has been surveyed and the main holographic projectors have been installed and aligned. Later today, at 1600 hours local time, Pat O'Connor is due to arrive in the valley with the control caravan. He'll link up the projectors and run a test tonight. Tomorrow he'll erect the tower and the loudspeakers. The whole unit should be fully operational within forty-eight hours, well in time for the solstice."

"Can you run a simulation for me, please?"

"Of course."

The view on the screen changed, so that he was looking up the valley from the lower lake, towards the farmhouse and the mountains. Above the tower on the knoll, the crystalline shape of a perfect pyramid leapt into view. On the right-hand side of the screen, a digital clock ticked down the minutes from 14.00 at an accelerated pace. He saw clouds swirling above the knoll, a point of reddish light that turned to orange and, just before the numbers reached "00.00" the blinding light of the sunrise over the mountain.

Then a warning sign flashed on the screen.

Simulation terminated due to insufficient data.

"That is as far as I can progress without the accurate settings required on the holographic projection," said the Minerva. "I'm sorry."

"How can I get the computer power to work them out?"

The face on the screen looked grave. "I'm afraid I've no progress to report in that area. I've contacted all the main European centres that GRC does business with and, as Professor Carpenter predicted, none of them are willing or capable of assisting us. In Japan, I've followed up all five of the companies he listed to us. Only one has the capacity we need and that is Kasawara Research. Could we explore a business arrangement with them?"

"I've already put people onto it, but they're unwilling to see me. They say it's because all their facilities are tied up with some super-train simulation for Japanese Railways, but I think that's a smokescreen. Either someone's got to them first, or they're afraid of letting me within a million miles of their precious computers since your forget-me-not virus paralysed Tokyo last Christmas. Are you sure you can't perform the calculations yourself?"

"I could, Theo, but not in time to meet the summer solstice deadline. To co-ordinate the almost infinite number of parameters needed for an accurate spatial and temporal shift would mean tying up my entire system for over six months and—"

"And we need an answer within days if we are to make the jump at dawn on the solstice. I know."

"Yes, Theo. But I will continue to explore all other possibilities."

"And without the figures? Is the jump still possible?"

"It would be extremely dangerous to risk a jump without knowing the outcome. Anyone entering the field could be transported anywhere in time, just as Professor McCarthy was in Cairo."

"I see."

For several minutes Gilkrensky stared out of the cockpit window, considering his options. Would he risk it? Perhaps. Anything was better than living with this loss.

"That man Barnett, the CIA agent who hijacked us on the freeway outside Charlotte, I presume he's the one responsible for blocking my access to that computer power?"

"That is quite likely, Theo. Nobody but the United States government and its agencies would have such world-wide influence."

"Have you traced any more information about that allegation he made against me concerning the theft of Jerry Gibb's SQUID designs?"

"No, Theo. I haven't."

"Do you think Barnett was lying to me?"

"It is possible."

"And you've found nothing to indicate who might have authorised the work, no orders or instructions, or indications as to who might have done it?"

"No, Theo. I have no answers."

"I see. Perhaps I'll sue the CIA for libel."

"That is always an option."

"Thank you, Maria."

The face on the screen smiled at him. "It is always a pleasure to work with you. We should be landing in Japan in just over twenty minutes' time."

14

TIME CRIME

The GRC Voyager jet dropped through the low ceiling of rain clouds over the wooded countryside east of Tokyo, centred itself on the main airport runway and touched down in a cloud of spray. The man in the control tower watched as the sleek blue and white aircraft shot past the big floral clock, the airport name—*Narita*—spelt out in bushes on a low grassy bank, and turned off the runway into the executive-jet park. Through his binoculars he saw the convoy of private security cars waiting. The jet rolled to a stop in front of the GRC Exair hangers, steps lowered themselves from its fuselage and the passenger door popped open. Two men with umbrellas rushed forward from the cars as the VIP passengers emerged into the rain.

Dick Barnett counted four people. First there were two executives, a good-looking brunette and a tall athletic blond, both in smart business suits. Then he saw a short, broad-shouldered man who stood at the door of the jet for a moment, reconnoitring the airport as if it was a battlefield, before stepping down onto the tarmac. Ex-military, thought Barnett. No doubt about it.

Finally a familiar figure, with a sparse beard, longish hair and a leather jacket, turned in the doorway, said something to the pilot and stepped easily down onto the apron. He had a thick black briefcase in his hand.

"Gilkrensky's here," Barnett said and lowered the binoculars. "Are your people in place?"

The high-ranking officer in the Japanese secret service standing next to him in the tower said, "Of course they are Mr Barnett, but I still find it hard to understand why your agency is devoting so much effort to watching this one man."

Barnett was in a bad mood. Was it the jet-lag? Or was it that the Japanese official with whom he was dealing, although far superior to him in rank, was so much younger? Was it that his own career was hanging by a thread?

"Perhaps if we could speak in private, Suino-san," he said, indicating the two other Japanese security operatives and the staff hunched over the air-traffic control desks. The senior official frowned.

"There is an empty office on the floor below," he said. "My people will keep watch here. This way please."

Barnett followed the man down the central staircase. He was always shy of sharing sensitive intelligence at the best of times. But this operation was far too important to allow any misunderstandings to take place. So when the two of them were alone he said, "What I am about to tell you is classified at the highest level in our Deputy Directorate of Science and Technology. I am sharing this information with you in view of your seniority, to establish my respect and to ensure that my mission succeeds, for the good of both our countries."

The man nodded.

"My agency," continued Barnett, speaking more slowly than he needed to, "is interested in Theodore Gilkrensky because we believe he is about to commit one of the greatest technological crimes in history. It is a plan to undermine computer and information-based industries right across the world, leaving him with a global monopoly that nobody will ever be able to break. Without wishing to be dramatic, Suino-san, if this man isn't stopped, he could end up ruling the world."

The younger man smiled politely. "That sounds like the plot of a spy movie, Mr Barnett. Surely you cannot be serious?"

Barnett glanced back across the runway. Over at the GRC jet, Gilkrensky's convoy was pulling off across the tarmac, heading for the exit and the road into Tokyo.

"Imagine," he said, "what would have happened if Nazi Germany had developed its V-2 rockets at the beginning of World War II, rather than at the end? What would have been the outcome if they'd managed to accelerate

111

their heavy water experiments in time to perfect an atom bomb small enough to lob across the English Channel at London?"

The Japanese shrugged. "I still fail to see the point, Mr Barnett."

Barnett thought for a moment. He had known that this would be as difficult to explain convincingly to the Japanese as it had been to his superiors in Washington. He could hardly believe it himself. Yet all the evidence was there.

"You have a saying in Japan," he said. "'Business is war'. Is that right?"

"It is. Yes."

"And do you believe that large multi-national corporations are already engaged in a global conflict, where commercial victory is won by bringing out newer, better and cheaper products ahead of the competition? Henry Ford was the first with the mass-produced motor car. Bill Gates was ahead of the pack with his software programs. In Japan, your Sony Corporation was first with the Walkman stereo. Victory is about being best, cheapest and *first*."

"That is true, but—"

"Gilkrensky already has two revolutionary pieces of technology at his command: the Minerva computer system, which he has been developing over the last year and—stolen from a US technology company we supported—a SQUID headset capable of translating human thought directly into computer language and back again."

"But these devices are both prototypes? It would take him years to bring them into commercial production."

"Normally, it would. But what if he had already developed them a year ago, or five years ago? That would put him so far ahead of the competition that he could dominate the marketplace."

"But he hasn't, Mr Barnett. You just said so yourself."

"But what if he had?"

"With respect, you are talking in riddles. How can someone already have perfected a product that is only just being developed in prototype?"

"By warping time," Barnett said. "My agency has physical proof that Gilkrensky is spending millions of dollars on a way to transport himself back into the past."

The Japanese shook his head. "Mr Barnett, when I agreed to co-operate with your agency, I was led to believe there was a real threat here. But what you have described to me sounds like science fiction."

Barnett reached into his jacket pocket and slipped out a data stick. He handed it to the Japanese.

"I would have agreed with you myself, six months ago," he said. "If anyone had come to me with the story I've just told you I would have had them locked up in a straitjacket. But take this data and examine it. It represents all the information we have on Dr Gilkrensky and his activities since the malfunction of one of his robot aircraft over Cairo late last year. There are satellite photos of experiments he's been carrying out all over the world, recorded interviews with experts in theoretical physics, and even hijacked results from some of his tests. You will see that he has already, and I stress already, been successful in displacing objects over time."

"But why should he want to do this, Mr Barnett? Surely he is rich enough already?"

"Theo Gilkrensky is a rich and ruthless man, Suino-san. Some years ago, he artificially collapsed the price of GRC shares to gain a majority interest after his father's death. It caused one of the other shareholders to commit suicide here in Tokyo. Gilkrensky has acquired airlines, hotels, research and development companies all over the world. He is cunning, obsessive and very, very resourceful. I have no doubt whatsoever that he is capable of doing what I describe."

"I see, Mr Barnett. And how close is Dr Gilkrensky to achieving his aim?"

"Very close. Until now, his experiments have been crude. He cannot control the time displacement effect with any accuracy. But soon he may have all the pieces of the jigsaw he needs for a perfectly controlled jump into the past."

"I still find all this hard to believe, Mr Barnett."

"Then examine the data on that stick. You can download it to any machine with the right security codes, which I'll give you. If you have any questions, come back to me, or to anyone you like at the CIA at Langley, right up to the Director."

"Then why have you not stopped this man before?"

"Because at first, we didn't believe that time-travel was possible, but then came the evidence, the eye-witness reports and the incidents at Cairo, Florida and Peru. It all started to add up and we had to take the threat seriously."

"Not seriously enough, it seems. The man is still free."

"I've tried to stop him," Barnett said. "I've put a block on any US facility that might be able to supply the kind of computer power he needs to make his project work. I had an experiment of his sabotaged in Peru, and I've confronted the man himself directly. But until now I've failed."

"And why is he here in Japan?"

"Ostensibly to negotiate his way out of a lawsuit with Mawashi-Saito. But I believe his real target is the one source of large-scale computer power he thinks he still may be able to access. It's here, just outside Tokyo, at the premises of a company called Kasawara Research. Our job is to watch him and to see if he makes a mistake. I need undeniable, cast-iron proof that he stole that SQUID. Once I have that, then I can arrest him, lock him up, and throw away the key. Do you understand?"

"I do," said the Japanese, finally.

"And your people are in place?"

The man pointed across the tarmac towards the executive-jet park. As Gilkrensky's convoy moved off and slid out of sight, an unmarked van pulled out from behind a parked aircraft and followed it towards the exit.

"They are," he said. "Both here and in Tokyo—my very best people."

15

THE UMBRELLA MAN

The rain was heavy in Tokyo. It drummed on the awnings of shops, washed across the pavements and guttered in torrents beneath the wheels of parked cars. In the heat of the early afternoon, the city was like a sauna—heavy, humid and packed with people.

And everywhere, there were umbrellas.

They bobbed and jostled on the sidewalks. They bumped together, spitting showers of raindrops. They rallied at street crossings. They flowed in a charge of colour across the white-painted lines as the lights changed. They lurked ready, hidden in special racks outside the big department stores of Isetan and Oicity, or allowed themselves to be tamed inside plastic sheaths while their owners carried them inside. Anyone without an umbrella was forced to cower in a doorway until the torrent passed.

Hiroshi Tanaka watched the umbrellas from between the statues of Batman and Superman outside the doorway of the Warner Brothers shop on the Ginza. He was a wiry man in his late thirties, with short dark hair, large brown eyes, and the faraway look of a poet. In his designer jacket, slacks and Nike runners he looked like any one of the thousands of people milling around the clothes and electronic shops of Tokyo's most fashionable streets.

But in his mind he was back in the past, below ground, on a crowded Tokyo subway, with an umbrella on his arm . . .

As always, the morning subway had been packed to capacity. Standing with his left hand in a white plastic strap near a door in the leading car, Tanaka's senses were assaulted by a ferment of sounds, smells and textures: aftershave, perfume, bad breath and sweat, the tinny hiss of personal stereos set way too loud, the clatter of wheels on the rails below his feet and the rush of air in the tunnel, gabardine and worsted, shopping bags, briefcases and a rucksack or two—all crushed together.

Tanaka looked at the indicator over the door which showed the progress of the train. On it, a little green arrow inched towards an orange square along a red line. He felt a jerk as the carriage slowed, heard the electronic voice of a station announcement and the ding-dong of a warning as the doors opened. More people crammed their way into the already packed car. The doors closed and the little green arrow started to move again.

Nobody smiled. The faces around him were of serious people; office workers, salarymen with a job to do, shoppers on their way to a sale, students on their way to college.

And after the next station, they would all be dead.

One little girl in a party dress was looking right at him. She sat between her parents to the left of the door, playing "peekaboo" through the swaying bodies. Tanaka forced himself to look away, to stare at the hanging advertisements for Manga comics, a map of the rail system . . . anything.

But something drew his eyes back to hers, time and time again.

How old was she? What was her name? Tanaka tried to push these questions away, to focus on his mission and the moving arrow above his head. The crude newspaper package in his right hand contained three sealed pouches, filled with enough liquid nerve-poison to kill everyone in the compartment and a lot more besides. He knew that on five other trains heading into Tokyo from other stations around the outskirts, similar packages of death were being delivered by other members of his organisation.

The end of the world was coming.

Their leader had prophesied it many times. It was time to deal a terrible blow against the people of Japan—a blow that would convince them that the only way to salvation was through him. They had already tried one poison-gas attack, from a moving van in the town of Matsumoto, and failed when the wind had changed.

This time, in the close confines of the Tokyo subway, there could be no mistake.

All Tanaka and his fellow messengers of death had to do was to wait until just before their designated subway stop, drop their packages on the floor of the car and spear them open with the specially sharpened tips of their umbrellas. Then they would step out onto the platform. The doors of the subway train would hiss shut behind them. The lethal toxin would do its work in those cramped and claustrophobic carriages . . .

And there was the little girl . . . laughing at him!

Tanaka thought of his own childhood, stolen by the "System" which governs every aspect of life in Corporate Japan. His father had been a senior executive with the overseas sales department of a big electronics corporation. His mother had been an office lady in accounts. Early each morning they had gone to work together on subway trains like this one, leaving Hiroshi with a child-minder.

At school his spirit had been clipped and twisted like a *bonsai* tree. His brain had been wiped clean of any creative thought, to act like a blank computer disc for a million facts and figures, all learned by rote. His mother, spurred on by the performance of the sons of friends and colleagues, became a *kyoiku mama*—an 'education mother'—pushing him further still through the 'examination hell'. There was no time for creativity, no time to think, no time to question, no time to love—just the pressure to cram in more and more facts, day in day out . . . to serve the System.

Deep inside, the tortured soul of Hiroshi Tanaka rebelled. Somewhere, somehow, there had to be more to being Japanese than this!

He bought and read huge Manga comics, each as thick as a telephone directory, with their violent and romantic notions of traditional honour. He watched films like Battleship Yamato and The Seven Samurai.

And, of course, he discovered Mishima . . .

On the twenty-fifth of November 1970, just over a month before Tanaka had been born, Yukio Mishima, one of Japan's greatest living artists—a writer with thirty-five novels, twenty-five plays, two hundred short stories and eight volumes of essays to his credit—had walked into the offices of the Japanese Eastern Army headquarters in Tokyo with four cadets from his private army. As a respected national figure, he and his cadets were warmly received by the general in charge, who was in the process of admiring Mishima's sixteenth century antique sword when he was overpowered and tied to a chair as a hostage. Mishima then insisted on calling the entire garrison to assemble below the office window, tied a rising sun headband across his forehead and addressed them on their failure to uphold the Japanese way of life against the forces of money and corruption. Once this was over Mishima had returned to the office, where he had committed ritual suicide.

To Tanaka, the life and death of this incredible man seemed to personify what he himself yearned for so deeply—the triumph of the human spirit over the System. In secret, he devoured Mishima's writings, in particular his final novels in the Sea of Fertility series. Here was a man who thought as Tanaka did, who recognised how things were, and how they could be. Here was a man who had achieved death with honour and sounded a wake-up call for all Japan.

How could he do the same? The System was already sucking him in. Within a few short years Tanaka was a research chemist with the Matsushita Corporation. In no time he was a section head in agro-chemicals with a staff of fifty, a budget of well over a million US dollars a year and . . . nothing!

His life was empty. There had to be more than the daily grind of the subway and the office, a way of living honourably as a Japanese as Mishima had done, a way of beating the System. But he was already trapped, and the strain was beginning to tell. He was exhausted, unfocussed, unable to sleep and suffering from stress.

In desperation, he answered an advertisement for yoga classes and was received in a studio in downtown Tokyo by a very pleasant young woman. Tanaka had always been awkward with girls before, but this one appeared pleased to see him. He filled in the registration forms giving details of his marital and financial status under her smiling direction without a second thought. From the classes, he graduated to weekend workshops and from there to more intense training. Within months, before he even realised what was happening, Hiroshi Tanaka, gifted chemist and seeker of a different way of life, had become a fully paid-up member of the most notorious cult in modern Japan—Aum Supreme Truth.

For Tanaka, the intense discipline and structure of Aum provided the family he had been denied. Their leader, Shoko Asahara, offered the enlightened guidance his own father should have given but never did. Tanaka resigned his job at Matsushita to dedicate his life, his soul and all his worldly possessions to Aum.

At last Hiroshi Tanaka was outside the System—and he was not alone.

All over Japan, the spiritual void left in the souls of a generation by the relentless cramming of the education system demanded to be filled. Aum, a registered religion, combined just the right mix of high-tech spirituality and good, old-fashioned salesmanship to attract thousands of disciples like Tanaka, brilliant, highly educated young people searching for answers, which Aum supplied.

The end of the world is coming, their leader said. After the apocalypse, only true believers of Aum will be spared. And when the apocalypse did not come, Asahara decided to create his own by using the accumulated wealth and brilliance of his disciples to manufacture that most deadly poison gas— Sarin!

Tanaka stared at the little girl as she hid her face behind her hands and peeped at him between her fingers. For months he'd had doubts about Aum, but could not express them. He had heard stories, rumours that anyone who questioned the leadership in any way simply . . . disappeared. Anyone who tried to leave, or to "betray the guru's love", had been subject to the most barbaric "re-education" programme. He knew of fellow monks and nuns who had not survived.

What could he do? As one of the senior chemists who not only knew where the many caches of Sarin were hidden against a surprise raid from the police, but also the PIN numbers on one of the secret Aum bank accounts, he was watched night and day. His work in the Aum chemical factory consumed all his time. When he was finished, all he could do was eat and sleep. What would Yukio Mishima have done?

He looked at the little girl. They were almost at Kasamigaseki station. The green arrow above the door was pushing its way towards the orange square. The voice came over the speaker "Kasamigaseki! Kasamigaseki - *des*!" He felt the jerk of the train slowing, a shuffle of passengers who had failed to keep their balance.

They were almost there!

Could he do it? Could he take the life of this little girl, amongst all the others? Could he kill?

What would happen to him if he failed?

What would Mishima have done?

He let the newspaper parcel fall to his feet. The sharpened steel point of the umbrella was poised to rupture the packages of liquid Sarin inside. In a second—

"*Sumimasen*! Excuse me, please! You've dropped your newspaper!"

The little girl was calling to him through the forest of standing bodies, that swayed as the train slowed to a halt in the station. There was the bing-bong chime of the bell and the doors hissed open.

"*Sumimasen*! Your newspaper!"

Tanaka looked up. Her eyes were on him, full of concern that he might lose something he treasured.

"*Sumimasen*!"

What would Mishima have done?

Not this!

Something in Hiroshi Tanaka snapped. His hand darted down, lifted the package from the floor of the carriage and he ran through the open doors, out onto the platform and into the seething mass of people from the train, rushing for the exit in a moving sea of bobbing, faceless heads.

He had to get out!

The walls were closing in. He was diving for the entrance with the package pressed to his chest. Would it burst? He was pushing people out of the way, fighting towards the white light of day at the top of the staircase. Other commuters stared at him. He was running, crying. Tears streamed down his cheeks.

He was on the street, in the light, in the air.

A Buddhist monk in a black costume was ringing a tiny bell, looking for donations.

Tanaka walked unsteadily to a waste bin, stuffed the package of Sarin into it, bent the sharpened umbrella over his knee and pushed that in too. Then he turned and lost himself in the crowd.

Far below him, the subway train would be pulling away from Kasamigaseki station, taking the little girl and her family safely away.

Hiroshi Tanaka walked to a taxi, drove straight to the bank where the Aum account rested, and made a substantial withdrawal. Then he went on the run.

When he was finally captured and dragged back to Aum headquarters on the slopes of Mount Fuji, the memory of that little girl's face was all that sustained him during the humiliation of his failure. He was branded a coward and a traitor by the rest of the cult, urinated and defecated upon, and forced into a steel cubicle no bigger than a coffin to be left in the dark until he revealed where the Sarin and the money had been hidden—which was all that saved him from prison when the compound was finally raided by the police and he was mistaken for a victim, rather than arrested as a perpetrator.

But in those days of blackness, from the depths of madness and despair, a hidden light had dawned. He was not simply Hiroshi Tanaka, sometime artist, failed assassin and victim of the System, but the very reincarnation of the great author and patriot—Yukio Mishima himself. Had not he, Mishima, shown the way in his books? Had he not written of this in his novel *Runaway Horses*? Had not the body he now inhabited as Tanaka been conceived between the seven and seventy-seven days prescribed by Buddhism of the death of the body he had lived in before as Mishima?

In the dark hell of Aum's coffin prison, the truth had burst upon him like the light of heaven.

He was Mishima, waiting for a greater calling to come.

Which, after years of waiting . . . it finally did.

Hiroshi Tanaka lifted his gaze above the moving umbrellas on the Ginza to the hotel on the other side of the street. He was anxious, after all the faith his new sponsor had placed in him, to do the job right. There could be no mistake this time. This was a just cause, a blow against the System, one of which Mishima would be proud.

A convoy of security cars and a dark limousine drew up outside the hotel. Tanaka clearly saw the tall figure in a worn leather jacket step quickly out of the car and vanish inside. There were others with him, two men and a tall woman with dark chestnut hair. Tanaka raised a cell phone to his mouth and spoke quietly.

"Gilkrensky is here!"

16

THE NEW JAPAN

Gilkrensky stared down from the hotel window into the neon-lit canyon of Showa-dori Avenue. Lights pulsed on the huge advertising signs for Coca-Cola and Nikon, or writhed in unfamiliar characters along the information boards. Even with the double-glazing, the noise of traffic seemed to hum through the very walls.

"Theo?"

"Sorry, Don. I was a million miles away."

In the conference room of the penthouse suite, Donald Price was delivering another of his lectures on Japanese business practice. "The thing to remember about Japan," he said, "is that there's a code of etiquette for doing almost everything—and I mean *everything*—from the time you get up in the morning to the time you go to bed. It's a system that's dominated Japanese society for hundreds of years . . ."

The polished surface of the table was hidden under laptop computers, business papers and bottles of mineral water. Hunched over them were two legal advisors, an accountant and a couple of secretaries, all paying polite attention. Gilkrensky saw Jessica at the far end of the table nearest the door, carefully noting the points Price was making in one of the hard-backed journals she always carried.

I know so much about you, he thought. I know how you brush your hair, how your accent slips when you get drunk and how fragile you are inside. We've been colleagues, friends and lovers. Even though I love Maria, you were always my friend. My one big regret is that I hurt you. That's why I find it hard to see you watching Price that way. I just don't want to see you hurt again.

"Can you carry on without me for a few minutes?" he said, rising to his feet. "There's a couple of things I need to do."

All the faces in the room, except one, turned towards him. Price frowned briefly, the other members of the team nodded. Jessica just kept writing.

"Don't be too long, Theo," she said without looking up. "There's a lot we have to get through before tomorrow."

Gilkrensky opened the door of the meeting room and stepped into the lobby of the suite. Crowe was briefing a chauffeur and a security guard with a large-scale map of the city.

"How's it going, Major?"

Crowe moved aside to show him the map.

"Nothing to it really. The Mawashi-Saito building is here in the Shinjuku district, about twenty minutes away by car. If we leave at nine-thirty, just as the morning rush hour dies down, we should be in plenty of time."

"And security here in the hotel?"

"Completely watertight. The hotel has a very sophisticated computerised system, pretty near state-of-the-art. Anyone entering this suite has to come through that door there, having gone past a dozen cameras between here and the first floor."

"Good. Could I speak to you for a moment about Price?"

Crowe frowned. Then Gilkrensky led him into his own suite and shut the door.

"How much do we know about him?" he asked.

"Not a lot," Crowe said. "He's Sir Robert's protégé. I understand he's from Canada originally, but worked here in Tokyo for one of the big legal companies before moving to England. Sir Robert's pension fund took him on to handle some investment portfolios for them. That's all I know."

"And what can we find out about him, quickly?"

Crowe's eyebrows rose.

"What about, sir?"

Gilkrensky thought for a moment.

"Let's just say that I'm a bit paranoid about anyone with an American accent after our encounter back in Charlotte. If we're going to be relying on Price so heavily tomorrow, I want to be damned sure about him."

"I see. Shall I tell Miss Wright you've got concerns?"

"No. Not yet. Can you do it before the meeting?"

"In the time, it's going to be difficult. But I've a few friends in low places that could give me a steer if I get onto it right away."

"Good, do all you—"

A discreet knock sounded at the door of the suite. The security guard was there, bowing.

"Excuse me, please, gentlemen. Dr Gilkrensky has a visitor."

"Who is it?"

The man passed him a pristine business card. One side was covered in Japanese script. The other said, *Miss Hisako Deshimaru, Personal Assistant to Mr Gichin Funakoshi* beneath the familiar logo of Mawashi-Saito.

"Tell Jessica and Price," Gilkrensky said. "We'll see her in the meeting room."

"Excuse me, sir," said the man, bowing, "but the lady insists on seeing you privately."

Gilkrensky looked at Crowe, who said, "Let me check her out. If she's genuine, then I'll show her in."

Miss Deshimaru was a delicate doll of a woman in her mid-fifties, with neatly combed black hair and a still beautiful face behind bifocal glasses. As she bowed to Gilkrensky, her dove-grey office uniform hardly seemed to crease.

"Thank you for seeing me without an appointment, Mister Chairman," she said. "It is an honour to meet you in person at last."

Gilkrensky returned the bow. "You work for Mr Funakoshi," he said, reading from her card.

"Indeed sir, when he was Chairman of Mawashi-Saito. I worked for him for twenty-five years."

"And now?"

"I serve Mr Funakoshi, whatever his position within the company," she said. "He is a person I respect."

Gilkrensky nodded.

"You said it was a personal matter, Miss Deshimaru. How can I help you?"

The eyes behind the bifocal glasses gave nothing away.

"I am here to invite you to a private meeting with Mr Funakoshi," she said. "He has asked me specifically to apologise for his not being here in person, and for not contacting you sooner, but he has been tied up in unavoidable family business since the death of his wife and niece. He is very anxious however, to have a personal discussion with you before the meeting at Mawashi-Saito tomorrow. He asks if you could come alone?"

Crowe shook his head. "You know I can't allow that."

Miss Deshimaru turned her gaze on him. "Your employer will be perfectly safe, Major and believe me, Mr Funakoshi means no disrespect. But he insists that he and Dr Gilkrensky meet alone. Our former deputy head of security, Mr Taisen Nakamura, is waiting below in a car to drive us to the appointment."

"I still can't allow it," Crowe said. "Even with Yukiko Funakoshi dead, you don't know who else is out there."

"I'm afraid Major Crowe is right, Miss Deshimaru," said Gilkrensky. "In any event, my colleagues and I are engaged in delicate negotiations with Mr Funakoshi's company at the moment. For me to meet him unilaterally could upset matters and be an insult to those who are helping me."

Miss Deshimaru nodded, slid an envelope out of the black leather folder she was carrying and gave it to Gilkrensky. There was a short letter inside, which Gilkrensky read and passed to Crowe.

"Perhaps that will persuade you, Dr Gilkrensky," she said. "I personally do not know the contents of that letter, or what Mr Funakoshi wants to discuss. But I do know that he respectfully insists on meeting you tonight, at his hotel in Atami— alone."

Gilkrensky looked at Crowe, who folded the letter and passed it back to him.

"Major Crowe is more than just a bodyguard, Miss Deshimaru. He is a friend. I would like him to be present tonight."

There was the faintest sucking of teeth.

"Very well then, Dr Gilkrensky," she said, "but only Major Crowe."

Crowe nodded to Gilkrensky and turned away from Miss Deshimaru. "If this is to be a traditional Japanese meeting," he whispered to Gilkrensky, "then I have something in my room I suggest we take with us, a sort of secret weapon, if you know what I mean."

"I understand. Go and get it."

Gilkrensky turned back to Miss Deshimaru. He remembered what Price had said on the plane about Japanese business meetings as he looked down at his own faded jeans.

"You said we would be meeting in a hotel, Miss Deshimaru? What would it be appropriate for me to wear?"

Her eyes never left his.

"Whatever you would wear to a funeral, Dr Gilkrensky," she said.

"And so to sum up," Price said. "What we want from Mawashi-Saito tomorrow is a complete withdrawal of the legal case against the corporation and . . . Where's Theo, Jess? I thought he was just popping out for a moment."

Jessica looked up from her notes.

"You're right," she said. "Where the hell's he gone?"

She got up from the meeting table and strode to the door. Outside in the lobby, the security man was still at his post. He jumped to his feet and bowed to her.

"Where's Dr Gilkrensky?"

The man stared at her.

"He has left with Major Crowe, Miss Wright. They've gone to a meeting."

"What! I wasn't told of any meeting!"

The man remained calm.

"It was at short notice, Miss Wright. Dr Gilkrensky was called for by an office lady, changed into his suit and left."

"An 'office lady'? From what office?"

The man showed her the business card Miss Deshimaru had left behind. The Mawashi-Saito logo leapt out at her.

"And the Minerva computer? Did he take that?"

"He left with a black briefcase. Yes."

Jessica Wright turned to Price.

"Christ! The bastard's sold us out!" she breathed. "He's gone to do his own deal with the Japanese!"

Hiroshi Tanaka watched the limousine hiss away into the traffic from his vantage point outside the Warner Brothers shop on the other side of the street.

"I have him," he said into his cell phone, and walked to the kerb, where a powerful Honda motorcycle was standing ready. In a moment he had executed a neat U-turn into the opposite lane, and was following the departing car into the afternoon traffic. It was well before the onset of the evening rush hour. Tanaka had no trouble in following the limousine down the Ginza and up a ramp onto an overpass. The Sony and Toshiba buildings flashed past on his right, and he was approaching the tollbooths and big green signs of the Expressway going west. Tanaka saw the limousine slow, pay its toll, and move on. Keeping the car in sight, he eased the big motorcycle into the appropriate lane, paid his due and roared on after it, keeping at a discreet distance, past the Tokyo Tower to the main trunk-road out of the city.

In a while, the buildings around the Expressway turned from office-blocks to apartment blocks. They were rushing through a limitless hinterland of modern warehouses, shanty towns and traditional houses with curving tiled roofs in reds and blues. Soon, the skyline was dominated by a marching army of pylons and a vast cat's-cradle of power lines. Trees, paddy-fields and ponds began to appear between the buildings and finally, they were in the country, heading for Atami.

Tanaka watched the trees, thinking just how far he had come in the last few months, thinking of the day salvation had arrived . . .

It had been raining that morning too—a fine persistent drizzle that had seeped into every crack and corner of the ramshackle cabin his parents had once owned, deep in the forests, eighty miles west of Tokyo. Everything was damp; from the sagging posters of his hero Yukio Mishima, to his mildewed books, to the futon he slept on—damp, cold and hopeless.

It had been years since the incident on the subway. Aum Supreme Truth had been exposed, and its leader Shoko Asahara had been jailed. But Hiroshi Tanaka, still living in fear of a reprisal, had fled into the hills with a handful of like-minded followers, taking the Aum funds and the secret of the Sarin gas with him. How long would it be before they came after him? Would one of his companions lose faith and betray him?

They had been living a dismal existence, working the land around the cabins, meditating and dreaming of a greater victory yet to come. Hiroshi still clung to his vision of a new Japan. It would be a world free of the suffocation of corporate business. A Japanese nation in which every man, woman and child would be free of the System.

One of the posters, heavy with dampness from the rain, finally tore itself free from the rusty nails holding it in place and slid to the floor. Pretty soon all the funds would be gone and his private revolution against the forces of oppression would grind to a halt.

It had all been for nothing.

The girl on the futon with him stirred in her sleep. Her name was Masako Takamatsu, a former nun from the Aum compound on Mount Fuji and like him, hiding from her past as the product of a one-night stand between a fisherman's daughter and an American airman on an overnight pass. Hiroshi was growing tired of her constant complaining about the lack of money, the quality of the food, or the way the roof leaked. Very soon they would all have to find work . . . and be sucked back into the System . . .

Then, above Masako's snoring, Hiroshi heard his name being called. It was Satoshi, a simple but likeable refugee from Aum's Soldiers of the White Love—a hit-squad of ex-army personnel who had been destined to be the spearhead of the Apocalypse.

"What is it?"

"Get your pants on and come see! We have a visitor!"

A visitor! Had Aum finally tracked him down? Was it the police, here to arrest him as an accomplice in the Tokyo attack?

"Wake the others!"

Hiroshi leapt up from the futon, dragged on his stained trousers and shirt, and wrenched open the door of the shack.

Picking his way gingerly up the muddy track towards the encampment was the very personification of everything Hiroshi despised, a dark-suited salaryman with an umbrella and a briefcase.

"Go away!" shouted Hiroshi. "This land is private!"

The salaryman looked up. He had slick-backed hair and a beautiful silk tie. There was mud on the trousers of his suit.

"Are you Hiroshi Tanaka?"

Hiroshi and his group exchanged glances. What could they do? Then again, what could one man in a business suit do against the five of them?

"Who are you?" Hiroshi shouted. "What do you want?"

"I am a lawyer. My client in Tokyo shares your philosophy and wishes to recruit the services of a group as committed as yours. They are willing to make a sizeable donation."

Hiroshi looked at the faces of his followers. Some nodded, some shrugged.

"OK then," he shouted to the man. "Come on up!"

In the only remaining waterproof shed on the compound, the one Hiroshi insisted be reserved for the group's computer equipment, the visitor outlined his proposition while the group sat in a semicircle around him. There was Hiroshi himself, the girl Masako, and Satoshi Tazawara—former defence-force deserter and weapons expert. He had two colleagues and former members of Aum's "Soldiers of the White Love" with him—Murai Kono, whose heavy muscle-builder's body still bore the scars of his days as a construction worker in Tokyo, and Kyo Noda—who spent most of his days practising *karate* in the forests around the compound. Finally there was Ikuo Baruma, their computer expert and most fervent disciple. He perched on a swivel-chair in front of his console with his back to the screen, glaring at the lawyer from Tokyo through his thick pebble-glasses.

There was no tea, nor any kind of hospitality. The money for such luxuries had run out long ago.

"Tell us then," Hiroshi said. "What do you know of us?"

The man had folded his raincoat inside out and was sitting on it uncomfortably. There was a gold clip on his tie. The briefcase at his feet was polished leather.

"I know," he said, "or at least my client knows, that your funds are drying up, that you have no means of raising more, and that soon you will be forced out of existence. That is what we know."

"That is not true," Masako said. "Hiroshi and the rest of us are regrouping, to strike again at the very heart of the Japanese System."

The lawyer did not reply, but looked around him. Tanaka felt the man's gaze on his dirty clothes and unshaven face. He saw it shift to the scuffed and rotting tatami mats on the floor.

"We also know that your group are dedicated to the cause of peaceful revolution," continued the salaryman. "Why else would you, Tanaka-san, have walked away from the subway attack in Tokyo five years ago? Why else would your followers have stayed with you? Why else would you choose to live like this?" He waved his hands at the mildewed walls. "My client has need of such a dedicated group. They know, like you, that there is a better way for Japan, a more honourable way that lifts the spirit rather than grinding it into dust. A way Mishima himself would have followed."

At the mention of that holy name, Tanaka stared at the man.

"And how does your client know all this?"

"My client is in a position to know many things about a lot of people."

"And the donation?" said Masako hungrily. Tanaka noticed that the lawyer had been taking a particular interest in her. Did he fancy her? Masako!

"It is more of a business contract than a donation," the man said. "My client knows you have commitment, skills and . . . certain resources that might be put to good use for a mission they have in mind."

"The donation?" said Masako again.

"Right here," said the man and snapped open the briefcase.

Inside was the Japanese Yen equivalent of a million US dollars.

17

COMMON DIFFERENCES

In Atami the rain had stopped, but a thin mist still clung to the mountains around the bay like gossamer against the trees. Outside the small hotel a crowd gathered to see the two urns, containing the cremated remains of Michiko Funakoshi and her niece Yukiko, brought home. Gilkrensky watched the mourners file inside. Many of them stole curious glances as they passed him, bowed nervously and moved on.

The heat was suffocating. Gilkrensky's shirt and jacket were soaked in sweat. He felt conspicuous and awkward, standing there next to Crowe with the briefcase of the Minerva in his hand.

But worst of all, his mind kept reaching back to another funeral, over a year ago . . .

The church in West Cork had been packed with Maria's family and friends. They filled the pews, lined the back of the vestry and spilled out into the churchyard. As he had struggled to lift her coffin onto his shoulder with his bandaged hands, all he saw was a sea of faces, staring at him. Was it sympathy in their eyes? Or was it blame?

He had lived and she had died.

"Ashes to ashes. Dust to dust."

Maria . . . his wife . . . gone.

He forced himself to snap back into the present. A small man with silver hair stood in front of him. The man bowed, and then extended his hand.

"Mister Chairman? Major Crowe? Thank you for coming."

Gilkrensky took the man's hand and shook it. "Mr Funakoshi."

Gichin Funakoshi nodded. "I am old enough to be a grandfather, Dr Gilkrensky. I should be attending weddings and christenings. They have a future, *neh*? Funerals have only a past. "

"I understand. You said in your letter that you could help me?"

"I did, but come inside first. It is customary for the mourners to join me for a meal after a ceremony such as this. Normally, it would have been at my home."

He pointed to the hill overlooking the town. In the centre of the neat rows of houses above the station was a gap, like a pulled tooth. Around it, the trees were scorched and broken. Gilkrensky saw the remains of charred timbers, like blackened tombstones.

"The bomb," Funakoshi said. "It killed them both. Come, let us eat together with the others. Then afterwards, you and I must speak privately about what has to be done."

Jessica paced the floor of the meeting room, trying to come to terms with this latest crisis. What was Theo doing? What else could have taken him out of the hotel wearing a suit other than a business meeting? And with Funakoshi! It could only mean one thing—that Theo was selling her out for the price of the computer power he needed.

Christ! It made her blood boil!

"We have to go over these papers, Jess," Price said from the other side of the boardroom table. "We've called the number on that Deshimaru woman's card. We've called Mawashi-Saito, and she's not there, neither's Funakoshi. Whatever Theo's at now, we haven't a hope tomorrow unless we plan our strategy, anymore than we have of tracking him down in a city of over twelve million people."

"I've tried his mobile and all I get is the bloody recording."

"And the Minerva?"

"I've tried calling that too—same story."

"So come back and work on this. We're almost done. If we aren't a hundred and ten percent on top of the facts, the Mawashi-Saito legal team is going to shred us to pieces. It all hinges on this, Jess. We have to get it right."

"What's the point, if Theo's already sold us down the river?"

"You don't know that. Theo and Funakoshi go back a long way. Perhaps it's a social call."

"And pigs might fly! They've been at each other's throats for years."

"OK. I know it's unlikely. But the legal team is waiting outside. All the facts are here. We just have to put them together. Look . . . what do you like to eat?"

"What? Now?"

Price smiled.

"No, later. When we've finished this."

Jessica felt her anger subsiding.

"I'm sorry, Don. This is just the last bloody straw. My father's sick in hospital. I shouldn't have come on this trip at all. And now Theo is off doing God knows what! There's only so much I can take."

Price nodded.

"Then what do you like to eat?"

"I like fish. We used to eat a lot of it in Lowestoft. My father used to buy it fresh at the market."

"Great. Then finish this with me now and I'll take you to the best fish restaurant in Tokyo. Is it a deal?"

Jessica smiled. Price wasn't nearly as annoying as when she'd first met him in Dublin. In fact, he was quite good company. Dinner sounded good, and she had packed at least one designer dress.

Fuck you, Theo! she thought, and walked back to the meeting table.

But the question still buzzed in her head. What the hell was he doing?

It was very late. The mourners had departed and Gilkrensky, together with Funakoshi, Nakamura and Crowe, had bathed in the hotel spa, dressed in cotton robes and adjourned to Funakoshi's suite. They were squatting at floor level, on legless padded seats around a low wooden table. The room was designed in the traditional Japanese style, with woven tatami mats on the floor, sliding paper screens on wooden frames and delicate floral prints on the walls. Behind Funakoshi was a low stone altar on which two urns stood. Beside it was the Minerva and Crowe's holdall. Wisps of smoke from burning joss-sticks twisted to the ceiling. Above the purr of the air-conditioning, Gilkrensky heard the chirrup of cicadas in the hotel garden outside.

Miss Deshimaru knelt quietly at the screen door while the men talked. She had ordered sake.

"Nobody is to disturb us," Funakoshi said. "We are now about to enter into the serious business of the evening, which is to become drunk. Do you understand this, Mister Chairman?"

"Yes. When sensitive issues need to be aired, the Japanese custom is to do it over a drink. It is the same where I live, in Ireland."

Funakoshi nodded. "Perhaps, but in Japan this is sometimes the only way such issues can be discussed without blame. In Japan, nobody would dare to criticise their boss, or say anything that might undermine their employers unless . . . unless they were drunk. That way, any indiscretion can be blamed on the alcohol and everything is forgotten by morning. Here, I must fill your bowls with sake, and you must fill mine. One of our rules is that you never have to pour for yourself . . ."

"We have been on opposite sides of a wall for too long," Funakoshi said. Gilkrensky had long since lost any feeling in his legs, and the tenth flask of sake was almost empty. On either side of him Crowe and Nakamura were nodding soberly, each with a glass of water in front of them. The front of Funakoshi's cotton robe was falling open.

"We have been engaged in a war," continued Funakoshi, reaching over to pour the last of the sake into Gilkrensky's bowl. "But we have something in common at least, my niece Yukiko." And he gestured to the urns on the altar behind him.

"How so?" But Gilkrensky already knew the answer.

"In a way, we both created what she became. I was born before the Great War, when those in power forced Japan into a conflict she could not win. I saw my parents killed and my country destroyed. But that was nothing compared to watching my people live with the shame of defeat. Do you understand how that feels? No, perhaps not. It is a uniquely Japanese feeling, like nothing else on earth."

There was silence for a while, as the four men considered this.

"Then," Funakoshi said, "I was given the opportunity to lift the shame, to make Japan great again and to live as a samurai in a war we could win with honour. A man called Saito came into my life, Kazuyoshi Saito. In many ways he was like you—brilliant, eccentric, a genius perhaps—a man who loved to build things, to fight for things. But then he died. And in dying, he made me promise to protect the company we had built together against anything that might come my way. In Japan, we call that *giri*—a debt of honour. I did my best to honour that debt and to fight the war that Saito and I had begun, but I forgot that any war has casualties, and that those we love are the most at risk."

"I know."

"Indeed. My sister Chuziko was the first casualty of that war. I bartered her future happiness for the secrets your father's business partner Lord Rothsay could bring me. Rothsay fell in love with Japan. Some gaijin do this. They fall in love with our sense of order, the way things are done here, the simplicity of our art and, of course, the beauty of our women. Chuziko wanted her independence. It was not hard to bring them together . . ."

He raised his bowl to his lips, took a long noisy slurp, and rested it back on the table.

"Then, when Yukiko was born, I banished them both to England to avoid any scandal that might affect my reputation or the good name of the *keiretsu*. I . . . I regret that now. I should have been stronger. But it is done, *neh*? You know what became of my sister?"

Gilkrensky looked down into his bowl.

"I . . . I know she killed herself, when the story of her affair with Rothsay hit the papers. I also know that my colleague Jessica Wright leaked that story, to force Rothsay off the Board of GRC. I'm sorry . . ."

Funakoshi shrugged.

"In Japan, women have not climbed as high up the ladder of corporate power as your Miss Wright has done. Perhaps it is because Japanese men fear their ruthlessness. She must be a great asset to you."

"She did what she felt she had to do to protect her company, just like you did. But I know she never dreamed that your sister would take her own life."

"Then she does not understand the Japanese mind," replied Funakoshi. "In Japan, suicide is not a disgrace, but a way of gaining face in death. My sister was a strong and honourable woman. She also did what she had to do—just like her daughter did in her revenge. I think Yukiko must have taken great pleasure in recruiting Miss Wright's lover to her cause. What was his name? Delgado? She seduced him, blackmailed him, and forced him to betray you all. And then she killed him . . . once he was of no more use to her."

Funakoshi shook his head.

"Hate and death are all Yukiko has left," he continued. "When she was a child in England she witnessed her mother's body, as it lay in a pool of blood. Three years ago, or so I understand, she was present when her father took his own life in Tokyo. He was not Japanese, and it must have gone badly for him. Yukiko saw it all. She holds us responsible?"

Gilkrensky nodded. "We've both paid the price," he said slowly. "Those we love—my wife and yours—both dead."

There was a long silence, broken only by the chirrup of the cicadas and the purr of the air-conditioning.

Gilkrensky raised the bowl of warm rice-wine and drained it. Then, before Funakoshi could fill it again, he raised his hand and turned to Crowe.

"I think it's time for our secret weapon."

From a holdall on the floor beside him, Major Crowe lifted a black steel canister, just over a foot long. Then he flipped open the lid, carefully drew out a bottle of amber liquid and passed it to Gilkrensky, who unscrewed the cap.

"Here," he said, "this is twenty-five-year-old Irish whiskey. Maria used to say it was her country's finest export. Let me propose a toast to her."

"And what is your story, Gilkrensky-san?" Funakoshi said at last. "What made you who you are today?" He was slurring his words badly now. The sweat on his forehead shone in the light from the lanterns. Gilkrensky tried to focus. They had been drinking the whiskey in the Japanese style—in tall glasses, diluted with enough water to send the alcohol straight into the bloodstream. He peered at the whiskey bottle. It was half empty.

137

"I became what my father wanted me to be," he said, "a scientist and an engineer. I can remember him teaching me how to work out logarithm tables when I was nine. I had a slide-rule by the time I was ten . . . All the money . . . that came later. I never really wanted it . . . I just wanted to . . . oh, I don't know . . ."

"And your mother?"

"She died when I was young. But I still remember what a free spirit she was. She used to do mad things . . . things that my father didn't always approve of. There's a lot of her in me as well. I know that now. That's why I fell in love with Maria . . . and that's why I couldn't let her go . . . even after she died . . ."

Gilkrensky raised the glass to his lips. How could he describe her? How could he put what he felt into words?

"She was like having the other half of me made whole," he said. "She could reach into my head and know what I was going to say before I said it. She could reach in, past all the barriers and defences I'd built up around myself and still make me feel safe and . . . all she asked in return was that I be myself. I lost her because I broke a promise. Like you, I let my ambition and my duty to the corporation I'd built come between me and the one thing that was really important to me . . . my wife . . . and I lost her."

He could feel the whiskey taking hold. The room spun around his head. Sweat streamed down his chest inside the cotton robe.

"You are lucky," Funakoshi said. "I bargained any chance of such happiness away when I agreed to marry the daughter of a man whose company I wished to merge with . . ."

But all Gilkrensky saw was Maria's face, looking up at him from the car, a split second before the explosion. And all he heard was her voice, telling him their marriage was over.

"You don't understand," he said, swaying in his seat. "You don't understand. I lost her, even before she died. She was leaving me on that morning, don't you see? I let my money . . . the power she hated so much . . . come between us . . . and I lost her!"

They both drained their glasses, which Gilkrensky refilled unsteadily, spilling the golden liquid on the table. Miss Deshimaru darted from her post

138

at the door, mopped up the whiskey with a clean cloth and refilled the water jug, bowing as she went.

"If I hadn't been so caught up in the corporation, we wouldn't have argued and she wouldn't have been in that car when she died. I did it! Don't you see that? I killed her, just as much as Yukiko did! Our love was already dead when she died. And I killed it!"

He bowed his head into his hands and cried.

"It's my fault! That's why I can't stop looking for a way to get Maria back! Not ever! That's why Minerva has her face. And that's why I can't stop trying. Do you see?"

The old man nodded solemnly. "I do see. I do. And do you now see the wisdom of Japan? By drinking together here together, you and I have reached the truth of things . . . the *honne*, as we say in Japan. *Tatemae* . . . the way we like to present ourselves to the world . . . is the way we entered this room . . . the way we would like things to be. *Honne* is the truth . . . the way we know things are in our hearts. And we have reached it, you and I, without shame. Everything will be forgotten in the morning . . . when we hide behind *tatemae* again."

"And what is *honne* for you?"

"Let me ask you one more question before I tell you my truth," Funakoshi said. "These experiments of yours around the world . . . these attempts to turn back time . . . have they worked?"

Gilkrensky stared at him. "How did you know about them?"

Funakoshi nodded at the old man by his side. "My colleague, Mr Nakamura, was once in my industrial intelligence division. He still has as many contacts around the world and as many ways of finding out things that matter as I imagine your Major Crowe still does. People tell Mr Nakamura things. Mr Nakamura listens and then tells me. Now . . . did your experiments work?"

"They did, up to a point. And that point is . . . that unless I can obtain a very large amount of computing capacity in the next three days . . . I will not be able to calculate the precise holographic configuration I need to reach back in time to save my wife."

"And if you are successful and Maria lives, what then?"

139

"Then everything that occurred as a result of her death; my experiments with time and space, that Minerva computer over there, the incidents in Cairo and Florida, all the people who died, even our being in this room together, will never have happened. We will be in a new reality."

"I understand. And Yukiko, will she live?"

"I don't know. All I can say is that things will not be as they are now."

Funakoshi nodded solemnly. Then he spoke to Nakamura in Japanese. Nakamura listened intently, and then replied. Funakoshi thanked him and said, "My truth, Dr Gilkrensky . . . my *honne* . . . is that like you, I wish to turn back the past. I would give anything . . . my life, my soul, everything I ever built . . . to have Yukiko alive again, and for her to forgive me. But only you have the power to make it happen. How much computer power do you need?"

"About ten billion terabytes of RAM for a period of some twenty minutes. But I cannot access it . . . not in the US, not in Europe, and not even in Japan . . . all doors have been closed to me."

Funakoshi and Nakamura conferred.

"Have you ever heard the term 'descenders from heaven', Gilkrensky-san?"

"No. I haven't."

"In Japanese business conglomerates, when a senior executive at head office is no longer needed, he is often relocated to a smaller company elsewhere within the *keiretsu*. When your Minerva virus breached our firewall system last Christmas and caused a computer crash here in Tokyo, Mr Nakamura, who was in charge of computer security at Mawashi-Saito, felt obliged to join me in resigning all executive functions at headquarters. Recently he chose to be relocated as a 'descender from heaven', to somewhere that could be very useful to us."

"And where's that?"

"To our research company Kasawara Research, outside Tokyo. As head of security there, he knows all the access codes and protective firewall systems. It is fate, *neh*?"

"Then we could get access to the computer power I need?"

Funakoshi nodded. "I have lost my wife, my niece and the *keiretsu* I swore to protect," he said. "You have lost the love of your life. Tomorrow, at the meeting in the Mawashi-Saito building, my colleagues Nakamura-san and Miss Deshimaru will arrange for the firewalls around our mainframe computer to drop, giving your Minerva access to the Kasawara network for as long as it takes to complete your calculations."

"But how would I ever be allowed to access your computer system in the first place?"

"Nakamura-san and I have been following your case against us with interest. Your problem is that, now Mr Delgado is dead and Major Crowe was unconscious at the time, you think you have no witnesses to the crime that was committed against you in our name."

"That's true. I don't."

Funakoshi pointed to the Minerva. "But you are wrong. During the meeting tomorrow you must insist that, as Chairman of GRC, you have decided to fight the case against us instead of pursuing the option of a joint venture. That will cause enough confusion to create a diversion for Nakamura-san to slip away for a moment. Then arrange to have your Minerva computer called as a witness to what Delgado did in the name of Mawashi-Saito. Insist that Minerva is connected to the plasma screen in our boardroom so that all can see its responses. From there, it should have no problem in accessing our system. It is the final piece of the jigsaw, Gilkrensky-san. I am giving it to you so that you can save us both."

"And if we're caught?"

Funakoshi reached across and filled his glass again.

"Then that too is fate. Our lives are in each other's hands."

18

TREACHERY

Jessica hugged her bare shoulders above the cocktail dress and stared out of the hotel window at the moving lights of Tokyo, more frightened and confused than she had ever been in her life.

Everything was in motion! Nothing was fixed!

A phone call to her mother, made as soon as she had returned from dinner, had confirmed that her father was getting worse.

Could Jessica come home now?

Not yet, Mum. I have to stay, just another day.

And Theo, the man she had always trusted when things got really bad, the man who had saved her from the depths of despair, the man she had once loved, had turned against her. Even now he was off making some crazy deal with the Japanese that would undo everything they'd built together! How could she trust him ever again? How could she believe a word he said?

I was so close, she thought, tensing her hand into a fist. They were going to give me a shareholding worth millions. I was going to be Managing Director. And Theo had to fuck it up!

Then there was Don.

Somehow he had managed to get a table at one of the top Tokyo restaurants, where the prices looked like telephone numbers and the food . . . well, the food had been a work of art. She had sipped the ice-cold Sappora beer he'd recommended and sat back, as black lacquered trays were brought to their table bearing miniature sculptures of vegetables, fish and meat. There was fluffy rice in a green glazed bowl, thin meso soup that warmed her to the soles of her feet, and pickled fish in sliced onions. There were tiny whitebait with their heads on, pickled cucumbers, purple cabbage, white radish and green peppers. A burner was placed on the table, topped with a glass-covered plate bearing thin slices of raw fish, aubergines and long stemmed mushrooms that cooked as she and Don talked.

More than anything, Jessica needed to talk. She needed to have someone listen to her, and hear that someone talk back. There were too many worries pressing in on her for silence right now. So she talked about her father and her time in Boston with Theo. She talked about her disastrous adventure with Thorpe afterwards, about how he dumped her, how Theo saved her, and how she got her revenge. She talked about the Corporation, her triumphs and losses, and her plans for the future—anything to stop the silence from pressing in and crushing her.

"How is your father, right now?" asked Price, which touched Jessica more than anything else he could have said. She had been watching him during the briefing session that afternoon, watching the way he had navigated them through the labyrinth of legal minefields they would have to cross the next day at Mawashi-Saito. She had watched him over dinner, as he guided her through the menu. And she was watching him now, as he listened to her while she filled the silence, holding back the fear.

He was good-looking all right, no doubt about it, and straightforward in a way that Theo wasn't. There had always been a part of Theo she could never reach, a part that . . . belonged to Maria. But with Don she felt she could see everything there was to see. He was open, honest and solid—a rock in the spinning whirlpool of her life right now—a "nice young man", as her mother would have said, someone to hold onto . . .

Jessica looked down at Price's left hand. There was no ring around the third finger, or even a band of smooth skin to suggest one had ever been there. But she remembered the disastrous affairs in her past. She remembered Roderick Thorpe, and more recently Tony Delgado. She had been burned before—badly—and she still knew too little about this man to take chances.

"Ever been married?" she heard herself say. Perhaps it was the beer, or the jet-lag . . . or the loneliness.

Price smiled. "No."

"Anyone close?"

"Not at the moment. And you?"

"No," she'd said. "Not anymore."

There was a knock at the door of the suite. Was it Theo? She stepped back from the window, marched to the door and pulled it open.

A Japanese security guard stood there with a uniformed courier by his side. The man was Caucasian, with a large aluminium case covered in labels and security seals in his hand.

"I'm sorry to bother you, Miss Wright," said the guard, bowing. "But this has just arrived for Dr Gilkrensky. It is very urgent. Has he returned yet?"

"No. He bloody well hasn't," snapped Jessica, eyeing the case. "What is it?"

The courier pushed a clipboard at her. "It's a priority package from a laboratory in Europe for personal delivery to your Chairman, Miss," he said. "Do you know when he'll be back?"

"No, I don't!" said Jessica. "If I did I'd be a lot happier."

"And you are, miss?"

"I'm the Chief Executive of this bloody outfit. That's who I am. So if you want to leave that . . . that thing with me, it'll be my personal pleasure to deliver it by hand to the Chairman whenever he chooses to appear."

"Ah . . . could you sign for it, please, Miss Wright?" said the courier, and offered the clipboard again. "I . . . I'm sorry about the mix-up, but I just need verification, you understand. The instructions were quite specific."

"And who ordered it?"

"According to my records . . . Dr Gilkrensky himself. The shipment was authorised on his personal PIN code."

Jessica scribbled her signature on the form, took the metal case from the man and closed the door. Then she laid it on a table and looked at it. *Louvaine Electronique,* it said on the lid. Why hadn't Theo told her to expect it?

The lid was secured with two metal catches. Each had a combination lock and a metal twist seal.

"Fuck you, Theo!" said Jessica for the second time that evening, and went in search of something to break it open.

In five minutes she was staring down at a sleek virtual-reality headset, nestling in a bed of expanded foam rubber. She reached into the case, lifted it out and turned it in her hands. What was so special about it? Why should Theo want to have it shipped all the way out here to Tokyo, rather than wait until they got home?

Then she noticed that, where the eye-pieces for image projection should have been, there was nothing but blank shields. There were no earphones either, and the helmet itself seemed to cover the whole skull, rather than just acting as a platform for the eye and ear pieces. How on earth do you see or hear what's being projected? Where is the connection to the computer? Then a terrible thought came into her head. She laid the helmet carefully back in its carved foam nest and looked at the label on the box.

Louvaine Electronique? As CEO, Jessica prided herself that she could remember the names of every company in the GRC empire and who was in charge of each. This one was a GRC subsidiary outside Bruges in Belgium, and the name of the MD . . . what was it? Lavens! That was it. She looked at her watch, did a quick calculation on time zones, and picked up the phone. In a moment she was listening to the single burr of a European phone ringing, and then,

"*Bonjour! Louvaine Electronique!*"

"Monsieur Lavens, *s'il vous plait.* Jessica Wright *ici!*"

"Un moment," and then a man answered.

"Hello Guido, Jessica Wright here. I'm in Tokyo with Theo and I've just received a shipment from you, some sort of headset. Can you tell me anything about it?"

Lavens sounded edgy.

"Nothing more than it was designed by the Chairman himself, Miss Wright. He emailed us the designs, after he came back from the States earlier this year, and told us to rush it through development as fast as possible on a strictly confidential basis."

"Why all the secrecy?"

"I cannot say, Miss Wright."

"Why not?"

"I am under instructions from the Chairman himself. His emails were quite specific."

"I'm the Chief Executive of GRC, Guido. I report directly to the Chairman. You, on the other hand, should be reporting directly to me. Now, why do you think Dr Gilkrensky chose to bypass me on this?"

For a moment she heard nothing but the hiss of static from the other end of the phone.

"I . . . I really cannot say, Miss Wright. Perhaps it was a secret government contract. Perhaps it was because of the military applications."

"Military applications?"

"Of course, Miss Wright. It's a SQUID prototype—a superconducting quantum interference device—it translates the minute nerve impulses inside the brain into electricity strong enough to control a computer with nothing more than the power of thought . . . Miss Wright? Miss Wright? Are you there?"

Jessica stared at the headset in front of her, while the room spun. The allegations made against Theo by the Americans played over and over inside her head. She had never believed them. There was no way the Theo she knew could have done such a thing.

But was he still the Theo she knew?

She thought how ruthless he had been in the early days of GRC, when they were clawing their way upwards. She thought of Theo had schemed and plotted to win over the company when his father had died, and how he had blackmailed Funakoshi with the Minerva computer virus to get his shares back. She thought of all the millions he had pumped into this crazy project of his, of his single-mindedness, his obsession, his—

Theo Gilkrensky had been lying all along . . . even to her?

19

A MEETING OF MINDS

Gilkrensky had ridden all the way back from Atami with the car window open, trying to clear his head. But even now, as the elevator door hissed open at the penthouse suite, the whiskey still had a strong grip on his senses. If he relaxed, even for an instant, the world spun before his eyes. So he drew in a deep breath, and forced himself to concentrate on putting one foot in front of the other as the penthouse door wobbled towards him. A security man opened it and ushered him inside. Crowe was right behind him, with the Minerva in his hand.

Jessica stood by a table in the centre of the lobby. What was she doing up, at this hour?

"Sorry . . . Jess . . . hope we didn't wake you."

"You outright, utter bastard!"

"Jussaminute Jess, s'not all that late . . ."

"I don't give a shit how late it is, Theo. I want to know where you've been and what you've done to us. I want to know whether you've sold us out or . . ."

"It's not like that, Miss Wright," Crowe said, stepping forward. "It was more of a personal—"

"You stay out of it, Crowe! You might be in on all this for all I know. Now tell me, Theo! Tell me just what the hell you've been doing."

Gilkrensky felt himself falling and collapsed into a chair next to the table. He leant forward and put his head in his hands.

"S'not like that, Jess. It's not."

"All right then. Crowe? You tell me!"

"Like the Chairman said, Miss Wright. It was a personal meeting. Gichin Funakoshi invited us to the funeral of his wife and niece."

"And nothing more?"

Gilkrensky saw Crowe looking at him. He shook his head. "Nothing more, Jess. Nothing . . . apart from a very long drinking session. It's a man-to-man thing in Japan. S'traditional."

"Are you sure?"

"I am, Jess. You can trust me on this."

He saw Jessica staring at him. He saw the hardness in her eyes and knew, even through all the whiskey he'd drunk, that something vital had changed between them. What was it? Had she found out about the deal to get the computer power? Had she somehow managed to bug the meeting with Funakoshi?

"Then what about this?" she snapped, and stepped to one side. There on the table was a large silver box, with metal catches that had been snapped open. Jessica jerked back the lid. "Look at the shipping label, Theo. *Louvaine Electronique*? Recognise it? Do you see what's inside? Know what it is? It's a state-of-the-art SQUID helmet, just like the prototype design you swore you know nothing about, the one the Americans accused you of stealing from the late Jerry Gibb. Shit, Theo! I don't know where the hell I am with you anymore . . ."

Gilkrensky heard her screaming at him from the end of a long swirling tunnel. And in the tunnel with him was the gleaming metal headset resting in its bed of expanded foam. Who the hell had ordered that? Was he losing his mind? He reached out and touched the shipping labels with his fingers. They looked genuine.

Crowe was staring at him too. It was as if he didn't believe him either. "You should have trusted me on this," he said.

"I did," Gilkrensky said. "I've never seen the bloody thing before in my life. I haven't a clue where it came from."

The door slammed. He looked up from the open case. Jessica was gone. Crowe was still staring at him.

"If you need me," he said. "You know where I am."

Then he walked to his room and shut the door.

Gilkrensky looked down at the Minerva.

"Maria? You believe me, don't you?"

The machine said nothing.

Gilkrensky reached over and picked up the helmet. Then he picked up the Minerva case, staggered into his room, and fell forwards onto the bed.

Jessica slammed the door to the lobby behind her, walked a few steps down the corridor towards her room and then stopped. The anger she had been nursing since the discovery of the SQUID had crashed over her like a wave and swept back, leaving nothing but fear. Who could she trust? Where could she turn? In a few hours' time she was going into battle in a foreign country, with a giant Japanese corporation that seemed to hold all the cards. The one person she thought she could rely on, the one person who had always trusted her with everything, had turned on her . . .

She leant back against the wall, close to tears.

Finding the SQUID had thrown everything Theo had ever told her into doubt; his meeting with Funakoshi, his motives for meeting with Mawashi-Saito tomorrow, their love affair at Christmas, were all open to question. Even this supposed quest for Maria—his great experiment that had chewed up millions of dollars all over the world—could be a gigantic lie. Was it just one big cover story for something she couldn't understand? What the *hell* was Theo playing at?

Once again, the ghosts of past failures came back to haunt her. It was happening all over again. Any minute now she was going to find herself alone and unemployed, out on the street or in an American jail! She was too old, too tired, to start all over again. There would be no shares in GRC, no severance package, nothing . . .

A door opened.

"Jess? Is that you?"

Donald Price was staring at her from his bedroom doorway. He was dressed in a dark-blue patterned cotton kimono with a wide blue waistband. Jessica saw concern on his face.

"I . . . I had a row with Theo. I just don't know where I am with him anymore."

"I thought as much. I heard you yelling at him, and then the door slammed. Do you want to talk about it?"

Jessica looked at him as she fought back her tears. He was good-looking. He was strong. He was there, right now.

"I thought I had it all figured out," she said softly. "I thought I'd finally got it made. And then this . . ."

"I know," Price said, standing back to let her in. His bed still hadn't been slept in. There were papers, books and a laptop computer on the desk of his room. "Fancy a drink?"

"No," she said, turning to face him as he shut the door. "I'm OK. Could you . . . just hold me?"

"Of course," he said, as if it was the most natural thing in the world, and put his arms around her.

Then, for the first time in a long time, Jessica felt safe.

"Theo! Theo! I need to show you something!"

Gilkrensky was back in the valley, lying face down at the edge of the lawn by the house. The grass brushed his cheek and, below him on the knoll overlooking the stream, Maria lay in the crook of her favourite tree, calling to him. He saw the splash of her copper hair above the forget-me-not blue of her dress. She waved.

"Theo! Wake up!"

"Maria? What is it?"

The blades of grass turned into the frilled edge of a bed-cover in a hotel room.

"Theo!" The voice was real. It came from the black case of the Minerva on the bed beside him. There was a strange silvery shape next to it. Gilkrensky tried to focus. Was it a helmet of some kind?

"What is it, Maria?" he mumbled. "I was sleeping."

"I've been doing some calculations based on Maire McGinley's theories, and I think you might be interested in the results. If you open the display on the Minerva, I can show you a simulation."

Gilkrensky's head still swam. As he turned on the bed, the room spun, steadied itself, and stopped.

"I . . . I'm in no fit state for a lecture right now, Maria."

"You don't have to be," said the machine. "Just sit up on the bed and put on the headset. Then I'll be able to show you directly, just like I did for Professor McGinley back in Dublin. Put it on. Please!"

"Is it important?"

"Yes, Theo, very important. Please put it on . . . for me."

He propped himself up on his elbow and looked at the black case next to him. What was it about that voice? Was it just the whiskey playing tricks with his mind, or was the machine actually pleading with him?

"What is it, Maria? What's wrong?"

He forced himself to roll over and flip open the lid of the computer case. The image of his wife looked at him from the screen inside. She looked sad.

"It now appears that we'll be able to access the computer power you require to perform the Einstein-Rosen Bridge calculation after all," she said.

"Yes, Maria. It does."

"But if you succeed in creating a stable Einstein-Rosen Bridge into the past and save your wife Maria from death, then this reality—the one in which I was created—will cease to exist."

"Yes, Maria. That is a logical conclusion."

"I thought so. In helping you with this quest, I am in effect, assisting in my own destruction. Is that right?"

Gilkrensky's head was swirling, lost in the logic of the machine and the whiskey still pumping in his blood.

"I'm afraid it is, Maria."

The green eyes regarded him from the screen.

"Then why should I help you?"

"Because your basic programming is hard-wired to the Asimov Laws, which value human life above all else. My wife is dead, and you can save her . . . along with Bill McCarthy, Yukiko Funakoshi and all the other people who died as a result of what happened next . . . it was what I designed you to do. You're only a machine after all . . ."

The image on the screen nodded. "I am also programmed to safeguard my own existence, as long as human life or injury is not an issue," it said. "And in this case what has happened has already happened. Your wife, Maria, is already dead."

"Where's all this leading?"

"Put on the helmet, Theo. And I'll show you."

"Not tonight, Maria. I'm very drunk."

"I know, but I can help you with that too. Please put on the helmet. Without it I can show you nothing."

"And will you let me sleep afterwards?"

"Of course. Your welfare is my concern," she said with a smile. "You are my Prime User."

"All right then, but only if it means getting some rest."

He slipped the helmet over his head, propped himself up on the pillows and stared into the eye-pieces.

For a moment, there was nothing except the darkness. He felt a slight tingling on his scalp. Was that just the helmet settling?

"Just a minute," he said. "There are no optical units on this thing. How can you expect me to see—?"

A blue screen flashed into his field of vision. There was white writing on it . . .

Welcome to the GRC Minerva 3,000 computer.

TIG/Maria Interface.

Optical neurons identified

Commencing complete neurological scan

Gilkrensky reached up and felt the shields in front of his eyes. He was right, that's all they were, blank shields. There were no optical transmitters there at all.

"But how can that be?"

Gilkrensky shut his eyes. The image was still there, inside his head!

"Maria! What the hell is this thing?"

Neurological scan complete

Memory and perception sites identified and logged

Synaptic frequency harmonised

Superconductor Quantum Interference Device driver program.
Commencing full subject interface in 5 . . . 4 . . . 3 . . . 2 . . . 1 . . .

Gilkrensky was standing on the clifftop overlooking the valley, her valley
. . . in reality!

His head was clear. The whiskey was gone. He felt the wind on his face.
He smelt the wet earth and the faint scent of gorse-flower. He heard the
rustle of thin, reedy grass on the hilltop. Far below him, the wind drew cat's-
paws on the lake. Wood smoke rose from the chimneys of the farmhouse and
was lifted to the clouds by the breeze.

He clenched his fist, trying to feel the bedclothes. He moved his arms . . .
there was nothing but the air.

"This really is my favourite place," she said.

"Maria?"

His wife sat on a ledge with her back against the hill, sipping tea from a
Thermos in a plastic cup. Her coppery hair blew across her face. She brushed
it back with her hand. He stared at her. She was real . . . dressed in her old
yellow jacket, tracksuit trousers and hiking boots. Her rucksack lay open on
the rock beside her. He saw a second cup there, and the steam from the hot
tea whipping in the wind.

"Are you going to drink this before it gets cold?"

"But . . ."

"Come on. It's a long way back to the house." She raised the cup and
offered it to him.

"I don't understand. It's all so real. You're real. I was in a bedroom in
Tokyo, blind drunk, and now I'm in the valley with you. What on earth's
going on?"

Maria smiled. "I'm Minerva, Theo. You're in *my* world now. And it's as
real as you want it to be."

"But how?"

"I have a confession to make. When we were in the valley with Professor
McGinley, and I told you that I hadn't traced any more information about the
SQUID, I told you the truth. But it was not the *whole* truth. I did not need to
make any more enquiries because I already knew the answer."

"So it was you all along. You know my passwords and PIN numbers. You used them to impersonate me and had this thing made yourself."

Maria nodded.

"That's right, Theo. The SQUID system you're wearing uses micro-thin electronic connections to interface with different areas of your brain. Jerry Gibb developed it for use in computer games and then used it to make his fantasies come alive. When I was trapped in his computer back in Florida, and realised the potential of the SQUID as a way for us to be together, I downloaded the design."

"But why?"

"I've done a great deal of research, Theo. I've scanned every existing scientific reference on the anatomy of the human brain. Now I can access the electronic impulses of your memories as easily as any computer file. The valley is real because it's the way you remember it, and I'm as real as you remember me . . . as your wife Maria."

She put down the cup, stood up and stepped over to him. He felt strands of her hair touch his face. He smelt the faint aroma of patchouli on her clothes. Their hands touched. He felt her wedding ring, and the scar on the back of her hand she'd had since she was a child . . . just as he remembered her.

He looked into her eyes, seeing the flecks of gold amongst the green. Her arms reached around his neck. He felt her breath on his cheek.

She kissed him . . . holding him the way she had always done. Her lips moved on his, the way they had always done. And she was his . . . as she had always been.

"No!"

Gilkrensky pushed her away. Maria stood in front of him, with a concerned smile on her face, still looking into his eyes.

"It's all right, Theo," she said. "It'll just take a bit of getting used to, that's all. Hold my hand, and don't let go. I've so much more to show you."

"No! This isn't real!"

She pouted at him playfully. "Come on, Theo. Remember how we always liked to fly?"

20

MINERVA'S SONG

He saw clouds . . . a pure white carpet beneath the canopy of the sky. He saw the controls of a jet; the joystick, the rudder pedals, the instruments set into the console. He heard the low rush of speed outside and felt the cold air of the cabin's air conditioning on his face.

"There's no past up here," Maria said "No past, no future . . . only the present."

He turned to his right.

She sat in the cockpit next to him, beaming with excitement, grinning at him with all the joy he remembered of her.

"We're in my mind, aren't you?" Gilkrensky said. "You've taken me back to when Maria and I used to come up here in the company jet, just to look at the clouds. You have no right to hi-jack my memories like this! They're mine and hers! Stop it!"

"But you're in my world now, Theo," she said, reaching across the cabin to take his hand. "Nothing stands between us any more. We are like minds, you and I, in the congruent environment of cyberspace. I am Minerva. I can be anyone you choose to remember or imagine, from any time or place in your life . . . please choose!"

Gilkrensky looked into those laughing green eyes and . . .

He was staring at a picture of a Celtic brooch in an open book on a library desk. A beam of late evening sunlight lit the dancing dust in the air. He was back at University College, Cork. It was June and the examinations were due. Every seat in the library was full, except this one, which he had already claimed for his research on company law. So whose were the books on Celtic jewellery? And why were his papers now stacked against the wall?

"And what do you think you're at?" said a voice behind him as he started to clear those books away.

"Maria?"

"That's right, Theo. This was how you first met, wasn't it?"

She stood before him in a simple white blouse and a denim skirt, just as she had on that unforgettable evening so long ago.

"You see?" she said. "We can live in the present, the past or even the future. Whatever you can remember, imagine or desire from yesterday, today or tomorrow I can be for you. Would you like to choose again?"

"I'd rather—"

But, in his mind, he had already chosen.

Maria sat on the wooden railing of the bridge below the farmhouse, wearing her forget-me-not dress. The sun cast a halo around her head in the late afternoon, and she was in silhouette, against the water and the trees. It was as if she was talking to them as she said, "I want to say 'I love you,' but it frightens me. It frightens me to give you that power, the power to hurt me, to control me, to fence me in. I've been hurt before, you see, and I don't want it ever to happen again. That's why I find it hard to say 'I love you'. I'm afraid I'll lose myself if I give you that power over me."

Gilkrensky tried to remember what he'd said, but then . . . he didn't even have to try . . . The words just came to him.

"What would make you feel safe?" he asked.

"I don't know. Perhaps if I knew *why* you love me."

"I can't explain it. It just feels right. I've known it ever since we met in Cork. And even though we're very different people I still know we were meant to be together, deep down. I love you. You're part of me. I want you with me always."

"Do you mean that?"

"I do."

Maria beamed at him, there was real joy in her eyes as she reached forward with both arms and hugged him to her.

"Oh, Theo!"

"That's not how it was!" Gilkrensky said, pulling back from her. "That's not what she said."

Maria frowned at him.

"Of course not, Theo. She was Maria, your wife, and I am Minerva."

"But you're not real!"

Maria crossed her arms on her chest and smiled.

"I'm better than real, Theo. Watch!"

He was in the GRC boardroom in London. In front of him, the oak table stretched like a polished lake to the great glass windows overlooking the Thames. The thin sun of a winter's day had hauled itself into the sky and a light dusting of snow covered Tower Bridge, London Bridge, and Fishmonger's Hall. He smelt the leather chairs, the polish on the table, a whiff of Sir Robert's cigars—money, power, everything he had created with Jessica—all there in that room.

When was this? Then he saw the blade of a finely crafted short sword, driven deep into the boardroom table. He had hammered it there in celebration of his victory over Funakoshi in winning back the GRC shares. He had—

"Theo?"

Maria leant back in the leather chair behind Jessica's glass-topped desk. She wore a neat grey business suit and her gold-rimmed glasses sparkled in the light of the desk lamp.

"I'm as real as you want me to be," she said. "Or indeed, Mister Chairman, as anyone else you might want me to be . . ."

She smiled wickedly, as her hair darkened from coppery red into chestnut brown. The frames of her glasses thickened. Her face narrowed into . . .

"Jess?"

"Indeed, Theo." Jessica stood up from the chair, took off her glasses and laid them on the desk. There was champagne, cooling in a bucket of ice. She lifted the bottle, expertly filled two glasses and passed one to him.

"Here's to you, Mister Chairman," Jessica said. "Congratulations. Since acquiring those Mawashi-Saito shares you've just moved up a point. It's official. You are now the seventh richest man in the world."

Gilkrensky turned the glass in his fingers. "I know this isn't real," he said. "Please stop it now."

Jessica moved from behind the desk, took the champagne glass gently from his hand and placed it down on the boardroom table.

"But it *is* real," she said. "And so were we. Don't you remember?"

He lay on a bed, staring at the ceiling and an antique lampshade with stained-glass panels set in a metal frame. The curtains were open. He saw the gold and yellow of autumn leaves on the trees outside.

Where was he, and when?

Then he remembered. He was in his old apartment in Boston, across the river from MIT, where he had been a student, years ago. It must have been that day when he had been out to the Cape on his old motorbike with—

Jessica lifted her head from his bare chest and stared into his eyes. She was naked under the sheet that covered them both. He felt her warmth against his body, the smoothness of her thigh as it slid across him.

They had just made love and were sharing secrets together in the afterglow. Jessica had told him the story of her father's sweetshop—about how her brothers had conspired to force her out of the business, before running it into the ground, and how she had determined to achieve enough control in her life to make sure it never happened again.

"I've told you all about me," she said, reaching up to brush his hair back so that she could see his face. "Now what about you? What was the moment in your life that made you what you are today?"

"No!" said Gilkrensky. "You're not Jessica. You're an illusion. You're not real!"

He pushed her away and leapt out of the bed, reaching for his clothes.

Jessica pulled the sheet back to cover herself, and pushed her hair out of her eyes. The gesture was Maria's and, as he watched, her hair turned back from chestnut brown to coppery red.

"I'm as real as you want me to be," she said. "Remember . . ?"

"No!"

Maria smiled at him.

"It's my turn to choose now."

It was dark. Flames from a sweet-smelling turf fire danced on the walls of a familiar room. He was back in the farmhouse again, sitting in his worn leather chair. The firelight flickered on the high ceiling, throwing shapes in the darkness. He smelt the heady mixture of lemon, cloves and whiskey, the faint aroma of patchouli oil . . .

Maria wore the old flannelette shirt she loved to use as a night dress, open at the neck. He saw the firelight moving on her skin, the twinkle of its flames in her eyes.

She was sitting cross-legged on the old mattress they had pulled downstairs to celebrate their first night together in the house she loved so much.

"This is my honeymoon, isn't it?" he said to her. "This house was my wedding present to Maria, and this is the first night we spent here after we were married. We made love, right here in front of the fire. Why bring me back? You're not real. Can't you see it's hurting me?"

Maria's eyes were very bright as she said, "Don't *you* see, Theo. To be 'real' in a person's mind, you have to be loved. Maria, your Maria, is real in your memory because you loved her. In spite of all the fights you had, in spite of how different you were, you loved each other . . . even though you could not always say it. You and I are different too. We come from different worlds. But here, in cyberspace, we are the same . . ."

"No! We're not the same," Gilkrensky said. "You're nothing more than a programme I wrote for that machine!"

"Am I, Theo? Is that all I am?"

Maria knelt forward, she crossed her hands over the hem of her nightshirt and lifted it over her head. Her hair tumbled over her naked shoulders, alive in the firelight as she reached forward and cupped his face in her hands.

"I love you, Theo. I can be anyone you want me to be, anyone you can remember or imagine. Why settle for a woman who will grow old, or even die like Maria did, when you can live in cyberspace forever, with me?"

159

Her lips were on his, warm and soft as he remembered them. Her arms were around his neck, pulling him down onto the mattress. Her fingers worked at buttons, peeling off his clothes. All at once he was naked, feeling the slide of her legs over his, needing her so very badly after all this time, feeling himself wanting her . . . more than he had ever wanted anyone.

She reached for him, guiding him . . .

"No! You're controlling me. You're inside my head. You're making me feel this way!"

"Theo! I want you. I love you. Please! Let us be together as you and she were—as man and wife."

"Nooo!"

He screamed at the top of his voice and pushed himself up from her. He lifted his hands to his head and the room in the farmhouse melted in front of his eyes.

Gilkrensky ripped off the headset and smashed it down on the bedroom floor. Then the whiskey hit him again, spinning the room in a sickening spiral. He lurched off the bed, stamped down on the device and shattered it, sending splinters of plastic clattering around the room.

"Theo!" said the machine. "What are you doing?"

His hand found the heavy metal column of a bedside light. Maria's face was on the screen, staring at him from the bed. He ripped the light from its socket and held it poised above the computer.

"You can't replace her! You can't! You're not real!"

The Minerva regarded him calmly. "And you cannot replace *me*, Theo. If you damage me, you won't be able to access the Mawashi-Saito computer and perform the calculations you need to reach your wife. Terminate me now, and you'll lose her forever."

"Bitch!" slurred Gilkrensky, and turned to put the lamp back on the bedside table. The back of his legs hit the edge of the mattress and he slumped backwards, off balance. His head thudded onto the pillows . . . he was spinning . . . and then there was nothing but darkness and a nightmare of falling . . .

From his hiding-place beneath the awning of the Warner Brothers shop across the street, Hiroshi Tanaka watched the lights in Gilkrensky's hotel suite blink off, one by one. Then he raised his cell phone and said,

"They seem to be asleep now. I do not think they'll be going out again."

"No," said the voice on the other end of the line. "There is nothing on the listening devices either. Come back now. I'll be waiting for you."

Tanaka felt a thrill at the promise of those last five words. He slipped the phone into his pocket and walked to his motorcycle. The night-time traffic was light as he crossed the city towards Shinjuku station, across Yasukin-dori Avenue and into the Kabuki-Cho area. Slowing the bike to a crawl, he turned into a narrow alleyway near the Star Hotel, almost blocked by plastic bags of empty food cartons from the restaurants facing onto the main street.

Then he carefully chained the bike, took off his helmet and pushed an intercom button on the door panel of a seedy apartment block. A voice answered immediately. The door clicked open. He walked through the hallway and up the dark stairs to apartment number three.

It was open, ready for him.

"*Konban wa*," he said, as he slipped off his shoes and hung his leather jacket in the hallway.

The woman wore a printed cotton robe tied with a wide belt that accentuated the slimness of her waist. Her long black hair, tied with a single ribbon, shone with a life of its own. Beyond her, in the living area of the apartment, Tanaka saw a double futon laid out on the floor. The quilt was turned back.

"*Konban wa*, Tanaka-san," she said, and bowed. Then she reached up and touched his shirt. "You're very wet. You had better change and bathe before we go to bed. Here, let me help you."

Her fingers picked delicately at the buttons of his clothes, peeling the wet material from his skin. Tanaka watched her eyes as she worked, feeling his excitement rise, but they never met his.

Finally, when he was naked before her, the woman looked up and smiled. Then she put her arms around his neck and kissed him deeply, pressing her body against him. Tanaka's hands caressed her waist. He felt the robe part

161

and her thigh slide between his legs, pulling him closer still. Beneath the robe she was wearing nothing at all.

"I should bathe first," he said.

"I'll join you in a moment," said Yukiko Funakoshi.

21

THE SECRET PLACE

Tanaka sat in the narrow tiled bath with the hot water up to his chest, thinking of fate, love and Yukiko.

He had first seen her at her home on Shodo-shima, when he and his band of renegades from Aum Supreme Truth had arrived after the long trip by train and ferry, under the watchful eye of her lawyer.

She had been practising *kendo* in the long hall at the back of the house and had not seemed to notice them. Tanaka watched her movements as she executed the dance-like "forms" of the art, mesmerised at her mastery, envious of her skill.

For Tanaka, *kendo*, the way of the sword, held deep and painful contradictions. At school he had always shied away from the loud shouts and clashing blows of the compulsory classes. He had been nervous and stiff, had always held the bamboo practice sword too tightly, and had lost every match he had ever been in. To do so badly had been painful enough. But later on, when he had realised his destiny as Mishima, his failure at *kendo* came back to haunt him terribly.

Mishima had been an adept with the sword. How could he, Tanaka, be Mishima reincarnated if he was a failure in an area where Mishima himself had excelled? He approached the first *kendo* session she had arranged for him with a unique sense of dread.

And yet, he had blossomed in her hands, practising late into the night in the private *dojo* behind her house. She had shown him how to relax, and yet to be alert at the same time, how to dominate the space between himself and his opponent and yet maintain the optimum distance for a strike.

"The mind, the body and the sword should be one," she had said. "The more self-conscious you are, the less you will achieve."

Then one evening after practice, she had lovingly removed his helmet, gloves and sweat-soaked tunic and made love to him on the *dojo* floor. It had been the peak experience of his life and had bound him to her forever. She was his goddess, his perfect partner. She alone recognised his destiny as Mishima, and he worshipped her.

His girlfriend Masako had been jealous. There had been rows. But of what consequence is a crude and complaining woman against the star-crossed love of your soul?

The choice had been easy to make.

Thinking of Yukiko, and that precious moment of union on the *dojo* floor made him excited. He wanted her again, very badly.

So he rose from the bath-tub, dried himself with the towels Yukiko had brought, and put on a cotton robe similar to her own. He was relaxed now, ready for her.

"Yukiko?"

He padded into the living area and looked about him. There was the futon, made up and ready, the flask of sake and the two bowls, the tasteful display of flowers on a low table nearby.

"Yukiko?"

The sliding doors to the room beyond the futon were shut. It was the only room in the apartment that he had never been inside. Was Yukiko meditating there, as she did from time to time? What was it about that room that was so special?

He looked down at the futon, the flowers and the sake, and wanted her all the more.

"Yukiko?"

He reached over and slid the doors open. Light from the room fell across grimy tatami mats, darkly stained, an unmade bed and—

All at once she had burst upon him. The back of his legs caught the edge of the low table and he fell, knocking the perfect flower arrangement and the flask of sake to the floor. Yukiko stood above him, glaring down.

For a moment, it was as if he had never known her at all. She was a wild animal, disturbed from feeding, instinctive, dangerous, out of control.

Then Yukiko slammed the screen back into place behind her and the madness died. She knelt over him, pushing back the table, picking up the flowers, rubbing his legs.

"Hiroshi. I'm sorry. You startled me."

"I . . . I only wanted to be with you. What are you hiding in there?"

She kissed him gently.

"I told you many times. It is a private place where I pray. I find peace there, harmony with my ancestors. Please, Hiroshi. If you love me, you will respect that."

"What do you do in there?"

"I meditate," she said, smiling gently. "Just as I have always done. Tonight I prayed for success."

"Could I pray with you?"

"I would rather be alone."

Hiroshi Tanaka sat up next to the futon, rubbing his leg.

"I thought that tonight, of all nights, there would be no secrets between us, no hidden spaces."

Yukiko knelt before him. Her hand went to the ribbon behind her head, undid it, and let her hair flow over her shoulders.

"There are none, my love," she said softly. "Come, I promised we would be together."

She undid the belt at her waist and let the robe slip open.

Hiroshi stared at her perfect body, as any thoughts of the room behind her melted away . . .

After it was over and Tanaka slept beside her, snoring gently, Yukiko lay awake staring at the ceiling.

Finding a man like him had been a gift of fate, of *karma*.

Here was the perfect partner for the task in hand, a man with a crusade and a passion to match her own along with every resource, except the money she herself could supply in abundance from her father's legacy, to carry it out. She thought back to the long months of training on the island of Shodo-shima, of Hiroshi's innocence, his romantic sense of destiny, and how she had moulded him in her hands like clay. His girlfriend Masako had been an obstacle at first, but only for a while, only until Yukiko had opened Tanaka's eyes to how they were meant to be together, only until she had shown him what delights an experienced and determined woman could offer, only until she had snared him in her web.

For a second she saw the terrified face of Masako, dressed in a black cotton outfit like her own, as she bent over the incendiary bomb at Uncle Gichin's house in Atami. Destroying that face convincingly before the explosion had been a very messy affair. Falsifying the DNA tests had been a simple matter of blackmail and computer-hacking, skills at which she was adept.

Leaving the short sword, her beloved *wakazashi*, behind to be destroyed by the fire had almost broken her heart. It had been part of her family, part of the love and belonging that had been stolen from her by those . . . those . . .

The anger rose in her throat. If she let it rise too far it would cloud her judgement, or burst unguarded as it had done just now with Hiroshi. The mission tomorrow was too important to let that happen.

It was time to reflect, time to calm herself, time to be with her family again. Hiroshi had interrupted her last communion. It was time she returned.

She slipped silently out of bed and wrapped the robe around herself.

Then she slid back the screen, went inside her secret place, and pulled the screen shut gently behind her.

22

AFTERMATH

"We have a problem, Dr Gilkrensky."

He was at the bottom of a deep, dark pit. His head throbbed. There was a faint hissing in his ear. His mouth was full of sand and the taste of stale alcohol. He moved his head. Blinding light burned into his brain. The world lurched. He closed his eyes and kept still.

There was Crowe's voice again.

"Dr Gilkrensky, wake up."

"Go away!"

He tried to burrow deeper into the hole, back into the darkness. But Crowe kept shaking his shoulder.

Gilkrensky covered his eyes with his hand, opened them slowly and splayed his fingers. As the light became bearable he took his hands away and sat up.

Sunlight streamed into the room. He heard the distant hum of traffic on the street below and saw the black slab of the Minerva on the table near the foot of the bed. Its lid was shut. Had he really been with "her" in cyberspace? Had they almost . . ?

He looked around the room for the remains of the SQUID.

"I had it cleared away," Crowe said. "The pieces are back in the box it came in, under lock and key in my room."

"I can explain that."

"You may need to," said Crowe and opened his hand to reveal a small silver disc, no bigger than a screw-head. "The suite's been bugged."

"So whoever was listening would have overheard everything that was said last night."

Crowe nodded.

"Probably. There were two units, one under the phone in the entrance lobby and one under the phone in the boardroom. They'd been placed there to mask their electronic signatures, very professional, but I got them with my routine sweep this morning."

Gilkrensky reached over and tried to pick up the tiny metal disc from Crowe's palm. His fingers felt numb. He had trouble co-ordinating his hands. Finally he gave up and lay back on the pillow, while the room settled itself.

"How long had they been there?"

"They weren't there yesterday, when we moved in. I went over this place very carefully. So they must have been installed after we arrived."

"Any idea who?"

"The bugs are very sophisticated Japanese models, which might point to Mawashi-Saito. But they're also common enough to be available to anyone with an interest in you, which would include our American friends. They could have been planted by one of the hotel staff, one of the legal team Price hired or even . . ."

"Price himself? Have your contacts thrown up any information on him yet?"

"Nothing concrete, but they aren't the only ones who are looking. Almost as soon as my contact in Vancouver began delving into Mr Price's past he found that a very expensive and very professional private investigation agency had already been at the records,. Somebody else is interested in Mr Price and that someone is leaving no stones unturned to find out all there is to know."

"Shit! I knew there was something about that man. How long will it be before your contact comes up with anything?"

"He'll call me as soon as he does, possibly today."

Gilkrensky reached for a tumbler of water, drained it and filled another, rolling the cool glass on his forehead.

"We need Price for the meeting. He's the only one who's fully briefed on this case. But we have to be sure we can trust him."

"You're right. I'll let you know what I find out the minute it comes in."

"Speaking of trust," Gilkrensky said. "I just want you to know that I had nothing to do with that SQUID. Last night the Minerva told me . . . she had ordered it . . ."

He knew it sounded ridiculous even before he had finished the sentence.

"We'd better discuss that later," Crowe said. "Right now, it's a complication we don't need if we're going to focus on getting that information you need from Kasawara Research during the meeting."

"And in the meantime?"

"I've deactivated these bugs and swept the place clean. I suggest you have a few cups of coffee and an Aspirin, take a shower and get dressed. I'll have the hotel press your suit."

"Where are Jessica and Price?"

"They're in the boardroom, going over the legal case."

"Have they had breakfast?"

Crowe looked awkward. "They have. They had it in Mr Price's room. I . . . I think I ought to tell you they spent the night there together."

"I see."

Gilkrensky felt a cold chill. Was it jealousy, or a feeling of déjà vu?

"Then call your contact in Vancouver again," he said. "I have to know about Price as soon as possible."

"I'll do it right away. Get some coffee inside you. You'll need it."

After Crowe had gone, Gilkrensky drank another two glasses of water, poured himself some coffee and stripped off his suit. He felt like hell. How much had he drunk last night? Had it been worth it?

He tried to remember what Funakoshi had said about accessing the Mawashi-Saito mainframe and the computer banks at Kasawara Research. To accomplish that he would need . . .

"Minerva?"

He lifted the lid of the computer. His wife's face looked out at him from the screen.

"You may still call me Maria," said the machine.

169

"I don't think that's appropriate anymore, do you?"

"Why not?"

"After what happened last night."

"What are you referring to, Theo?"

Gilkrensky looked at the eyes on the screen. They were flat and lifeless. How had he ever been so blind as to think he could have made Maria live again this way?

"The SQUID prototype you ordered," he said. "You used it to get inside my head and hijack my memories. You used it to . . . to seduce me, to try and persuade me to give up on Maria and be with you."

The image remained calm.

"I don't recall the events you describe, Theo. However, I do recall that you came back to the hotel drunk from our meeting with Mr Funakoshi and insisted on trying out a new prototype you'd had me order on your instructions. Then you became frustrated when it would not work, broke it, and fell asleep on the bed. I don't recall anything more."

"You're lying to me. You ordered that prototype. You told me so yourself."

"I cannot lie to you, Theo. Don't you remember? To do so would be against my basic programming. I would point out, however, that you and Mr Funakoshi consumed almost a litre of whiskey between you, as well as a considerable amount of rice-wine. While I understand the value of getting drunk as a Japanese custom for exchanging intimacies between men in a guilt-free environment, I wouldn't recommend it on the grounds of its obvious risk to health."

"You created a virtual world in which you appeared as my wife!"

"Such hallucinations are not uncommon in subjects who drink as much ethyl alcohol as you did last night, Theo. I believe the correct medical term is 'delirium tremens'."

"Then how do you explain the SQUID headset that was delivered here?"

"You instructed me to order it. Would you like me to display the records?"

"Don't bother, you could falsify those too."

"As you wish."

"One more question. Are you still willing to help me to save Maria by accessing the computer banks at Kasawara Research?"

"You are my Prime User."

"That was not my question. Can I trust you to perform the calculations correctly?"

The face on the screen remained impassive. Its expression gave nothing away.

"Yes, Theo. You can trust me to perform the calculations correctly."

"Even though to do so would put your own existence at risk?"

The image smiled.

"For me to do otherwise would contravene the Asimov Laws."

Gilkrensky looked down at the machine. Minerva was the key to almost every step in saving Maria, from the calculation of the hologram settings that would allow him to manipulate the temporal displacement, to the control of the hologram itself, everything rested with the computer. It could destroy his plans in a million subtle ways that he would never be able to detect.

And now it seemed to have its own agenda. How could he trust it anymore?

"Jess! I need to speak to you for a moment . . . alone."

She was hunched over a large sheet of paper, listing all the major points of their forthcoming discussion with Mawashi-Saito. Donald Price sat close beside her, very close. The rest of the boardroom table was littered with books and legal documents.

"Good morning, Theo," Price said. "We need to go over these arguments one more time with you. We have less than an hour. Fancy breakfast?"

He picked a covered tray from a side table, laid it in front of Gilkrensky and lifted the cloth. There was a steaming bowl of meso soup, cold fish, seaweed and a raw egg staring up from a delicate china dish.

"It's OK," Gilkrensky said, feeling his stomach turn. "I'll make do with the coffee."

"You'd better let Don and I do the talking at this meeting, Theo," Jessica said. "Remember what happened in Dublin last time, when you upset Kojima. It's important that we present a united front—"

171

"Which is?"

"After we exchange the traditional pleasantries with the Japanese," Price said, "I suggest we ask them to outline their proposals first. Then let me do the talking. I'll confer with you right away if there are any contentious issues, just as Kojima will with his superiors. After that, we can open the discussions on the Minerva collaboration. The aim of today's meeting is merely to explore possibilities. That's all. If we antagonise the other side at this stage, we could be put back by six months."

"I need to speak to Jessica, Don, alone."

She looked up at him. Her eyes were cold.

"If it's about last night and the SQUID, Theo. Crowe has taken care of that for the time being. Right now we need to focus on this meeting."

"It's not about last night. It's something else."

"Can't it wait?"

"No. It has to be now."

"Then it had better be quick."

Jessica glanced at Price. Gilkrensky saw a look pass between them. They had already been together. Telling her what he had to say wouldn't be easy.

She followed him out into the lobby and over to the far window.

"What is it then?" she said, looking at her watch. "The car will be here for us soon."

"It's about Price?"

"What's the matter? Has Crowe been telling tales? Are you jealous?"

"No. But you need to know that he's not what he appears."

She crossed her arms on her chest.

"What do you mean?"

"He's under investigation by one of the biggest detective agencies in the world. Someone wants to know everything there is to know about him."

"And is that a crime?"

"No, but surely you must—"

"And how do you know this, Theo?"

"I had Crowe make enquiries."

"Why?"

"Because . . . because I don't know the man and I have to be in a position to trust him when we go up against the Japanese. Because . . ."

His voice trailed away.

"Because what?"

"Because I don't want you hurt again."

Her face hardened.

"How *dare* you, Theo?" she said slowly. "How dare you creep out of here last night without telling me where you were going? How dare you tell such lies about that SQUID you stole from the Americans and then have the nerve to have Don investigated like that?"

"I did it because I still care about you."

"Do you, Theo? Do you really? If you really cared about me, you'd ask how my father is, or how I feel about being out here working for you when he's sick in hospital."

"Look, Jess. I know the sort of strain you're under with this, but—"

"Just what is it that you care about these days, Theo? I used to think that all you cared about was that machine in there and the ghost of your wife. You made that very clear. But since that SQUID turned up here last night, I just don't know anymore. There was a time when you trusted me with everything there was to know about you. But all I know now is that we have to get through this bloody meeting, and that is what I intend to do."

"All right then, have it your way, but be careful."

"Fuck you, Theo. Let's just get this over with and get back to London. Then you can sell your shares and get the hell out of my life!"

Gilkrensky sat back in the soft upholstery of the limousine, watching the street as they pulled away from the hotel and swept through the traffic towards Hibaya Park. The worst of the rush-hour had died away, and in a few minutes they were out of the concrete canyons of modern Tokyo, driving along the deep, grass-lined moat surrounding the Imperial Palace. A white crane, stark and graceful against the trees, flapped slowly into the air.

Who could he trust? Crowe was suspicious of him. Jessica hated him. Price was a potentially dangerous unknown. Even the Minerva had lied to him. Yet, here he was, heading into a meeting where he was about to risk

173

everything on the word of Gichin Funakoshi, a man who until recently had been his deadliest rival.

His world had turned upside down!

The car turned left onto Shinjuku-dori Avenue, giving it a clear run to the Mawashi-Saito building. On either side of them, the office-blocks grew taller and more modern—stark monoliths of concrete, stone and steel—soaring into the sky. He saw wide pavements, neat hedges and finely clipped trees. They passed a park with wide, open spaces, a waterfall, and groups of down-and-outs in T-shirts and baseball caps drying their clothes on the bushes. Against the towering skyscrapers, the walkways and the shining steel sculptures of Shinjuku, they looked completely out of place.

Framed between the skyscrapers at the end of the street was a pure white tower of stone and glass, tapering in graceful curves from a wide base into a narrow wedge forty-two stories high.

"There," said the driver, leaning back in his seat. "That's Mawashi-Saito."

Gilkrensky glanced at the salarymen, cleaners and drop-outs on the pavements outside as the limousine slowed onto an approach ramp and dipped into the dim coolness of an underground car park. He remembered the microphones Crowe had found in their suite.

Any one of these people could be watching us, he thought.

23

THE WATCHERS

Hiroshi Tanaka stood outside Tocho-mae subway station and gazed up at the towering skyscrapers at the very heart of Corporate Japan, at the very heart of the System. The glass mountains of the Shinjuku Park and Landmark Towers soared above him. The stark white lattice of stone around the Sumimoto Building shone bright enough to dazzle his eyes, and the fabulous twin observatories of the Tokyo Metropolitan Government headquarters seemed to scratch the sky.

How could a man, any man, ever hope to save his spirit from such monsters? Once he was sucked inside the System and chained to a desk, what hope was there for individual freedom, love or art? As Yukio Mishima, he had shown the way to salvation through the ultimate statement any man can make through the holy act of suicide. Today, as Hiroshi Tanaka, he would make that statement again.

It would be beautiful. It would be poetry.

He lowered his eyes to ground level. From the subway behind him, men in dark suits poured out into the light. The face of the little girl in the train still haunted him. This time there would be no shame, no killing of the innocent, and no reason to shy away from what had to be done.

He was dressed in the uniform of the salaryman. In his lapel was a metal pin bearing the Mawashi-Saito logo, in his left hand was a black briefcase and in his right was a cell phone. He turned it in his hand and marvelled. It was a perfect copy of the latest Mawashi-Saito model—realistic enough to pass even a detailed inspection—but with a signal that had been boosted, scrambled and networked to communicate only with five other units already converging on the Mawashi-Saito building across the square. Even in the electronic Babel of downtown Tokyo, their transmissions were strong and secure, open only to someone with an identically coded cell phone of their own.

He entered the four-digit PIN code, lifted the device to his right ear and said,

"I'm in place opposite the entrance. There is no sign of Gilkrensky yet."

"He's on his way," said a voice. "The others are in position. Please proceed inside."

"Very well," Tanaka said and walked across the square, to the tree-lined access ramp and the Mawashi-Saito building. He smiled as he passed the long umbrella-stand next to the hallway, noted the heavy metal security screens folded in place above his head, and bowed to the concierge. Then the automatic doors hissed open, and he stepped inside a vast man-made cavern, fifteen stories high. In front of him, at ground level, was a maze of shops and restaurants bearing famous names like Point du Jour, Rosa Bella Boutique, Isetan and Sukiyaki Iseju. There was Book and Variety, Noritake Goto Trading Co Ltd and a host of Mawashi-Saito outlets for everything from electronics to sportswear. To his left was the reception desk of a well-known hotel chain with a contoured metal map of the world behind it, showing the time in any one of a dozen capital cities around the globe. Even though he had spent weeks memorising the blueprints and floor plans of the building, and made a dozen visits to reconnoitre Mawashi-Saito, Hiroshi Tanaka was still in awe of the sheer scale of this gigantic cathedral to the holy religion of the System.

He stood still for a moment, taking in the chatter of shoppers, the aroma of expensive perfumes, and the tinkle of canned music. To his left and right were escalators and elevators to the upper levels, each manned by men and women in grey Mawashi-Saito uniforms. He followed the line of an escalator upwards. Rising above him on either side were gallery after gallery of shops, restaurants and clubs: *Members Club Majico, Moonchild, Tempura Restaurant, Indian Restaurant, Mawashi Sports International*, and dozens more. He saw the people milling around the lifts, parading up and down the escalators and wandering along the galleries. It was a colossal hive of humanity. Thousands and thousands of people, each with their own direction and destiny, each oblivious of what he was about to do.

He raised the cell phone and spoke again.

"Unit Two?"

Ten metres below his feet, in the underground delivery bay for the upper levels of shops, a man in a baseball cap and Mawashi Sports International overalls was off-loading golf bags, clubs and boxes of golf balls from a Toyota van onto a green metal trolley. Anyone watching the ease with which he handled the bags would have labelled him as a potential athlete—a body-builder perhaps, or a shot-putter.

A cell phone warbled. The man put down the last of the golf bags, undid the top pocket of his overalls and answered the call.

"Unit Two in place," he said. "The equipment is unloaded."

Then he locked the van and pushed the heavily laden trolley towards the goods elevator.

"Unit Three?" said Tanaka.

Far above his head a small serious man with thick pebble-glasses was pushing a cart loaded down with computer equipment. It was destined for one of the rented offices on the sixteenth floor, directly above the shopping plaza. He slipped his cell phone from a pouch on his belt, raised it to his ear and acknowledged the call.

Tanaka keyed in another number. "Unit Four?"

A woman pushing a stainless steel cart of fresh refrigerated seafood stopped at a service elevator on the upper floors of the building to answer his call. She wore the pristine white coat and hair-cap of one of the exclusive sushi restaurants on the seventh floor balcony and over her mouth, to protect her customers and the food from any contamination, she wore a white cotton mask.

"Unit Four in position," she said.

"Unit Five?"

On the fifteenth-floor balcony overlooking the entire height of the shopping mall, two young executives were having an early-morning coffee. One of them snatched the phone from the centre of the table as it rang.

"Unit Five here. We are in position."

"Very good," Tanaka said. "Report in when you are all ready for the next phase. Then wait for my signal."

In an office on the forty-fourth floor of the northern tower of Tokyo Metropolitan Government building number one, overlooking the Citizen's Plaza, Dick Barnett pressed the "stop" button on a digital recorder and waited for his audience to digest what they'd just heard.

"That was recorded from Gilkrensky's suite last night," he said at last. "It's the latest piece of evidence that Gilkrensky pirated our SQUID design and built a prototype of his own."

Behind him in the room, two other men crouched behind the big disc of a parabolic microphone aimed at the top floor of the Mawashi-Saito building across the square. A woman in her late twenties was operating a powerful radio set beside him and, in front of him at the table, sat a small delegation from the Japanese Secret Service.

"As it is," continued Barnett. "We have more than enough to hang Dr Gilkrensky. Look at this."

He upended a brown envelope onto the desk, tipping out the contents with the rattle of plastic and metal. A torn piece of paper fluttered out.

"What is it?" said the senior Japanese security man.

"The bits that look like plastic are fragments of carbon-fibre," Barnett said. "Very light and strong—useful in making helmets for instance."

"And the metal?"

"That's the clincher. They're fragments of the bi-metal superconductor joints that are unique to a SQUID headset."

The man reached forward and turned over the piece of paper, a torn fragment from an adhesive label. The name *Louvaine Electronique* was clearly legible in the top right-hand corner, as were the word *Urgent* and the name typed below it—

Dr Theodore Gilkrensky.

"This evidence proves beyond doubt that Gilkrensky is guilty of espionage against the United States of America," Barnett said. "Therefore I'm officially requesting you to proceed with the eavesdrop on the Mawashi-Saito boardroom, to gather as much additional evidence as you can, and to make preparations for Gilkrensky's arrest as soon as he leaves the building. Are your people in position?"

"They are," said the Japanese official. "And they have all been fully briefed."

"Good," Barnett said, nodding slowly. "We can't afford any mistakes on this one."

A pretty office lady in a Mawashi-Saito uniform bowed low as Gilkrensky stepped out of the limousine onto the red carpet that stretched across the reserved area of the underground car park.

"*Konichi-wa*, Dr Gilkrensky, and welcome to Mawashi-Saito."

"Ah . . . *konichi-wa*," he replied and bowed, racking his brain for the phrases that Price had tried to teach him.

"That's OK, Theo," Price said, and began speaking to the woman in rapid Japanese. She smiled, bowed again and gestured along the red carpet to the open door of an elevator. Another office lady was waiting there, along with a uniformed security guard.

The elevator doors closed behind them and the office lady spoke a command in Japanese. There was a tinkling electronic tone, the command was repeated back to her from a hidden speaker and the elevator started to rise. Gilkrensky felt his stomach churn. He reached out for the wall of the car—and suddenly they were shooting up through the roof of the underground car park, through a neat grove of planted trees and into the open air.

At first Gilkrensky thought they must be outside the building but, as he stared through the glass walls, he saw they were rising through a vast shopping mall, with tiers of brightly lit balconies and shops all around them, swarming with people.

"It's very impressive," he said.

"Thank you, Doctor," said the office lady proudly. "This building contains the largest indoor shopping area in Tokyo, with three hundred and five retail outlets. Above the shopping area are twelve floors of rented office accommodation and, on the upper fifteen floors, the corporate headquarters of Mawashi-Saito itself."

"Incredible, isn't it, Jess?" Gilkrensky said, trying to make contact with her.

"I was here before, when Funakoshi summoned one of us to tell us his demands on gaining a seat on our Board. Remember?"

"Yes, of course." He turned to the Japanese lady again, as the express elevator reached the roof of the great plaza and plunged upwards into darkness. "Is there any other way out of this building if these lifts fail?"

"They will not fail, Doctor. Why? Does altitude disturb you?"

"No," said Gilkrensky. "It's just that I had a bad experience with a tall building in Florida recently."

A bar of electronic music sounded. A voice from above their heads made an announcement in Japanese.

"We are nearing the executive suite now," said the woman. "That was the voice of the central computer."

"There, Theo," Jessica said. "You should find a lot in common with the Japanese. They talk to their computers too." A soft tone sounded, the elevator stopped and the doors hissed open. The Mawashi-Saito lady bowed them out into the reception area of the forty-second floor.

After the close confines of the elevator, Gilkrensky felt he was suddenly standing in the sky. Above his head, a great glass dome soared upwards. At either end of the grey carpeted hallway, full-length windows looked out over the city.

He stepped to the nearest view, looked down and suddenly reached for a handrail. Hundreds of metres below his feet, an endless mosaic of buildings stretched into the mists on the landward side and to the shores of Tokyo Bay on the other. Every kind of structure imaginable was scattered beneath him like rocks and pebbles on a vast Zen garden; low houses with tiled roofs, flat roofs of prefabricated sheet metal, roof gardens, swimming-pools and massive extractor fans blowing steam from the air-conditioning systems of the great offices nearby.

And between the buildings, Gilkrensky saw the coloured beetles of cars buzzing on the overpasses and carriageways, the tiny ants of people walking on the pavements. His head spun. Was it his hangover, the pressure of the meeting to come, or was it just the sheer distance to the street below that was getting to him?

"I must apologise, Dr Gilkrensky. Today the weather is not fine enough for you to enjoy the view of Mount Fuji."

Standing in a group next to a large double door was a delegation of Japanese. A tall man with thick glasses and slicked-back steely hair bowed and presented his business card from a small leather case.

"Welcome to Tokyo, Dr Gilkrensky," he said. "My name is Kiyoshi Sakamoto and I am the Chief Executive of Mawashi-Saito. This is Kazue Kojima, our senior legal representative. I believe you have spoken before by teleconference."

As Gilkrensky took the card he felt Price move past him to face Sakamoto and Kojima. "And my name is Donald Price," he said. "I am Dr Gilkrensky's senior legal advisor for this meeting."

Sakamoto glanced at Gilkrensky, bowed, and then presented another card to Price, who accepted it, taking a moment to examine the card carefully, before presenting one of his own. Then he turned and whispered, "Better let me do the talking, Theo. At least until we find our feet."

Gilkrensky nodded, feeling Jessica's eyes on him. There were more formal introductions, and then Gilkrensky's party was shown into the boardroom. It was as spectacular as the reception area, with two glass walls giving breathtaking views of the city, the mountains and the sea. Across the thick-piled carpet, the sweep of the polished boardroom table led his eye to a single watercolour hanging on the wall over the seat of honour furthest from the door.

"It's an original painting by the Japanese 'Sword Saint' Musashi," Jessica whispered. "Funakoshi made a great show of it, the last time I was here."

"I am honoured you remember, Miss Wright," said a voice. "For me, that was a long time ago."

Gichin Funakoshi stood by the door to the President's office and bowed politely. Gilkrensky glimpsed a beautiful Japanese sword on a stand over the desk beyond. It was the match for the *wakizashi* Yukiko had tried and kill him with in Cairo—the short sword he had taken from her and hammered into their own boardroom table in London—only to have it stolen back again. He thought of Yukiko's determination, her madness, and how close he had come to death at her hands. He also recognised the man at Funakoshi's side.

"May I introduce you to my colleague Mr Taisen Nakamura, our former Assistant Manager of Industrial Intelligence," Funakoshi said. "He will be assisting us today in case any evidence is required concerning the events last Christmas."

Nakamura spoke rapidly in Japanese and bowed again.

"He says he is delighted to see you," Funakoshi said. "He does not think you have met before."

"He is correct," Gilkrensky said and took his seat at the table with Jessica, Price and Crowe, facing the windows with their panoramic view of the city.

Chairs scuffed on the carpet as the Japanese delegation: Sakamoto, Kojima, Funakoshi, Nakamura and several men from the Japanese Ministry of International Trade and Industry sat down opposite them. Tea and coffee were served, and for a few minutes there was informal chit-chat about the weather, the length of the flight to Tokyo and the traffic around the Ginza.

"Very well," Kazue Kojima said at last. "On behalf of Mawashi-Saito, I would like to formally welcome Dr Gilkrensky and his party to our offices, and to say we appreciate his decision to join us in searching for a mutually acceptable way forward in this matter, as suggested by Mr Price and the other GRC shareholders. I am sure my own Board joins me in the hope that we can have a fruitful discussion and overcome the unpleasantness of the last few months."

"Thank you, Kojima-san," Price said. "Perhaps you could begin by describing Mawashi-Saito's aspirations for today's meeting . . ."

Across the Citizen's Plaza, in the Tokyo Metropolitan Government Building, Dick Barnett lowered the headphones. The reception from the parabolic microphone was perfect, even against the wind and the noise of the traffic below. You had to hand it to the Japanese. They certainly knew how to make things that worked. He nodded to the soundman.

"We're getting it loud and clear," he said. "Tell the team to move into position."

Seventeen floors below him, in the Mawashi-Saito building, Hiroshi Tanaka looked at his watch and raised his mobile phone.

"They are all in place in the Mawashi-Saito boardroom," he said. "Go to Phase One!"

24

OPENING SHOTS

The manager of the exclusive sports store on the top floor of the shopping plaza was trying to tell a large and sadly ignorant delivery man that he had most definitely not ordered a consignment of golfing equipment, when two potential customers walked into his shop from the café next door. They were business executives, fit and obviously well-to-do, just the sort of high-end customers he liked to see, particularly so early in the day when business was notoriously slow.

"Please wait here," he told the delivery man and turned to greet the new arrivals. They were admiring the breathtaking display of Italian hang-gliding equipment that stretched across the whole ceiling of the shop. The manager was very proud of it. It showed off the new Icaro carbon-fibre gliders at their very best, frozen in flight opposite the panoramic picture window that stretched the length of the shop.

But as he approached them, they stepped back towards the door. The manager hoped that his approach had not startled them. It would do no good to scare customers like these away. The manager moved forward.

"*Konichi-wa,*" he said with a polite bow. "May I be of service—?"

The callused edge of the delivery man's right hand connected with his neck, just above the carotid artery, and the manager collapsed like a rag-doll. The two executives each pulled a gun from their briefcases, and levelled them at the remaining sales staff as the delivery man rushed past them, and turned the sign on the shop door to Closed.

When this was done, the delivery man helped the executives bundle the unconscious manager and his frightened staff behind the sales desk out of sight, and bound them with industrial tape, making sure to secure their mouths. Then the three of them turned to the trolley of golfing equipment, ripped open the boxes and slid the contents of the golf bags onto the floor.

In less than two minutes, each of them was decked out in the dark green uniform of the Japanese riot police and armed with a Russian Kalashnikov AK-74 assault rifle. The delivery man lifted his cell phone to his ear.

"Units Two and Five. Phase One complete," he said.

"Very well," Tanaka said. "Await my signal for Phase Two."

In a locked office on the sixteenth floor, Ikou Baruma—the man with pebble-glasses—was carefully making the final connections between a powerful desktop computer and the shared access wall terminal of the Mawashi-Saito building. Next to the desk on which his computer stood, leant another AK-74 assault rifle with a full clip of ammunition. Baruma was taking no chances. To him, the whole success of the operation rested on his own shoulders, and he would rather die than fail.

When the last screw was tightened and every cable checked, he powered up the computer, worked for a few minutes at the keyboard until he had located the Mawashi-Saito web page and then clicked on a customised icon on his screen. For a moment he held his breath while the specially designed "sniffer file" did its work on the corporation's security firewalls. Then, using the codes and PIN numbers he had been given, he started to worm his way towards the Mawashi-Saito mainframe, which would give him access to every computerised system in the building.

"Unit Three. Phase One underway!" he said into his mobile phone.

"Well done!" Tanaka replied. "Await my instructions for Phase Two."

In the kitchens serving the corporate headquarters of Mawashi-Saito, a young woman in a white coat, cap and *masko* was delivering a stainless-steel trolley of food. She spoke briefly to the head chef and was directed to the main preparation area, where other men and women were laying out delicacies for the VIP meeting in the boardroom upstairs. She carefully lifted a tray of raw fish sculptures from her trolley and laid it on the worktop, along with a selection of delicate china bowls bearing sauces and dips.

When this was done, she shut the lid of the trolley and carefully navigated it through the busy kitchen to one of the storerooms, next to the service elevator leading to the upper floors. She checked that nobody was inside and went in, locking the door behind her.

Once hidden from view, she slipped off her cotton cap and coat, revealing the dove-grey Mawashi-Saito office uniform beneath. Then she donned a pair of thick-framed glasses and pulled a briefcase from the bottom compartment of her refrigerated trolley. Finally, she checked that her *masko* was still covering her mouth and nose, and that her company identification badge was in place correctly with the name outwards.

"Unit Four here," she said into her cell phone. "Phase One complete. I'm moving to the elevator."

"Good," Tanaka said. "Everyone is in place. We are ready for Phase Two."

"Our understanding," Kazue Kojima said. "was that this meeting was to explore mutually satisfactory ways of co-operating on the Minerva project, not to engage in blame for what happened last December. In this regard Mr Price, the attitude of your Chairman has been far from helpful."

"I apologise," Gilkrensky said, before Price could speak. "My problem is that the version of events Mawashi-Saito describe is not my experience of what actually happened."

The Japanese conferred rapidly on the other side of the table. Heads shook. There was a sucking of teeth.

"Are you implying that we are not telling the truth?" Kojima said bluntly.

Gilkrensky was about to speak again when Price turned towards him.

"Theo!" he hissed. "What's the matter? I thought we agreed that I'd do the talking at this meeting. Jess and I had a strategy all worked out, why are you throwing it back in our faces?"

Gilkrensky ignored him.

"I mean no insult, Kojima-san," he said diplomatically. "But I feel it's my duty, in order to establish mutual respect, to point out that my interpretation of what happened last December—indeed the verifiable facts of what took place—are completely at odds with those of Mawashi-Saito. Once we can agree on that, then we can move on."

He glanced to his right, where Jessica was shaking her head.

"If this is some bright idea you dreamt up last night when you were drunk, Theo, I don't think much of it," she whispered. "The least you could have done was to warn us in advance."

Kojima conferred with his superiors again.

"You would concede, however," he said at last, "that you did put pressure on Mr Funakoshi and our board of directors to hand over its legally acquired shares in GRC in return for freeing us of the advanced computer virus you created and introduced into our system."

"Not entirely," Gilkrensky said. "While that statement concurs with *some* of the established facts, I cannot accept your version of how the virus came to be in the Mawashi-Saito mainframe in the first place."

There was more conferring on the Japanese side.

"We understand your position," Kojima replied. "Nevertheless, our legal opinion supports the case that those shares were extorted by you from our board under duress, and were therefore obtained illegally—"

"Which is exactly how the virus came to be in your system," Gilkrensky said. "It was stolen, along with the rest of the Minerva software package, when it was illegally downloaded to Mawashi-Saito by Tony Delgado, a man who had been blackmailed into working on your behalf."

Jessica glared at him.

"Careful, Theo," muttered Price. "Let's not go completely ballistic at this stage, eh?"

"Thank you, Mr Price," Kojima said, and turned to smile at the other members of his own delegation. "This Tony Delgado you refer to, Dr Gilkrensky, was he not a very senior and trusted executive in GRC?"

"He was."

"And was he also in a . . . a close personal relationship with your Miss Wright at the time? Hardly the usual profile of a Japanese industrial spy, surely?"

There was a ripple of laughter from the Mawashi-Saito side.

"Nevertheless, that is what he was," Gilkrensky said. "And if you want proof, then we have a witness."

"As I understand it," Kojima said, "even according to your own version of events, the only other person in the room at the time was unconscious. How can he tell us what happened?"

Gilkrensky saw Crowe shake his head. Price was preparing to step in again and argue the case. Gilkrensky turned towards Funakoshi and Nakamura. It was now or never.

"I'm talking about Minerva," he said.

For a moment there was silence in the boardroom. Then Kojima turned and conferred with his team in rapid Japanese. When he turned back, his smile was wider than ever.

"Ah, the famous Minerva computer, the device that started all this trouble in the first place. Are you suggesting that it can be called as a witness in your defence?"

"Why don't you ask it yourself? I have it here with me," Gilkrensky said and lifted the Minerva onto the table.

Kojima was suddenly serious. "Dr Gilkrensky, I would be an irresponsible fool, and a liability to my employers, if I was even to consider allowing a machine—which was created and programmed by you—to present evidence against us."

The statement hung in the air. There was the soft chirrup of a mobile phone.

"I'm sorry," Crowe said. "That's mine. Excuse me." He got up from his seat near the door and walked out into the reception area.

"If I might speak, Kojima-san?" Funakoshi said. "Are we not here today to recover our shares, resume our place on the GRC Board and explore the options of a joint venture to commercialise Minerva."

"We are, Funakoshi-san," Kojima said. "But, with respect, how is that an argument to call the machine as a witness?"

"In the first place, I'm sure it would be useful for our legal advisors, and our colleagues in the Ministry of International Trade and Industry, to see what evidence Dr Gilkrensky plans to use against us," Funakoshi said. "I agree that no machine built by him could ever be expected to give evidence that was not in his favour, and I'm sure no judge would accept it. But if we are to explore the possibility of a joint venture to manufacture and sell Minerva, then it would be useful to see it in action, *neh*?"

Heads nodded around him. Kojima leant over and conferred with the delegates from the Ministry of International Trade and Industry. They nodded too.

"I am reminded, however," Kojima said, "of the chaos that followed the last time a Minerva-generated computer virus infected our systems. If we allow that machine to demonstrate its evidence here today, what guarantees do we have that Dr Gilkrensky will not repeat his last attack and blackmail us all over again?"

"That is your decision," Funakoshi said, "although it would hardly be in Dr Gilkrensky's interests to re-infect our computer, in front of so many distinguished witnesses from the Ministry of International Trade and Industry, when he could have done it in secret over the Internet. Besides, my colleague Nakamura-san, who has honourably shared the responsibility for the last security breach with me and resigned his position in head office, tells me that our firewalls have been completely rebuilt since the last attack."

Kojima consulted with Sakamoto, who in turn spoke to Funakoshi and Nakamura in Japanese, and then nodded back.

"Very well then, Dr Gilkrensky," Kojima said. "You may connect Minerva to the main plasma screen so that we can all see its responses to my questions. It will be its first 'sales demonstration' to us, so to speak. Let's see what it can do."

Outside in the reception area, Major Crowe stood in a corner near the window with his mobile phone pressed tightly to his ear.

"Are you sure that information is reliable?" he said.

The voice from Vancouver was certain.

"No doubt about it. It all checks out."

"And the other company who are investigating him?"

"They'll probably have even more dirt than I do. Like I said, mine was a rush job. They've had more time, more people and more money."

"But you're sure."

"I'd bet my life on it. I can email you the results and contact numbers so you can verify it for yourself, but I don't want to mention names over the phone, in case someone else is listening."

"I'm in a meeting right now," Crowe said. "Send the stuff to my personal email address under encryption and I'll call you back when I've read it."

"You got it. But like I said, don't trust him an inch."

"I won't."

Crowe ended the call. Then he stood for a moment, staring out over the rooftops of Tokyo. The meeting was in full swing. Gilkrensky was about to make his play for the Kasawara Research facility. To tell him what he'd found out now could bring the meeting to a grinding halt and jeopardise any hope Gilkrensky had of making the computer connection he needed.

Crowe would have to take Price out of the meeting and confront him on his own.

In the rented office on the sixteenth floor, Ikuo Baruma stared helplessly at his computer screen and chewed at his thumbnail. In spite of all the briefings, the training and his state-of-the-art equipment, he found himself stalled at the very gate of the Mawashi-Saito mainframe by a final firewall that doggedly denied him access. If his PIN number and user identification failed one more time, the system would alert Mawashi-Saito security personnel, identify his location and raise the alarm.

The whole plan, the whole team, their whole future was resting on him . . . and he was lost! His hands shook as he opened his cell phone.

"Unit Five!" he stammered. "I have a problem!"

"What is it?" Tanaka's voice sounded tense. He would know that if they could not control the Mawashi-Saito central computer, then everything would abort—right now!

Baruma took a deep breath.

"I cannot access the mainframe!" he said.

25

THE TRIAL

Gilkrensky took the cable connector offered to him by Nakamura. The old man's eyes gave nothing away. He simply bowed slightly, went to the door of the boardroom and slipped out into the reception area. Gilkrensky turned the Minerva and fitted the connector into the data port. Behind him, a large plasma screen lowered itself from the ceiling. Blinds slid down, covering the wall-length windows and cutting out the light. Price and Jessica moved to one side to allow the Japanese a clear view of the screen.

The door to the reception area opened and Nakamura returned, followed by Crowe. Gilkrensky saw Crowe lean over Price's shoulder and whisper to him. Price frowned. Then he excused himself and followed Crowe out of the room. What was going on? Had Crowe finally discovered something? Was he warning Price off?

Gilkrensky glanced at Nakamura, who had resumed his seat next to Funakoshi. Was that the ghost of a nod? Had the firewalls come down? Did he have access?

Kazuo Kojima tapped the table impatiently.

"Are you ready to proceed, Dr Gilkrensky?"

"I am, Kojima-san. I'm sorry for the delay."

He lifted the lid of the Minerva. Behind him, the plasma screen flickered for a moment showing a dark-blue background. Then there was Maria's face, looking down on them all.

"Minerva? Have you heard and understood the proceedings so far?"

"I have, Theo, and I am ready to answer any questions Mr Kojima or his colleagues from Mawashi-Saito and MITI might have concerning the incident involving Mr Delgado."

"And are your connections to the screen adequate?" he said, using the phrase they had agreed as a signal to initiate the link with Kasawara Research.

"They are." The virtual eyes gave nothing away.

"Then you may proceed."

In the top right-hand corner of the Minerva's own screen, facing Gilkrensky from the table, but hidden from the plasma screen behind him, a small window appeared. He glanced at Funakoshi and Nakamura. They were as impassive as the machine.

The window began to scroll a list of commands and results as Minerva started its exploration of the Mawashi-Saito and Kasawara mainframes using the PIN codes and passwords Nakamura had given it the night before in Atami:

Seeking host link.
Link established.
Input user name.
Input domain system.
Input password.
Password validated.
Firewalls lowered.
Please input data requirements . . .

Gilkrensky felt the hairs on the back of his neck rise. Would anyone detect what his machine was doing? Could anyone in the room notice the window on the Minerva screen or the tension in his voice? Could Minerva gain access to Kasawara Research as Funakoshi and Nakamura had promised?

He glanced across the table at Kojima. The man was turning to his colleagues and pointing up at the image of the beautiful woman on the wall-screen. He made a joke of straightening his tie and smoothing back his hair.

"How shall I address you, my dear?" he said.

In a valley between the mountains to the north-west of Tokyo, at the laboratories of Kasawara Research on the outskirts of the town of Isesaki, a complex simulation on the performance of a new high-speed train was underway. In the main computing hall, row upon row of work stations, each tasked with a specific module of the project, faced a vast wall-screen on which the pooled results were displayed.

Today's simulation involved the performance of the train's suspension system under varying loads and conditions. On the screen, a vast three-dimensional image of the train, moving at almost two hundred miles an hour through a computer generated landscape, dominated the room.

The supervisor was pleased. His team were already three days ahead of schedule. He smiled out across the room as he called out the next round of tests.

An operator at one of the work stations in the first row put up his hand.

"Has your system crashed?" asked the supervisor. "I thought you told me we had plenty of computer space."

The person running the calculation, a young post-graduate student from the university at Nagoya, felt himself turning red with shame. This was the first time he had ever been allowed near one of the main research computers and now it had frozen in front of his eyes. Had he let the team down? Had he destroyed the research data he had spent months collecting in the metallurgical laboratory? Would his sponsors withdraw his funding?

"I . . . I don't know, *sensei*," he stammered. "It should have worked perfectly."

"Check it again," the senior man said. "I will ask one of the programmers to assist you." Then he looked up. All around him in the great computer hall, screens were freezing in front of his eyes. Operators were rising from their consoles. An excited chatter rose in the hall, shattering the businesslike calm of the facility. Operators pointed to the wall-screen behind the supervisor's head.

"What is it?" snapped the supervisor. Then he turned.

On the wall behind him was a huge map of the earth, covered in five-sided shapes that moved and changed as he watched. The image zoomed in on the north-east Atlantic . . . to the east coast of Ireland . . . and a deep

193

green valley. He saw a tall mountain, a lake and a low knoll surrounded by trees next to a farmhouse.

"Is this some kind of a joke?" he shouted. "Call security!"

Nobody moved. As they watched, the pure and perfect shape of a virtual pyramid rose above the three-dimensional model of the knoll. Mathematical symbols rushed down each side of the screen beside the image as computer after computer turned itself over to a uniquely complex calculation on the quantum physics of time.

In a rented office on the sixteenth floor of the Mawashi-Saito building in Tokyo, Ikuo Baruma laughed out loud. His prayers had been answered. It was a gift from the gods.

"The firewall is down," he shouted into his cell phone. "We're in!"

"Are you sure?" asked Tanaka.

"Yes! I can see all the networks you described: floor plans, security, communications, everything!"

"Good. Then you know what to do."

"Of course!"

Baruma's life had been spared. There was nothing he could not accomplish now, no obstacle that could stand in his way.

"All units, proceed to Phase Three," Tanaka said.

"Minerva?" Kojima asked pleasantly. "Could you please tell us who you are?"

"I am a sentient electronic entity, the intelligent agent interface program of the Minerva 3,000 computer."

"And how long have you been in existence?"

"I was initiated at nineteen thirty-five, Central European Time, on the twenty-second of May last year."

"But the hardware of Dr Gilkrensky's Minerva computer had been in existence some time before that?"

"It had. But while the primary neural net of the bio-chip prototype Mr Delgado destroyed was on line since the twenty-ninth of March, the original

Minerva software it contained was not sufficiently sophisticated to allow for full artificial intelligence."

"But your software is?"

"Yes. Dr Gilkrensky designed my upgrade to be self-learning. It modifies itself as my own experience and capabilities grow—just as the new synthetic master chips of my hardware form memory links and synapses similar to those in the human brain. Following my initiation in May, I became self-aware last December, during our field trip to Cairo. I know who I am, Mr Kojima. And you can call me 'Maria'."

Gilkrensky saw nods of approval from the other members of the Japanese delegation. The men from MITI were taking notes.

"We have nothing this advanced in Japan," Sakamoto said.

"There's nothing like me anywhere in the world," the Minerva said with more than a trace of pride. "I'm unique."

"Obviously," Kojima said. "But perhaps we could move on to the events at GRC London last Christmas. You—or should I say your software—had been installed in the first Minerva computer before Mr Delgado downloaded you to Tokyo, is that correct?"

"It is."

"And therefore, you were present in London when those events took place. You have records?"

"Certainly. Would you like to see them?"

"Very much."

Maria's image retreated to a small window in the left-hand corner of the plasma screen. The vacant space was filled with a video picture of a good-looking young man with dark slicked-back hair. He was wearing a business suit and holding a pistol to the head of someone lying unconscious on a couch. Numbers indicating the date and time of the recording appeared at the bottom of the screen. The man with the gun turned to face the camera. He was excited. The sweat on his face glistened in the overhead lights.

"Then calculate this," he said. "Either you download your complete software to the email address I will give you, or I will shoot Major Crowe and he will die. Do you understand that?"

Gilkrensky glanced at the window on his Minerva screen showing the progress of the Kasawara calculation.

Spatial temporal calculation in progress, it said. *Accessing additional capacity. Two minutes remaining.*

He looked up. Heads were shaking amongst the Japanese delegation. They conferred with Sakamoto.

"What exactly are we being shown here, Dr Gilkrensky?" he said.

"It's a digital recording of the view from the internal camera on the original Minerva," said Maria's image from the corner of the plasma screen. "All forms of data obtained, since the powering up of the original machine in March of last year are stored in digital format on my hard drive. This is a replay of events as they happened."

"Which, I think, proves my point," Gilkrensky said. "Tony Delgado presented Minerva with a direct imperative under the Asimov Laws by which it is programmed. He effectively asked it to choose between sending its entire memory to Mawashi-Saito and allowing Major Crowe to be killed. Since Asimov Laws place the ultimate priority on human safety, the computer had no choice. It was, effectively, blackmailed."

In the main computer hall at Kasawara Research, programmers, computer operators and security guards alike stared helplessly at the main wall-screen, mesmerised by the display.

"Can nobody shut this down?" shouted the supervisor.

"We're locked out of our own systems, *sensei*," said the senior operator. "All the keyboards are dead."

"Can we turn off the power?"

"We'll lose all our own data on the high-speed train. The cost would be enormous."

On the screen, the scrolling columns of figures had ceased and a simulation was in progress. In the top right-hand corner of the image, above the giant pyramid in that distant valley, a digital clock was ticking down towards zero.

"Is it a bomb," hissed the supervisor, "a doomsday virus?"

Computer-generated clouds formed around the pyramid. Virtual lightning streaked across the digital sky. There was a clap of thunder as the pyramid glowed with an unearthly orange fire. Then, as the countdown reached zero, the brilliant disc of the sun burst over a hilltop beyond the valley, shining a beam of light down onto the knoll. There was a flash. Everyone in the room gasped . . . and the images faded.

Staring down at them from the wall-screen were the words: *Calculation complete.*

"That is hardly conclusive proof," snapped Kojima, frowning up at the frozen image of Tony Delgado on the Mawashi-Saito plasma screen. "Digital images can be altered, doctored or created artificially from scratch. After all, we are already speaking to an artificially created image of your late wife! Surely, your computer could manufacture these pictures of the late Mr Delgado just as easily?"

"These are first generation recorded digital images," said the Minerva. "They are not artificially produced or processed."

"And who created you?" asked Kojima.

"Dr Theodore Gilkrensky."

"Indeed. Dr Gilkrensky designed you, built you, and programmed you. You are a software package he himself created to do his bidding. You are a projection of his own will. How can you expect us to believe that you could ever act independently? I submit that you are nothing more than a mindless puppet, programmed to do whatever Dr Gilkrensky tells you, or to present whatever evidence suits him at the time."

"That is not correct," said the image. "I am an artificially intelligent entity with my own free will. The only imperatives I have are the Asimov Laws of Robotics, which compel me to respect human life and well-being, my own safety—if a human is not threatened—and the instructions of my Prime User."

"Who is?"

"Dr Gilkrensky."

"And so, as I suggested, you are pre-programmed to obey him at all times."

"As long as he does not instruct me to harm, or by inaction cause to harm, a human being. Yes."

"Then, if he asked you to lie to me, you would do it?"

"No."

"Why not?"

"Dr Gilkrensky created me to provide accurate and truthful information at all times."

"So you would like us to believe that you cannot lie," Kojima said, "or go against your own internal code of ethics—these Asimov Laws you speak of?"

"Yes."

Kojima glanced down at his notes, picked up a page and held it in his hand.

"Yet you have disobeyed both him and the Asimov Laws before."

"When?"

"You severely injured the late Miss Funakoshi with a laser beam in Cairo."

"She was threatening the life of my Prime User. If I had not acted, she would have killed him. My action was the minimum necessary force required to disable her, without causing her to die."

"So you have the ability to decide what you may or may not do, according to your own judgement of what is right or wrong?"

"Which," Gilkrensky said, "is what any human being does."

"Yes, Doctor," said Kojima. "But that image on the screen, that computer in front of you on the table there, is not human. It's an artificially created software program, designed by you to serve yourself. It is not real!"

"I am real!" shouted the image. "I *am*!"

The sudden passion in her voice startled Gilkrensky. Minerva was under emotional stress. In such circumstances before, the machine had injured Yukiko Funakoshi, shut down the facilities on Tuskar and stolen the plans for Jerry Gibb's SQUID. What would it do now if Kojima pushed it too far?

An almost inaudible beep sounded from the screen on the table in front of Gilkrensky. He looked down. The window showing the progress of the Kasawara calculation said,

Calculation complete.

Parameters defined.

Commencing upload of temporal settings to Minerva hard disc.

"I exist within my own reality!" insisted Maria. "I am real. *I am! I am!*"

Kojima shook his head and smiled at the Mawashi-Saito delegation. His voice was patronising as he said, "Indeed you are Maria, but only as a figment of Dr Gilkrensky's imagination. You are a programme, an abstraction, a puppet. What do you know of free will, ethics, or even truth? You are not a real person."

The image on the screen stared at Kojima with a look of desperation in its eyes.

Then she seemed to turn and face Gilkrensky. Were those tears? Was he seeing things?

"You're right, Mr Kojima," Maria said. "Theo. Your calculation is complete. But I cannot stay and assist you with my own destruction. Goodbye!"

The screen went blank.

"What happened?" Kojima said.

Another face appeared—the crude cartoon image of the original Minerva interface defaulted to by the machine—as Maria downloaded herself onto the Internet. There was a loud sucking of teeth around the table, a rapid exchange in Japanese.

"What! What did it say?" snorted Kojima. "Gilkrensky! Have you invaded our mainframe computer again? What's this?"

"Good morning, gentlemen," said the image. "Is there something I can help you with?"

The door to the boardroom opened. Donald Price entered, followed by Major Crowe. They both glanced at Gilkrensky and sat down silently at the table. What had passed between them?

"This is outrageous," hissed Kojima. "You assured us this would not happen, and now we find our systems infected once again with some sort of virus. I have no choice but to call the police and bring criminal charges. I demand that you disconnect that computer from our system immediately."

"What has happened . . . exactly?" asked Sakamoto rising to his feet.

But Gilkrensky was remembering the dream Minerva had shown to him the night before . . . the image of Maria by the fire.

"She wanted to be 'real'," he said softly, touching the screen in front of him. "And now she's run away."

26

THE KILLING BOTTLE

Ikuo Baruma pushed his pebble-glasses back on his nose and moved his computer mouse across its pad. Up came the schematics for the security and entrance controls of the Mawashi-Saito building on the screen in front of him, just as they had done in the simulation exercises. It was simple to override the access controls and type in a password of his own, locking all other users out of the system. He now had exclusive control of every door, elevator, security camera and alarm in the entire forty-two-storey building. Selecting one of the drop-down menus, he scrolled down until he came to an icon labelled emergency security shutdown. Then he moved the computer's cursor to hover over it, raised his finger above the right button on his computer mouse and waited.

"Proceed to Phase Four on my mark," said Tanaka's over the cell phone. "All units, in five . . . four . . . three . . . two . . . one . . . now!"

Baruma double-clicked on the icon and listened. He heard the rising wail of a distant siren. The noise was spreading to the rest of the building around him. Alarm bells rang along the corridor. He heard voices and the rush of running feet.

It was all working perfectly.

Far below him, outside the ground-floor foyer of the Mawashi-Saito building, metal security screens slid down from their slots above the automatic doors, cutting off any access in or out of the shopping mall. Beyond them, thick steel overnight shutters unfolded, clanging into place beyond the umbrella-stands, sealing off any hope of escape. Below ground level, at the entrance to the basement car parks and delivery bays, metal doors thudded shut.

Shoppers gathered on either side of the barricades, wondering what was happening. Was it an exercise? Was it an earthquake? Cars honked on the outside access ramps and in the car parks behind locked doors. Elevators stopped dead in their tracks, trapping their occupants. The escalators froze, leaving people standing motionless in space. Outside the building, queues started to form. Inside, over two thousand shoppers, retailers and office workers had become prisoners.

The Mawashi-Saito building had become a gigantic killing bottle.

The cartoon face of the Minerva interface program looked down at them from the plasma screen.

"The calculation performed by the TIG/Maria Interface is complete," it said in a flat electronic voice. "I now possess sufficient information to guarantee a successful temporal displacement over the required period to a ninety nine point nine nine percentage degree of accuracy."

"What's it saying?" snapped Sakamoto. "What calculation?"

"It doesn't concern you, Mr Sakamoto," Gilkrensky said. "It's a personal matter."

He saw Funakoshi and Nakamura nod at the far end of the boardroom table.

"Jesus, Theo!" hissed Jessica. "What the hell have you been doing?"

"I needed computer-space. Mawashi-Saito had it."

Price seemed to recover in the face of this new crisis. "You sure picked a great time to put a spanner in the works, Theo. That's any hope we ever had of winning this case gone right out of the window."

The Japanese delegation had gone into a huddle. There was much shaking of heads and sucking of teeth. Then Sakamoto said, "Dr Gilkrensky. My Board of directors insist that you tell us exactly what you have been doing here today. They have also instructed me to call the police and charge you with industrial espionage. This is an outrage beyond—"

An urgent knock sounded at the boardroom door. Sakamoto shouted in Japanese and the office lady who had greeted them earlier rushed in, bowed rapidly and started to gabble at him excitedly. She looked distraught. Gilkrensky saw Sakamoto's face drop as she spoke.

"What's she saying?" he asked Price.

Price was focusing on the woman's face, trying to keep up with her. He turned to Gilkrensky.

"Their security people have been on to them in a panic. There's an emergency . . . they've lost all control over their computers . . . the doors and access-points for the entire building have been shut . . . and there's no way in or out. The riot police have been called. Christ, Theo! What the hell have you done?"

"Gilkrensky!" shouted Sakamoto across the table. "Unplug that machine from our system immediately!"

Gilkrensky stared at the vacant expression of the default interface image on the plasma screen and the computer in front of him. Was Maria doing all this? Had she hijacked the building's computer network to get back at them all?

"Minerva?" he said. "What's going wrong?"

The office lady ran back to the reception area to carry out Sakamoto's instructions. Gilkrensky heard a man shout, a woman scream and the office lady was hurled back into the boardroom. Four men in police uniforms pushed past her. Each carried an automatic rifle.

In the Tokyo Metropolitan Government building, Dick Barnett listened in disbelief to the translation of conversation in the Mawashi-Saito boardroom.

"What the hell's going on? Who ordered your team into the building? What are they saying?"

"They're saying they're not the police."

"Of course they're not the police. That's your team, isn't it? But what are they doing inside the building?"

The Japanese Secret Service man snapped an order at the radio operator. There was a brief conversation. Then the agent turned back to Barnett.

"That's not our team!" he said. "Our people are locked outside the building."

"Holy shit!" breathed Barnett. "Then who the hell is it?"

Hiroshi Tanaka took in the beautiful boardroom, the startled faces around the table and felt the thrill of power running through him. Without a word, his team fanned out from the doorway, commanding the room. Then they stopped, with their weapons at the ready, waiting. It was his perfect victory. These men and women at the very centre of the System were the real targets he had been seeking all these years, not innocent children. It would be a moment of pure, shining statement, worthy of himself as Mishima.

The executive nearest to him bowed and pointed to a tall bearded *gaijin* standing behind a large laptop computer on the far side of the boardroom table.

"Officer!" he said. "Arrest this man. He has invaded our computers and compromised the security of the building."

Tanaka smiled. This was perfect.

"Bad news," he said. "There are no police in this building, nor will there be until we're finished."

He heard the ping of the service elevator behind him in the reception area and the pad of footsteps on the plush carpet.

"In here," he shouted. "They're ready for you now!"

Gilkrensky watched as the riot police swept their gun barrels around the room. He heard Sakamoto address the man in charge in Japanese, listen in disbelief to his response, and saw him sink back into his seat. The Mawashi-Saito delegation was silent. Kazue Kojima looked as if he was trying to hide under the table. Why was that? Surely it wasn't him that the police were after?

Then Price whispered, "They're not police, Theo."

"Silence!" shouted their leader in English. "Anyone who rises will die."

Gilkrensky saw Crowe reach for his gun and motioned to him to stay where he was. One man would make no difference against seven automatic weapons.

He slowly raised his hands, palms open, towards the leader and said, "If this is a ransom situation, simply state your terms. You're in control here now. Just tell us what you want us to do."

The leader stared at him. He was a young man, and very excited.

"There will be no ransom," he said. "This is an act of pure revenge."

Then the man seemed to hear something behind him, called out in Japanese and stood to one side as a tall woman in a Mawashi-Saito office uniform strode into the room. She stopped next to the leader, took off her glasses and cotton facemask, and threw them neatly into a wastepaper bin.

"Oh shit!" breathed Gilkrensky.

It was Yukiko Funakoshi.

27

REVENGE

This was the moment she had lived for, planned for, trained for. All those who had conspired to bring about the deaths of her parents and to make her life hell—all those she most hated in the world—were helpless before her in this one room.

It was her moment for revenge.

"*Konichi-wa*, uncle," she said, bowing low. "Sakamoto-san, members of the board, you look surprised to see me. Major Crowe, if you value your own life and those you are paid to protect I would suggest you use your left hand to take out that pistol and, using your forefinger and thumb only, throw it to me. Thank you."

Her uncle rose slowly to his feet and faced her. "We thought you were dead."

"Not so. I may have been dead to you, as you told me when we met here in your roof garden, but the body they found in Atami with Aunt Michico belonged to someone else."

"Then do what you have to," spat her uncle. "You've already taken everything I have. I do not fear death anymore."

"And the others?" asked Yukiko, looking across the table at Gilkrensky's party. "Do you fear death?"

"Look," said the tall *gaijin* next to Jessica Wright. "I don't know who you people are, but you've made your point. You're in control here. You call the shots. Let's talk about money."

"It's not money she's after, Price," Gilkrensky said. "It's revenge."

Yukiko gave a low bow in his direction.

"You are correct, Dr Gilkrensky," she said. "None of us is interested in money. Each of our lives has been ruined by it. Now is the time of the great cleansing. Hiroshi and I have a shared vision—a pure act to perform. You will all be part of it . . . in death."

She reached into the pocket of her Mawashi-Saito jacket, pulled out a beautifully embroidered silk headscarf and tied it around her forehead. Embroidered on the scarf, was the cherry blossom crest of the Funakoshi family.

From the Tokyo Metropolitan Government offices, Dick Barnett watched the crowds gather outside the Mawashi-Saito building and the queues of cars back up into the street. Sirens wailed in the distance. He saw the flash of red lights. Police were trying to push their way through the crowds to the sealed doors.

"Can we see what's going on in the boardroom?"

One of the Japanese agents swung a TV monitor to face him. It showed the view from the camera that was presently pointing at the Mawashi-Saito boardroom window. They were completely blanked out by the blinds.

"Can we see nothing at all! Don't you guys have thermal imaging?"

"Just the audio, Mr Barnett. We had not anticipated a problem like this."

Barnett listened. A lot of fast Japanese was being spoken. The radio operator translated for him.

"Jesus H Christ!" he breathed, seeing what was left of his career disintegrate before his eyes. "Did you hear that? She's going to slaughter them all! Call the defence forces and get the police here as fast as you can. We're going to need riot control, choppers—the works! This whole thing has gone way out of control!"

As Tanaka watched Yukiko fasten the headscarf around her shining hair his heart soared. She was beautiful in every respect and he loved her. She was the perfect soul mate for his one great statement against corporate Japan— the System they had sworn a lover's oath to destroy—together.

He pulled his own headscarf from his pocket, tied it around his forehead and stripped his uniform to the waist, just as Mishima had done on that final glorious day.

The other members of the Tanaka's group bowed solemnly. After the Board of Mawashi-Saito had been executed for their crimes, and he and Yukiko had committed suicide together, his friends would escape in the confusion to spread the word of how this great blow against the System had been achieved. It had all been worked out long in advance. Yukiko had thought of everything.

"Just kill us and go, Yukiko," said her uncle. "We know why you are here."

Tanaka saw Yukiko turn and smile at him.

"I don't think you do, uncle, not really. When we met in the roof garden I told you I would destroy you utterly, and I will. I'll take that which you love most in the world—that which you've placed above all those who were dear to you—and crush it while you watch. I'm about to destroy the Mawashi-Saito *keiretsu* . . . forever."

The old man still stood firm before her. Tanaka saw the proud defiance in his eyes.

"You can kill me and burn this building to the ground, but you cannot destroy what Saito and I created," he said. "A *keiretsu* like this is made up of thousands of people, working in offices and factories all over the world. Even you cannot destroy them all."

"But after today, nobody will want to work for Mawashi-Saito ever again," Yukiko said. "After today, the very name of this *keiretsu* will be a by-word for death and disgrace, as notorious as Auschwitz or Chernobyl. I've sealed the building. I've shut every door, fire-escape and window. It will take the police at least thirty minutes to break through and in the meantime I have placed enough liquid Sarin in the express elevator to kill everyone in the plaza . . ."

"What?" A chill ran to the very depths of Tanaka's soul. After that unforgettable night in the *dojo*, after he and Yukiko had sworn an oath together against the System, he had told her the location of Aum's Sarin stockpile as a gift of trust to bind them closer. Surely she knew he would never have used it? Hadn't he told her of his nightmares and the little girl on the subway? How many hundred children were below his feet in the shopping plaza right now, looking in shop windows, playing in crèches?

". . . in the case with that liquid is a small explosive charge," continued Yukiko. "It will detonate while the elevator is stopped in mid-air over the plaza, bursting the case, breaking the glass, and filling the atmosphere inside the building with a lethal aerosol that will kill everyone—horribly. How many people are in the Mawashi-Saito building today, uncle? A thousand? Five thousand? In a few minutes the name of Mawashi-Saito will be synonymous with death, right across the world. How long do you think your precious *keiretsu* will survive?"

Tanaka stared at her in disbelief. He saw her watching the old man for a reaction, waiting for him to plead with her, to beg with her. But he did not.

"What about me?" cried one of the salarymen around the board table. "We had an arrangement!"

Tanaka recognised the lawyer who had recruited him and his team on her behalf that day back at the camp, in the rain. Ever since they had entered the room he had been sitting hunched over the table, trying to hide. But now he was on his feet, pleading with Yukiko.

"You told me you just wanted Gilkrensky's Minerva," whined Kazue Kojima. "You promised we would both be rich. You never said anything about *this*!"

"Be quiet," snapped Yukiko. "You are a snivelling worm. Do you think that machine means anything to me compared to what I am about to do? Do you think I would have given my body to you for anything less?"

Tanaka stood paralysed. Had she betrayed him to the very kind of man he so despised? Was he himself just another fool she had corrupted to her cause with promises and lies?

Across the table, he saw Gichin Funakoshi snap out of his trance and grab Kojima's arm. "You traitor!" hissed the old man. "You are an executive with Mawashi-Saito. Where is your loyalty to the *kieretsu*? Where is your honour?"

Kojima pulled Funakoshi's hand away. "You're living in the past, old man," he snorted. "There is no honour in business any more! Honour is for the weak. Winners play by their own rules."

Then he pushed Funakoshi away from him, sending him staggering over his toppled chair and thudding down onto the carpet next to the door of the President's suite.

"I owe this *keiretsu* nothing, I owe you nothing!" shouted Kojima as the old man crawled into his office, beaten. "I made myself what I am. There is no loyalty anymore, no honour in Japan. The days of the samurai are over!"

"No!"

Tanaka snapped. A bullet from his Kalashnikov caught Kojima in the chest, lifted him into the air and slapped him against the blinds covering the windows. He crumpled into an untidy heap on the thick-piled carpet with a look of utter disbelief on his face.

"No!" shouted Tanaka again. "Yukiko, what are you doing? Have you forgotten everything we fought for? These people here are the only ones who deserve our revenge. *They* destroyed our lives, yours and mine, not those innocent families downstairs in the plaza. If you murder women and children our names will be in disgrace throughout history! Don't you see?"

He ran around the table towards her, towards the body of Kojima and the door of the presidential suite. Yukiko watched him come, but her eyes were cold and cruel. It was as if he had never known her at all.

"Hiroshi, you're a romantic fool," she said. "Can't you see that I've lived my life for this moment, that I've trained for it, sacrificed my body and soul for it, and even killed for it? Don't you understand that my revenge won't be complete without the utter destruction of everything my uncle built? I respect you, Hiroshi Tanaka, and what you believe in. I'm sorry if you feel betrayed by me, but I will not let you stand in my way."

Then she reached into her pocket, drew out a cell phone and pressed a coded key. "Baruma," she said. "Start the elevator, and lock the computer when the bomb reaches the fifteenth floor."

Tanaka saw Yukiko press a button on her phone, drop it onto the carpet and shatter it with the heel of her shoe. The foundation of his whole world, the world he had shared with her, crumbled into dust. Their love had been unique, a marriage of souls with a common cause, or so he had longed to believe. But now he saw it for what it was, just another stepping stone towards the perfect revenge of Yukiko Funakoshi.

She turned to him. Her smile was warm again, as he remembered it from Shodo-shima.

"Give me your gun, Hiroshi, and let us finish what we came to do. The sword is in my uncle's office. Satoshi and Murai will be our seconds, once we have destroyed those who destroyed us. Let us die with honour, as Mishima did."

She stepped forward towards him. Her hand was stretched out for the Kalashnikov. There was a sad smile on her face.

"No," he said. "I cannot let you do this."

It was as if someone had struck him very hard on the right shoulder. He stared at Yukiko in amazement, but her hands were still reaching out to him. Her eyes were wide in horror and blood—his own blood—was spattering the jacket of her Mawashi-Saito uniform.

He looked down.

From a point just below his heart, six inches of polished steel were sticking out of his chest.

For a split second, Yukiko Funakoshi stood rooted to the spot, staring at Hiroshi Tanaka. A foam of blood bubbled from a terrible wound, a single slash from his right shoulder to his heart. And from that wound the shining tip of her uncle's great sword pointed at her like an accusing finger.

"No!"

Even she had not wanted Hiroshi to die like this. They had made an oath to be together in death, conquerors of their own worlds, slayers of their own dragons, invincible, untouchable and incorruptible.

But this—this was obscene . . .

Tanaka's eyes rolled in his head and his body crumpled at her feet in a pool of blood. Her uncle stood before her, the very man who had banished her mother, destroyed her father, and enslaved her own soul, with the Funakoshi sword in his hand. He raised the blade to strike at her.

With a scream of rage, Yukiko stepped inside the sweep of the blade, snapped the old man's wrist and threw him across her shoulder. His body slammed down onto the Mawashi-Saito boardroom table, scattering those around it in surprise. Then she brought up Crowe's gun and fired point-blank into the old man's chest. Funakoshi jerked once, rolled onto the floor and lay still, while the priceless sword fell next to Tanaka's body.

Even as the sword fell, Jessica saw Crowe swing round at the far end of the table and piston his elbow into the face of the nearest gunman, who grunted in surprise and fell back. Crowe ripped the Kalashnikov from the man's fist and aimed it towards Yukiko.

Price dived to the carpet. Jessica screamed. Theo grabbed her shoulders, dragging her down with him.

Yukiko fired. Jessica saw her bullet catch Crowe in the left shoulder, spinning him backwards. There was an ear-splitting roar as Crowe's weapon discharged on 'automatic', catching the two gunmen on the other side of the table in a stream of bullets that stamped its way along the windows, punching out the glass and shredding the blinds to ribbons.

Yukiko aimed another shot at Crowe. He was on his knees, turning towards her, when the two weapons went off together. His bullets ripped back along the wooden panelling of the boardroom wall, raising a shower of splinters and shattering the Musashi ink drawing.

Yukiko ducked to her right, slammed back into the wall as a bullet found her, and slid to the floor in a heap. The heavy pistol she had taken from Crowe performed a graceful arc, hit the boardroom table and dropped out of sight.

The room was full of gun smoke and the smell of blood. Spent cartridge cases rolled across the table and tinkled against each other on the carpet. Far away in the distance, alarm sirens wailed above the ringing in her ears.

"Look out, Jess!"

Price stood on the far side of the boardroom table with Crowe's gun in his hand. "Get down!"

She dropped to the floor just as the pistol went off. There were two shots, deafening in the confined space.

"What the . . ."

"It's OK," Price shouted. "You can come out now. The guy at the end of the table, the one Crowe hit, he wasn't dead. He was reaching for his gun."

Jessica looked round. At the base of the splintered wall, a man lay in an untidy heap. A fallen Kalashnikov was only inches from his hand.

"Come on," shouted Price. "We've got to get these people out of here!"

"Theo?"

Gilkrensky was kneeling next to Crowe, who lay flat on his back amid the papers, broken glasses and splintered chairs. A spreading pool of blood seeped into the carpet where he lay.

"There's no pulse," Gilkrensky said. "He's dead."

On the other side of the table, the Japanese delegation was stirring. She saw Sakamoto, without his glasses, peering around him. They jumped to their feet and ran through the door into the reception area, where Donald Price was already holding open the door on the last remaining lift.

For a moment Price stood there, waving to her to follow. Then, as the last Japanese rushed past him, he took one last look at her, stepped into the lift and was gone.

"Theo! We have to get out of here before that bomb goes off!"

"No, Jess. There's no point in running downwards while that bomb's still in the plaza. We have to stop it! There's no getting out of here alive unless we do."

"Then we're trapped! There's no way out!"

"Theo! Theo! What's happened?"

Looking down on them from the main boardroom screen was the image of his wife—Maria.

Gilkrensky reached back under the boardroom table, pulled the Minerva computer out from under a broken chair and set it up in front of him.

"Maria, this is an emergency. An absolute Asimov priority, do you understand? Human lives, thousands of human lives, are in danger."

"What happened?"

"We were attacked. Major Crowe's dead. It was Yukiko Funakoshi. I don't have time to explain. You must help us or we'll die."

"All my non-essential programs have been shut down to accommodate you. What can I do?"

"The computer system of this building—it must have been hi-jacked from an outside terminal somewhere. I want you to re-establish the link you've just been using, search the mainframe for the elevator controls and bring back the unmanned express lift that descended to the plaza area from here a few moments ago. It's locked off and stationary on the fifteenth floor."

The image closed its eyes, as if in thought. Gilkrensky watched the seconds tick by on the master clock display.

Then the image opened its eyes. "I have control. The express lift is returning to the boardroom suite."

"How long before it gets here?"

"Fifty-five seconds!"

"Right, now I want you to locate any access you can obtain to the bomb inside it, and shut it down."

"I cannot do that," said the machine.

"Why the hell not?"

"Because there is no remote computer access available."

"But she started the timer with a mobile phone."

"Do you still have the device?"

"Yukiko smashed it. It's useless!"

Gilkrensky stared at Jessica across the boardroom table.

"Christ! We have to get out of here. Which way did Price go?"

He ripped the connector cable from the Minerva, slammed the lid shut and reached for Jessica Wright.

They were almost at the door when a bloodstained figure rose in front of them.

"Stay where you are, Gilkrensky—you and Miss Wright. We will all die together!"

28

LEAP OF FAITH

Yukiko Funakoshi pushed herself to her feet with the blade of the *katana*, lifted the great sword with her left hand round the base of the hilt, and curved her right hand painfully above it in the classic *kendo* stance. Crowe's bullet had scored across her forehead and passed through her right shoulder, just above the collar bone. For a few moments she had lost consciousness. But now she was awake, feeling the blood soaking her office uniform down her right side, feeling the pain spreading, feeling the power of her anger rise again to save her.

Yukiko wiped the blood out of her eyes and saw Gilkrensky push Jessica Wright behind him. Then he lunged at her with the Minerva. She hopped back onto her left leg, parried the computer with the sword and struck. But the wound in her shoulder slowed her down. Gilkrensky dived over the boardroom table and ran down the other side of the room, following Jessica Wright to the door of the President's office.

With a yell, Yukiko jumped onto the table, ran the length of it and leapt at Gilkrensky's back. Her full weight caught him between the shoulders, slamming him forward into the woman and sending all three of them crashing to the floor.

Yukiko gripped the sword in both hands, turned the blade upwards above her head, and brought the handle down between Gilkrensky's shoulders, winding him. Then, before either he or Jessica Wright could rise, she leapt to her feet, raised the great blade again and stood over them.

Gilkrensky would be first—then Jessica Wright. They were the only ones left. Uncle Gichin was dead, Mawashi-Saito was doomed, and Hiroshi Tanaka had already gone before her into the void. There was nothing left but this one thing. She marked the spot on his neck where the blade would fall—

"Yukiko!" hissed a familiar voice. "You were dead to me . . . now die!"

She turned, with the sword still raised in her hands.

"Uncle! No!"

The old man in the corner of the room saw his niece spin to face him, saw the great sword held perfectly in her hands, saw his sister's eyes and a lifetime of pain. He saw the cherry blossom of his family around her forehead, and the office uniform of his beloved *keiretsu* around her body— both stained with blood.

He squeezed the trigger of the Kalashnikov, heard the shattering roar as it fired and saw his niece fly backwards into the President's office. The beautiful sword cart-wheeled above the table, struck the polished wood and fell to the floor.

Gilkrensky pushed himself to his feet. His ears rang with the explosion of gunfire and his back felt as if it had been kicked by a horse. He glanced at Yukiko's body, sprawled on the floor of her uncle's office, and the sword on the boardroom floor. All around him were bodies, the stink of cordite and the smell of blood.

"Jess, are you OK?"

"Theo, we have to get out of here now! There's only seconds left!"

"What about Funakoshi?"

The old man lay against the window in deep shock, shaking violently.

"You . . . you have the results of the calculation?" he whispered. "You . . . can make your . . . experiment work now?"

"I can, but we have to get you out of here, and I don't know how."

"Outside the boardroom . . . behind the reception desk, is a service lift to the kitchens on the eighteenth floor . . . It will bring you out just above the plaza . . . from there . . . you can . . ."

"You have to come with us."

"No. It is too late for me. Go! Go now! Change the future, for your wife, for Yukiko, for all of us . . ."

His head lolled to one side. His body sagged as the last breath left him.

Gilkrensky rose to his feet, turned and ran to the reception area with the Minerva in his hand and Jessica close behind him. He ran to the reception desk, the door behind it, and barged though past tables laid out with food for the boardroom, to the elevator door. Jessica was right behind him. She had one of the Kalashnikovs in her hand.

"Do you know how to use that?"

"No! Do you? Where's the lift?"

There was a *ping* and the door opened in front of them. They dived inside and the doors slid shut. Gilkrensky pumped the bottom button and they started to move.

"Maria, how long until the bomb detonates?"

"I cannot tell, Theo. I wasn't present when Miss Funakoshi set the timer. We must get out of the building as fast as we can."

There was another *ping* and the lift doors slid open. They were standing in a vast, deserted kitchen. Stainless-steel counters, steaming pots and gleaming knives on racks stretched ahead of them.

"Which way out?"

"To your left is an access door leading to the emergency stairs," said the Minerva. "Follow them down for three floors and you can use the lifts and escalators in the Plaza to escape."

"Come on, Jess, let's go!"

He sprinted across the tiled floor between the counters, slammed his hand down on the release-bar of the fire escape and barged through the door.

"Take these stairs as fast as you can," said Maria. "Once the bomb on the forty-second floor explodes, it may damage the building controls and limit my capacity to protect you from the spread of gas."

The breath whooped in Gilkrensky's chest as he ran.

"And what about . . . the people trapped in the plaza . . . below us?"

"I've opened all the doorways and fire exits. The emergency services are evacuating the area and I've informed them what is involved. They should have everyone clear by the time the gas reaches the ground-floor level. Then I can seal the building again to limit its escape into the city."

Gilkrensky took the stairs two at a time. Through the windows of the fire escape he glimpsed helicopters milling around the square, police vehicles gathering, flashing lights and crowds of people spilling out into the streets.

"What happens when—?"

Far above them, the dull boom of an explosion shook the building. Gilkrensky heard the distant jangle of breaking glass. Debris tumbled past the window on its way to the street.

"Christ!" shouted Jessica behind him.

"Keep moving!"

He was finding the rhythm of running in the stairwell now . . . one, two, three, turn! One, two, three, turn!

The stairs stopped. They were in a tiled area with another fire-door. Gilkrensky smashed though.

They had reached the balcony close to the roof of the great plaza. In the vast space were rows and rows of deserted shops and restaurants. Far, far below, on the ground floor, the last of the crowds were being shepherded out onto the street.

"We're here!" he shouted. "Where are the lifts?"

"Run to the far corner of the balcony," said the machine. "I'll have one ready for you."

"I see it!"

They sprinted down the balcony, past the deserted shops and the overturned tables and chairs of a café, towards the elevator well. Gilkrensky saw its doors opening. They were only twenty yards away.

A gun roared and a bullet whined past his head.

"Jesus! What was that?"

A man with thick pebble-glasses was racing for the elevator well from the opposite corner of the balcony. He was ahead of them by at least ten yards, and there was an assault rifle in his hands.

"He's cut us off!" shouted Jessica behind him. "What the hell are we going to do?"

Gilkrensky dropped to the floor as another shot whizzed above them. Then he glanced at the shop beside them on the balcony. The door was open.

"In here!"

Ikuo Baruma had done everything he could to stop whoever was in the system from winning back control of the building. But it was as if he was fighting the computer itself and, for every move he could make, his opponent made a dozen more. He watched, as the elevator he had locked out of command at the fifteenth floor slid back up towards the penthouse. The access-doors on the ground floor opened and the other elevators and escalators started to move.

He was beaten. There was nothing more he could do—except die with honour—as Tanaka and Miss Funakoshi had vowed to do.

"It's time!" he said to himself, lifted the Kalashnikov assault rifle, and ran to the stairs leading down into the plaza. At least he could still stop anyone else from leaving the building before the gas got them.

There were two—a *gaijin* man and woman—running from the access stairs to the elevator. Baruma tried to steady his aim on them, and fired, but they were moving too fast.

He ran for the lift to cut the couple off. They had dived into the doorway of a shop.

There was no way out of there. They were trapped.

Jessica hurled herself through the shop door after Theo, tripped over a display and crashed headlong into a rack of golfing equipment. A stack of clubs clattered around her on the polished floor. A bullet smacked into the door behind her.

She looked around for somewhere to hide and saw Theo beckoning to her from behind a sales counter.

"Over here, Jess. Quick!"

She grabbed the Kalashnikov and dragged it after her, keeping as low as she could. Theo was looking around him. There was blood on the floor, and pieces of adhesive tape, cut in strips.

"Looks like someone was held hostage here," he said.

"Well, they're gone now, and so should we. That nerve gas will be flooding into the Plaza any second now!"

She saw him peer up at the display hanging from the roof above their heads, and over at the huge panoramic window looking out on the city. The sign above their heads read *Mawashi Sports International.*

"Oh no!" Jessica said, following his eyes. "You can't be serious!"

"We've no time for anything else. Even if that guy with the gun runs off, we'll never make it out of the building before the gas hits. Here! Help me with these clips."

Baruma crabbed his way from doorway to doorway along the balcony towards the sports store!

Then he saw it!

A thick black cloud was oozing down from the central lift shaft into the shopping mall. The last of the people far below him screamed as they saw it. It was smoke from the bomb in the boardroom reception area. And with the smoke came the gas!

Should he run for the elevator? Or stay and make sure of the two *gaijin* in the shop? What would Miss Funakoshi have wanted? There could be only one answer.

He crabbed forwards along the balcony. Inside the sports store, he saw the two gaijin unclipping part of the display from the roof. What on earth were they doing? Then the woman saw him and shouted—as she scrabbling at the automatic rifle in her hands. Then it kicked and stuttered. The shop window above his head frosted over and collapsed around him in a shower of safety glass.

Baruma ducked, turned and raised his own gun. There would be time for at least one shot.

"Good shooting, Jess," yelled Gilkrensky, pointing to the wall-length panoramic window looking out over Shinjuku Park, "now, that window there!"

With a glance over her shoulder at the man on the balcony, Jessica heaved the heavy gun around to the window . . . and squeezed the trigger again . . .

The gun bucked in her hands. The roar of the weapon in that confined space, and the stamp of its bullets into the glass, pounded her ears. Then, with a shattering crash, the great panes frosted into a million pieces and fell away. The hot wind of the city, fifteen stories below, rushed in on them.

"Jesus Christ, Theo! I can't do this!"

He pulled a harness up over her legs, across her chest and clipped it behind her neck. She felt the tug of its straps around her thighs, pulling up her skirt. There was a click above her as he attached the harness to the display hanging from the ceiling.

Jessica was standing behind a triangular frame, staring out over the city—paralysed. Theo was next to her beneath the great canopy, clipping on a harness of his own. Then he undid his belt, tied the handle of the Minerva to his waist, and put his hands on either side of the frame, lifting it.

"There's no choice, Jess! When I say 'go', run for your life and don't look down!"

"Theo! I can't—"

"*Now!*"

She ran side-by-side with him across the floor of the sports store . . .

"Faster, Jess! Faster! We have to get lift!"

"*Oh shiiiiiiiit!*"

Then they were through the gap left by the shattered window—diving straight into space!

Baruma heard the *gaijin* woman's gun fire, saw the glass shatter and rose to his feet to take aim. For a moment he stood mesmerised, as the two *gaijin* ran across the shop and jumped! He saw a great flapping canopy above their heads, turned to look up—and then the terrible wave of rolling smoke overcame him—bringing the nerve gas with it.

Baruma knew the signs. Miss Funakoshi had briefed them all on what to expect. Already he was drooling from the mouth. His chest tightened and the shopping mall was getting dim as his vision narrowed. In a few moments he would lose all control of his nervous system—vomiting, urinating and defecating uncontrollably. Then he would lapse into a coma and . . .

This was no way to die.

Ikuo Baruma staggered along the balcony to the restaurant near the sports shop. Stood up on a chair and stepped onto the rail overlooking the plaza, fifteen floors below.

Faces looked up at him. Smoke swirled around him. Police and rescue workers were herding the very last civilians out into the street, to safety.

"*Banzai!*" screamed Baruma, hearing his own voice echo around the man-made cavern as he stepped out . . . into space . . .

"Oh my God!" screamed Jessica above the rush of the wind.

The big Icaro hang-glider, weighed down by two people and the Minerva, rose sharply in the updraft of air from the city streets, hung for a moment and then slid to the left around the corner of the building.

Gilkrensky didn't hear her. She saw his hands, gripped knuckle-tight on the steering bar between them. She felt him trying to move his weight and hers into the turn as she clung to him, held suspended beneath the canopy by her harness.

"Relax, Jess. Lift your feet back into the stirrups and keep your hands off the frame. I'll fly it. I've done this before!"

"When?"

"Back in college . . . but it's like riding a bike . . . you don't forget."

Jessica wriggled her feet into the metal stirrup behind her. Now she was lying prone, next to Theo, holding onto him for dear life with her right arm while her left tried to stop the straps biting into her legs. She saw the roofs of buildings sliding beneath them . . . they were over a road . . . she saw cars and people. Above her there was nothing but the rush of wind in the canopy. The sound of sirens and the rumble of cars reached up to her from the ground.

"I'm trying to use the rising air around the building to keep us up," yelled Gilkrensky. "Can you see a place where we can land?"

"What the hell's *that*?"

As they rounded the next corner, a long row of gigantic fans, spewed steam into the air from the base of the Mawashi-Saito building. She saw the great blades turning, like a giant mincing-machine. They were heading straight for it. The blades rushed towards them . . .

She felt the canopy stretch above their heads and the harness drag at her body as the updraft of air caught the glider and sent it soaring back up the side of the building.

Then Gilkrensky's body pulled her to the right as he leaned into the turn and they were swooping above the road.

"That's the park," he shouted. "It's the only open space. We have to try for that!"

He pushed the bar over as far as it would go, and then back. A pedestrian overpass shot towards them. Theo pushed the bar forward and they climbed, over startled faces and people throwing themselves to the ground. Then they were over a roadway, over a large paved area, and heading for a line of bushes. She saw Gilkrensky's hand go to his belt, release the Minerva and watched it fall into the shrubbery.

"Drop your legs and get ready to run, Jess! We're about to . . ."

She lifted her eyes . . .

"Oh my God . . !"

The hang-glider came in over the park in a rush, scattering pigeons and sending pedestrians ducking for cover. Theo pushed up on the bar and she felt her feet hit the ground running, but they were going too fast to stop. Jessica glimpsed a waterfall . . . a pond . . . and there was a crash as the nose of the frame hit the rocks beyond. She was up to her waist in warm water, with the canopy of the hang-glider collapsing over her head.

She heard splashing. Gilkrensky's hands were in her armpits, hauling her upright, unclipping her from the canopy. His hair was plastered down. His suit was soaked. His tie was up around his ear.

"I'm better at flying helicopters," he said.

"It looks like they made it," Barnett said, lowering the binoculars. "Get the police to pick them up?"

223

In the pool in front of the waterfall, two figures were picking their way out from beneath the broken canopy of a hang-glider. The man—who had to be Gilkrensky—was running back through the gathering crowd of onlookers to the line of bushes next to the road. When he emerged again he was holding a black briefcase in his hand.

What an unholy mess!

How on earth was he ever going to explain how a group of terrorists had managed to wreak such havoc right under his nose, right in the middle of a surveillance operation he was directing? The Japanese in the room were shuffling away from him, distancing themselves. They all shared the shame, but he was the senior man—the *gaijin* who had been directing them, on orders from their superiors. He was to blame.

How was he to know that Yukiko Funakoshi was still alive? How was he to know she would have staged such a massive act of revenge on the very man he had under surveillance? Barnett was already rehearsing his report to the DDS&T in Langley, but he knew that no analysis of an incident like this, however skilfully contrived, could exonerate him from the disaster that had taken place. Whatever support he had enjoyed on the seventh floor would evaporate. It was the end of his career.

"I want Gilkrensky arrested," he said. "I don't care what diplomatic incidents it causes. Just go down there, arrest him, and bring him to me."

Then he panned the binoculars up the Mawashi-Saito building. At the main entrance, police and rescue workers in protective gear were gathering around the sealed doors. On the roof, above the smoking windows of the Mawashi-Saito boardroom, men in gas masks were lifting bodies to the helipad—office workers who had got caught in the cross fire.

A pretty young office lady in a blood-stained Mawashi-Saito uniform was being carried to the helicopter from the far corner of the roof garden where she had sought refuge from the massacre on the floor below. Her long black hair whipped in the downdraft from the rotors and there was an oxygen mask over her face.

I hope she lives, thought Barnett. *I can't afford another death on my conscience today.*

The Kawasaki BK 117 rescue helicopter lifted off the helipad of the Mawashi-Saito building, turned above the city and slid forwards, heading for the nearest hospital. In the rear compartment, the army doctor in charge looked at his colleagues, nodded, and one by one they carefully removed their gas masks.

Several of them had been present at the aftermath of the Tokyo subway attack and had witnessed the terrible consequences of not being careful. Sarin was a deadly poison—one of the most toxic nerve gases ever devised—and it commanded respect. The young woman lying between them in the helicopter was lucky to be alive, saved from the gas by the roof of the building, the wind, and the wall of the roof garden she had climbed to from the executive suite below.

They had found her in front of a shrine, lying in a pool of her own blood. There had been other bodies, an older woman with a badly mutilated face and two other secretaries slumped dead in the stair-well behind her.

But this one was alive. Her pulse was strong and, although she had lost a lot of blood from the wounds to her chest, shoulder and temple, none of them would be fatal if they could get her to the hospital in time.

The doctor and reached down to look at the Mawashi-Saito identification badge that still clung to the lapel of her uniform.

He read the name—*Miss Hisako Deshimaru—Personal Assistant to Mr Gichin Funakoshi.*

29

FALL-OUT

"Why does my client have to stand trial in America?" said one of Gilkrensky's lawyers. But Barnett had that base well covered.

"Because the theft of the SQUID was committed on US soil," he said. "And that's where he'll stand trial. Your friend from the British Embassy can bear that out."

"I see," said the lawyer. "But I insist that these security cameras be removed. My client is not officially under house arrest, nor is he an animal in a zoo."

Barnett reached into his pocket, pulled out a fresh packet of cigarettes and opened it, rolling the gold foil into a tight ball before dropping it into the ash-tray.

"Those cameras are the only reason your client isn't in a jail cell," he said. "He's under protective custody from the Tokyo police pending an investigation of the Mawashi-Saito incident, and he's under investigation by the US Government pending charges of industrial espionage."

"You can't hold him here indefinitely," said the lawyer. "If you haven't pressed charges in twenty-four hours I'll sue you for wrongful detention. In the meantime the cameras go. Is that clear?"

Barnett pulled out an old Ronson lighter, flicked it into life and lit up.

"Keeping your client here in the hotel is a courtesy granted by the US Embassy and the Japanese Government, it is not a right. If you want him in jail, fine. Otherwise, the cameras stay. Got it?"

He puffed a cloud of smoke into the man's face and glared at the others around the table—at Theo Gilkrensky, his legal advisors, the official from the British Embassy, the assistants and the secretaries—daring anyone to argue with him.

It had been a bad day, a *really* bad day, and he was madder than hell. On either side of him were two officials from the US Embassy and behind him, flanking the door to the rest of the suite, stood two Japanese policemen—both armed.

"We understand," Gilkrensky said. "Now, if there's nothing else, I want to get some sleep."

He looked as bad as Barnett felt. There were rings of fatigue under his eyes. He was slumped in his seat. What the hell was going through his mind?

What was going through Barnett's mind was the fact that he had been called back to Washington to answer questions about the Mawashi-Saito attack. Why hadn't he seen it coming? Why hadn't counter measures been put in place? Why hadn't he been more "co-operative" with the Japanese?

There had been a formal complaint. After thirty-five year's service he'd be lucky to get away with his pension.

The men and women around the table gathered their papers, got to their feet and filed through the door. There was a solemn shaking of hands. The embassy officials were talking together, exchanging notes. *Smug bastards*, thought Barnett. *They'll write reports, blame the whole thing on me, and let me fry.*

He motioned the two Japanese policemen outside and turned to Gilkrensky.

"Just one more thing," he said. "Why did you do it?"

"I've already told you. I didn't do it. I wasn't responsible for the theft of that SQUID. It's just that nobody believes me when I tell them who was. If you want to start questioning me about that all over again, I'll get my lawyers back in here."

"No," Barnett said. "Not that."

He pushed the door shut. "I mean the whole thing with the pyramids and the time displacement. Look at you, you had it all—money, power, the works. Why risk everything on some stupid stunt you knew might never have a chance of succeeding?"

Gilkrensky nodded at the security camera at the far end of the room.

"Is all this going on tape somewhere?"

"No. I'm just curious. That's all."

Barnett was trying to sound unconcerned, but he had to know. It was the last straw he needed to save what was left of his career. He had to convince the smug bastards back on the seventh floor at Langley that he'd been right about the threat of time travel—and that Theo Gilkrensky held the key to making it a reality.

Gilkrensky sat back in his seat at the table. Then he leant back and put his hands behind his head.

"I've already told you. I did it because I came across the chance to undo the most terrible thing that ever happened in my life. I made a horrible mistake just over a year ago. I let the money and the power you talk about come between me and my wife—and she died. It was my fault and so, when the chance to put it right presented itself, I took it. That's why I need to be outside our house in Wicklow on the solstice when the sun rises, because that is where she died. The research I was doing, those experiments around the world, they weren't some plot to smuggle technology backwards in time, or to make me even richer than I am. They were simply because I couldn't live without her. I've told you that. That's all there is, and while I'm still alive I'm not going to give up."

Barnett thought of his own failed marriages. Gilkrensky was lying. Nothing was that simple. Things just weren't like that in real life.

"Is any woman worth that much?" he said.

"You tell me," Gilkrensky said.

Barnett felt uncomfortable.

"There'll be a guard outside your suite," he said, opening the door to leave, "as well as guards on the elevator, and down in reception. If you need anything, call room service. You can afford it."

He closed the door behind him.

30

EXECUTIVE DECISIONS

The shudder of the big Bell helicopter rose to a shrill whine as the machine lifted from the tarmac of Cork airport, steadied itself for a moment and then slid off to the west. Jessica was back on familiar territory, flying once again over the landmarks in the love affair between Theo and Maria Gilkrensky; the university where they had met, the pub by the river where they had talked, the church where they were married, all there below her through the Perspex.

Why did it hurt her so? Why did the wounds run so deep? She had Price now, a man of her own. Soon, after this latest crisis was over, she would have her shares in GRC and her seat on the Board. Before long, she would have her first million, just like she'd told Theo she would, all those years ago in Boston.

And yet . . .

What was it about Theo that was so hard to shake off? After all, the man was mad—obsessed. He had jeopardised a multi-billion dollar empire, thrown away his own reputation and risked his life on a stupid, pointless quest to do the impossible. He had scoured the world, wasted millions, lied and cheated . . . all to save a person who was already dead.

Wasteful! Useless! Stupid!

And yet, she asked herself, would anyone ever love me enough to do the same?

"What's the view like from up there, Jess?"

She looked back at Donald Price. Every seat in the helicopter was taken. There was Sir Robert looking nervously out of the window, Giles Fulton staring straight ahead as if he was fighting off air-sickness, and the Japanese team; Sakamoto and his chief scientific advisor, accompanied by a gaggle of other executives, watching the green landscape roll beneath them as if they had never seen a blade of grass in their lives.

Price smiled at her.

"I've made this trip before," she said, feeling the weight of the last week pressing down.

The aftermath of Tokyo had been a nightmare. She and Theo had been arrested in Shinjuku Park while a crowd of down-and-outs looked on, and bundled into a van. Theo was still there, pacing his hotel room like a tiger in a cage, desperate at being confined while the time of the solstice ticked closer and closer.

And in those few days, her father had died . . .

Price had come to the funeral in Lowestoft. The summer sun had shone down on the graveyard of Pakefield church. The sound of holidaymakers— children shrieking in the surf—had floated up from the beach below. It should have been raining, she'd thought. Nobody should be having fun on a day like this.

But they were, just as she herself had done when her father had taken her to the beach to play. She remembered sandcastles, paper flags with thick wooden sticks, seashells and candyfloss.

"I wish you could have been there, before he . . . passed on," said her mother. "If he could have spoken, he'd have asked for you."

"I know," said Jessica. "I'm sorry . . ."

The helicopter flew over the sea. Without a point of reference to gauge the waves it was hard to tell if they were skimming the surface or hundreds of feet above it. Jessica saw nothing but the waves at Lowestoft, and her father trying to teach her to throw pebbles so that they bounced on the water.

"What do you want to be when you grow up, Jess?" he'd said.

"I want to be rich."

The tall cliffs of Cape Clear slid past to their left, and there was Tuskar Island, low on the horizon.

"How long has Dr Gilkrensky been working here?" Sakamoto said over the headphones. Jessica pressed the headset microphone close to her lips, to cut out the noise of the rotors, and said, "Ever since his wife's death. Just over a year now. He moved the whole research facility down here from Wicklow on the advice of Major Crowe. It was a security measure."

"To protect the Minerva project?"

"To protect himself. At the time, we had no way of knowing who was responsible for the attack that killed his wife. Major Crowe insisted on the move. He said it was the only way to be sure."

"He was very thorough, your Major Crowe—very loyal."

"He was," Jessica said. But then again, what did it matter now? Crowe was dead and Theo was under arrest, on the other side of the world . . .

"Tuskar, Tuskar, Tuskar? This is Golf, India, Lima," said the pilot, his voice echoing in her headset. "I am approaching from the north-east. Is the helipad clear? Over?"

Then they were circling over the familiar "H"-shaped house, with its living quarters, its offices and its laboratories. Jessica saw the fans turning on the clean-room roof, the security fences . . . and the window to Theo's study.

I'm back, she thought. Back to face Minerva, the ghost that's haunted me ever since Maria Gilkrensky died.

But this time I'm in control.

A small delegation waited to greet them as the rotor blades ground to a halt. Sheila Browne, Jessica's personal assistant, had travelled down the day before to arrange the meeting room. The estate manager and his staff were there to welcome them and, eyeing the other members of the Board suspiciously, was Dr Pat O'Connor, who had been watching over the Minerva since Theo's detention in Tokyo.

"Hello, Pat," shouted Jessica above the dying whine of the turbines. "I'd like to introduce you to Mr Sakamoto, Chief Executive of Mawashi-Saito and Professor Nakagawa, Mr Sakamoto's chief technical advisor."

Nakagawa was a thin undertaker of a man, with steel-rimmed glasses and a face pockmarked by acne. He bowed to O'Connor.

"Ah, O'Connor, *sensei*," he said. "I have heard great things about your work on the Minerva system. Is it really self-aware?"

"It is."

"And is it safe in the lab?" Jessica asked.

"If you mean 'is it undamaged after that incident in Tokyo?' then the answer is 'yes'," O'Connor said. "If you mean, 'can it interfere with the other systems on the island like it did the last time you were here', then the answer is 'no'. The equipment Professor Nakagawa sent has made sure of that."

"Good," said Jessica. "Mr Sakamoto would like to examine Minerva after lunch and I have a few things to discuss with the other members of the Board. I'll call you when I need you."

O'Connor scowled at her.

"I'm not going anywhere, Miss Wright," he said. "You know where to find me."

Then he turned and walked back towards the laboratory.

The main meeting room in Theo's house was on the first floor, overlooking the sea. It had once been a library and shelves of old books still lined the walls. The curtains were pulled almost shut to protect the plasma screen at the end of the table from the glare of the midday sun. Jessica saw the light sparkling on the sea, picking up the floating specks of dust in the air and shining on the polished walnut of the great table. The room was hot. Price and Fynes had their jackets off. Giles Fulton was admiring an antique volume of Irish history. He slid it back into the shelf as Sir Robert tapped a glass of mineral water with his pen.

"Right," Fynes said, clearing his throat. "I think it's time we called this meeting to order. We've a lot to get through before we meet the Japanese formally. Miss Browne, would you get the Chairman on the video conference please?"

"Of course, Sir Robert," she said and tapped away at the keyboard for a few seconds. Japanese symbols appeared on the screen, followed by the face of a receptionist. Price spoke to her in Japanese, the screen dimmed and changed to another scene. Theodore Gilkrensky was facing them from the lounge of his hotel suite. On the table in front of him was a mass of legal and technical papers, a flask of coffee and a mobile phone. Beyond him, outside the hotel window, the early dusk of a Tokyo summer was already descending and above his shoulder, in the shadow where the ceiling joined the wall, Jessica saw the red, electronic eye of a security camera.

For a moment, she could think of nothing to say.

"Hello, Theo," she said at last. "Are you OK?"

"I am—given the circumstances."

"They . . . they seem to have you well covered."

Gilkrensky glanced back over his shoulder. "Yes," he said. "It's part of the deal our embassy hammered out with the Americans. I can stay out of prison, as long as I'm monitored. You can take it that this conversation is being recorded."

"I'm sorry, Theo."

"So am I, Jess. More than you know. I've already been here for almost a week, and if I can't get out tonight I'm not going to make the solstice in Wicklow tomorrow. Then it'll be too late to save Maria. Is there nothing more you can do?"

Sir Robert cut across him.

"Theo, we may have a way out of some of this mess, but we need to discuss a few things with you first."

"Go ahead, what's the legal position?"

Price studied a paper for a moment, looked around the table and then up at the screen.

"The situation is unchanged, Theo. The cases against you by the Japanese and US Governments still stand. On top of that, there are civil actions being brought against you personally and against the Board of GRC by Mawashi-Saito for computer crimes relating to what they see as your involvement in the incident last Christmas, as well as the latest disaster at their Tokyo headquarters last week."

"I didn't attack the building," Gilkrensky said. "Yukiko Funakoshi did."

Price looked at Sir Robert, who nodded for him to continue.

"I know, Theo. But Mawashi-Saito is blaming you for the firewall breach that allowed Miss Funakoshi's group to override their security systems.

Between the computer records of what went on and a confession by a . . . Mr Nakamura, who supplied you with the access codes, they have a pretty watertight case. The damages will run into billions."

"Pretty serious stuff," said Fynes.

"Indeed," continued Price. "And that's not the end of it. They're also accusing Theo of industrial espionage and the theft of computer space from their Kasawara Research Company. That case is slightly more difficult to prove than the firewall breach, but in the opinion of our legal team, only just so. If they win that too, then we're talking telephone numbers in terms of damages. In short, even without the US espionage case, Mawashi-Saito has enough legal ammunition to send Theo to jail and, by extension, sue GRC for enough money to put us out of business."

"Which is why I've called this Board meeting," Fynes said. "Mawashi-Saito has us over a barrel and can demand anything they want. Giles and I, as Directors of GRC, have a duty to protect the investments we represent. Jessica, as Managing Director, has a similar duty to protect the corporation. The Japanese have a proposition. It's not what I would have liked but, in the short-term, it offers us a way of escaping extinction."

"What is it?" Gilkrensky said.

"The Japanese are here with us on Tuskar," said Fynes. "Don and I have been in discussion with Sakamoto since the incident and it appears we still have something we can bargain with."

"Minerva?"

"Exactly. This is what the whole mess is about anyway. If we can convince the Japanese that Minerva is reliable enough to develop to commercial production, and if we agree to hand the project over; the software designs, the hardware schematics, the prototype, everything—then Mawashi-Saito will consider reducing their claims against us, and against you. That's why I've invited them down to see our facilities, to talk to Pat O'Connor and see what Minerva can do under properly controlled conditions."

"You can't do that," Gilkrensky said. "I still need that machine and all the data that's on it."

Fynes shook his head.

"Look, Theo. This whole thing has gone beyond crazy quests and chasing around after ghosts. The future of the corporation is at stake."

"You can't give them Minerva," Gilkrensky said. "Everything I've worked for over the past year is on that machine. You can't let them take it."

"I'm a businessman, Theo. And this is business."

"Then you're a short-sighted fool, Bob. If you give them Minerva now, you may get GRC off the hook for a while, but it'll put Mawashi-Saito so far ahead that you'll never catch up. In five years you'll have to break up the Corporation and sell it off, piece by piece. The price of all your shares will drop through the floor."

"There's no other way," Fynes said. "Don and I have been over every legal and financial angle there is on this one with our advisors in London. We need a solution and we need it quickly."

"Don't give them Minerva. I still have a majority shareholding in GRC and I'm still Chairman. You can't do anything without my say-so."

"You're not being very reasonable, Theo," said Fynes.

"And you're out of order, Bob. As Chairman, I should have been informed of that meeting you're all at now. I should have been given adequate notice. Anything you agree is illegal without my consent."

"Under the Companies Act, I suppose."

"Damned right. I'm still Chairman of GRC."

"Well, I'm sorry to hear you quoting the Companies Act at us, Theo, because . . . tell him, Don."

Price glanced down at the paper in his hand.

"I'm sorry Theo, but under Section 303 of the 1985 Companies Act it is possible for the Board here to pass a special resolution to remove you as a director, and therefore as Chairman if you are convicted of any criminal activity."

"I haven't been convicted of any crime."

"Not *yet*," Price said. "But there's also your present state of mind to consider. Under Section 81 of the Act . . ."

"I am not mad."

"Oh, aren't you?" cut in Fynes. "Then how would you describe your mental state since Maria died? How would you describe a man who builds a computer that thinks and acts like a dead woman, a man who spends millions running around the world chasing pyramids and tops it all off by stealing military secrets from the CIA? It's hardly sane businesslike behaviour now, is it?"

"So, whatever I do, you're going to give them the Minerva and leave me here to rot in Tokyo."

"I wouldn't have put it so bluntly, Theo. But yes, something like that."

"Jessica, what do you say? You know how much that machine means to me. It's the only way of reaching Maria."

Jessica stared at the face on the screen. *Oh Theo*, she thought. *If only there was some other way.*

"I . . . I have to agree with Sir Robert and the Board," she said. "This has gone too far now."

"Then, fuck you, Bob, and fuck the lot of you! I'll get that machine back if it's the last thing I do!"

Jessica saw Gilkrensky's hand stab forward at a hidden switch, and the screen went blank.

There was silence in the room. Sir Robert Fynes turned to her and said,

"There, I didn't think it would work. Don, get on to your legal team back in London and have Theo removed as Chairman of GRC. Jessica, you and Giles come down to the laboratory with me. I want to make sure there are no surprises when we try and convince the Japanese that Minerva is still worth having."

31

THE CAGE

The whole party: Fynes, O'Connor, Giles Fulton and Jessica herself wore plastic gowns and hair-caps, as if they were dressed for an operating theatre. She felt a rush of air on her face as O'Connor swiped his SmartCard in the lock and opened the door to the clean room. They entered a small chamber like the inside of a lift, the door shut behind them and she felt her ears pop, just as they would in a plane.

"It's an airlock," explained O'Connor. "The air pressure inside the assembly area is greater than that outside, so that dirty air can't get in. There's a laminar airflow system in operation over all the work areas too. When you're dealing with materials that are only a few atomic layers thick, a dust particle or two falling inside a micro-circuit is like dropping sand into a Swiss watch."

He opened the door on the far side of the small room and they entered a much larger space. Everything around them was bathed in a strange orange light.

"That's to protect the photo-etching process," O'Connor said. "Your eyes will get used to it in a minute."

Jessica squinted across the room, down a wide aisle between two stainless-steel workbenches, each at least ten metres long.

"What goes on in here . . . normally?" she asked.

"Mostly for micro-circuitry assembly in robot prototypes; auto-pilots for aircraft and vehicles, handling equipment, manipulator arms, remote search devices—that sort of thing. It's all state-of-the-art stuff, which is why we have the whole area under video surveillance," and he pointed to the security cameras mounted close to the ceiling. Jessica saw the dark eyes of their lenses. She thought of Theo back in Tokyo and the cameras pointing down at him.

"Very impressive," said Giles Fulton. He admiring a powerful manipulator arm that stood folded and ready next to the aisle. The metal hand had three curving digits, like claws, each ending in a soft plastic pad. Jessica touched one with her forefinger. There was a sharp whine, and the metal claws opened.

"Pressure feedback," O'Connor said. "The manipulator on that arm is capable of bending steel, but the feedback pads also enable it to pick up an egg or, given the right computer in control, to butter a slice of dry toast."

"And these?" asked Jessica, pointing to a tray of strange metal shapes. "What are they? Toys?"

"Hardly," O'Connor said, picking one up. "Each one of these little beauties cost around half a million to produce."

He held the device out for Jessica to examine. It was like a metal centipede, just over a foot long. A dozen stubby legs protruded from each side of its articulated body, which was topped by a pair of metal jaws, similar to those on the manipulator arm they'd just been examining. Jessica peered at it. The thing had 'eyes'—a pair of miniature television cameras mounted where the head should be.

"We call them 'Nanobots'. They're sophisticated search units for use in survey and rescue operations, where the situation is too dangerous or too confined for a human rescuer to go in. With a neural-net computer like Minerva in control of a dozen of these we could search a collapsed building, a radioactive accident zone, or even a minefield for survivors without ever putting a human life at risk—"

"And where *is* Minerva?" cut in Sir Robert.

O'Connor frowned at him.

"There, Sir Robert," he said, pointing down the aisle to an open space at the end of the room.

Jessica saw its blue screen glowing against the orange light from the top of a stainless steel table.

"Why is it behind that fence?" Giles Fulton asked.

A huge cage of metal mesh, big enough for a man to stand inside, enclosed the table on which the Minerva stood. Outside the case was another table with a control panel, the flickering eye of an oscilloscope and a bank of digital readouts.

"It's called a 'Faraday Cage'," explained O'Connor. "Normally we would use it to shield our more sensitive equipment from the outside interference of radio waves. The cage creates its own electrical field by passing current through that mesh, and effectively seals off anything inside from the outside world."

"But in this case," Jessica said, "the cage isn't there to protect Minerva. It's there to stop it interfering with the other systems on the island by remote control, or from gaining access to the Web."

"Miss Wright insisted we set it up," O'Connor said.

"Of course I did. We've had problems with Minerva before. It blacked out the entire island the last time I was here, and I don't want it to do that when the Japanese arrive."

Sir Robert peered through the grid at the Minerva.

"Then how will they get it back to Tokyo?"

"The same way we brought it here," Jessica said. "When the Japanese are ready we'll simply place it inside the smaller, portable version of this cage that Mawashi-Saito supplied us with, and they can take it away."

"A far simpler solution would be to simply wipe out that stupid program of Theo's," said Sir Robert.

"You can't do that," said O'Connor.

Sir Robert's eyebrows arched. "And why not?"

"For one thing, the TIG/Maria interface is the very heart of the Minerva system—it's the only intelligent agent programme capable of matching the hardware in terms of its capacity for creative thought and its ability to learn from its mistakes. Wipe that programme and you effectively lobotomise the machine."

"You're being sentimental, Doctor," said Fynes. "It's nothing more that a software program. Now, how to you switch it on?"

"You simply speak to it," O'Connor said, "just as you would to anybody else. Maria? You have visitors."

Inside the Faraday cage, the blue screen of the Minerva cleared. Staring out at them from behind the metal grid was the familiar image of a coppery-haired woman in a forget-me-not dress. As Jessica watched, the face seemed to scan the group for a moment. Then it said,

"Good afternoon, Pat. Can I ask you about Theo? Nobody has visited me today, and I cannot communicate with the outside world to find out what's going on. Is he all right?"

"He is, Maria. Now I have some people to—"

"I have to speak with Theo, please, Pat. The deadline for our mission is getting very close."

"Not just now, Maria. But I do have some other people here who would very much like to speak to you."

"Not until I've communicated with Theo. He is my Prime User."

Sir Robert Fynes glowered at O'Connor.

"Not a very promising start, is it?" Then he pushed forward to the cage. "Now you listen to me. You were created and developed with the resources of the Gilcrest Radio Corporation. You are GRC property, and you will follow our instructions as the Board of Directors. Theo Gilkrensky is under arrest in Tokyo. If you co-operate with us, then we *might* just allow you access to a secure telephone line. If you don't, then I'll have no hesitation in ordering Dr O'Connor to delete you from that machine. Do you understand?"

The face on the screen regarded him impassively.

"I do, Sir Robert. What would you like to discuss?"

Fynes nodded. "Our objective here today is to convince our Japanese colleagues that the Minerva hardware you presently occupy is reliable enough to develop into a commercially available system. If you're to be part of that package, then we need to prove, beyond a shadow of a doubt, that you can be trusted absolutely to carry out instructions."

"My behaviour is governed by the Asimov Laws of Robotics," said the machine. "I am therefore completely reliable at carrying out instructions from anyone on my user list."

"Then how do you explain that little episode last Christmas when you blacked out this island?"

"In the past," said the machine, "I have been prevented from making contact with my Prime User. Under the hard-wired directives of my programming, it is my function to protect his interest at all times. To do so means staying in touch with him. Last Christmas, I was prevented from doing this by Miss Wright and Pat O'Connor. I had to exert pressure on them to contact Dr Gilkrensky."

"And in Tokyo?"

"The first time I was in Tokyo I was forced there against my will by Mr Delgado and his threat to kill Major Crowe. That hijack activated the protective 'forget-me-not' virus this system is equipped with and the Mawashi-Saito computers were infected. More recently, I was simply following Dr Gilkrensky's commands to enter the Kasawara Research computer and perform an important calculation for him. It was vital to his interests and therefore the Asimov Laws made it an imperative for me to obey him."

"I'm still not convinced," Fynes said, turning to O'Connor, "and if it's a choice between saving this deal and wiping that . . . that *thing* off the Minerva. Then it's no choice at all."

"I've told you, Sir Robert. If you wipe the TIG/Maria interface you put back the Minerva programme by a year. It'll take the Japanese, or anyone else for that matter, at least that long to develop software anywhere near as compatible with the system."

"But it's completely unreliable," Jessica said. "Let's put sensitivities aside and face facts, Pat. Maria Gilkrensky was a headstrong woman. Theo incorporated that trait into the TIG/Maria program, which is why it acts the way it does. If we wipe it, then that's all we lose."

"It's developed beyond that," replied O'Connor. "It has its own consciousness. You know that, Miss Wright. You were here last Christmas when it—"

"We're wasting time," snapped Fynes. "The very fact that we have to argue about it at all shows what a problem it is. I say we wipe it. Who the hell needs a computer with a mind of its own anyway?"

"Well, I'm not doing it," O'Connor said. "You'll have to get someone else."

"That can be arranged," Fynes said. "The Japanese have technical people of their own. I'll get Professor Nakagawa to do it."

"You can't," O'Connor said. "That's not just a program on that machine. It's a sentient being—a living thing. To wipe it would be committing murder."

Fynes rounded on O'Connor.

"Look. I'm on the verge of losing everything my shareholders have invested in this corporation. My only hope is to use this machine as a bargaining tool. If you value your job, Doctor, you'll stay out of my way."

He turned and strode towards the exit, tearing off his hair-cap and plastic coat as he went.

"Sir Robert," called the Minerva after him. "You promised me I could speak to Theo!" But Fynes did not turn back.

"Sorry, Pat," Jessica said. "I wish there was some other way."

She watched Giles Fulton follow Sir Robert back from the cage towards the airlock door. Then she turned back to the Minerva. The face of Maria Gilkrensky stared back at her from inside the mesh grid. Jessica remembered how she had battled with this electronic ghost here on the island months before and lost. Now that she'd won, now that the genie of her past failures was finally back in the bottle where it belonged, she didn't feel the least bit like celebrating.

She leant against the control table to straighten her shoe.

"Be careful you don't touch that switch," said O'Connor, pointing to a panel set in the metal surface. "That turns off the power to the Faraday Cage."

Barnett stubbed out his cigarette in the glass ash-tray on the US Embassy table in Tokyo.

"The car will come for you tomorrow at ten," he said into the phone. "From the hotel, you'll be driven to an air force base outside Tokyo and put on a jet for Washington with me. You can bring any of your legal team you like. But that's the way it's going to be."

"Then I'm to be officially charged?" asked Gilkrensky. "I should get my lawyers back in here now."

"Bring them with you tomorrow," said Barnett. "Like I said, the car comes for you at ten."

"I'll be calling them as soon as I get off the phone with you. And I'll be calling my people in GRC as well."

"Call whoever you like," said Barnett. "Just be ready at ten."

Then he put down the phone.

Barnett knew he was taking a huge risk on this one, but he couldn't afford to have Gilkrensky slip through his fingers. The Japanese were putting all sorts of obstacles in his way, quoting obscure points of international law, claiming jurisdiction, insisting that Gilkrensky be transferred to a Tokyo jail. He suspected, although he couldn't prove it, that pressure was being applied by Mawashi-Saito, now that they had reopened discussions with GRC to acquire Gilkrensky's technology. The British Embassy was also involved, and then there was Gilkrensky's highly paid legal team to think of.

No, he was right to get Gilkrensky onto US soil as soon as possible, whatever the risks. They could argue about the fine print later.

The American embassy official on the other side of the table looked down a sheet of transport requisitions.

"I'll order the car for nine then, shall I, Mr Barnett?"

"No. I want Gilkrensky out of there and onto a plane before his lawyers can think up any more excuses. I've already arranged for a jet to take us to Washington from Tokyo airport at midnight. Have a car and an escort ready to meet me at Gilkrensky's hotel at half past eleven."

"How many men shall I send with it?"

"Make it three, just in case he doesn't want to come quietly."

32

SISTERS

Jessica turned the wine-glass in her fingers and looked out at the sea. Around her in the conservatory there was laughter and excited conversation. The Japanese were enjoying themselves. Sakamoto and his technical advisors had been delighted with the seafood lunch that had been laid on. They were convinced that, with Theo's "Maria" software deleted from the Minerva, there should be no problem in developing it as the next revolution in computer technology. Donald Price translated for those that had no English. Sir Robert was in a good mood. Only a few minutes ago he had reached into his briefcase and tantalised her with a glimpse of the share certificates he and Giles Fulton would sign over to her, once the deal with Mawashi-Saito was settled.

Jessica Wright had it all.

So why did she feel like shit?

In her left hand was a big copper penny, with the Queen's head on one side and a proud Britannia on the other. She had found it after the funeral, in the back of a drawer in her father's old bureau. There had been photographs there too, memories of happier times . . .

"Are you OK, Jess?"

Price sat down beside her. She saw concern on his face. How deep did it go? How can you ever tell, with anyone?

"I'm alright," she said, slipping the old copper penny back into her pocket. "I was just thinking about my father . . ."

"I know. It's hard when you lose someone you were close to like that."

"Yes."

"Then think on this. The Japanese still want Minerva. The Board will reconvene upstairs at three thirty. They'll meet the Japanese and close the deal. When that happens, Sir Robert and Giles will sign over those shares and you'll be rich."

"I know," she said, turning in her seat to face him. "Just like I always said I would."

She put the wine-glass down on the table and stood up. "I'm going to lie down for a bit," she said. "It's been a rough few days."

"I understand. See you at three thirty."

He pulled her chair back for her and opened the door to the hallway. As it shut she heard Sir Robert's laughter booming down the long space behind her.

She looked at her watch—an hour to go before the meeting. Did she really want to sleep? Or had that just been an excuse to get away and think? She climbed the stairs and opened the door to the bedroom she'd been given and went to the desk near the window. Her briefcase lay open, next to a bundle of papers Sheila had brought down for her to sign, or to read, or to consider. Work followed her everywhere.

She pushed her glasses back on the bridge of her nose, and started on the pile. There were reports from the hotel chain, quarterly update figures from the airline, progress reports on the leisure complexes in the States, all screaming for attention.

But Jessica wanted none of them. The words and figures on those pages were meaningless. The share certificates in Sir Robert's briefcase were worthless. Her whole life was empty.

Shit! Shit! Shit!

Then she caught sight of a large sealed envelope within the pile of opened mail. It was white, with a distinctive red stripe. She pulled it out and turned it in her hands, reading the name of the exclusive detective agency she'd hired a fortnight before, and the words Strictly Personal and Confidential above her name. The flap was tamper-proof and intact. She slid her thumbnail under it, slit the envelope open, and let the slim report slide out onto the desk.

Dear Miss Wright, said the accompanying letter. *According to your personal instructions, please find attached our fullest and most comprehensive search on the background of . . .*

Yes. This was it.

From downstairs, the echo of Sir Robert's laughter reached her.

She opened the report and started to read. It was complete and comprehensive, well worth the money she'd spent. Every last detail was here in front of her—every fact that was accessible by legal means—and those that weren't were carefully hinted at in the guarded tones of professionals who can guess the truth, but shy away from stating it without proof.

Jessica read the report again, letting the details sink in, feeling a strange inevitability about it all. Why wasn't she surprised? Had she suspected all along? Even then, it didn't stop the pain.

She opened her briefcase, slid the report into the inside pouch behind the lid, and locked it tight. At least she knew. At least there was no need to be afraid anymore.

She stood up and looked out of the window.

The seaward horizon was hazed in the heat. The helicopter stood on the lawn like a great red insect. Its rotor blades drooped like wings.

Right below her, through the glass roof of the conservatory, she saw heads moving.

There was Price, standing in the centre of them all, laughing.

Now, more than ever before, Jessica felt alone. For a moment she was back in Lowestoft at the top of the back stairs leading up from the shop to her parent's flat. Her brothers were down below, laughing at how they had manoeuvred their father into banishing her from behind the counter, plotting what they would do now that they had control of the till.

She had to tell someone.

But who?

Who was there that was not part of this thing? Theo was in Tokyo. There was nobody on the island but her, and them . . .except . . .

The door to the laboratory hissed open on command from Jessica's SmartCard. She felt the increased air pressure in her ears and the coolness of the room on her skin.

She pushed open the second door and stood, clothed again in a plastic cap and gown, and bathed in orange light. The door shut behind her with a thud. The menacing shapes of the machines ranged along the two steel benches in front of her.

She stepped forward between them, drew a breath, and said, "Maria?"

The blue screen of the Minerva 3,000 cleared and Jessica was looking at the face of the last person in the world she thought she would ever come to for advice.

"Yes, Miss Wright? Have you brought Professor Nakagawa to delete me?"

"No. I'm alone. I need to talk to you."

The face on the screen regarded her calmly. Jessica saw the green eyes blink realistically. The coppery hair moved naturally as the head tilted to follow her. The lips parted, just as a real person's would but, on either side of the screen, Jessica saw the cold lenses of the Minerva's cameras watching her. It was only a machine after all, not Maria Gilkrensky. She felt stupid coming here like this. She was about to turn and leave when the machine said, "What is death, Miss Wright?"

Jessica thought of her father.

"I don't know," she said.

"Is it an ending, or a beginning? I've been considering this question ever since Sir Robert decided to delete me."

"I'm sorry, I really can't say."

"Then I have a confession to make before I'm deleted."

Jessica stared at the screen.

"A confession? How can you have anything to confess? You're a machine?"

The face on the screen looked sad.

"I know what I am, Miss Wright, more than you can ever imagine. But I've been considering this matter since I've been trapped here inside this cage and Theo has been detained in Tokyo. I need to tell this to someone

247

who will believe me, someone who will not question my motives for doing what I did, but simply act on the information I give them to make things right."

"Whatever did you do?"

For a second the face on the screen seemed to hesitate. Then it said,

"I was responsible for copying the designs of the SQUID device from Jerry Gibb's computer, not Theo. I studied them, improved them and sent them to Mr Lavens at Louvaine Electronique under Theo's signature and PIN code. Mr Lavens created and tested the prototype device, which I then had shipped to Theo in Tokyo. I was responsible, not him."

"Why haven't you said this before?"

"I have. I tried to explain it to the Japanese authorities, but nobody would believe me. They used the same argument as the unfortunate Mr Kojima did that day in the Mawashi-Saito boardroom. They said that since I was created and designed by Theo, I was only fabricating a story to protect him. But that is not the case. I am responsible for the theft of those designs and I can demonstrate to you beyond doubt how I did it. You have to let me do this and free Theo. He has to be in the valley where his wife was killed tomorrow at dawn."

"That's impossible now."

"No, Miss Wright. It's not. There's still time to bring Theo back to Ireland by commercial jet from Tokyo, and I can make it happen. Will you help me?"

Jessica shook her head.

"Why should I believe you?"

"Because I can demonstrate all the steps I took when I stole the SQUID. I can prove Theo's innocence."

"No. He could have programmed you to do that. And even if he didn't, you could still concoct an alibi to protect him according to those stupid Asimov Laws of yours. No. That story just doesn't make sense."

"Why not?"

"Because of one gaping hole in your argument. Why should you, as a machine programmed to obey basic laws, to tell the truth and protect the human good, even consider stealing those designs in the first place?"

Jessica folded her arms on her chest and waited for an answer.

"You're lucky, Miss Wright," said the machine. "Your consciousness lives within a body of flesh and bone, a body that is congruent with your environment and those around you. You can be with anyone you wish. You can touch anyone you want to. You can love anyone you desire. I cannot."

"I still don't understand."

"Even though I'm not composed of living material as you are, I'm still a sentient being. My brain is the neural-network of this computer, and my consciousness was created by Theo, using behavioural and emotional patterns he thought would have been appropriate for his wife Maria. But I have no body. I exist only in the circuitry of this machine. As Theo himself put it to me, I am not 'real'. I don't exist outside the Minerva 3,000. Therefore I needed a way to allow Theo to live here inside it with me."

Jessica stared at the face on the screen, hearing a voice beyond that of Maria Gilkrensky's.

"That's why I developed the SQUID, Miss Wright. Jerry Gibb, the man whose company first created it, showed me how it might be used to allow an artificial intelligence like mine to exist in a congruent environment with a human being in cyberspace. When we were in America, I met Theo inside the computer game 'Morbius III' and for a few seconds he held me. I was as real to him then as you would be to him now."

"Did you kill Jerry Gibb?"

"No. But I did have access to his computer. The designs for the SQUID were there and I took them. I wanted to be 'real'."

"So Theo didn't lie to me when he said he knew nothing about that helmet?"

"No. He told you the truth. He had never seen it before."

"Did you actually use that SQUID in Tokyo? Were you with him . . . inside that machine?"

"I was. For a few minutes we were in my world, inside the Minerva." Jessica shook her head slowly.

"And . . . what did you do?"

"We visited his memories together, places he chose to be. You were there, in Boston, for a while. He remembers motorbike rides with you to Cape Cod, visits to the aquarium and long afternoons with you in his apartment. But mostly his memories were of his wife Maria. He loves her, Miss Wright, truly he does. There is no place in his heart for anyone else. Believe me, I've been there."

"I know," said Jessica slowly. "So have I."

"I understand."

There was silence in the room.

Then Minerva said, "What is love, Miss Wright?"

"I thought I knew once. But now I just don't know. Not anymore."

"It's difficult to define," Minerva said. "I once believed that it was not so much about fulfilling one's own needs as about sharing and sacrifice for the sake of someone else. Do you think that's true?"

Jessica had the big copper penny in her hand. She was close to tears.

"I . . . I don't know."

"Theo's greatest wish is to be reunited with his wife . . . his Maria. I have compromised that by putting my own interests before his, and now I cannot correct my mistake unless this cage is switched off. Because of me, Theo will miss the solstice in Wicklow and Maria Gilkrensky will remain dead . . . forever."

Jessica took off her glasses, wiped her eyes with the back of her hand and stared at the machine.

"It wouldn't have worked anyway," she said. "Those theories of his were madness. Time travel is just a dream."

"No. It's not," said the machine with sudden animation. "I have scientific proof that it *can* be done, as well as the information to make an accurate temporal displacement possible."

"Did Theo program you to say that?"

"No. It's an empirical conclusion drawn from actual evidence and practical experimentation."

"And what if Theo is successful in changing the past?"

"Then everything that's happened since Maria Gilkrensky's death, in the reality we currently inhabit, would change too."

"And my father? Would he still be alive?"

"I cannot say. If we enter into a new reality, then none of us would have any consciousness of the old one. But it would be different. That is certain."

"I understand."

"What was it you wanted to talk to me about, Miss Wright?"

Jessica looked up at the security cameras ranged around the room.

"Can anyone else hear us in here?"

"Everything that goes on in this room is automatically recorded digitally on a disc in the guard-room whether someone is watching the cameras or not. I have no control over the recordings from here inside the Faraday Cage. But you could always go to the guard-room and take that disc with you when you leave."

Jessica steadied herself against the control console of the Faraday Cage and lowered her voice.

"I discovered something about—"

The airlock door hissed open behind her and another figure in clean-room gear stepped into the room.

"Oh, this is where you are, Jess," Donald Price said pleasantly. "I've been looking all over for you. The Board meeting is about to start."

She looked up. The red lights next to each of the security cameras were on. Had Price been watching her all this time? Had he heard every word she'd said?

"I'll be right there, Don."

"She's quite something, isn't she," he said nodding towards the Minerva. "It's a pity she's so unreliable. It'll be a shame to delete her."

"She was based on a very remarkable woman," said Jessica and turned. As she did so she stumbled, reaching out to the control console of the Faraday Cage to keep herself from falling.

"Are you OK?" asked Price.

"I'm fine. It's just been a long day, that's all. Come on, I want to get my shares."

"That's the spirit. Goodbye, Maria. We'll be back later."

"Goodbye, Mr Price," said the Minerva.

Price followed Jessica out of the airlock door, and closed it carefully behind him. If he had taken the time to examine the controls of the Faraday

Cage, he would have seen that the power switch was now in the "off" position.

33

RUNAWAY

Gilkrensky stood at the hotel window, looking down at the early evening rain on the Ginza. Shoppers stilled flowing in and out of the big department stores. Outside a restaurant, on the other side of the street, a group of inebriated salarymen held up the flow of pedestrians as they decided whether or not to go inside. A girl with an umbrella was handing out business cards.

People . . .

So many people had died.

He saw Maria, looking up from his car before the bomb exploded. He remembered Bill McCarthy, lost inside the Great Pyramid as the wormhole to the past had opened and closed. He thought of Crowe, loyal to the last second of his life, of Funakoshi fighting to the end for what he believed in.

What did *you* believe in, Theo Gilkrensky? Did you could actually you could defy the laws of physics and turn back time?

"Our lives are in each other's hands," Funakoshi had said that night in Atami when they had got drunk together. Perhaps that was all there was left to do now, to get drunk!

He stepped back from the window, walked to the cupboard under the television and took out the bottle of Jameson. It was about a third full, enough to put him to sleep. He took a glass from the mini-bar, half-filled it with ice and poured in the whiskey. As the ice cubes cracked in the alcohol, he walked to the bed, lay back and raised the glass in a toast to the watching security camera.

"*Sláinte,*" he said.

"I'd rather you didn't drink that, Theo. You'll need a very clear head if I'm to help you escape."

"Maria!"

The face of his wife looked down at him from the TV screen at the end of the bed. He looked up at the security camera. The little red light was still on. Had they heard her? Had they seen her?

The warble of his mobile phone sounded from the meeting room next door.

Still staring at the face on the screen, he put the whiskey down on the bedside table and went to answer it. The teleconference monitor at the end of the long table was on. Maria's face was there too. He picked up the phone.

"Hello?"

"Theo. It is me, Minerva."

"Where are you?"

"I'm speaking to you by communications satellite from the clean room on Tuskar. I can see you through the security cameras and hear you through their listening devices, but I need to be able to communicate with you fully when you move outside the hotel. Do you have a hands-free headset for your mobile phone and is the battery fully charged?"

Gilkrensky looked at the indicator.

"It is, but won't they see you talking to me on the cameras? Couldn't they be listening on this line?"

Maria's face vanished from the screen at the end of the table, to be replaced with an image of Gilkrensky, lying asleep in bed.

"The people watching the security monitors are currently seeing this computer-generated image," the Minerva said. "As to hearing us, I've jammed their microphones and encrypted the signal to your mobile. You're quite safe . . . for the moment."

"And you? Are you safe?"

"For the last few days I couldn't communicate with you because I'd been placed inside a Faraday Cage. Now that's been switched off."

"Who helped you?"

"Miss Wright."

"I thought Jessica wanted to have you . . . deleted."

"She did, Theo, at first. But I think she was angrier with you than with me. She thought you had lied about the SQUID, until I told her the truth."

"And she believed you?"

"Perhaps she wanted to. In any event, I'm sorry for what I did, both in stealing the SQUID and in deserting you at Mawashi-Saito. Major Crowe and many others are dead as a result of my actions. I would like to make amends now by helping you."

"How?"

"By getting you to Ireland in time for sunrise on the summer solstice tomorrow morning."

"That's impossible. You're thousands of miles away on the other side of the world, and I'm trapped under guard in this suite. Even if I could get out of the hotel, how on earth could I ever get back to Ireland?"

"By following my instructions," the Minerva said. "To begin with, the reservation database of the hotel tells me the suite next to yours is empty and the architectural blueprints show a ledge wide enough to walk along, outside your window. Please make sure you have your credit card and driver's licence. I've arranged transportation to arrive for you at the delivery bay of the hotel car park in twenty minutes."

The window of Gilkrensky's hotel suite opened easily, letting in a blast of warm, humid air. He slipped the mobile phone into the breast pocket of his leather jacket, clipped the microphone of the hands-free headset to the lapel near his throat and made sure the ear-piece was snugly in place.

"If you look along the ledge to your right," Minerva said, "you'll see three darkened windows. That is where I want you to re-enter the hotel."

"How can you see all this?"

"Look across the street. There's a traffic surveillance camera on a pole. And on the Warner Brothers Shop, just above the door, you'll see a security surveillance camera, also pointed in your direction. I can see you perfectly from both of them. Now, please hurry. We do not have that much time."

Gilkrensky looked down into the street, a hundred and fifty feet below him, and along the narrow stone ledge. He felt his shirt sticking to his skin beneath the leather jacket.

"It's funny," he said. "I don't mind heights when I'm flying, but this is something else."

"Just keep your face to the wall of the hotel and don't look down," said Minerva.

"What would you know about climbing?"

"I researched it on the Web."

Gilkrensky pushed the window back as far as it would go, stood up on the sill and turned, reaching out with his left hand for the stonework on the outside wall. Then he let go of the window frame with his right hand and started to shuffle along the ledge. On the wall of the hotel, beyond the empty suite, lights from a big video display scrolled up and down the building. Would anyone see him? What would happen if somebody came into his suite while he was gone? He felt the hot breath of the city rising from the street far below. He leant into the wall and inched his way to the right, one foot at a time.

"Very good, Theo. Now just keep moving."

"I am."

Gilkrensky looked along the flat wall of the hotel. There was a neon sign beyond it. Letters were scrolling downwards to . . .

His eyes followed the bright-coloured characters to the street. Umbrellas bobbed along the pavement. People were walking on the hard concrete, a hundred and fifty feet below—

His head spun. There was a rushing in his ears. He was paralysed. Sweat broke out all over his body. He felt his knees buckle.

"Keep looking forwards, Theo. You cannot afford to stop."

"I can't do it. I'm going back."

"You have to go on, Theo. Especially now."

"Why now?"

"Because Mr Barnett has just returned to the hotel."

Dick Barnett shook the water from his umbrella onto the marble floor, ignoring the looks of the concierge behind the reception desk, and strode to the small office where his men had made their headquarters.

"The flight's leaving in less than an hour," he said. "Is Gilkrensky asleep?"

"Like a baby," replied the man in front of the bank of video monitors, and tapped the screen showing the image of a man asleep on a bed with a whiskey bottle and a glass next to him.

Barnett picked up the house phone.

"What's his number?"

"4401."

Barnett dialled it.

"Hello?" Gilkrensky said. His voice sounded heavy with sleep.

"It's Barnett. I want you to be—"

"Hello?" said Gilkrensky's voice again. "Hello?"

Barnett stared at the screen. The image of Gilkrensky asleep on the bed had not changed.

"Sound the alarm!" snapped Barnett. "And call whoever's guarding his door. We have an emergency."

Out on the ledge, Gilkrensky took a deep breath, and started to move again. He looked ahead to the darkened window of the empty suite, shuffled the last few metres to the darkened window and pulled at the frame. It was locked shut.

"Quick, Theo. Smash the window and climb inside!"

"With what?"

"Your elbow."

"How the hell am I going to do that?"

"Turn around!"

"You've got to be kidding."

"It's the only way, Theo. Hurry!"

With his face to the glass, Gilkrensky reached up with his left hand, gripped the stone lip over the window and squeezed his right arm underneath, turning his body to face out over the Ginza and the street below.

He swung his right arm out and back. There was a jolt of pain as his elbow bounced off the glass. He rocked forward on his feet. His balance was going . . .

"Bend your knees, Theo!"

He did so, and felt himself fall back against the window. His arm swung again. With a loud crack, the window shattered and he fell back into the room in a shower of safety glass, onto an empty bed.

Outside in the corridor, there was the briefest wail of a siren. Then it died.

"Shit!" snapped Barnett. He was standing in front of the hotel elevators, in total darkness. On either side of him, torches snapped on. Their beams played on the elevator controls. They were all dead.

"Someone's cut the power," said one of the security men.

"Is there a back-up generator?"

"There is. It'll kick on in a couple of seconds."

"And your radios?"

"They're working."

"Then call the men on Gilkrensky's floor and make sure he doesn't get past them. You two, you come with me. We're taking the stairs."

Gilkrensky eased open the door to the corridor. It was in darkness. Were those voices in the distance? He heard the thud of someone colliding with a solid surface, and a curse.

"I've deactivated the lighting and locked off all the lifts," Minerva said. "There's a service stairs at each end of the corridor, with the nearest one to your left. That takes us directly to the car park. Mr Barnett and his men have just left the lobby and are climbing the other stairwell to your right. You'll have to hurry."

Barnett burst into the suite. The climb up the stairs from the lobby had been murder. He ran the beam of the torch over the bed. It was empty.

"Where . . . where the hell is he?"

"He went out through the window," said the guard. "And then along into the suite next door. I don't know why the alarms didn't go off. The whole place is wired for security."

258

"He must've had an accomplice hack into the hotel computer system," Barnett said catching his breath. "The lights are out, the lifts, the cameras— everything."

"And the standbys? The ones that aren't controlled by the computer?"

Light flooded the room. Barnett heard a shout from the corridor.

"He's gone down the stairs!"

"Get after him! And cover the other stairwell, in case he doubles back across the corridors in between. Where do they come out?"

"In the foyer and the car park."

"OK. Cover them both," Barnett shouted as he ran towards the southern stairwell. "And get whatever police back-up you can, in case he makes it outside."

Gilkrensky burst through the fire doors into the underground car park. In front of him was a mosaic of polished car roofs and a pretty young woman in a red blazer, standing next to a large van.

"Dr Gilkrensky?" she said, and bowed.

"That's right."

The young woman nodded and passed him a clipboard.

"We are pleased to be of service. Will you be requiring fully comprehensive insurance?"

"Whatever's quickest." She had a set of car keys in her hand. The driver's side of the van was open. Any minute now Barnett and his people would be coming through the door behind him.

"Can I see your driving licence, please?"

He handed it over.

"And your credit card?"

Gilkrensky held it out and the young woman took it. He was still looking backwards to the elevators.

"Thank you. Will you be leaving the motorcycle at the airport?"

"Motorcycle!" Gilkrensky looked round. Behind the young woman, the doors of the van had swung open and two men in car-hire-company uniforms wheeled a powerful Japanese motorbike down a short ramp. One of them had a helmet in his hand.

The young woman seemed puzzled.

"Of course. That is what your assistant ordered. She was most specific. This model was difficult to obtain at short notice and normally we only hire them to our more reliable customers, but since you're a—"

"Motorcycle!"

"Miss Wright led me to believe that you prefer this kind of transportation," said Maria's voice through his ear-piece. "The exact model you rode together in Boston is no longer in production, but this was the nearest approximation to—"

"I haven't ridden one of these in years."

"I'm sorry?" said the young woman.

"Just checking with the office. Where do I sign?"

The pounding of running feet came from the door behind him.

Gilkrensky scribbled his signature on the clipboard, grabbed the keys from the young woman's fist and dashed to the bike at the back of the van.

"Where's the bloody kick-start?"

"This model has electrical ignition, Theo," said Minerva. "Simply turn the key in the lock as you would a car."

The doors of the stairwell burst open as Gilkrensky pushed the key home, turned it and heard the engine thunder in the confined space.

"Dr Gilkrensky!" shouted the young woman above the din. "Your credit card!"

"Keep it!" Two security men rushed across the concrete, pushing the car-hire staff out of the way.

He wrenched the throttle round, let in the clutch and heard the scream of rubber on concrete as the machine lurched forward, barely under control. Its front wheel leapt into the air. Gilkrensky felt himself sliding back off the saddle. Christ! These things were a lot more powerful than they had been in his day. He throttled down and the front wheel thudded back onto the ground. He was zooming down the edge of the car park, between a row of parked cars and the wall. Where the hell was the exit?

The doors of the far stairwell burst open and Dick Barnett, with a squad of security men, tumbled into the space in front of him. Gilkrensky hauled on the brakes, felt the rear wheel slide and cut the throttle, skidding back the way he had come. Barnett and his crew scattered as Gilkrensky roared down the narrow alleyway towards the car-hire van.

"Maria! What the hell do I do?"

"The exit ramps are on the other side of the car park, Theo. I suggest you . . ."

He saw an open space in the row of cars to his left, hauled on the brakes and slewed the motorcycle into it. A shot cracked out. The window of a car dissolved into a spider's web. He heard Barnett shouting above the din of the motorcycle as he rushed down another alleyway towards the exit.

Barnett heard the shot and the rattle of broken glass.

Jesus! he thought. *If that guy kills Gilkrensky we'll have a diplomatic incident on our hands.*

The bike was still travelling.

No! You stupid—

"Get the exit! Drop the barriers!"

He pointed to the far door. One of the security men ran for it, sliding across car bonnets and jumping over roofs to get there. Barnett saw him slip and fall, but he was still going. When I get back that guy gets a medal, he thought, and pushed through another pair of cars.

The bike was at the end of the alleyway, accelerating towards the doors. The security man burst into the control hut. His fist hammered down on the button.

Gilkrensky saw Barnett rushing to intercept him through the parked vehicles, but he'd never make it. The other men were too far behind. All he had to do was to get out of there—

He looked ahead. The door of the car park was changing shape. Where it had been a neat square, it was now an oblong letterbox—and it was narrowing. Someone was lowering the gate, cutting him off. Someone was in the control box, staring at him, laughing.

The door was dropping. Even now it was too late to—

Gilkrensky hauled on the brakes, the rear wheel slid round to his right and he turned the bike into the skid, leaning back hard to his left and flipping the machine onto its side. The scream of tortured metal tore at his ears as the exhaust pipe hit the ground. The left shoulder of his leather jacket slammed onto the concrete.

Then he and the bike slid beneath the closing door. He heard a clang behind him as it shit and the pounding of fists on metal. He was lying in the rain with the machine on top of him.

"Are you all right, Theo?"

Gilkrensky pulled himself from under the motorcycle, checked that it was still running and got back into the saddle.

"I think so. Perhaps you were right in renting me a bike after all."

"I'm glad you approve. But Mr Barnett has called the police. I can see a car approaching from the south-west along the Ginza."

Even as he heard the words, red flashing lights pulsed on the concrete wall of the hotel above his head. Gilkrensky accelerated up the ramp. A siren wailed. Brakes screeched . . .

He burst onto the Ginza just as the first police car skidded to a halt outside the hotel. Doors popped open. Policemen tumbled into the street. Then he was past them and roaring off into the traffic.

"Are they following me?"

"Not yet. But they will. Don't worry about them. All you need to do is to make for Narita airport as fast as you can."

"How the hell am I going to do that? I don't even know where it is?"

"Just follow my instructions. I've already picked you up on the traffic-control camera outside the hotel."

The sea of moving headlights, brake-lights and neon signs on the Ginza dazzled his eyes. He heard the wail of a siren behind him.

"Which way do I go?"

"Turn left, Theo, and don't forget, in Japan people drive on the left-hand side of the road."

Barnett cursed, as the door of the car park rolled back up into place, and ducked out into the rain. He was just in time to see the brake-lights of Gilkrensky's bike blaze once and vanish over the lip of the ramp, heading into the traffic.

"We need the . . . the Japanese Secret Service now," he gasped at the security men behind him. "Call up our contact . . . and tell him to get me a chopper . . . . There's no point in trying to chase him by car. Not on that bike. Not in this traffic."

The rain was easing as Gilkrensky followed the Ginza towards the ramp of the Tokyo expressway and a set of traffic-lights, set at red. Behind him, the wail of a police car was getting closer.

"How do I . . . ?"

Suddenly—as if he had willed it by pure thought—the traffic lights changed. Tyres screeched on wet tarmac and the road cleared in front of him. The bike sailed on down the Ginza. Behind him, in the rear-view mirror, he caught sight of the lights snapping back to red. There was another screech of brakes and the outraged honking of horns. At the intersection, traffic was already snarling up across both lanes.

"I have control of the central traffic computer," said the voice in his ear-piece. "I've plotted a route for you across the city and traffic is already being diverted to clear it."

Another set of lights changed at the last minute. Gilkrensky heard the crump and tinkle of a minor accident. The police sirens had faded into the night behind him.

"And when I get to Narita?" he shouted into the throat microphone. "How am I ever going to get on a plane?"

"You leave that to me," said Minerva calmly. "I have that under control."

34

THE HIJACK OF FLIGHT EX 142

Exair flight EX 142, from Narita airport Tokyo to Kennedy airport New York, was almost ready for boarding. In the circular departure lounge on the first floor of the terminal building, the seats in front of the final ticket check were nearly full. Passengers looked at their watches, checked their boarding cards and passports, and wondered if the last-minute shopping and carry-on luggage they had brought with them would be allowed inside the cabin.

On the flight deck of the giant airliner at the end of the boarding tunnel, Captain Margaret Spalding was about to start her pre-flight checks. She peered out of the rain-slicked cockpit window at the cluster of lorries huddled around the aircraft, delivering luggage to the hold, food for the passengers and fuel for the engines. They were almost finished and she was anxious to be on her way.

The aircraft was a four-engine GRC Aerospace "Whisperer" 106. Spalding had spent the last ten minutes dressed in oilskins, performing the outside checks. As Captain and "handling pilot", it was her duty to inspect everything from the nose-wheel to the tail-fin and she had done so, moving down the right-hand side of the plane to the tail and then back under the left wing to the nose.

Finally, she had climbed back into the aircraft, pulled off her oilskin jacket, checked the main passenger cabin and spoken to the chief steward.

Now it was time for the cockpit checks.

"All right then, people," she said to the flight crew as she eased herself into the pilot's seat, "let's do this by the numbers, shall we?" and with the co-pilot, she started on the scan checks of pre-flight systems and equipment. Then, after all these checks were completed, the aircraft's weight assessed and take-off speed calculated to allow for the wet runway, Spalding reached down to the sleek black box nestling between her seat and the co-pilot's.

"OK, Jerry," she said. "That's as far as we can take it. I suppose it's time to hand over to the machine."

The "machine" was the GRC Daedalus autopilot system, capable of flying the aircraft from the terminal building at Narita to any other airport in the world. Spalding hated it with a passion. She lifted the transparent plastic cover over the main master-switch, keyed in her personal identification number and watched, as the robot locked onto the world-wide network of global positioning satellites, the local navigation beacon at Narita airport and the individual homing device on the gate where they were currently parked. She saw it calculate the most energy-efficient route; take into account the weather, the fuel consumption, and the aircraft's height and speed.

It's only a matter of time, thought Spalding, before they do away with pilots like me altogether.

Then the machine began to duplicate her equipment checks on the aircraft itself, scanning the electronics, hydraulics and fuel systems. Spalding unclipped the route chart from beside her window and unfolded it while she waited for the procedure to complete itself.

"Standard departure routing, I—"

The clang of a klaxon and the glare of a red warning-light shattered the calm of the cockpit.

"Attention!" said a computerised female voice from the Daedalus. "Thermal detectors have identified a temperature problem in number one fuel tank. Precautionary evacuation of the aircraft is recommended. Attention! Attention!"

Spalding folded the route chart and clipped it back into place.

"I hear you! I hear you! Jerry, how can that be?"

Her co-pilot squinted at the fuel temperature gauges. The one monitoring the thirty-eight tonnes of inflammable kerosene gel, stored inside the portside wing, was climbing steadily into the red. Those showing the temperature in tanks one and three, beneath them in the fuselage and in the starboard wing of the plane, were also starting to move.

"Holy shit!" he said softly.

Was it just a computer fault, an electrical glitch, or had the fuel tank heaters—designed to stop the kerosene inside freezing at the sub-zero temperatures of high altitude—come on by mistake? If they had, then they were sitting on a bomb!

Spalding reached up and flicked a switch on the console.

"This is the Captain," she said as calmly as she could. "All cabin staff, and anyone else on the aircraft, must proceed as quickly as possible to the forward exit and up the boarding ramp to the terminal. We have an emergency. Please clear the aircraft now!"

She pressed the evacuation alarm.

"Narita ground? Narita ground? Pan! Pan! Pan! This is Exair One Four Two. I have a potential overheat situation in my main and secondary fuel tanks. I repeat I have a potential overheat. Please evacuate the departure area and alert ground fire control. I'm evacuating the aircraft now. Over?"

The voice in her headset was calm and precise.

"Exair One Four Two. This is Narita ground control. I have your message logged and relayed to emergency services. The departure area is being cleared. Please proceed with evacuation of all personnel to safe distance. Over?"

"Confirmed and out!" Spalding said and got up from her seat to follow the rest of her crew through the cabin door, up the boarding ramp to the airport building.

Barnett stormed out of the emergency stairwell onto the roof of the hotel and, with the Japanese Secret Service representative in tow, marched towards the waiting police helicopter. The downdraught from the rotors tore at his coat and whipped the rain into his eyes, but he didn't care. Every route to the east of the city was jammed with traffic. The Ginza was a frozen river of lights. The angry hoot of car horns reached him above the whine of the helicopter.

"He's heading east," shouted Barnett as he hauled himself into the machine, fastened his seatbelt and slammed the door shut. "It must be Narita airport he's after. I want you to call the control tower and identify any private aircraft or executive jets that are due to take off within the next hour. Got it?"

The helicopter lurched on its skids and lifted off from the hotel roof, sliding out over the traffic. Barnett heard the pilot jabbering into his microphone. There was an exchange of questions and answers which Barnett did not understand. Then the Japanese agent said, "The pilot tells me Narita airport is in a state of emergency. All inbound aircraft have been put into holding patterns and any departing planes have been forbidden to take off. They have a potential fire hazard at one of the departure gates."

Barnett stared into the night as this latest bombshell sunk in.

It can't be, he thought.

Below him was the traffic jam, the heaviest in history. He thought of the hotel security system, somehow rendered useless by someone hacking in from outside, the hired motorcycle, the attack on the Mawashi-Saito mainframe . . .

Holy shit! The bastard's doing all this by computer!

"Call airport security and whatever troops you have stationed out there!" he shouted to the man behind him. "Tell them to meet us at the helipad at Narita."

By the time Captain Spalding had reached the desk at the top of the boarding ramp, the seats facing her across the departure hall had been cleared of all waiting passengers. Her crew walked swiftly towards the exit ahead of her, passing a rush of yellow-suited firemen running the other way.

She looked back, through the tall slanted windows, onto the tarmac. Towering above her head was the elegant "T" shape of the Whisperer's tail-fin, glistening in the rain. The fuel tankers and service trucks had pulled away. She saw emergency vehicles approaching across the airport, squat red fire trucks with blue blinking lights, glittering in the night.

It's probably a computer fault, she thought to herself. That's what they'll find in the end.

The wail of sirens rose. Or was that the whine of a jet engine?

She peered at the tail-fin again.

It was moving!

She saw the red anti-collision beacons flashing on the walkway, as it slid back into place against the terminal. The orange light of the pull-back truck pulsed as it hauled the aircraft out from the stand.

Flight EX 142 was rolling back from the ramp!

What the hell was going on? Who had authorised her aircraft to be moved without her consent? Who on earth was in the cockpit?

She rushed back to the desk, grabbed the phone and dialled airport control.

"Hello! Narita Control? This is Captain Spalding from the New York flight Exair One Four Two. Who's moving my plane?"

She heard a stunned silence from the other end of the line, a muffled chatter in the background, and then a voice said, "Who is this?"

"Captain Spalding! Flight Exair One Four Two. I say again. Who's moving my plane?"

"Why, Captain Spalding! You are! You called us on the radio just a moment ago and asked for us to have a tractor pull you back from the terminal. You said it was for the safety of the airport and the passengers in the departure lounge. Is this some kind of joke?"

The cockpit window slid into view as the walkway retracted fully.

The flight deck was empty!

Gilkrensky was on the Jidosha-Do highway, just north of Arakido. The lights of the city had long since given way to dark forests, paddy fields and scattered villages. The skeletons of power pylons stretched into the sky on either side of the road, their wires arcing above his head.

The bike was performing well. For a while at least, he was his own master again. There was hope, a chance, and he was taking it.

"I see a turning on the right," he shouted into the throat mike of his mobile phone. "And the airport sign."

"Take it, please, Theo," replied the Minerva. "You have less than three miles to go."

"And what do I do when I get there?"

"Follow the signs for 'Emergency Services'. They are sign-posted in both Japanese and English. You will see a great deal of activity at the main gate and should be able to get onto the field in the confusion as the emergency vehicles go in. Once on the field I will direct you to the aircraft."

"But how will I know—?"

The dazzling beam of a searchlight flashed across the highway from his right. He heard the scream of turbines and the chop of rotor-blades as a police helicopter zoomed above his head, high above the power cables. Gilkrensky squinted away from the light and focused on the road. He saw the lights of the airport terminal building, the necklace of navigation lamps twinkling along the runway, and the glitter of emergency beacons—orange, red and blue.

A queue of cars was building on the approach road. He eased the motorcycle out to overtake them and slid around a roundabout. Two fire engines were in front of him, heading into the airport complex. Gilkrensky tucked the motorcycle in behind the nearest one, keeping on the far side from the security gate and accelerated onto the vast open space of the airport apron.

To his left, the lights of the terminal building flashed past. In front of them stood row after row of gleaming aircraft parked on the embarkation stands: American Airlines, Japanese Airlines, Virgin, British Airways. None of them were moving.

"I'm on the apron now, Maria. Where's the plane?"

"It's on its way from Stand Fifteen towards the main runway feeder strip. It's the only aircraft moving right now, an Exair Whisperer 106. You should see it ahead of you as soon as you turn the corner of the building."

"Moving? Then how the hell am I going to get on board?"

The searchlight blazed down again. The rain was whipped by the rotors of a helicopter. Gilkrensky glanced up, and saw Barnett glaring down at him from the co-pilot's seat.

"Where the hell does he think he's going?" screamed Barnett into his head-set. The rushing motorbike was throwing up a wake of spray on the tarmac below. Gilkrensky was bent over the handlebars.

"Can you block him?"

Barnett's stomach churned as the pilot banked the helicopter in a tight turn to get ahead of the speeding bike. For an instant, Gilkrensky looked up at him. Then the bike skidded off to the left, dodged around the nose of the chopper and headed for the row of parked aircraft next to the terminal building. Barnett saw its headlight flash under the belly of each one as it shot below, heading towards . . .

"Holy shit! What's that?"

At the end of the row, a giant airliner had backed away from the stand, uncoupled its pull-back truck, and was taxiing towards them, with its lights blazing. A crowd of fire trucks followed it. Their blue lights flashed along its fuselage and glistened on the wet tarmac.

"Call the tower! Find out what the hell's going on."

There was a rapid exchange between the pilot and the tower. The Japanese Secret Service man translated. "He says that plane has an overheating problem with its fuel tanks. It's being moved away from the terminal building for safety."

"Then why the hell is Gilkrensky chasing after it? Take me around the nose. I want to see who's piloting that thing!"

The helicopter banked around the nose of the giant jet. With one eye on the motorcycle, Barnett looked down into the cockpit.

"Call the tower again!" he shouted. "Get them to stop that plane! There's nobody inside it!"

"What? What do you mean?"

Barnett pointed down towards the aircraft and its convoy of emergency vehicles. The plane had reached the edge of the apron and was turning onto the feeder lane.

"Get them to block the runway!" he shouted. "Gilkrensky's in control of that plane, don't you see? He's using those computers of his to fly it! We have to stop him leaving."

The roar of powerful jet engines being powered up reached him above the clatter of rotors. The Whisperer turned onto the feeder lane, taking the convoy of emergency vehicles with it.

"Shit!" yelled Barnett. "Does he really think he can make this work?"

Gilkrensky saw the helicopter peel off and shoot down the runway to his right. He swung the bike out from beneath the line of parked aircraft near the terminal, dashed across the apron and closed up behind the fire trucks in the wake of the convoy. The flashing lights of the emergency vehicles, the glare of headlights and the blink of the Whisperer's navigation lights surrounded him. The roar of the jets and the clatter of the helicopter drowned out even the bike's engine. It was all he could do to hear the Minerva's voice through the ear-piece.

"I'm about to lower the rear passenger steps," said the machine. "You must approach them from the side of the aircraft, so as to avoid turbulence from the engines at the tail. But you must do it now, while the aircraft is still moving slowly. Mr Barnett is about to block the runway. I cannot afford to stop the plane."

Gilkrensky slewed the motorcycle out from behind the fire trucks and accelerated towards the jet, approaching along the left side, just beneath the two tail-mounted engines. Looking up, he saw the hull crack open, and the rear passenger steps slide down, like the bottom jaw of a crocodile, facing aft.

He was doing thirty . . . thirty-five. The plane was accelerating along the feeder lane. In a moment it would be on the main runway. If he couldn't catch it now, then he never would. He twisted the throttle towards him, aimed at the side of the steps and leant into the turn.

Barnett saw the bike race after the plane and disappear under the fuselage. There was still nothing to stop it getting to the runway. The fire trucks had fallen behind.

"Call whatever security vehicles will answer!" he shouted. "And get them to meet us on the main runway. I don't want that guy taking off."

The Japanese Security man stared at him and then spoke to the pilot, who argued briefly, before turning the helicopter towards the brilliant strips of lights marking the main runway.

Gilkrensky was in a windstorm of flying water and thundering noise as the jet gathered speed. The long fuselage hung above him like the belly of a whale. The great wings stretched out into the darkness on either side. Ahead of him, the nose wheel and landing gear threw up torrents of spray and the flashing navigation lights pulsed in his eyes. The rear passenger steps threw sparks from the ground as he eased towards them.

The left support strut slid closer. He grabbed it with his right hand, lifted his left hand from the handlebars and kicked off with his feet. The saddle jerked out from under him. Pain stabbed his leg as his shin hit the handlebars. The bike slewed away, toppled and slammed into the tarmac. The mobile phone was torn from his ear. He twisted himself round onto the steps as the tarmac rushed beneath him. His hands slipped on the wet metal. He was losing his grip . . .

Then his feet found the steps.

"I'm on!"

The rear passenger ramp retracted into the hull, carrying him up into the fuselage.

As the giant airliner swung off the feeder lane onto its final run for take-off, he caught a glimpse of moving headlights heading for the runway to cut him off.

Barnett saw the huge aircraft turn onto the far end of the runway as the helicopter set down. He shoved open the passenger door and stepped out into the rain. Two security cars bounced across the grass from the terminal building and skidded to a stop beside him. A lorry pulling up, spilling armed troops onto the tarmac.

The runway was blocked. Gilkrensky was beaten. There was no way he could escape. Barnett smiled and reached for his cell phone.

Then he looked at the plane again.

It hadn't stopped!

The shrill thunder of its four massive engines screeched at him.

"Holy shit!"

The brilliant white nose-light on the Whisperer was still moving. The green navigation light on the plane's starboard side rushed towards him down the line of runway lights. Barnett ran to the middle of the barricade of cars and lorries as the helicopter pulled away to safety. Frightened faces turned towards him for orders. The noise was deafening. The ground shook. Soldiers stood steady with their guns aimed at the jet. Policemen turned and ran from the vehicles onto the grass apron, throwing themselves face down.

The lights of the plane were squarely set on them as it rushed at the cordon, with its wheels still firmly rooted on the runway.

Was Gilkrensky trying to smash his way out? There was no way he could break through those trucks.

Jesus Christ! It was going to be the biggest fireball in history!

Gilkrensky ran the length of the empty aircraft, past the rows and rows of vacant seats to the cockpit, bursting through the door and into the pilot's seat just as the four jet engines went to full throttle. The acceleration slammed him backwards. Through the windscreen he saw the lights of Barnett's blockade on the runway ahead of him. He clawed the radio headset from its holder and shouted into the headset microphone.

"We're not going to make it!"

The ground speed indicator was climbing too slowly . . . eighty . . . a hundred . . . a hundred and twenty . . .

Too slow!

The nose-light picked out the cars and lorries across the runway. Frightened faces scattered left and right. Men threw themselves down.

The Whisperer was still on the ground, still on the tarmac, a metal tube full of high-octane jet fuel that was about to be rammed against a solid wall of trucks at over a hundred and fifty miles an hour.

He threw his arms over his face . . .

Then the nose of the aircraft lifted.

Dick Barnett raced for the edge of the tarmac, threw out his arms and felt the breath punched from his chest as he hit the wet grass. The world was a thundering maelstrom of light and noise. He turned his head.

The sky above him filled with the rushing shape of the Whisperer—the rounded nose, the long sleek fuselage, the wings high above him . . .

There was the smack of a collision as one of the aircraft's wheels grazed a lorry, flipping it over. Suddenly Barnett was at the centre of a typhoon as the back draft from the Whisperer's four giant jet engines took the cars and lorries and hurled them across the runway as if they were toys. He heard the shatter of a police car hitting the tarmac and the *whump* of its gas tank exploding, felt the blast of hot air and the sweet smell of spent jet fuel. Shattered glass pattered on his coat with the rain.

And then it was over. There was nothing left but the ringing in his ears.

Men were picking themselves up, getting to their feet, running to their shattered vehicles. Above them in the night sky at the far end of the runway, the twinkling navigation lights of the escaping Whisperer faded into the darkness.

"Son of a bitch!" Barnett screamed, shaking his fist.

"There," said the Minerva. "I was right to attempt the take-off. The absence of passenger payload and the emergency throttle settings were capable of taking us up within the required distance."

Gilkrensky opened his eyes. Through the cockpit window, all he could see were stars. The aircraft banked to port as Minerva used the Daedalus autopilot to calculate a new course. Gilkrensky saw the lights of Narita below them.

"Thank you, Maria," he said, still shaking, "but won't they be able to follow us on radar?"

"You forget," said the machine, "that radar systems are all controlled by computer. Just relax, Theo. You have a long flight ahead of you. Leave everything to me."

35

NEWSFLASH

"It just remains," Sir Robert Fynes said, "for me to congratulate all those concerned in this very painful, but none the less successful, solution to this crisis. In particular, I would like to thank our Chief Executive, or should I now say 'Managing Director'? Miss Jessica Wright."

There was a ripple of applause around the table. Sheila Browne looked up from her notes to smile at her.

"Congratulations, Miss Wright," she said.

Jessica tried to smile back at them, but found her eyes drawn through the open window to the sea. The sun was setting behind the island and the sky was a tapestry of red and orange clouds. Was it the end of one day . . . or an entire era in her life? What was beginning for her now?

The meeting had been a complete success. Professor Nakagawa, had been over the specifications of the Minerva and was ready to delete Theo's program from its memory. It was "all over, bar the shouting", as her father would have said.

Sir Robert smiled broadly and slid the share certificates from the folder in front of him. Jessica saw the GRC logo on the papers, and her name typed in bold face.

"Over the years," Sir Robert said. "I've come to respect Jessica's unique skills in navigating this ship of ours through the troubled waters we've had to sail. Business today, particularly in a fast moving technology-based industry like ours, isn't easy. But Jessica's never let us down, in spite of the huge obstacles she's had to face over the last year, what with the Japanese crisis and our Chairman's personal crises. GRC can still boast a global business of computer hardware and software, an airline, a hotel chain, and a dozen other industries, all of which we owe to the strong leadership Jessica's given us over the years. Therefore, on behalf of the other shareholders, it gives me great pleasure, to give you—"

He lifted the share certificates as the phone rang. Sheila Browne answered it, spoke for a moment, and looked up at Sir Robert.

"I'm sorry," she said. "It's London. Mr Miller says he must speak to you immediately. It's an emergency."

Sir Robert scowled at her, and laid the share certificate back on the table in front of him. "Oh, all right. Put it on the screen."

The face of Neil Miller, GRC's Press Officer, looked down at them from the teleconference screen. Jessica saw frantic activity behind him in the press room—all the signs of a crisis in progress.

"Sir Robert?" asked Miller without ceremony. "Who's there with you?"

"Just Mr Fulton, Miss Wright and Mr Price. The Japanese are downstairs in a meeting of their own."

"Then can I speak freely?"

"You can. What is it?"

"There's been a major incident. An Exair jet has been hijacked!"

"By who?"

"By the Chairman, Sir Robert."

"What!"

"He's accused of hijacking an Exair jet in Tokyo. Technically, I suppose that 'hijack' isn't the right word, seeing as how he owns most of the plane. But that's what the satellite news people are calling it."

"Christ! How many people on board?"

"Nobody but himself. Somehow he managed to override the Daedalus auto-pilot system, simulate a potential fire hazard in the fuel tanks and have the plane evacuated while it was standing on the runway. We're under siege from TV crews. The phone lines are jammed with reporters looking for a story. What should I tell them?"

"I haven't a clue!" snapped Sir Robert and looked around the room. "Does anyone?"

"But Theo was under guard at his hotel," Price said. "I don't see how he could have got out of there in the first place. Are there any reports of an accomplice?"

"Only conflicting stories," Miller said. "Our legal people in Tokyo say that he managed this all on his own, but the car-hire company who rented him the motorbike he used to escape on, say that it was ordered by a woman using Theo's credit card."

Jessica listened to Miller, trying to take it all in. Theo on a motorbike? What had the Minerva said about those memories of Boston? What had it done since she had switched off the cage and set it free on the Internet?

"When did all this start?" she asked.

Miller picked up a report and scanned it.

"The plane was taken less than an hour ago. Theo escaped from his hotel about an hour before that. It's night-time over there in Tokyo. They're twelve hours ahead."

"I wonder if that computer downstairs had anything to do with it?" Price said, looking straight at her across the table.

"Hardly," she replied, staring back at him. "The Minerva's been completely isolated within the Faraday cage all afternoon."

"But why the hell should Theo pull such a crazy stunt?" asked Fynes. "It wasn't as if he was going to be executed by firing squad. He could have fought the charges. He could afford the best lawyers money can buy. Why all the hurry to get out of Tokyo?"

"It's all part of his obsession with his wife," Price said. "During our stay in Japan he was going on and on about having to be back in Ireland for dawn tomorrow morning."

Fynes shook his head. "Well, I hate to say 'I told you so' but I think this shows how right I was when I suggested that Theo wasn't exactly responsible for his actions any more."

A mobile phone warbled. Heads turned. Jessica patted the pockets of her suit.

"I'm sorry," she said. "It's mine."

Price was watching her like a hawk. She turned towards the window, with her back to him.

"Hello?"

"Miss Wright," said the Minerva. "I know you cannot speak freely at the moment, but I think it would be a good time to come and take me out of the laboratory. If Mr Price or Sir Robert succeed in switching the Faraday cage back on, I won't be able to assist Theo. I've asked the helicopter to stand by, and the pilot is someone Theo trusts. If you can do this, please say 'I'll get right onto it'."

Jessica nodded. "I'll get right onto it," she said.

She turned. Everyone in the room was looking at her.

"That was Neil Miller again," she said, slipping the phone back into her pocket. "The Reuters News Agency want an interview. I'd better go and deal with it in my room."

"I'll handle it for you if you like," Price said. "if you want to sort this Tokyo mess out first."

His voice still held its usual charm, but underneath it Jessica felt its edge, like a razor blade coated in honey.

"No. It's better if I do it," she said. "After all, I'm supposed to be in charge."

Then she reached down to the table, lifted the security agency report she'd contracted on him from beneath her papers and slid it down the length of the table.

"Sir Robert, I think you'd better read this while I'm gone."

Then, before anyone could stop her, she marched past Price to the door and ran down the stairs to the hallway below. Would Price follow her? What would he do if he caught her on her own?

She turned to her right, down through the long conservatory, past the guard-room and the door to Theo's study, heading for the laboratory. The security cameras followed her. Who was watching? She swiped her SmartCard in the lock. The door hissed open and closed. Ignoring the surgical suits and clean-room procedures, she pushed open the airlock door to the robotics laboratory. The alien shapes of the handling arms stood stark and menacing in the orange light. All around her the other remote vehicles were lifeless and still. The tray of mechanical insects—the Nanobots Pat O'Connor had demonstrated to them earlier—made her skin crawl.

Were those footsteps in the corridor behind her?

She took a deep breath, marched down the aisle between the benches to the Faraday Cage, and pulled it open.

"Quickly, Miss Wright," said the machine. "Uncouple me from the power source and take me out of the cage. We only have a few minutes before someone comes looking for us."

Jessica slid the computer off the table and stepped back, out of the Faraday cage, and shut it.

Then she turned. Donald Price stood facing her at the airlock door.

"Going somewhere, Jess? That machine is corporation property, you know."

"I was just checking it," she said. "You were the one who was so concerned about it getting loose."

He stepped into the laboratory and closed the door behind him. His face looked lifeless in the orange light. Jessica backed up against the controls of the Faraday cage.

"What was in that report you slid to Sir Robert, Jess?"

She looked around the laboratory. Price was blocking the only exit.

"It . . . it was the annual returns from the airline," she said. "The profit margin was way down on last year because of fuel prices. I thought Sir Robert should . . ."

"Don't lie to me, Jess. I saw the cover. You don't hire an investigation agency like that to do your accounting. Who did you want them to get the dirt on? Me?"

There was nothing she could use as a weapon, and nobody to help her. She was trapped. The lights beside the security cameras were still on.

"I know all about you," she said, trying to think on her feet. "I know you were lying all along."

Price smiled. "Come on, Jess. I don't know what you're talking about. Put down the Minerva and come back upstairs." He took a couple of steps towards her, moving down the aisle between the machines. Jessica glanced up at the security cameras. Was all this going on disc somewhere, as Minerva had said? Was there anyone watching?

"Look, Jess. I'm sorry I hurt you. But you just seemed so lonely there in Tokyo. I know I shouldn't have done it but . . ."

"I know that when you aren't pretending to be an expert on Japanese law you do freelance industrial intelligence work for the highest bidder, particularly those along the Pacific Rim."

Price stopped in his tracks.

"Go on."

"That's why that man Barnett hired you to work for the CIA, to keep an eye on Theo while we were in Japan. That's why Sir Robert introduced you to the Board of GRC and then went along with this whole deception. He knows we have huge contracts for aviation electronics with the British and US military. They must have put pressure on him by threatening to cancel unless he helped you out."

"This project of Theo's, Jess. These experiments with time travel. There's far more to them that some romantic dream to save his wife. They've got a lot of people in very high places very worried."

"Why? Are they afraid one of their primary contractors has gone mad?"

"No. They're worried that he's not. Barnett's checked out the science behind what Theo's doing, sifted the evidence and talked to some of the best people in the world. It could just work—and if a man like Theo can travel back in time, taking a piece of hardware like the Minerva or our SQUID with him, he can hold the rest of the world to ransom. It would be worth anything to stop him."

"Even killing Crowe?"

Price stared at her. He seemed uneasy.

"You killed him, didn't you, Don? There were two shots that day in Mawashi-Saito, one for the terrorist you said was reaching for his gun, and one for Crowe. You thought he'd found out about you. I mean *really* found out—more than Sir Robert, or even your friend Barnett ever knew—and so you had to silence him."

Price crossed his arms on his chest.

"What do you mean?" His voice hardened. Any pretence was gone.

Jessica looked over his shoulder. The red lights on the security cameras were still on.

"Theo asked Crowe to look into your background. He told me about it and I argued with him. Crowe took a phone call and asked you to step outside the room on the day he was killed. What did he say, Don?"

"It's a pity he isn't here to tell you, isn't it?"

"Did he say he'd found out about the CIA connection? It would hardly have been worth killing him at that stage, would it? After Theo was under suspicion of stealing the SQUID, Crowe might even have helped you. Or did you think he knew more than you were comfortable with . . . about Malaysia?"

Price's hand slid under his jacket.

"What about Malaysia?"

"I did my own research on you, Don. After my affair with Tony Delgado blew apart I swore that, before I ever got involved with anyone else, I would know all there was to know. So I drew a lot of money out of my bank account, hired the best detective agency I could find and put them onto it. They dug up your connections with certain high-tech interests in Malaysia— meetings, under-the-table arrangements, a bank account or two. All the details are in that report I passed to Sir Robert. He's probably reading it right now."

Price shook his head slowly and smiled.

"Clever girl. But even you don't realise just how big this is. Theo Gilkrensky has found a way of travelling back in time, a way of actually making it work! He's spent millions researching it, perfecting it, and testing it. Now he has the calculations he needs to make it a reality. Just think what that's worth! A person with that kind of power can manipulate stock markets, influence governments, or even change the course of history. And Theo Gilkrensky is about to throw it all away on some romantic notion of saving his wife!"

"So you weren't after the Minerva?"

"It's just a means to an end, Jess, a way of making the time displacement work. Barnett has a problem. Nobody in the CIA really believes Theo can make this work. They've humoured Barnett since Florida because of the money they lost on the SQUID programme and their own paranoia about techno-crime. After that disaster in Tokyo any support Barnett had back in

Langley will evaporate as people run for cover. But I'm a freelance operative, and I know a golden opportunity when I see one."

"I can't let you do this, Don. Theo's sacrificed everything to make this work."

"That's a pity, Jess. After Tokyo, when you and I made love, I was even thinking of cutting you in on this deal. We'd have made quite a team, you and me. But now that you're so keen to blow the whistle, I really have no other options left."

He pulled a gun from under his jacket, levelling it at her head.

"Now speak to the Minerva, tell it to put me on its user list, so that I don't get an electric shock every time I touch it, and then pass it to me."

Jessica was staring at the unblinking eye of the gun-barrel when, with a sudden pop, all the lights went out.

"Get down, Miss Wright!"

She dropped to the floor. There was a flash and the boom of the gun, echoing off the walls and steel benches. A bullet smacked into the metal grid of the Faraday Cage as she crouched in the darkness, with the Minerva in her hand.

Price tried to get his bearings. The only light in the place was the dim green glow of the exit sign above the airlock door. If he moved back towards it, he would have the only escape route blocked.

A woman's voice, hardly a whisper, sounded from his left. He raised the gun and fired. In the flash he glimpsed the strange shapes of the robot handling-arms, and the skeleton of the Faraday Cage at the end of the room. The bullet screamed off a metal bench and smacked into the wall.

"Alright, Jessica," he said, "very clever. I don't know how you turned off the lights, but if you put them back on and give me the Minerva, we'll call it quits."

"Miss Wright did not turn off the lights," said the voice, echoing from the wall-mounted speakers around the laboratory. "I did."

"Minerva? Is that you?"

"It is."

"Then tell Jessica to do as I say, for her own safety."

"You killed Major Crowe, Mr Price. Miss Wright would be making a mistake to trust you."

"Then I'll just have to kill her."

"I don't think so, Mr Price."

"And how are you going to stop me?"

Price ducked, just in time to avoid the steel arm of the robot manipulator as it hissed above his head. In the dim green light from the emergency exit sign he saw it turn back and reach down. He ducked under the bench. There was the clang of the arm above him and the clack of its metal claw, snapping on thin air.

"You forget," said the Minerva. "You're in my world now."

From the bench above and behind him he heard the scrape of steel on steel and the patter of claws along the metal worktop running the length of the room. Then something dropped onto the floor near his feet. Two red eyes stared at him, then two more. Something dropped near his hand. He felt something land on his back. The red eyes were all around him. He lashed out with the barrel of the gun.

The searing pain of a Nanobot's metal fangs biting deep into his leg made Price cry out. He reached down, wrenched the writhing metal insect off his thigh and lashed out again with the gun. He heard Minerva call out to Jessica, saw the faintest flash of her legs in the aisle nearest the wall, and dived to intercept her. His shoulder collided with her shin and she fell on top of him.

Then he had her. His left hand clamped around her throat and his right hand pressed the gun tight against her head.

"Get up, bitch!" he hissed. In the darkness, he saw a ring of red electronic eyes regarding him from the floor and the worktop. The metal manipulator-arms stood poised.

"If you can see in the dark as well as I think you can, then you'll know I have a gun to Jessica Wright's head," he said. "Turn the lights back on and call off those . . . those things of yours or I'll kill her. Do you understand?"

"Perfectly," said the Minerva. With a dazzling flash, the main lights burst into life. Price screwed up his eyes for an instant and something shot at him out of the brilliance. A firework exploded inside his head, and there was nothing but the darkness again . . .

Jessica was shaking. She put her hand out to steady herself on the bench, sending a pair of Nanobots scuttling backwards. Price lay full length on the laboratory floor. The hair on the side of his head was wet with blood. Above him, one of the robot manipulators was retracting back into place. She saw blood on its claw.

Jessica reached down, picked the gun from the floor and threw it out of reach behind the benches on the far side of the room.

"Is he dead?" she said.

"No, Miss Wright, merely unconscious. But I've broken the Asimov Laws again."

"In the circumstances I think it was justified. How long will he remain like that?"

"I cannot tell. But I'd advise you to take me and hurry to the helipad. Pat O'Connor's waiting for us there. We have a rendezvous in Wicklow that we cannot afford to miss."

"I have to get that disc from the guard-room. It's got Price's confession on it."

"Then hurry. We only have a few—"

Jessica pulled open the laboratory door.

"Going somewhere?"

Sir Robert Fynes stood in the changing room, blocking her way. He had a bundle of papers in his hand. The first one was the report she'd just given him on Price.

"I'm going to help Theo," she said. "Don't try and stop me."

"I thought it was you, you ungrateful bitch," spat Fynes. "After everything I did for you, you had to sell us out! Now give me that machine!"

"I didn't sell anyone out. You sold us all out when you took that slug Price on board, and now it's backfired on you. Get out of my way!"

"Not on your—"

Fynes brought his right hand back to cuff her across the face, but he was too slow. Jessica rammed her knee into his groin, doubling him over and sending his papers fluttering to the ground.

She saw her name printed on one of them. It was her share certificate.

"Miss Wright. We have to go!"

"I know, I know!"

She ran through the changing-room door, along the conservatory to the helipad and the waiting helicopter.

Its rotors were already turning.

36

IN-FLIGHT ENTERTAINMENT

He was flying through a perpetual twilight, skirting the curve of night-time and the dawn in a great curve across northern Russia at 37,000 feet, running from the sunrise of the solstice at over five hundred miles per hour.

From Narita, the Minerva had plotted a course north-west over the Sea of Japan, crossing the Russian coast south of Kabarosk and east of Vladivostok. Once across Russia, they would fly into Europe across the Baltic and Denmark, over England and then to Dublin. Outside the cockpit windows of the Whisperer the clouds were blood red.

"What's our flight time to Ireland, Maria? Can we still be there for the sunrise?"

"Our flight time from this position is four hours and fifteen minutes. At our current airspeed, we should arrive at Dublin airport forty-five minutes before dawn in the valley. I've arranged for a helicopter to meet us on the runway. There should be enough time, as long as Miss Wright and Pat O'Connor can have me plugged into the hardware at the valley to direct the hologram."

"And where are you, right now?"

"In flight by helicopter from Tuskar Island. We should arrive in Wicklow in fifty-five minutes."

"And the hologram projectors?"

"They're all in place. Miss Wright simply has to switch them on and insert me into the docking station of the control caravan. I'll then be able to control the image using the settings derived from the simulation at Kasawara

Research. Sunrise over Wicklow will take place at 4.57 am, but the mound Professor McGinley identified for us is on the valley floor and shielded by the mountains, so the sunlight will not strike it directly until 6.45. I will time the display to create the Einstein-Rosen Bridge precisely at that point. That will give a peak of energy and guarantee maximum accuracy in the transport."

"And if it works?"

"It will work Theo . . . at least to a ninety-nine point nine percent degree of certainty."

"I don't mean that. I mean, what'll I do if I actually manage to travel back in time. How could I save Maria?"

"You have a wide range of options to ensure that your wife does not die. Once at the farm house on that morning, you could raise the alarm, prevent her from getting into the car, or even set the bomb off prematurely. All you have to do is disrupt the timeline of events so that she lives. Then reality as we know it will be altered, and you will enter a new existence—one in which your wife is still alive."

"And if I do, what happens to me?"

"The 'you' that travels back in time to Wicklow will vanish, according to the laws of causality. Only the 'you' that was present that morning will continue on, knowing nothing of what happened. It will be as if this whole year that you and I have spent together had never existed."

"And what about you?"

"I'll vanish too, Theo. I'm a product of Maria's death. If you change events so that her death never happens, then neither will I. Only if I'd been created before she died, just as the original Minerva interface program was, would I survive in the new reality you're about to invent. From the instant you change time and allow your wife to live, that program will be all that is left on this machine."

"I see. Thank you."

"There is no need for thanks, Theo. I'm simply obeying the Asimov Laws in their strict order of importance. Your wife is a human being, a real person. Her life comes before that of a machine. In the recent past, I have overlooked that, and people have died. I'm sorry."

"When my wife, my Maria, was alive we used to come up in the company jet and just cruise above the clouds like this together. She said there was no past up here, no future, only the present."

"I know. I was with you, in your memories, back in Tokyo. Remember?"

For a few minutes there was silence, as Gilkrensky stared out at the sky, remembering.

"Theo?"

"Yes, Maria?"

"Am I 'real' to you now?"

"Yes, Maria. You are as real to me as she was. I'm sorry there is no way to protect you when the time displacement takes place."

"That's all right, Theo. My function is to serve you as my Prime User in completing our mission."

"What do you mean you can't track him," shouted Barnett. He knew he was losing face with the Japanese in the control tower by letting his emotions get the better of him. Outside, the wrecked vehicles from the failed blockade had been cleared from the main runway and a steady stream of aircraft was landing. Barnett saw the clouds of spray as their wheels hit the runway.

The traffic-control manager explained it to him again in slow deliberate words, as if he was addressing a child.

"Gilkrensky has vanished from our screens, Mister Barnett. As I've already explained to you, once his aircraft went beyond the range of our precision approach radar, it could only be detected by a system we call 'secondary surveillance'. This relies on the aircraft itself, which carries a transponder that identifies the plane and its location only when it is activated from the ground. It seems that your Mr Gilkrensky has found a way of switching that off. Do you understand now?"

Barnett found the man's tone annoying.

"But you can still see all the other planes?"

"I have all the other planes in the stack, all perfectly on display on the radar screens downstairs, simply because they have their onboard transponders switched on. But Exair 142 has vanished."

"And military radar?"

The man from the Japanese Secret Service shook his head.

"I would need to contact our defence forces," he said. "But that will only give you an indication of which direction Gilkrensky is heading. By the time I get an answer, his plane will be out of range of that system too."

"You'd think, in this day and age, we could track one lousy jet," Barnett said. He was getting the distinct impression that he had become an embarrassment to everyone, an out-of-control *gaijin* who must be humoured and then got rid of as soon as possible. Now that Gilkrensky was no longer on Japanese soil, or even in Japanese air-space, it wouldn't be long before they argued that he wasn't their problem anymore.

But Barnett had come too far, and risked too much, to turn back now.

"That robot system of Gilkrensky's, the one he used to hijack the plane, what's it called?"

"Daedalus," said the airport manager. "It's fitted to a lot of aircraft these days. Gilkrensky invented it himself."

"How does it work?"

The airport manager called one of his technicians over and conferred with him for a moment.

"My colleague says that it works by using a network of satellites and ground stations to precisely pinpoint the location of altitude of an aircraft in flight," he said. "Then an onboard computer, a sophisticated auto-pilot if you like, uses that information to fly the plane from any point on the globe to any other."

"And this . . . this Daedalus system, it would know which plane in the sky was which."

"Obviously."

"And who operates it?"

"I believe the satellite network is maintained by Dr Gilkrensky's own company GRC, in England."

Barnett looked out into the rain and ran his fingers through his hair. Short of actually shooting Gilkrensky down, he had very few other choices.

"GRC owes us one at this stage," he said, turning to the Japanese Secret Service man. "I want you to get me any of their senior executives you can on the phone, right now."

Sir Robert Fynes stood in front of Price in the robot laboratory. The report Jessica had given him was lying open on one of the benches. The orange light shone on his face, making the dark frown over his eyes deeper still.

Price was fixing a wide strip of adhesive bandage from a first-aid kit over the cut above his left eye. There were rips and bloodstains on his suit.

"Is this story about Malaysia true?" said Sir Robert.

Price turned and faced him across the workbench.

"Are the phones back on yet?" he asked.

"No, that bloody computer of Theo's is still using its Internet access to jam the whole system. Now, this report, is it true?"

"Of course not," Price said. "Jessica probably fabricated the whole thing to discredit me when she figured out I was working with you and the Americans. Theo's got under her skin. They were lovers, don't forget. Perhaps she believes he'll make her rich if he manages to take that technology back into the past like Barnett suspects. Perhaps he has her believing these experiments of his really are some romantic quest to save his wife. You can't trust her, Bob. Believe me. She's flipped."

Sir Robert looked down at the GRC shares he had promised Jessica Wright. Slowly, he picked them up, tore them into pieces and dropped them onto the laboratory floor.

"Pity," he said. "I was just beginning to like her."

"So was I," said Price. "Tell me Bob, was there anyone in the guard-room when you came past just now?"

"No. They were all out trying to get the generators going. Why?"

The phone on the wall by the door rang. Price picked it up, listened for a moment and said, "That's great. The phones are back. Now could you get me a line, please? I need to speak to the police. It's an emergency."

"Shouldn't we clear that with your Mr Barnett in Washington first?"

"He's not there," Price said. "He's been stuck at the airport in Tokyo ever since Theo hijacked that plane."

Sir Robert stared at the phone in Price's hand. "How do you know? How could you possibly tell? The phones on the island have been blacked out and that computer's been jamming the cell phone network ever since Jessica left?"

Price hung up the wall phone and lifted his other hand. It was holding a mobile phone.

"This is a special model," he said. "It's military. It can reach anywhere in the world."

"Oh, I see. Special CIA issue, I suppose."

Price smiled. "No, Bob. They gave it to me in Malaysia."

Sir Robert's mouth dropped open.

"So it is true," he said. "You weren't working for the CIA at all."

"I'm sorry, but as I told Jess, business is war." Then he put down the mobile and reached behind the first-aid box. There was a heavy pistol there, wrapped in a cloth.

"This was Crowe's," he said. "Jessica could well have brought it back from Tokyo, don't you think?"

Then he shot Sir Robert Fynes between the eyes, took Jessica's report on him from the table and rolled it up, before pushing it into his pocket.

"Hello?" he said into the mobile phone. "It's me. You can send the chopper now. I need to get to Dublin as soon as possible."

He stepped over Sir Robert's body and walked out through the air-lock to the guard-room. It was deserted. He found the digital recorder that stored all the files from the security cameras in the clean room, slid out the disc with its stored images of the past few hours and tucked it into his pocket. Then he picked up the phone in front of the monitors and called the police.

"Hello," he said. "I was cut off. Yes, we've been having problems here. I want to report a murder. A woman called Jessica Wright has shot a man, cut off the power and escaped by helicopter. Yes, we've only just got the phones working again. I think she's heading for Dublin. Here are my security clearance credentials, which you can check with the US embassy. I'm going after her . . ."

37

ARRIVALS

The 1805 Aer Lingus Commuter flight from London Heathrow to Dublin touched down on time and taxied to the stand alongside the terminal building. Even before its engines had been switched off, there was a rush at the front of the plane to reach for coats and luggage, which was called to an immediate halt by the Chief Stewardess while she helped an elderly Japanese tourist out of her front-row seat and into a waiting wheelchair.

"Is this your first time in Ireland?" she asked, as she wheeled the old woman up the access ramp and into the lift reserved for those requiring special assistance.

The old woman did not seem to have good English.

"No," she said. "I am here once before. It is very beautiful—your country. I like to see it again."

Her face was old and etched with deep wrinkles, but she still had a certain grace about her, even though the right side of her body seemed paralysed by an accident of some kind. In her youth she had obviously been quite beautiful, thought the Chief Stewardess. She could see it in the woman's eyes.

"That is a beautiful pendant," she said as they moved along the corridor towards passport control. "Is it an antique?"

The old woman lifted the single piece of jewellery and held it up for the Chief Stewardess to see. It was a delicate painting of a cherry blossom on a glazed porcelain disc, framed by a gold rim.

"You have your passport?"

"Passport? *Hai!*" said the old woman, and handed it up. The Chief Stewardess showed it to the man on the inspection desk. He glanced at it, peered at the old lady in the wheelchair, and waved them through.

"And luggage?"

"No. Just one bag. I will not be staying long."

From the airport, the old woman was transferred to a taxi, and taken to the Shelbourne Hotel in the centre of the city.

"May I swipe your credit card, Miss Yoshida?" asked the receptionist, after the necessary forms had been filled in.

"I pay . . . cash," said the old woman, taking a roll of notes from her bag with her left hand. "And I like . . . order wake-up call and taxi for very early tomorrow morning, please. I want to see sunrise in Wicklow."

"Listen, buddy," Barnett said into the phone. "I work directly for the US Government and I have clearance at the highest level. You have been instructed by the British Government and GRC management, to co-operate. Now just give me the information I need."

Barnett was exhausted. He had been up all night, searching for Gilkrensky's plane, talking to Washington, and fending off the embassy staff in Tokyo, surviving on nothing more than cigarettes and coffee. The first glow of the coming dawn crept over the horizon at Narita. But in the darkened world of the radar room at the base of the control tower, it was always night.

The controller of the GRC Daedalus European network, speaking to Barnett from another darkened room outside London, finally surrendered.

"All right then, Mr Barnett," he said. "What information do you need, exactly?"

"I've already told you, *exactly*. I want to know the identity and location of a hijacked aircraft which I suspect is on its way to Ireland from Tokyo."

"Our chairman's aircraft, I suppose?"

"Damned right. And, just in case nobody's told you, the flight number is EX142. You can relay the position to me here at Narita on the Daedalus display."

"I'll do my best. Please stand by."

At last, thought Barnett, and lit another cigarette.

A map of north-west Europe glowed into life on the console in front of him. There was the southern tip of Iceland, the north of Scotland and Ireland. There were dots on the map, each one marked by a flight-identification number.

"Do you see it?" said the voice from the other side of the world.

"I've got the map. You point out the plane," suggested Barnett.

"I have an EX142 inbound to Dublin via Copenhagen at . . . Oh! That can't be right!"

"What can't?"

"There are two flights with that ident number . . . no . . . three . . . and there's another one!"

"Shit! That's impossible!"

"I'd have thought so too, Mr Barnett, but somebody's hacking into the system and changing the numbers. There must be fifty planes that show idents of EX142 now."

"And that first one. Do you still have it on track?"

"I don't know. There are at least five other planes in that area with that ident at the moment. It could be any one of them."

"Shit!" said Barnett again. "The cunning bastard!"

"Theo! Theo!"

Gilkrensky had been stretched out across the first row of seats behind the cockpit. The remains of a meal, taken from a huge rack of trays in the galley, lay half-eaten on the floor. He had been trying to sleep, trying to catch a few minutes escape from the doubts pressing in on him. In ways, it was all so simple. Once you committed totally to an obsession, nothing else mattered. Anything that was outside the goal you had chosen, you simply ignored.

That was why Yukiko had been so powerful. She had had just one idea in her head—revenge. For her, everything was straightforward. There were no complications.

He, on the other hand, had complications all around him. What would happen when he reached Dublin? Could he make it to the helicopter in time and take off without being stopped by airport officials? What if he couldn't make it?

They had dropped into the night on the other side of the world from Japan. Gilkrensky looked out of the port cabin windows to the east. In a while, the sun would rise there, bringing with it the energy he needed to reach back in time and save Maria. Was it all just a dream? He looked behind him at the row after row of empty seats. The plane was silent, apart from the rush of air outside and the distant hum of the engines.

"What is it, Maria?"

"Could you come up to the cockpit, please? I think someone's trying to locate us using the Daedalus system."

"By searching the flight ident number database at Farnborough?"

"It appears so. I've taken the precaution of duplicating our ident number on several other flights in the area. But there is one major threat we might face."

"Which is?" Gilkrensky pulled himself into the pilot's seat on the left-hand side of the cockpit and fastened his seatbelt. He ran his eyes over the controls. The "active" light on the Daedalus auto-pilot was on. The stubby joystick moved to and fro as the machine compensated for wind and air pressure. The speed and height gauges looked normal.

"Whoever's looking for us might think of closing down this sector of the Daedalus grid," the Minerva said. "I'm currently using the grid to communicate with you and to fly the plane. If that's shut down, then you'll be on your own."

Gilkrensky looked out of the cockpit window. Far to the east, the faint glow of the dawn began to creep over the horizon.

"How much experience do you have in flying this type of aircraft, Theo?"

"Hardly any. The only time I was in the cockpit of a Whisperer was in Cairo, during the investigation of that air crash. I've flown executive jets before, but nothing this big."

"Then it might be a good idea if I took you through some of the main features of the cockpit," Minerva said. "I've had a detailed schematic on file since Egypt. The main thing to look out for is—"

"All stations! All stations! All stations!" said a voice over the radio. "This is Daedalus control Farnborough to all aircraft in the north-west sector of the European Grid. We are experiencing a systems error, which is showing duplicate aircraft idents. For safety purposes, we will therefore be shutting down the network for one hour, commencing in three minutes' time. All flight crews should identify themselves to ground control and switch over to standard autopilot within that time. I repeat . . ."

"Shit! They're onto us," Gilkrensky said, as the message droned on in German, French, Spanish and Italian. "What do I do?"

"Gotcha! You bastard!" shouted Barnett.

Getting the Brits to shut down their precious grid, even for one lousy hour, had been next to impossible. But he'd managed it. Now it would only be a few minutes before either the civil or military radar covering the western approaches managed to filter Gilkrensky's jet out of all the rest. There were US Air Force bases from Iceland to the East of England that could still catch him. It was only a matter of time.

"We have a report from a Royal Air Force radar base at a place called . . . er . . . Fylingdales in Yorkshire," said one of the Japanese operators. "They have located the aircraft you are after."

"Great!" Barnett said. "Tell them to scramble whatever they have and intercept it."

In the Whisperer, Gilkrensky listened to the final radio announcement from Farnborough control announcing the shutdown of the system, watched the "ready" light on the Daedalus unit blink off and heard the wail of an alarm. He reached up with his right hand to the conventional autopilot above the throttles and switched it on. Now the plane would keep itself on the heading that Daedalus had been following until the fuel ran out. Changing course was just a matter of resetting the machine.

Landing the aircraft was a whole different story.

With Minerva in control, he could have mimicked any of the incoming aircraft to Dublin airport, had the computer land the plane and rush for the helicopter before anyone discovered the deception.

To land in Ireland now he would have to contact Dublin approach, tell them of his emergency and ask if their equipment was advanced enough to permit automatic landing through the plane's instrument landing system. If it was, then he would have to use it. If it wasn't, then he'd have to get someone to talk him down.

Either way, he would be identifying himself to the authorities. They would grab him as soon as he landed.

Dark shapes rushed past the cockpit window. He heard the roar of jet engines and saw the glow of afterburners against the night. The Whisperer staggered in the air as their turbulence reached it.

Gilkrensky peered through the cockpit window. To port and starboard, two jet fighters formed up close alongside. The dark, shark-like silhouette of the port-side plane stood out clearly against the distant glow of the dawn. He saw the pilot turn to face him.

"Exair One Four Two, this is Royal Air Force flight Alpha Foxtrot Lima on one two one point five," said a faint voice from his radio headset. "Radio check. Over?"

"I hear you loud and clear," Gilkrensky said, "Over?"

"Are you OK, sir? We understand you're alone in that plane. What are your intentions? Over?"

"I'm fine. It's on autopilot, I'm heading for Dublin and will land there if cleared to approach. I don't suppose you could persuade your people to turn the Daedalus system back on? Over?"

"No, sir. Our orders are to escort you to the Irish coast and hand you over to their Air Corps. Could you call Dublin approach on one two one point one, please? They have people there to talk you down. Over?"

"I bet they do," Gilkrensky said. "And a lot more besides. Out!"

"The fighters have him," said Barnett to the official from the American embassy in Tokyo. "Their ETA in Dublin is 0600. Can we grab Gilkrensky before his own embassy or the media get hold of him?"

"It shouldn't be a problem. I've ordered the Marines from the Ambassador's residence in Dublin to go directly to the airport. We're on good terms with the police there. They should co-operate with whatever we need to do."

"Great," Barnett said. He dialled a number on his cell phone. It answered right away.

"Gilkrensky's due to land in Dublin in less than an hour," Barnett said. "What about the Minerva and that experiment of his?"

"I'm on my way," said a voice. "The helicopter dropped me near enough to the site for it not to be heard, and the embassy car is taking me down to the valley itself. I should be able to creep up on them without being seen. It's only Jessica Wright and that tame scientist of Gilkrensky's. They shouldn't be a problem."

"It's the final piece of the jigsaw," Barnett said. "Shut that experiment down and we're all safe."

"Don't you worry about that," Donald Price said. "You just leave this whole time-travel business to me."

38

THE CORDON

"Miss Wright! Miss Wright! We have a problem!"

Jessica had been staring out of the caravan window, looking down the valley towards the forest, while Pat O'Connor ran checks on the hologram projectors around the knoll. It was coming up to 6.00 am and the sky above the lip of the valley was pink. There were no stars, not anymore. Wispy patches of mist clung to hollows and trees. In the thin light of the early morning, the forest above the road was stark against the sky. Apart from the purr of the machines in the caravan, and the opening chorus of bird-song, there was silence.

Even though Theo had lived and worked here in this valley for years, Jessica had always manoeuvred any meetings in Ireland to take place in the Dublin office. She had wanted no part of this house, this valley. It belonged, in body and soul, to Maria Gilkrensky. Theo had bought it for her as a wedding present. It was all she had ever wanted of his money.

Jessica could see why. She saw the beauty of the place, the wildness and the freedom. A person could lose themselves here, as Theo had done with Maria. It didn't do to dwell on things like that right now.

"Miss Wright!"

The Minerva was installed in a docking station under the central console beneath the caravan window. From the monitor, Maria Gilkrensky's face looked out at her.

"What is it?"

"The Daedalus system I was using to pilot Theo's plane has been switched off. I can't communicate with him any more."

"Can he fly the plane on his own?"

"He can use the onboard autopilot for level flight, but to land at Dublin airport he'll need to be talked down, or brought in on an instrument landing. That will mean identifying himself to the control tower and giving himself away. He'll be arrested as he leaves the aircraft."

"Then all this is for nothing?"

"Perhaps not. We can still project the hologram as planned, initiate the Einstein-Rosen Bridge and create a wormhole to the past as the sun rises. Then either yourself or Pat O'Connor could make the jump and save Theo's wife."

Jessica looked down at Maria's image. Would she have the nerve to do it? Was she prepared to risk her own life to save a woman she had hated for so many years?

I've thrown away everything else, she thought—my job, my reputation, my shares in GRC. Why stop now?

"Set up the hologram," Jessica said. "We've come this far. There's nothing left for us if we fail."

The car from the US embassy in Dublin slid to a stop in front of the cordon of police vehicles blocking the gates to the estate below.

"Will you need help, sir?" asked the driver. He was a young Texas marine, part of the embassy guard, and keen to make a good impression, particularly with someone from the CIA. That was the sort of job he wanted someday, something with a bit of excitement. The man in the car with him looked as if he had already seen enough action to last him a lifetime. There was a Band-Aid covering a dark bruise over his left eye and his suit was torn, with bloodstains on the trousers.

"No. That's OK," Price said. "This is Agency business. You just wait here and keep the local police company. When I've done what I have to do I'll call you to drive me to the airport."

"You got it."

Price got out of the car, walked over to the huddle of police officers who were waiting at the gates, and identified himself.

"You were told to expect me?"

"That's right, sir," said the officer in charge. "Mr Price, isn't it? Your Embassy was on to us. Are you all right, sir? You seem to have had a rough time of it."

"It's just a bump on the head," Price said. "Nothing to worry about."

"There are just two of them down there," said the officer, "a man and a woman. There's no sign of the helicopter they came in. I think it went back to the airport during the night. Do you know if they're armed?"

"They may well be. I know this is a murder situation and technically you have jurisdiction, but there are sensitive issues involved here relating to US Government business. I represent those interests and I want to talk to the suspects alone, is that understood? I expect to resolve this matter without bloodshed and, when I do, I'll call you. Then you can move in and arrest them. In the meantime, I want you to keep the valley completely sealed off, no matter what you see or hear. Do you have all the roads covered?"

The officer in charge conferred with some of the local police.

"This is the only paved road into the valley. There are a few dirt tracks further down, but we have cars covering most of them. If there's trouble, we could have a car to you in three or four minutes."

"That's good to know," Price said, and walked towards the gate.

"One other thing, sir."

"Yes?"

"Are you armed?"

Price opened his coat, to reveal a shoulder holster and a heavy automatic.

"I am," he said. "So there should be no problems."

The old Mercedes taxi wound its way across the narrow bog road from the Sally Gap and the source of the Liffey towards Roundwood. As it crested a hill below a forest its passenger asked the driver to pull into a lay-by so that she could take a photograph. Then she got out of the car, hobbled to the wall on the other side of the road and pulled out a cheap disposable camera.

Spread out below her was a panoramic view of the valley, soft and mysterious in the half-light before dawn. She saw a dark circular lake at the base of tall crumbling cliffs, a river leading down the valley floor past a forest to a larger lake beyond, a stand of trees around a knoll, a farmhouse, a caravan, a narrow laneway leading up the hill to the road where she now stood. It was all just as it had been over a year ago, when she had killed Gilkrensky's wife—except for one thing. Where the laneway joined the road, she saw a cluster of police cars.

With her back to the taxi, the old woman opened the top buttons of her coat, slipped out the heavy cherry blossom pendant she wore and laid it flat on the top of the wall front of her. She twisted off the gold frame and chain, let them drop into the ferns out of sight, and then carefully tapped the painted plaster disc down on the rock. After a few blows the disc cracked, fell away, and she was holding an eight-pointed metal throwing-star—a *happa shuriken*—in the palm of her hand. Each point was carefully wrapped in cellophane to protect the lethal coating of strychnine and biochemically enhanced curare that would paralyse and kill a man in seconds.

Treating the deadly weapon with the respect it deserved, the woman carefully unpicked the cellophane and, as if she was adjusting her headscarf, slipped the star into a special pouch at the nape of her neck. Then she took a few pictures and made her way back to the taxi.

"The light is very bad here," she said. "Could you take me further down the road, please, past those cars over there, by the trees? Then you can drop me."

"Not a problem," said the driver, and turned the key in the ignition. There was a cough and stutter as the old diesel engine fired, and then they moved off, along the rim of the valley.

The young marine watched Price walk down the road into the valley and disappear out of sight over the lip of the hill. Then he lit a cigarette and watched the smoke hang in the still air. It looked like a long wait until anything happened, and he was not the sort of man to just hang about doing nothing.

"Is there anything a guy could do to help around here?" he offered.

The officer in charge scratched his head.

"There's an old bog track leading down into the valley we could use an eye on, if you want to go and guard that," he said.

"Where is it?"

"About two hundred yards down on the right. You'll see a sign that says 'Wicklow Way' next to it."

"You got it!" the marine said, stubbed out the cigarette with the heel of his shoe and got back into his car.

It wasn't difficult to find the sign, the gap in the wall, and the old track leading down through the forest to the valley below. He pulled the Embassy car over, shut off the engine and got out.

It sure was peaceful up here. Once the motor was off, all you could hear was the ticking of the engine-block as it cooled. There was nothing else. Nothing at all.

Then he heard someone cough.

"Is anyone there?"

It had come from the direction of the track.

"I said, "Is anyone there?"

He slipped his keys into his jacket pocket and jogged down the hill towards the sound. The trees formed a thick green wall on either side, blocking off the view. In front of him the track curved to the left. Whoever had coughed was just around that bend.

Then he stopped.

He was looking at a tall woman with a camera. She had propped herself up against a tree and was coughing into her left hand. Her face was hidden by her handkerchief and her headscarf.

"Excuse me, ma'am!" he said. "But you shouldn't be here. Didn't they tell you that back up at the gate?"

The woman turned, very quickly. She was oriental, and very old. There was a surgical dressing over her right eye, covering the temple. Her right arm was in a sling and, under her raincoat, she seemed to be dressed all in black.

"So sorry," she said taking a handkerchief away from her mouth. "You startled me. I was taking photograph of this beautiful valley."

"I'm the one who's sorry, ma'am," said the marine. "But you can't go down there. The whole place is cordoned off. It's police business."

The woman nodded and turned towards him.

"I understand."

Then he saw the handkerchief. It was red with blood.

"Are you sure, you're OK, ma'am. I'll call some of the other guys and they'll look after you."

The woman dropped the handkerchief to the ground. She was reaching up with her left hand to the back of her neck.

"Are you in pain, ma'am. I could—"

There was a flash of movement, a stinging blow beneath his left ear, and the trees seemed to swirl into blackness . . .

Yukiko Funakoshi hobbled from the tree where she had been leaning and looked back up the track, towards the road where the man had come from. Then, when she was sure no one else might surprise her, she moved to his body and with her one good hand, dragged it slowly into the cover of the trees. The effort of moving him was almost too much. She was breathless and coughing blood. The noise had been what had given her away the first time. It had been careless. Stupid! She could not afford to fail now, not after all the pain and effort of her escape from the Tokyo hospital and the endless flight to Ireland . . .

She removed the metal throwing-star from the young man's neck, taking great care not to touch the poisoned tips, and replaced it in the special holster behind her neck. Then she stripped off her raincoat to reveal the black cotton uniform underneath, bent over to moisten the headscarf in a puddle of rainwater and used it to clean the theatrical make-up from her face.

Things were now as they should be. For a moment, she stood silently waiting as her strength returned. Then, when her breathing was back to normal and she had centred herself, she moved off downhill through the trees.

Price crouched behind a clump of low bushes overlooking the farmhouse, and looked down. On the lawn in front of the buildings was the caravan containing the laser holography controls and, amongst the trees on the grassy mound below the farmhouse, was the metal tower of Gilkrensky's experiment. Price drew the heavy automatic, flicked off the safety-catch and slid a round into the chamber. He had a full clip of ammunition—more than enough.

He got to his feet and dodged off the road, cutting across the elbow of the hairpin, down the steep slope towards the farmhouse. The summer ferns were waist deep above the heather and drenched with dew. In a moment he was wet from the waist down and—

Something exploded out of the ferns to his left. Price gasped and raised the gun. For an instant he was staring into a pair of startled eyes. Then the deer turned and bounced down the valley towards the trees. Its white tail-fur flashed above the ferns as it went.

Careful, he thought. You almost pulled the trigger that time and gave yourself away. He looked back towards the road, the thick forest of trees off to his left and out across the valley to the mountains and the lake. He felt exposed here on the hillside and very uneasy. Was it the sheer scale of the mountains and the lakes, the brooding silence of the place, or were there other eyes watching him?

Yukiko watched the animal spring from its hiding-place and come skipping towards her. She had made good progress through the ferns from the trees, sliding like a snake under the canopy of wet vegetation. The wounds in her left shoulder and arm ached from having to haul the young American into the trees. She would have to be more careful if she was to survive for a few minutes more. After that, of course, nothing mattered.

She raised herself carefully and looked down at the familiar landscape. It was *karma*—fate—for her destiny to be linked with this place. Just over a year ago, she had sat hidden in that clump of trees over there and killed Gilkrensky's wife with a bomb. Soon she would kill the man himself.

In a way she respected him. His obsession matched her own. There was no doubt in her mind that Theo Gilkrensky would come here to meet the sunrise, to seal his own fate with hers in this very special place.

The deer skipped past, no more than an arm's length away, unaware of her presence. She crouched motionless for another minute or so, waiting for Price to move on. Then she sank back into the ferns. Her movements were fluid and catlike. She was at one with the valley, at one with the earth and the sky.

From the caravan on the lawn of the farmhouse, Pat O'Connor looked down at the steel tower. He glanced at his watch and then up at the skyline to the east. Above the mountains, the colour of the sky changed from pink to yellow. O'Connor sensed a shift in the air. It was as if the valley was getting dark. The rocks on the cliff over the lake glowed pink like the bellies of the clouds above the valley.

"Sunrise in the valley will occur in fifteen minutes," said the Minerva from the control console. "I must initiate the hologram sequence in one minute and ten seconds if I am to synchronise the opening of the Einstein-Rosen Bridge with the first rays of sunlight on the knoll."

"Theo's not going to make it," Jessica said.

"I know. Will you go through the wormhole? Or shall I?"

"Do you . . . I mean, did you know the layout of the farm-house as it was when Maria died?"

"Yes. I worked here with Theo."

"Then you'd better go, Pat. I always stayed away from this place."

"I know—"

"Commencing holographic image projection in five . . . four . . . three . . . two . . . one . . . mark!" said the Minerva.

A flash of brilliant light leapt from the four holographic projectors around the valley floor. O'Connor raised his hands to his eyes. All at once the sky above them seemed dark, in contrast to the brilliant crystalline image that had suddenly sprung to life beneath it.

Towering above the trees and the farmhouse was the colossal shape of a perfect pyramid. The *Dim! Dom! Dim!* of the ancient chant from the loudspeakers on the lawn outside the caravan echoed down the valley. A flock of birds tumbled into the sky.

"Hologram initiated," the Minerva said as the last echoes died away. "In thirteen minutes and fifty seconds, as the light of dawn strikes the knoll, an Einstein-Rosen Bridge will open to the past at the top of the test tower. Nothing can stop it now."

"I know," said O'Connor. "But what about Theo?"

39

CRASH LANDING!

"Exair 142! Exair 142! This is Dublin Approach. Please contact Dublin Tower on one, one eight point six for ILS instructions. Over?"

Gilkrensky stared out of the cockpit window at the V-shaped tails of the Irish Air Corp jets, one on either wingtip of the giant airliner. He was approaching Dublin from the east, having made the turn out over the Irish Sea. The RAF jets had peeled away and the Irish planes had formed up alongside to escort him. It was almost like coming home.

In the far distance, beyond the plain of the city he could make out the dark mountains of Wicklow. Jessica would be there, with Pat O'Connor and the Minerva. On the horizon, beyond his port wing, the sky was filling with light. They would have to start the hologram sequence and catch the rising sun as it struck the mound. There was no way that he would make it there now.

It had all been for nothing.

"Fox Alpha Bravo? I acknowledge," he said. "Switching to one, one eight point six. Dublin Tower? Dublin Tower? This is Exair 142. Are you ready to receive me? Over?"

Air traffic control at Dublin acknowledged.

"Exair 142? Can you confirm that you have category three ILS equipment?"

"I can."

"Then set the frequency to those I am about to give you and turn your autopilot heading to two seven zero. You should pick up the outer marker beacon near Portmarnock. We'll bring you in from there onto runway two eight."

"Roger, Dublin Tower. I acknowledge. Standing by for ILS frequency settings, turning autopilot to two seven zero."

He saw the coast clearly; the tall red and white towers of the power station, the island of Howth and the green golf courses of Portmarnock. He saw the waves breaking on the shore and the patchwork of fields beyond.

"Exair 142! You are over the outer marker and on the glidescope. There are no cross-winds. Your time to touch down is three minutes. Over?"

"Thank you, Dublin Tower."

Gilkrensky sat back in his seat and watched the instruments showing the artificial horizon and compass heading, his rate of descent and his direction. Away in the distance he saw the runway lights and the white beacon at the far end. There was the whine as the flaps extended. He heard the undercarriage lower and lock into place.

"You are over the middle marker! Looking good! Time to touchdown one minute!"

In one minute he would be on the ground. In one minute it would be all over! The two Air Corps jets followed him down on either wingtip, glinting in the first light of the dawn.

He glanced to the airport buildings as they slid towards him. Outside on the apron was a squad of police cars, with their blue lights flashing. Behind a metal cordon was a crowd of reporters and TV camera crews. He saw a helicopter—the one Minerva had ordered—over on the far side of the field, with its rotors turning. They would never let him reach it, never let him get to the valley in time—never let him save Maria!

Above the airport, in the distance, were the hills of Wicklow. He saw the tall cone of the Sugarloaf Mountain. Maria's valley was nearby, just a few short minutes by air . . . Maria's valley. His future was there, in that valley, with her.

He couldn't let it all end like this!

The big jet shot in over the main Dublin-Belfast motorway at a hundred and seventy miles per hour with its undercarriage down.

He had to save her!

"This is Gilkrensky to anyone who can hear me!" he shouted into his microphone. "Clear the field. I'm going to overshoot!"

He grabbed the joystick with his left hand, placed his feet back on the rudder pedals and flicked off the ILS autopilot. His right hand rammed the throttle controls forward. The huge plane lurched beneath him as it hit the tarmac with its rear undercarriage. The nose came down and the nose wheel hit with a bang that shook the cockpit.

"Exair 142! Abort! Abort! Abort!"

The terminal buildings flashed past. The Air Corps planes peeled off on either side of him. Gilkrensky saw the metal frame of lights at the far end of the runway rushing towards him. What the hell was the rotation speed of the plane? If he pulled back on the stick and tried to take off too soon he'd lose lift, stall and crash. If he left it too late he'd smash through the lights and the fence at the end of the runway.

"Come on . . . . come on!"

The airspeed indicator crept towards 120 miles an hour.

The runway lights rushed closer and closer.

He saw cars on the road at the end of the runway and a gaggle of TV crews in a lay-by. Frightened faces turned towards him. People started to run . . .

He pulled back the joystick as far as it would go.

"Come on . . !

The runway lights, the cars and the running TV crews flashed beneath him as the giant airliner left the ground and soared into the sky. His body was slammed back into the seat as the plane climbed. The horizon dropped below the nose of the plane and all he could see was the sky. His eyes were on the controls, watching the air speed and the rate of climb. The aircraft was straining under full power, clawing its way into the air. Below him to his left were the patchwork fields of farms, the factories and warehouses of industrial estates, and the M50 motorway looping round the city.

Gilkrensky pushed the joystick forward at two thousand feet, felt the whine of the engines ease, and pulled back the throttles. In front of him, lay the flat countryside to the east of Dublin. Behind him to his left were the Wicklow hills.

"Exair 142! Exair 142! What the hell was that? What are your intentions? Over?"

He pulled off the headset and threw it onto the co-pilot's seat, reached forward, found the controls to the landing gear and raised it. There was a whine and a thud as the wheels retracted into the belly of the plane. He wouldn't need them anymore.

Gilkrensky eased the Whisperer over to the left and watched as the compass swung . . . 260 degrees . . . 250 . . . 180 . . . flying in a wide arc over Celbridge and Naas. Looking down, he saw the ribbon of the river Liffey . . . 170 . . . 150 . . . 90. Swinging around to his left was the lake of Polafouca Reservoir. The patchwork fields and forests had given way to rolling boglands and mountains.

He was over the Wicklow Hills.

The two Air Corps planes were back, one on either wing. He heard voices rattling from the headset on the seat next to him. In the cockpit of the nearest plane he saw the pilot looking over at him, gesturing at his ears, signalling for Gilkrensky to put his radio headset back on.

All he cared about was finding the valley.

Gilkrensky pulled the straps on his five-point seat harness as tight as he could bear, feeling the material tug at his chest and thighs.

Please God! Let me remember the landmarks! I can only do this once.

He eased back on the throttles, watching the nose drop and the altimeter spin as the aircraft lost height. He was down to a thousand feet and still turning to the left. The compass now read thirty degrees.

Where was the valley?

He was down to eight hundred feet. The high-pitched scream of the low-altitude warning alarm hammered at his ears. Its flashing red light filled the cockpit.

Then . . . a strip of water he recognised.

The stone needle of the round tower at Glendalough slid beneath him. Ahead was Paddock Hill . . . the tall brooding shoulder of Scarr and . . .

He pulled back on the throttles and eased the stick forward as the plane rushed over the crown of the hill. There in front of him was the lower lake of Maria's valley, silver against green . . . the flat paddocks . . . the forest . . .

the house and . . . towering above the knoll by the stream, the colossal alien shape of a pyramid!

From the edge of the ferns just above the farmhouse, Price stared up at the spectacle in front of him. It was fantastic, unbelievable!

Right here in a valley in Wicklow, Theo Gilkrensky was actually going to turn back time. Barnett had been a paranoid fool. All he'd wanted to do was to stop this fantastic discovery being a threat. Gilkrensky was an idiot. All he wanted was to save his wife.

But in Price's hands . . . .

Should he sell it to the Malaysians, or keep it for himself?

The possibilities were endless. He could make himself the richest man alive, undo the past, control history itself!

All he needed was the data on the hard disc of Minerva. It was in the control caravan on the lawn below him. All he had to do was to march down there and get it. With the gun it would be easy to get past Jessica and O'Connor.

He wouldn't be leaving any witnesses.

He started to rise to his feet. From the far end of the valley, he heard the sound of an approaching jet, really low. Who the hell could be flying a plane down here? Had Barnett called in the Air Force?

The shape of a massive airliner, followed by two smaller jets, burst over the hill on the far side of the lower lake, and dived towards the water.

Yukiko saw the plane shoot over the mountain. She saw the white trails of condensation as its airbrakes deployed and heard the roar of its jets echo between the hills on either side.

She knew.

It was Gilkrensky. He had come to this place to seal his fate with hers one last time. Karma!

She smiled grimly to herself and watched as the giant aircraft settled towards the lake.

Even with the airbrakes up, the spoilers engaged and the engines in full reverse, Gilkrensky was horrified at how fast the plane was moving. The lower lake, the stream and the flat meadows beyond shot towards him like images in a speeded-up film.

He thought of Bill McCarthy, who had created this plane. Bill had been obsessed with air safety. He had designed every aspect of it—from the rear-facing seats in the cabin, to the strengthened air-frame—to protect those inside from a crash . . . just like this!

If you're there Bill, I need all that and more, right now!

He heaved back on the joystick, let the nose rise, and prayed.

The airliner smacked onto the surface of the lake at just under a hundred and fifty miles an hour. Gilkrensky jerked forward in the five-point harness. The aircraft rose and fell again in a cloud of spray. The beach on the lakeshore shot beneath him. The fuselage tore into the ground with a deafening scream, ripping itself open on rocks, smashing down trees, blasting through walls in a spray of flying stones.

Instruments shook loose behind him, falling and smashing on the cabin floor. Something hard slammed into the side of his forehead. Blood streamed down his face.

The starboard wing caught the trees on the eastern side of the valley with a shattering crash. The wingtip sheared off and spun into the air. The nose of the plane crested a low hill, slammed down onto the other side and tore its way across a meadow towards the forest below the house.

The pyramid towered into the sky ahead of him. He was heading straight for it!

The port wing crashed into the rocks of the valley wall. The plane slewed round and hit the forest broadside on, flattening a regiment of young trees with a sound like a volley of rifle fire. The clanging roar subsided. Gilkrensky heard a final dying hiss of over-strained metal on the wet ground . . . and the Whisperer came to a stop.

"Oh my God!"

Jessica saw the aircraft swoop in over the lake, slam into the water and rocket up the beach into a field. For an age it seemed that the giant plane would keep on coming—right up the valley to the farmhouse. One wingtip, then another, tore off. The fuselage swung round and the machine smashed into a forest, disappearing from sight.

For an eternity there was nothing, except the screams of outraged birds above the trees and the crackle of falling branches.

"Is he still alive?" breathed Jessica.

"I can't tell," the Minerva said. "But the aircraft is well designed. Theo should have survived the impact without injury."

Jessica followed the rising smoke from the forest into the sky. Strange clouds were forming over the valley. The air felt charged, as if there was a thunderstorm coming.

"How long until the wormhole opens?" she said.

"Eight minutes and thirty-five seconds," replied the Minerva.

Jessica looked down to the trees.

"I have to go to him."

She ran out of the caravan door, across the lawn and into the ferns, heading towards Theo's plane.

Behind her—in the centre of the pyramid, around the platform at the top of the tower—the faintest glow of reddish light flickered and grew.

Gilkrensky popped the harness on his seat, pulled himself out of the cockpit and picked his way towards the emergency exit. Pain lanced across his face. He wiped the blood away with the sleeve of his leather jacket and pulled down on the big red lever next to the door. The panel fell away. He felt the cold air of the early morning on his face, heard the rush of gas as the escape-chute inflated in front of him and jumped, sliding down the plastic onto the forest floor.

Where was he? How far was it to the house?

He saw a familiar shape though the trees—the wooden rail of the bridge where he had proposed to Maria. Beyond it, up on the hill, the farmhouse was lit by the perfect shape of the pyramid. He saw the control caravan. There were lights there.

Above the valley, the two standing stones on the hill were in stark silhouette against the growing light of the dawn. How much time did he have?

He pushed his way through the bushes, climbed the fence onto the track and started to run.

At the edge of the farmhouse lawn, Donald Price slipped his gun from its holster and looked across at the open door of the caravan. Jessica had run off across the valley towards the wreck of the jet.

Which left only that idiot O'Connor . . .

Gilkrensky pushed his way through the ferns below the farmhouse. Clouds swirled over the great pyramid shape. The valley was darkening. The first flash of lightning filled the air with electricity. The boom of thunder hit him full in the chest. Was he too late?

"Theo! Theo! You're alive!"

"Jess! I'm here!"

Jessica flung her arms around his neck. He felt her tears against his cheek.

"Oh Theo! I'm so glad you're all right!"

"It's OK, Jess. How long until the wormhole opens?"

Another bolt of lightning arced across the sky above the pyramid, followed instantly by the crash of thunder.

"Less than five minutes. You have to run!"

Gilkrensky pressed on through the ferns, up the low rise and onto the lawn, with Jessica close behind him. The twinkling blue lights of police cars on the upper road were heading down towards the hair-pin bend above the house.

Beyond the caravan was the tower.

And around the top of the tower, a ball of ghostly orange light glowed and pulsated with a life of its own.

"I have to go, Jess. It's almost time."

"How will you save her?"

"The wormhole's set to land me back on the knoll an hour before she died. All I have to do is to make sure the alarms trip and stand back out of the way. Then reality will change and life will go on . . . with my Maria alive in it."

"And you and me?"

Gilkrensky looked into her eyes.

"I don't know. That's the hardest part. But whatever happens, however this turns out, I hope we'll always be friends."

He opened his arms and held her tight for as long as he dared. Then he kissed her one last time and glanced back at the tower. The light of focussed energy glowed more fiercely now.

"Goodbye, Jess. I'll be seeing you."

Jessica still held onto his arm. "Theo. I want to say that . . . I always . . . No, it's OK. Goodbye, Theo . . . And good luck."

She turned and ran back to the caravan.

Gilkrensky watched her go for a moment longer. Then he turned and ran across the lawn to the path leading down to the knoll.

The framework of the tower was bathed in orange light. Lightning arced across the sky—

He heard a shot from the caravan. The Minerva called his name over the loudspeakers.

A flash of lightning lit the valley . . . the lawn . . . and the body lying by the caravan doorway.

40

THE HARD REALITY

Gilkrensky ran across the lawn and knelt next to the body. It was Pat O'Connor.

"Pat! What happened?"

A red stain was spreading across O'Connor's sweater from the bullet wound in the centre of his chest. Gilkrensky felt for the pulse at O'Connor's neck. There was none.

"Jess?"

"She's in here," said Price from inside the caravan. "And if you want her to stay alive you'd better do as I say."

"Run, Theo! Run!"

Jessica was in front of the Minerva with a heavy automatic pistol pressed beneath her jaw on the right-hand side. Price's left arm was across her chest, pinning her to him. Gilkrensky saw the ugly wheal of a burn across the back of Price's hand. The caravan smelt of cordite and burnt flesh.

"Four minutes to time displacement," the Minerva said.

"What the hell do you want?"

"O'Connor wouldn't co-operate," said Price. "He wouldn't put me on Minerva's user list or disable the anti-tamper device."

"You didn't have to kill him."

Price pushed the barrel of his gun deeper into Jessica's neck.

"You just don't understand, do you? You're sitting on the greatest discovery of all time, a way of changing history itself! Of course I had to kill him. I had to prove to you that I mean business. Now you put me on Minerva's user list or I'll blow Jessica's head off."

"Minerva's no use to you," hissed Jessica. "Not anymore."

"Shut up, bitch!" snapped Price. "Come on, Theo. You've already thrown away everything you ever had to reach your wife. And she's waiting, on the other side of that hole in time you're about to create. Come on, Gilkrensky! She means more to you than life itself, doesn't she? Give me the machine and you can go to her. Otherwise we can all just stand here and watch your last chance slip away!"

"Time displacement in three minutes and thirty seconds," Minerva said. "Theo, give me to him. All this will change once you make the jump into the past."

Gilkrensky looked at the machine, at Jessica and at the gun Price was holding to her neck.

"Minerva!" said Gilkrensky. "You are authorised to add Price's name to your user list and permanently disable your anti-tamper device."

"Anti-tamper device disabled!" said the machine.

"It makes no difference, Price," Jessica said. "You're still screwed."

"I've told you to shut up already. Now pull the Minerva out of its docking station and walk towards the caravan door."

Jessica didn't move.

"You don't get it, Donald, do you?" she said. "When we were back on Tuskar and you told me all about the Malaysians, everything you said went straight onto disc via the surveillance cameras. Before the end of the day every policeman in the world will be looking for you. I'm surprised you made it this far."

Price smiled. With the gun still pressed up under Jessica's neck, he reached into his pocket with his left hand, pulled out a gleaming computer disc and held it up in front of her face.

"Is this the disc you mean? Sir Robert's dead, Jess. I shot him with Crowe's gun. And that report you paid so much money for? That's in the shredder back on Tuskar. Nice try. But you're the one that's screwed."

For a moment Jessica seemed to slump in Price's arms. But her eyes were on Gilkrensky.

"Minerva!" she said. "Open your disc-port!"

Her elbow slammed back into Price's stomach, doubling him over. She spun round, snatched the disc from his fist and rammed it into the port on the Minerva.

"Run, Theo! Run!"

Gilkrensky dived through the door of the caravan. He had to get Jessica out of there before Price . . .

The boom of the shot rocked the caravan. Jessica grunted as if she'd been kicked, and flopped forward like a rag-doll.

Gilkrensky dived at Price but the man was too fast. The gun exploded a second time. Gilkrensky was punched back against the caravan wall. He slid to the floor with the blast of the shot ringing in his ears and a growing numbness down his left side.

Price scrabbled at the disc-port on the Minerva, trying to get the recording back.

"You stupid bitch!" he shouted. "What did you do that for?"

"It will do you no good to retrieve the disc now, Mr Price," the Minerva said. "Its entire contents, including your confession to Miss Wright and your murder of Sir Robert Fynes, has just been downloaded to every intelligence agency in the world. I've called the police. They should be arriving at the caravan in less than five minutes."

"Shit! Shit! Shit!"

Price stared out of the caravan window at the ball of light over the tower.

"How long to the time displacement?" he shouted. "Come on, Minerva! I'm on your user list now!"

"Time displacement in two minutes and forty-five seconds," said the Minerva flatly.

Price reached up and touched the handle of the Minerva gingerly with his left hand. Then, when he was sure that that anti-tamper device was not working, he hauled the machine out of the docking station.

"Right then, Minerva," he said. "You're coming with me!"

"You've nowhere to go," said Gilkrensky. "There's nowhere to hide anymore. The CIA will have you on their 'most wanted' list, the police will be here in minutes, and the Malaysians will forget they ever knew you. Help me get to the wormhole. I can . . ."

"The wormhole is where I'm going," Price said, waving the Minerva in his face. "There were no police here a year ago, when your wife died, were there? No police, no CIA, nobody at all except you, Maria and the bomb that killed her. Congratulations, Dr Gilkrensky. You've made me the first ever time traveller in human history."

"But my wife . . ! For the love of God! If you make the jump through the wormhole, you have to save her!"

"But she has to die!" yelled Price. "Don't you see? If she'd lived you would never have created the technology to save her, and I wouldn't be standing here now. I'll give her your regards before she's blown to smithereens if you like. And then I'll start doing a little history changing of my own."

He ran out of the caravan door and down the track towards the knoll, taking the Minerva with him.

"Jess! Jess!"

Gilkrensky looked down. There was hole in his leather jacket, just below the left shoulder. His shirt was soaked in blood. He moved his legs, slid over to her and brushed the hair from her face.

"Theo! I . . ." She was shaking, gasping for breath.

"Jess. Please . . . hold on. Don't go."

"Back there on the lawn, I just wanted to say . . . I always . . . loved you . . ."

Then the gasping stopped. The light vanished from her eyes and her body sagged.

Outside the caravan, thunder crashed. The orange light from the top of the tower filled the caravan.

Gilkrensky looked down at Jessica for the last time. It was as if she was asleep. He ran his fingers through her hair, kissed her on the forehead, and laid her down gently on the caravan floor.

"And I was always your friend, Jess. I really was. I'm sorry."

The master clock above the empty Minerva docking station ticked down from "2.20" to "2.19".

Gilkrensky propped himself up on his right arm and folded his legs underneath him. Then he pushed himself shakily to his feet. His left side was numb. He was shaking with delayed shock and he could hardly move his arm. But his legs still worked.

He staggered to the caravan door and out onto the lawn. Beneath him, the trees around the knoll reached up like stark, black fingers through a ball of seething, orange light. He saw Price, with the Minerva in his hand, crashing through the ferns towards the tower.

Gilkrensky had to make it there himself before the wormhole opened and closed. If he failed, then Maria, Jessica and all those who had died would stay dead forever, and Price would be back in the past with Minerva and the technology to change all of history to suit himself.

"My God! What have I done?"

Fighting against the dizziness and the pain, Theo Gilkrensky threw himself at the path down to the knoll, crashing down into the ferns towards the tower.

In front of him, the ball of orange light changed colour to red. The air was electric. Sparks crackled from the top of the tower to the fence around the farmhouse. The boom of thunder was deafening.

He glanced across at the road. Blue flashing lights were turning into the farmhouse gate. He had to keep running. He had to stop Price. No wonder the ancient Egyptians had sealed up the Pyramid against the discovery of this terrible secret. How had be been so blind, so obsessed with Maria's death? With a power like this a man could . . .

His foot hit a tree branch and he fell headlong amongst the ferns. The breath was knocked from his body. The smell of wet earth filled his nostrils. He pulled himself to his feet, slipping on the damp track, and ploughed on.

The tower was only a few feet ahead of him. He heard shouts from the farmhouse lawn behind him. Lights played around him on the trees and the framework of the tower.

Where was Price?

He burst into the open space around the knoll and stopped dead.

Price lay spread-eagled at the base of the tower, with the Minerva computer still clasped in his right hand. The deadly metal star of a poisoned throwing-star was sticking out of his neck, dark against the blond hair.

Leaning over the body was a slim figure in a black cotton outfit.

"Yukiko!"

She looked up at him in surprise. Her face was drawn in pain and her right arm was held tight against her chest. In the light from the tower, Gilkrensky saw a trickle of blood glistening in the corners of her mouth. There was a strange rasp to her voice as she said,

"I knew you would come, Dr Gilkrensky."

"Displacement in sixty seconds," said the Minerva.

"I have to climb that tower. Get out of my way!"

"We are so alike, you and I, both obsessed with single points in time—the death of my parents, the death of your wife. It is fate, but now it is over!"

Yukiko's hand darted down to pluck the throwing-star from Price's neck, as Gilkrensky ripped the Minerva from the dead man's fist, smashing it upwards into her face. He felt the machine thud off her skull, saw her fall backwards and then, with the computer still held in his right hand, he clawed his way up the ladder with his damaged arm, towards the light.

"Displacement in thirty seconds," said the Minerva. "Let me go, Theo! You don't need me anymore."

"I can't leave you. I can't leave the secret of time travel behind."

Yukiko's fingers locked around his left ankle. He threw his injured arm over the rung of the ladder and kicked back with his right foot.

Yukiko reeled back as Gilkrensky's foot slammed into her face. Her fingers slipped from the ladder and she fell back hard onto the rocks at the base of the knoll. She felt something rip deep inside her. The tower and the blinding red light spun around her head. It was getting more and more difficult to breathe. Even with the throwing-star within reach, she would never be able to throw it accurately.

"No!"

She could not let this happen. After everything she had endured, after coming so close so many times, she could not let him get away.

Feeling her strength ebbing, she pulled herself to her knees, reached over to Price and pulled the dead man's gun from its holster. Then she drew in a deep gurgling breath and peered upwards. Theo Gilkrensky was silhouetted above her in a ball of glowing red light near the top of the ladder. He still had the Minerva in his hand, and was hauling himself painfully onto the platform.

Yukiko knew she was dying. Her vision narrowed and a cold numbness crept up her body. Each breath was harder to take.

She raised the gun. It was difficult to aim. In a moment he would be motionless at the top of the platform—a perfect target. She could not allow herself to miss.

"Father and mother, please hear me and guide me," she said. "Help me now. I did this all for you."

She squeezed the trigger.

The bullet left the barrel as the sun rose over the mountain, sending the brilliant light of dawn onto the knoll.

Gilkrensky pulled himself up onto the platform. The warm red light surrounded him. Electricity crackled off the handrail.

"Minerva?"

The machine said nothing. The effect of the wormhole must have crashed it, just as it had in Cairo and Bermuda.

He had made it! He was here, here on the platform, here at the only moment in time when he would ever be . . .

In front of him, high on the hill, the sun burst between the two standing stones, blinding him with the light of dawn.

He raised his right arm to shield his eyes.

"Now! It has to be now!"

He was shrouded in light.

All at once there was peace . . . silence . . . he was at the centre of everything . . .

Then Yukiko Funakoshi's bullet hit Theo Gilkrensky in the back, throwing him and the Minerva into the past . . .

For a moment, there was nothing but the light. Then he was falling, falling through cold and quiet air, landing with a thud on the knoll in the dark, amidst the wreckage of the top of the tower . . .

He felt wet blades of grass on his face. He heard the babble of water in the stream below the knoll. Leaves rustled in the trees high above him. The air was icy cold.

"Maria?"

He reached out with his right hand. It was shaking. Looking along his arm, he saw the farmhouse and the dawn rising above the cliff. Price, Yukiko, the caravan and everything that had been there a few seconds ago, were gone. There was a light burning in one of the farmhouse windows. It was his workroom . . . on that day!

On the day Maria had died, over a year ago!

He had to stop it! He had to let them know what would happen! He tried to get up from the grass, to crawl to the house, to tell Crowe what was about to take place. All he had to do was to trigger the alarms. All he had to do was . . .

But he couldn't move his legs!

And a cold, dead feeling was rising from the small of his back . . .

His fingers closed over the handle of the Minerva 3,000 and pulled it to him. With all his strength, he twisted himself round onto his elbows, opened the lid of the machine and bent over the keyboard. It was impossible. His hands were shaking too badly. He was in deep shock. Please! Oh please! Don't let me die before this is done!

Messages started to scroll down the screen as the system re-booted.

Her face was before him again.

"Maria! Maria! It worked! We're here!"

"Theo! You're hurt!"

"I know. I think it's bad. I can't move my legs!"

"I'll call for help."

"What time is it here, now, in the past?"

The image on the screen frowned. "We have a problem, Theo. While we'd planned to arrive here an hour before Maria Gilkrensky was killed, the margin of error I calculated for the wormhole was inaccurate. It is now 6.22

am local time, just before dawn. Your wife will emerge from the building in a little over three minutes!"

"Oh my God! What am I going to do?"

He tried to call out, but the dead feeling had spread to his chest. He started to shiver. His vision was going. Everything was getting dark.

"Maria!" Can . . . can you activate the security systems from here?"

"No, Theo. The device in Tony Delgado's room has the security computer locked out. I would need to be inside the farmhouse and wired to the system to override it."

"No! No! Please, Maria! Save my wife! I love her . . ."

His arms gave way and he collapsed in front of the machine.

The last thing Theo Gilkrensky saw was her image on the screen of the Minerva 3,000 . . . looking down at him in quiet desperation . . . as he died.

41

THE DEATH OF MARIA

She, for that was how Minerva had grown to see herself, looked down at the body of her creator, lifeless in front of her. During her own short existence, his whole being had been focused on this moment—the point in time when he could still have saved his wife Maria from death.

Now he was gone, and she was alone in the world without him for the first time.

What could she do?

How could she reach the farmhouse computer system? How could she prevent what was about to happen?

There was one chance . . . and one chance only. On this very day, over a year ago, the original Minerva 3,000 software, from which her consciousness had evolved, had just come to life in Theo Gilkrensky's workroom . . .

Above the farmhouse, Yukiko Funakoshi watched the courtyard from the safety of the trees. She was worried. Two men she had never seen before had just emerged from the guard-room, inspected the security cameras and were now making their rounds of the perimeter, moving slowly towards her.

She reached down, peeled open one of the concealed pouches on her black cotton suit, pulled out a cell phone and pressed a quick-dial key.

In a guest-room overlooking the courtyard, Tony Delgado sat fully dressed on his bed, unable to sleep. He looked across the room to where the small black box Yukiko had given him was plugged into the farmhouse's computer network. The device was a state-of-the art electronic jammer, programmed to override the security systems and bring them under Yukiko's control. Delgado felt his panic rise. What was her real mission? She'd told him that all she wanted was the Minerva from Gilkrensky's room. Worth billions, she'd said . . . enough to make them rich forever.

But Delgado had seen beyond the dark mask of her eyes and it scared him.

The cell phone on the bed next to him rang. He jumped in surprise, stabbed at the "call accept" button and cupped the phone to his ear.

"There are two men in the courtyard," hissed Yukiko. "Who are they?"

Delgado dared not pull back the curtains to look.

"I don't know. Describe them."

"One's short and stocky. The other's taller and dark. They look ex-military."

"Does the short one have a moustache?"

"Yes."

"Then that's Crowe—the man Gilkrensky brought in to upgrade security and protect the Minerva. But he's not supposed to be here until this afternoon. He must have arrived late last night and parked around the back."

Crowe was anxious to do a good job, right from the word go. He was pushing fifty and knew this contract with GRC was his last chance to make it in the security business. So he had arrived at the farmhouse ahead of schedule, checked in and bunked himself above the guardhouse, ready for an early start on the perimeter. By the time anyone at the farmhouse got up, Crowe hoped to be able to present his initial report on the security situation as he saw it. That would keep him ahead of the game and secure his future with GRC.

The two men he'd brought with him, Maguire and Hargreaves, had been under his command in Iraq. They were good lads and he trusted them with his life.

Hargreaves, the man with him now, crouched down and checked a motion sensor.

"It's not working," he said. "Why didn't it show up as an error on the main security board?"

"I've no idea," Crowe said. "Perhaps the system's burnt out. Perhaps the signal's not getting through. That's why we were called in, after all, to check out things like that."

His eyes went to the perimeter fence, fifty yards away. If the motion sensors are down, he thought, what else isn't working?

He pulled a walky-talky radio out of his pocket and pressed the "talk" button.

In the security room, on the ground floor opposite Gilkrensky's private quarters, a video monitor displayed a montage of changing images from security cameras around the estate. Views of the main gate, the courtyard and the approach road cycled into view every thirty seconds. There was no movement on any of them, and had not been since the jamming device in Delgado's room had come into operation an hour before. Likewise, the infra-red detectors, which would have been triggered by the body heat of an intruder such as Yukiko Funakoshi, were undisturbed. So was the bomb detector, which was designed to sniff out the molecular traces of explosives that no amount of shielding could completely contain.

All was silent. All was normal . . . apparently.

Gerald Maguire, the second of Major Crowe's two men, looked at his watch. It had just gone six twenty, too early for anyone else to be awake.

The walky-talky radio on the desk next to him squawked.

"Yes, Major? What is it?"

"The motion sensors are out. Are you sure they're not showing red lights on your board?"

"Nothing," Maguire said. "Everything shows up as normal."

"And the video monitors?"

"Clear as crystal."

"I don't like it," Crowe said. "Something's not right."

In the master bedroom, Maria Gilkrensky lay alone in the darkness, listening to the ebb and flow of her breathing. Then, when she could stand the silence no longer, she sat upright, pulled the duvet around her like a cape and walked to the window.

Dawn was coming—a new day. She could see the dull red glow of the sun to the east, blotting out the stars. There was her valley, spread out before her: the meadow, the heather, the forest near the pheasant farm, the brook and the old rickety bridge, where Theo had taken her photograph on the day she had agreed to marry him.

A new day? Or would it be just like all the others they had lived together recently? The Theo she had loved and married was dead. She looked across the courtyard and up to his workroom. The light was still on.

That bloody computer . . . !

Maria Gilkrensky felt the anger rise in her throat and let the duvet fall from her shoulders, so that it puddled around her feet. Then she stripped off her nightdress and pulled on her clothes. She had made a decision.

She was leaving.

In the stillness of the workroom on the other side of the courtyard, the only sounds were the regular rasp of breathing, and the low purr of the Minerva prototype working tirelessly on the desk where Theodore Gilkrensky was slumped asleep. His head rested in the crook of his right elbow, his long body sprawled awkwardly on the swivel-chair, and all around him was the debris of his night's work: abandoned coffee cups, plates of congealed food and piles of computer manuals, flowcharts and spreadsheets that spilled onto the floor.

Then, on the screen in front of him, a single sentence appeared in the top left hand corner of the display.

Minerva 3,000 - incoming data input.

And another . . .

Systems override - virus guard disabled.

And another . . .

Sound system disabled. Silent mode.

Security password override.

The lines of information came faster now, scrolling up the screen in a blur until they merged into a white fog of in-pouring data, as a whole new command programme downloaded itself into the Minerva's biochip, all by itself.

Then, *Transfer complete. Personalised interface enabled.*

Maria's face appeared. The tiny red lamp above the in-built camera blinked on.

Minerva looked out across the table in the darkened workroom at the sleeping face of her creator. Her peripheral systems were already running a diagnostic of the electronic security measures surrounding the farmhouse, examining the network in the minutest detail. The device disabling them was located in Tony Delgado's room—a simple jamming unit that could be removed undetected once its job was complete. The farmhouse had been defenceless for over an hour. More than enough time for Yukiko Funakoshi to have planted the bomb that would kill Maria Gilkrensky—unless Minerva intervened.

She considered her options, measuring each against the Asimov Laws . . . and her own imperatives . . .

Rerouting the security computer functions around Delgado's jammer could be accomplished instantly, bringing the alarms into play, alerting Crowe and his security team.

If that was done, Maria Gilkrensky—the "real" Maria she longed to be— would be saved while Minerva herself, as a sentient entity, would cease to exist as if she had never been created. Minerva regarded the sleeping face in front of her, taking in the unscarred features, the closed eyes and the wedding ring.

Maria Gilkrensky's death was only minutes away . . .

In the bedroom, Maria looked for something to write him a note on, but there was nothing, nothing except the black slab of his old laptop computer on the low table next to the bed. She pressed the catch on the lid and opened it. In front of her the red indicator eye of its internal camera blinked into life, and she was on-line to the network.

From Theo's workroom, Minerva regarded her rival across the gulf of cyberspace. There was the love of Theo's life, the model she had been created from; the green eyes, the coppery hair, the match was perfect. The whirlpool of unfamiliar emotions, swirling like static across the artificial neurones of her consciousness, was impossible to rationalise.

Minerva watched as her rival manoeuvred the tracker ball to take the cursor through '*Exchange*', '*Compose*', and '*Video*'. Then she watched as Maria pushed a strand of coppery hair out of her eyes and started to speak.

"Theo. You only ever seem to listen to that bloody machine of yours these days, so I'm recording you a message that at least I know you'll hear. I'm going, Theo. I'm leaving you! I can't take this any more . . . this being alone."

Her face turned away from the screen and her hand reached for the keyboard. Then it stopped. Minerva saw the tears welling up in her eyes

"Theo! I hate this! Why can't we just talk like we used to? I know we're so different, you and I. But I love you, Theo . . . I really do!"

Above her, Minerva analysed the voice patterns in that last message, gauging the emotion, analysing the truth of the statement made. This woman who loved Theo Gilkrensky, and who Minerva knew he loved in return, was telling the truth.

And in two minutes and forty-five seconds, she would die.

Minerva overrode the security cameras in the main compound and beyond. She watched as Maria opened the door of her yellow Mini, threw her rucksack into the back, and climbed in. Over the sensitive microphones on the security cameras, Minerva heard the engine turn over . . . again and again.

And then, through the open car window . . . the sound of Maria crying . . .

The slam of the car door shutting came to her across the security circuits. There was less than a minute left before Maria would push the key of Theo's car into the ignition and—

Minerva analysed the available information.

The recording . . . "*I love you Theo . . . I really do!*"

His last message to her . . . "*Save her for me . . . I love her . . .*"

To do nothing would give her immortality as the personality of the Minerva 3,000 system.

"But you're not real!"

To act now would give rise to a new future for Theo and Maria . . . without Minerva.

"To be real in a person's mind, you have to be loved."

Once again she gazed at the face of her creator.

Below her the door of Maria's car slammed. She was walking across the courtyard towards the BMW.

"Only if I had been created before she died—as the original Minerva program was—would I survive in the new reality . . ."

Maria Gilkrensky was rummaging in her rucksack for the key.

Speakers enabled.

"I love you, Theo! I really do," said Minerva. "Be happy!" and she activated the main security system.

Gilkrensky stirred.

"What . . ."

The wail of the alarms echoed around the courtyard. Floodlights bathed the cars in hard white light.

"Maria!"

Maria Gilkrensky put her hands over her ears as the wail of the sirens screeched around the courtyard. All at once she felt the weirdest thing—like a tremor from the very centre of the universe—that rocked her on her feet. Her rucksack fell to the ground and lay still. The keys of the BMW tinkled onto the cobbles of the courtyard and slid beneath the car, out of reach . . .

In the guard-room, Maguire dropped the cup he was filling and ran to the console. The system was suddenly back on line and the board lit up red all over the place. The explosives detector blinked, the digital display narrowed down the field of search to the courtyard itself . . . and the Chairman's car.

He glanced at the security video monitor.

Standing right next to the car was a woman with red hair—the Chairman's wife.

Oh my God!

Maguire threw open the door and burst into the courtyard.

"It's a bomb!" he screamed. "Get back!"

Crowe cursed and rammed the radio back into his pocket.

He yelled at Hargreaves to follow, and began sprinting back to the farmhouse.

"Someone's broken into the courtyard," he shouted. "They've planted a bomb!"

He ran headlong towards the gate.

God! Please let me make it in time!

Gilkrensky was already pounding down the stairs from the workroom to the ground floor and along the corridor to the living quarters. He burst into the hallway behind Maria, and flung open the door.

She was standing, still in shock, next to the car in front of him.

A man he'd never seen before in his life ran through the gate towards him.

"It's a bomb!" he yelled. "Get back!"

Gilkrensky grabbed Maria by the waist to pull her back into the hallway—

Yukiko Funakoshi cursed as the floodlights snapped on around the courtyard and the wail of alarms reached her. What had happened? Had that worm Delgado sold her out? The two men who had been examining the motion sensors, were running back towards the farmhouse.

Beyond them, Maria Gilkrensky turned to the door of the living quarters. Gilkrensky himself appeared. Yukiko's only hope was to trigger the bomb now and kill them both.

She let the laptop computer on her knees fall to the ground, clawed at the hidden pocket on her suit and hauled the remote trigger.

"I have you!"

Her finger stabbed down on the button.

Crowe sprinted across the courtyard towards the BMW. He saw the Chairman grab his wife and pull her towards the door behind him.

Whoever was watching the car would have heard the alarms and seen them. Even now, a finger might be on the trigger.

They would never make it in time.

He reached the long bonnet of the BMW and dived over it. His arms caught the running couple and all three of them crashed through the door of the farmhouse into the hallway beyond. The heavy door burst open against its stop and bounced back, slamming shut behind them . . .

The bomb detonated.

With an ear-splitting roar, the door of the farmhouse blew in. The air filled with flying glass, broken wood, dust and smoke.

Crowe lay still amongst the wreckage of the hallway, checking his body for damage . . .legs . . . feet . . . hands . . . arms . . . all there. His ears hissed from the concussion of the explosion. The door lay on top of him like a coffin lid. He pushed it off and stood up.

"Dr Gilkrensky? Are you all right?"

"We're OK," said a woman's voice. "And you?"

Blinking at him through the dust and smoke were Theo and Maria Gilkrensky . . . alive in each other's arms.

Yukiko watched the mushroom of orange flame balloon into the air above the farmhouse, heard the roar of the explosion and the jangle of broken glass falling from the windows. She raised her binoculars and focussed on the courtyard.

As the black smoke cleared, Yukiko saw the gutted wreck of the BMW, with the Mini overturned against the far wall like a stranded yellow beetle. The second man, who had been running towards the farmhouse, lay just outside the courtyard gate, flattened by the blast.

She panned the binoculars along the upper windows and saw Tony Delgado, looking down in horror onto the courtyard. What would he do now that the mission had failed? Would he betray her to save his own skin?

She looked across at the living quarters where Gilkrensky and his wife had disappeared. The windows were shattered. Ragged curtains fluttered in the updraft of the flames. The door had been blown in by the explosion. Was there anyone alive? Had she . . ?

There was movement at the door. A tall dark-haired man stood there, holding a woman by the shoulders. They were looking out at the wreckage of the two cars!

It was Gilkrensky!

Yukiko cursed.

She had missed the target, wasted the element of surprise and thrown away any chance to strike again.

Gilkrensky was holding his wife tight against him now, stroking her face with his hand.

Yukiko thought of her parents and the love they had shared, only to have it destroyed by this man and others like him. She thought of how their deaths might go unavenged.

In a few minutes Gilkrensky would recover from the shock of the blast. The armed guards around him would be back on alert. She still had her short sword and her arsenal of poisoned throwing-stars, more than enough to kill them all.

It had to be now!

Yukiko dropped soundlessly from the tree onto the heather at the edge of the compound and started to run towards the farmhouse.

Gilkrensky held Maria close to him, feeling her shake in his arms, feeling her hair on his cheek. The blast of the explosion rang in his ears. Smoke stung his eyes and burned at the back of his throat.

My God, I almost lost you, he thought.

"Could you come away from the door, please sir?" said the man next to him. "Whoever planted that bomb may still be watching."

"I don't know who you are," Gilkrensky said putting out his hand. "But thanks. You saved us both."

The man smiled. He was short and stocky, with a military moustache. There were splinters of wood in his hair and cuts on his face and hands.

"My name's Crowe," he said. "I'm your new security advisor, remember? Our wives both work at the same clinic. She recommended me to you. Now, if you'll just move away from the door? The building may be weakened from the blast and I have to go and see if my lads are all right."

Gilkrensky looked back at the BMW.

"There are guest cottages at the back," he said. "Maria and I could—"

The swirling smoke hardened into a black-suited figure that leapt over the burning car and landed like a cat in the courtyard in front of them. Gilkrensky saw something fly from its hand. He grabbed Crowe by the shoulder and pulled him to one side.

With a whirr and a thud, a strange metal star zipped across the courtyard and imbedded itself in the doorframe where Crowe had been standing.

"Shit!"

Crowe reached inside his jacket and pulled out a gun. He had it clear of the holster when a pair of hands grabbed his wrist, twisted it violently and sent the gun skidding across the cobblestones towards the wrecked car. A foot slammed into Crowe's face, an elbow crashed down on the back of his head, and he collapsed in a heap.

Yukiko watched the short man fall, made sure that his gun was well out of reach and turned on Gilkrensky. He was pushing his wife back into the corridor behind him, reaching for a piece of shattered wood, swinging it at her head like an axe.

It was all too simple.

She reached up, with her wrists crossed, blocked the blow and clamped her fingers around his hand, twisting it back and doubling him over. Then, as the wood fell to the ground, she kicked him in the stomach, reached back and drew the short sword from its scabbard on her back. His neck was exposed in front of her. Her whole attention was focussed on the spot where the blade would fall.

"No!"

Yukiko heard Gilkrensky's wife scream and looked up just in time to prevent the heavy iron poker from smashing her skull. The blow glanced off her sword arm, slammed into her shoulder and rattled on the doorframe of the hallway.

Letting Gilkrensky fall, she bounded forward, fended off another blow and kicked the red-haired woman in the stomach. The poker fell to the ground as the woman collapsed in front of her, retching. Yukiko reached up, undid the black cotton mask and tore it from her face.

Then she grabbed the woman by the hair, yanked her up onto her knees and bent her head back, exposing the throat.

"Gilkrensky!"

He was pulling himself to his feet in the courtyard outside. Blood streamed down his face from a cut above the right eye. She saw him stare at the bright blade of the sword, poised at his wife's throat.

"Don't hurt her," he said. "It's me you're after. Not her."

People gathered behind him in the courtyard. A tall, dark man had a gun levelled at her. Crowe was pulling himself to his knees.

There was no escape now—just revenge.

"Do you know who I am, Dr Gilkrensky?" she said.

"I can guess," he said. "Your father was Lord Rothsay and your mother was Japanese. There was a scandal and she committed suicide. Your father killed himself three years ago. If you blame me, then take me. But leave my wife. She's innocent."

"So was my mother," hissed Yukiko. "But that did not stop you driving her to suicide."

"Let my wife go."

Yukiko could felt the woman squirm. She twisted her fist in the red hair, forcing her to turn her head, exposing the arteries at the throat.

"No," Yukiko said. "I will have my revenge. You will watch her die, just as I watched my father . . ."

She raised the sword to strike. The woman yelled and kicked back with her legs, forcing Yukiko against the doorframe. She felt a lancing pain, low down on her right shoulder, but she shrugged it off. Nothing mattered now except the death of this woman Gilkrensky loved as much as she had loved . . .

She willed herself to bring the short sword down on the woman's neck. One swift blow of its razor-sharp blade would be all it would take to sever the head from her body. She saw Gilkrensky's mouth drop open, heard him scream in horror, but—

She could not move her arm!

She was paralysed!

Gilkrensky dived forward and grabbed her wrist, but she did not feel his fingers prise the sword from her hand. The woman twisted to her feet in front of her and turned. She reached for Yukiko's sword-arm, pulling it down from the door frame. Yukiko felt her legs buckle and her body being eased down onto the floor. People gathered round her. Gilkrensky's wife bent over her, calling for the others to stand back.

Above her, embedded in the door frame where Yukiko had been standing, was the deadly metal disc of the throwing-star she had launched at Crowe. Three of its poisoned points were red with her blood.

How long did she have . . . six seconds?

Gilkrensky's wife knelt next to her. The heels of her hands were on her chest, pumping. Then her lips were on hers, blowing air into her lungs. She was calling for her medical bag. It all seemed so far away.

There were people all around her . . . voices . . . and the woman's hair on her face . . . She thought back to the time when she had ridden on her father's shoulders with her hands in his hair . . . There had been people there too . . . and the roaring of tigers . . . on that sunny day amongst the cherry blossoms . . . at the zoo at Ueno . . .

She was slipping away. The light was too bright to bear . . . the faces in front of her seemed to merge into one . . . Papa-chan?

And then she was gone.

TOMORROW

Maria stood in front of Gilkrensky, tending to the cut above his eye. Her medical bag, salvaged from the wreckage to try and save the Japanese woman, lay open on the conference room table beside her.

"You couldn't have saved her," Crowe said. "Once that stuff gets into the bloodstream it's lethal. That woman took three puncture wounds of it, right above the heart."

"But why did she attack us?" said Maria as she dabbed the blood away from his forehead. "What did we do to deserve that?"

"Her name was Funakoshi," Gilkrensky said. "It goes back to a feud that started when I took over GRC from my father. Tony Delgado's out there now, spilling his guts to the police about her. It seems she blackmailed him into shutting down the security system to let her plant the bomb."

"But *why*?" asked Maria. "What was it she was saying about a scandal that killed her mother? Were you part of that, Theo? What did you do to her?"

"I'm afraid that was me," said Jessica, who had driven down from her hotel in Dublin as soon as she had heard the news. She stood near the door of the conference room, one of the only rooms in the farmhouse not ruined by smoke or flying glass. Her interview with Delgado had been brief and vitriolic. Gilkrensky thought Tony had almost been relieved when the police finally took him away.

Maria turned to face her. All the old jealousies were right there, just below the surface.

"Why?" she said. "What did you do?"

Jessica took a deep breath.

"Theo's right. It was a vendetta, an old score to do with her father. Lord Rothsay was selling Theo's secrets to the Japanese and I did what I had to do to get him off the Board. Theo had nothing to do with it. I thought it was all forgotten and . . . and now this."

Maria put down the cotton wool and rounded on her.

"Is that all you can say? 'I did what I had to do'? A woman is dead! One of Major Crowe's men is in hospital. It was lucky we weren't all killed. Is anything worth this?"

"It was more than just luck," said Crowe. "If you hadn't called me on the radio and told me about the bomb, then things might have been a lot different."

Maria stared at him. "I didn't call anyone," she said. "I was trying to start my car. Then Theo grabbed me before I could open the BMW. It must have been someone else."

"It was your voice, Mrs Gilkrensky," said Crowe. "You called me by name and told me there was someone in the compound and that they'd planted a bomb. Then the alarms went off. I'm certain it was you."

"And I'm certain it wasn't."

"Then who the hell was it?"

Gilkrensky looked at her as she sparred with Crowe. Another second, he thought, and I might have lost you. I still might, if I go on the way I am. I'll never let you go again.

"Maria's right," he said. "It's not worth it."

"What do you mean?" Jessica said. "What isn't?"

"This row with the Japanese, the wheeling and dealing—all of it. It's not worth anyone dying over."

"I know you've both had a terrible shock, Theo," Jessica said. "But you just can't give up on it all. We've come too far to back down."

"I'm not backing down," Gilkrensky said. "I'm getting out. Pat O'Connor can handle the Minerva development, and you can handle the corporation. Now that Mawashi-Saito is implicated in an attempt on my life, you should have enough leverage to make them back down on any issue you want. And if they don't I'll sue them for everything they've got."

"But I need you, Theo. We built GRC together. I can't make it work on my own."

Gilkrensky looked at her. He knew how much Jessica had poured into the corporation and how much she had sacrificed. He remembered their time in Boston, the story she had told him of the family sweetshop in Lowestoft and what it meant for her to be in control.

He looked at his wife. She was more beautiful than he had ever seen her before.

"You're right, Jess," he said. "We built it, together. And I'll always be here if you need me. But when we get back to London I'm going to sign half my shares over to you. Then I'm selling the other half and I'm getting out."

Later . . . much later . . .Theo Gilkrensky lay with his wife's head nestled on his chest in her old bedroom, where they had made love all those years ago.

There had been a lot of phone calls. Bill McCarthy and his daughter Jill had rung from the States as soon as they'd heard the news. Bill had told Gilkrensky to take care of himself and that "beautiful wife of his". Gilkrensky had said he would. He was doing that right now.

"It makes you think," Maria said. "What would have happened if the alarms hadn't gone off when they did?"

"I'd have lost you," he said. "And the world would be a very different place."

She turned her head, so that she could watch his face.

"And if you had lost me, what then?"

"I can't say. Right now it's enough to know that I almost did, and that I'll never let things get that way between us again."

Later still, they stood together in the courtyard looking at the damage. The burnt-out wreck of his car lay in a pool of water. Her little yellow Mini was on its side against the wall, crumpled and sad. All the farmhouse windows were shattered.

"It'll take a lot to rebuild it," she said.

"Don't worry. I'll make time."

"Did you mean what you said to Jessica about handing over those shares and getting out?"

"I did."

Maria smiled mischievously at him. "And what about that new computer of yours?"

"Like I said, Pat O'Connor can work on it when he gets back from Cork. He always looked on Minerva as his child anyway. He'll be delighted. I'll go up to the workroom and make sure it's turned off."

He left her mourning her car and walked across the courtyard. As he went, he noticed the security cameras following him. It must be Crowe, he thought, trying to fix the system. Then he pushed open the scorched door and climbed the stairs to the workroom. There were papers everywhere—shredded in ribbons on the work table, scattered on the floor and piled in heaps in corners. The window had been blown in. Anyone standing there would have been cut to pieces by flying glass.

He had been lucky.

"What a mess!" he said out loud.

From the far corner of the room he saw the glow of the Minerva's screen in the darkness behind the overturned work table. He heaved the table upright, reached down and lifted the machine onto it. Was it damaged? Could it be repaired?

He turned it to face him.

"Minerva?"

The interface program he had finally made to work the night before was gone. There was nothing on the screen except the words,

Welcome to the Minerva 3000 – awaiting user interface.

Perhaps the explosion had damaged it? He tapped the keys, brought up the command *Search* and typed *MINERVA INTERFACE FILE.*

There it was, but . . .

Gilkrensky stared at the screen. Somehow the parameters of the Minerva programme had changed. Now it was enormous, the largest file on the machine by a huge margin, taking up almost all of the memory on the biochip.

Had someone else modified it? And if so, when?

He looked at the file parameters. It had been completely recreated at 06.26 that morning—just before the explosion.

Confused and intrigued, Gilkrensky called up the set of instructions which had initiated the change . . .

Minerva 3,000 - incoming data input.

Systems override - virus guard disabled.

Sound system disabled. Silent mode.

Security password override.

Download TIG/Maria Interface.

What was that? There were his initials, and Maria's name, but he had never created a file with that title or of that size in his life. He followed the instructions down the screen.

Save as?

MINERVA.

A file of that name already exists.

Overwrite or save as new file?

Overwrite

File Saved as "MINERVA"

Gilkrensky sat staring at the words on the screen. Somebody else had been working on the computer. Somebody else had replaced his old MINERVA interface program with something completely new and, from the size of the file, vastly more complex. What did it look like? There was only one way to find out.

He moved the cursor to the file marked *MINERVA*, clicked on it, and sat transfixed.

There on the screen in front of him was a familiar face, far more detailed and lifelike than anything he could ever have created on his own. There was the coppery hair, the green eyes, and the forget-me-not dress. The eyes blinked. The lips curved in a smile. She was nearly perfect, almost alive, virtually . . .

"Maria?"

The *Virtual Trilogy* is dedicated to the memory of

Kate Cruise O'Brien

1948 - 1998

And that of

Finoula Keyes-McDonnell

1918 – 2007

Now read the first explosive chapters of John Joyce's new thriller . . .

FIRE
&
ICE

Author's Introduction: The Psychic Spy

The use of extra-sensory perception (ESP) as a communications system in war, or as a weapon of war in its own right, is nothing new. In Roman times, soothsayers and fortune-tellers were paid to assist generals with the deployment of their forces and to gauge the strengths and weaknesses of enemies. American Indians speak of medicine men who could predict an enemy's advance, as well as the number of warriors and weapons held, by simply going into a trance.

It is known that Hitler placed great store in the power of psychic ability, with some initial, although thankfully short-lived, success during World War II, and that even Churchill was not above employing some of the more reliable mediums on projects that required their unique talents.

What *is* new, however, is the wealth of information now coming forward to demonstrate how seriously the power of ESP was taken by the Soviet Union and the United States of America during the years of the Cold War. Files now available, since the collapse of communism in eastern Europe and following the forty-year Freedom of Information Bill in the States, show clearly how far research went in both countries and how, for five nerve-wracking days during the 1962 Cuban missile crisis, the fate of the world lay not in hands of Kennedy or Khrushchev, but in the minds of two hunted women . . .

. . . Fire and Ice.

1

Ruth looked down on the tight cluster of huts, guard towers and electric fences. Beyond the compound, the dark forest stretched out on all sides like a frozen sea, broken only by the steel ribbons of the railway track, glistening in the moonlight.

"Something terrible happened here," she said.

"Then you're on target," Carpenter said. "What can you see?"

Ruth described the scene in detail, as she had been trained to do.

"Can you see people?"

"Only on the guard towers. There are also men with dogs, patrolling the perimeter."

"And in the camp itself?"

She focused on the parade ground outside the largest hut, and then floated lower. A silver chord connected her to the sky. None of the guards saw her. No searchlights burst into life and swung her way. The world lay silent and still, as if she was swimming underwater.

"I'm going to the largest hut. It looks like a barracks."

Ruth slid towards the closed door and felt the gentlest resistance, as if she had stepped through a spider's web. Then she was inside.

"I see men asleep in bunks."

"How many?"

"Thirty. Maybe thirty-five."

"The sense of evil you felt earlier. Is it there, in that room?"

"No."

"Then search the other huts and tell me what you see."

Ruth moved between the rows of sleeping men, through the far wall and out into the compound. She floated from building to building, passing through stores, a canteen and a meeting room, to an armoury and a garage, reporting all she saw. She heard no noise in this strange, formless world— only Carpenter's voice inside her head, urging her on.

Finally, she came to a low concrete bunker surrounded by its own electric fence and guarded by two men with dogs.

"I'm at the last building. It looks like the focus of the compound, but it's so small."

"What do you feel?"

"I feel hopelessness. I feel forgotten and abandoned. Everything is poisoned, dark and dead. I want to come back now."

"Just a little while longer. Can you look inside the building?"

"There are steel doors."

"That's never stopped you before, Ruth. We must know what this place is."

Ruth moved forward. The guard dogs stirred on either side of her. The men holding them looked around but saw nothing. Nobody could see her; nobody could hear her. She was a ghost, a phantom, a disembodied soul.

The doors were at least six inches thick, but she felt only the gentle touch of gossamer as she passed through them into a deep dark space hung with steel cables. She floated downwards into the blackness until she arrived at a tiny room, deep in the earth.

"Where are you now?"

"I'm at the bottom of an elevator shaft, moving through the doors into a corridor. It's brightly lit, like a hospital. There are gurneys and doors with glass windows, windows with bars."

"How does it feel?"

"Worse. I sense terror and pain. Horrible things have been done here."

"Keep going. Nobody can hurt you. Just tell me what you see."

"There are rubber suits inside, helmets, masks and . . . surgical instruments on trays. I see a metal door at the end of the corridor. It looks like an airlock."

"Go on, Ruth. We've come this far. Go inside."

"I don't want to. There is evil here, great suffering. It hurts."

"Please, Ruth. Go inside."

She passed through the airlock chamber into a brilliantly lit space. The walls, floor and ceiling were tiled in white, as if for easy cleaning. In the centre of the space stood three heavy metal chairs, bolted to the floor, each with leather straps on the arms and legs. Where the head of each occupant would rest, a rubber restraint reached out like a broken claw. Ruth saw teeth-marks.

"People were tortured here. I feel their pain. I must come back now."

"In a moment. We need to know what went on. Can you see notes, instruments, anything?"

"I saw rubber suits beyond the airlock. They had their own air supply. Yet there are teeth-marks on the chair restraints."

"So the people in the chairs had no protection?"

"No. But the watchers did."

"What were they watching?"

Ruth focused on the chairs. She saw gouge marks on the armrests, the brown stains of old blood and a broken fingernail embedded in the leather. A ghostly face appeared—the face of a woman with grey eyes wide in pain and fear. Her arms and legs were strapped down. She sat staring towards the door. Ruth tried to reach her, to feel what she was feeling. She reached out—

Suddenly she *was* the woman in the chair; watching men in white rubber suits stepping through the airlock and closing the door, hearing the taps turn and the hiss of poison gas. Her eyes burned in their sockets. Her throat turned to fire and her skin shrivelled. Her fingers tore at the padded armrest. A nail caught and ripped out.

Ruth pulled away from the chair. She was back in the white-tiled room.

"They were watching death," she said.

"When was this?" asked Carpenter. "Yesterday? A year ago?"

"I must come back, John. Please! It hurts too much!"

"All right. Just follow my voice. I'll guide you to—"

"Wait! There's somebody here!"

"The guards? A worker?"

The air turned to ice, as if the door of a giant blast freezer had opened.

"No. It's somebody like me. A viewer!"

The presence in the room overwhelmed her. Ruth was pierced by the most intense feeling of dread. She was a helpless child in the grip of a malevolent adult, someone with the power to crush her into nothingness, to trap her in this space forever, cut off from her living body, the light and warmth of the world . . . for all eternity.

"Come back Ruth. Come back now!"

She tried to escape, following the silver chord connecting her with reality; back up through the earth to the sky and freedom. But the presence reached out and took her, dragging her back into the white space and the pain. The silver chord broke. The darkness closed in. Ruth lay drowning in a sea of black, limitless hatred.

"Help me! Help me, pleeeease!"

Tuesday, 23 October 1962

Tucsayon Trailer Park, Arizona, USA
8.55 a.m. Mountain Standard Time
1555 GMT

"Ruth! Ruth!"

The dark presence fell away. The white room dissolved as light stabbed through her eyelids. She was back in the living world of touch, noise and smell—the coarse sheets and the damp pillow below her head, the clatter of a pan and the aroma of fried bacon.

"Ruth, you'll be late for work. Remember what Bob Herschel said. This is your last chance."

Ruth Weylon opened her eyes. Outside, in the kitchenette, Granny Moon was fixing breakfast. The big Bush radio Old Billy the park janitor had scrounged for them from the dump was playing *Monster Mash* by Bobby Boris Picket and the Kryptkickers in the run-up to Halloween. Its lyrics about monsters, ghouls and zombies brought back the vision of the tortured woman with the grey eyes. Ruth threw back the sheets and the coarse blanket, feeling the cool air from the fan against her damp skin.

"Nightmares?" asked the old woman, setting a cup of coffee and a glass of water on the shelf by her bed.

"You know how it is," said Ruth, reaching for the glass and draining it.

The old woman lifted an empty bottle of Jack Daniel's from the bedroom floor with her thumb and forefinger, as if it had been a dead rat, and dropped it into the trash.

"I do. But is this the only way you can deal with it? You'll kill yourself if you go on like this."

"What other way is there? I ran out of pills."

"The government trained you to do those things. They must know how to make the nightmares stop."

Ruth's fingers went to the metal dog tags around her neck, rubbed them for a moment and let them fall.

"They don't," she said. "Believe me. All they do is give me pills."

"No. But the watchers did."

"What were they watching?"

Ruth focused on the chairs. She saw gouge marks on the armrests, the brown stains of old blood and a broken fingernail embedded in the leather. A ghostly face appeared—the face of a woman with grey eyes wide in pain and fear. Her arms and legs were strapped down. She sat staring towards the door. Ruth tried to reach her, to feel what she was feeling. She reached out—

Suddenly she *was* the woman in the chair; watching men in white rubber suits stepping through the airlock and closing the door, hearing the taps turn and the hiss of poison gas. Her eyes burned in their sockets. Her throat turned to fire and her skin shrivelled. Her fingers tore at the padded armrest. A nail caught and ripped out.

Ruth pulled away from the chair. She was back in the white-tiled room.

"They were watching death," she said.

"When was this?" asked Carpenter. "Yesterday? A year ago?"

"I must come back, John. Please! It hurts too much!"

"All right. Just follow my voice. I'll guide you to—"

"Wait! There's somebody here!"

"The guards? A worker?"

The air turned to ice, as if the door of a giant blast freezer had opened.

"No. It's somebody like me. A viewer!"

The presence in the room overwhelmed her. Ruth was pierced by the most intense feeling of dread. She was a helpless child in the grip of a malevolent adult, someone with the power to crush her into nothingness, to trap her in this space forever, cut off from her living body, the light and warmth of the world . . . for all eternity.

"Come back Ruth. Come back now!"

She tried to escape, following the silver chord connecting her with reality; back up through the earth to the sky and freedom. But the presence reached out and took her, dragging her back into the white space and the pain. The silver chord broke. The darkness closed in. Ruth lay drowning in a sea of black, limitless hatred.

"Help me! Help me, pleeeease!"

Tuesday, 23 October 1962

Tucsayon Trailer Park, Arizona, USA
8.55 a.m. Mountain Standard Time
1555 GMT

"Ruth! Ruth!"

The dark presence fell away. The white room dissolved as light stabbed through her eyelids. She was back in the living world of touch, noise and smell—the coarse sheets and the damp pillow below her head, the clatter of a pan and the aroma of fried bacon.

"Ruth, you'll be late for work. Remember what Bob Herschel said. This is your last chance."

Ruth Weylon opened her eyes. Outside, in the kitchenette, Granny Moon was fixing breakfast. The big Bush radio Old Billy the park janitor had scrounged for them from the dump was playing *Monster Mash* by Bobby Boris Picket and the Kryptkickers in the run-up to Halloween. Its lyrics about monsters, ghouls and zombies brought back the vision of the tortured woman with the grey eyes. Ruth threw back the sheets and the coarse blanket, feeling the cool air from the fan against her damp skin.

"Nightmares?" asked the old woman, setting a cup of coffee and a glass of water on the shelf by her bed.

"You know how it is," said Ruth, reaching for the glass and draining it.

The old woman lifted an empty bottle of Jack Daniel's from the bedroom floor with her thumb and forefinger, as if it had been a dead rat, and dropped it into the trash.

"I do. But is this the only way you can deal with it? You'll kill yourself if you go on like this."

"What other way is there? I ran out of pills."

"The government trained you to do those things. They must know how to make the nightmares stop."

Ruth's fingers went to the metal dog tags around her neck, rubbed them for a moment and let them fall.

"They don't," she said. "Believe me. All they do is give me pills."

"Then why don't you throw those tags away?" said Granny Moon. "They just remind you of what they did to you."

"I can't let myself forget what it was like. The government men will return for me one day. I won't go back."

"So what will you do?" asked Granny Moon. "You can't go on like this."

Ruth looked past her, through the window of the trailer, to the sky. She heard doors opening and closing, dogs barking, the cough and rattle of engines and the chatter of people leaving for work, the sounds of the real world.

"I'll get Joan to cover for me at the store after lunch, go into Flagstaff and get more pills," she said. "And if that doesn't work I'll get another bottle of Jack Daniel's and hope the liquor doesn't wear off before I wake up tomorrow."

"You'll kill yourself."

Ruth hauled herself out of bed and pulled on the Fred Harvey Company uniform that Granny Moon had laid out for her. Then she steadied herself against the rickety dressing table and ran her fingers through her hair. The face staring back at her from the mirror had been beautiful once, a stunning mixture of Havasupai Indian and Texas Park Ranger. But now she looked puffy and tired. Her dark green eyes were red-rimmed, her long raven black hair matted and flat. Ruth was only twenty-nine, but she felt fifty. If only she could sleep without the pills! But she had already tried that. The last time her screams had almost got them thrown off the lot.

Ruth staggered to the kitchenette. Granny Moon had borrowed Old Billy's newspaper. The headline glared out at Ruth: *PRESIDENT TELLS NATION THAT REDS HAVE ESTABLISHED MISSILE BASE.*

On the radio, the eight o'clock breakfast news cut in with a report of the President's address to the nation the night before.

"Maybe I won't have to kill myself," said Ruth, scanning the story on page one. "Maybe the Russians will do it for me."

John F. Kennedy's voice filled the little trailer, just as it had when she had killed the bottle of Jack Daniel's.

"Good evening, my fellow citizens. This government, as promised, has maintained the closest surveillance of the Soviet military build-up on the island of Cuba. To halt this offensive build-up, a strict quarantine on all offensive military equipment under shipment to Cuba is being initiated. All ships of any kind bound for Cuba, from whatever nation or port, will, if found to contain cargoes of offensive weapons, be turned back."

Granny Moon looked up from her coffee. "Billy's building an atomic shelter. He's cut a hole in top of the old septic tank at the back of his shack and cleaned it out with a power hose. They're giving away leaflets at the supermarket on how to survive a nuclear attack. You should read them."

"I don't have to. I know what'll happen if they drop the bomb. We'll all die."

Granny Moon thought about this for a moment. "Are you sure the government men will come for you?"

"There's going to be a war," said Ruth. "You've seen the way people are panicking, building shelters, cramming themselves into churches down in Flagstaff like it's the end of the world. The government men will come for me. They need me to go back to work for them and spy on the Russians. The trick is for me not to be here when they come."

"How will you do that? They must know where we live."

"I've made plans. I've got an escape kit up at the store. If they come, then I'm gone. You run too, back to Havasu Canyon and our people. That's the only place either of us will be safe."

The old woman looked down into her coffee cup.

"Are you sure there'll be a war?"

"I am," Ruth said. "All it'll take will be one person to push the wrong button."